The Two Confessions

John Whitbourn

'All is lost. Monks! Monks! Monks!'

(Dying words of King Henry Tudor *'VIII-and-last'*.)

Published 2013 by Spark Furnace Books, an imprint of Fabled Lands LLP.

www.sparkfurnace.com

The right of John Whitbourn to be identified as the author of this book has been asserted by him in accordance with the United Kingdom Copyright, Designs and Patents Act 1988.

ISBN: 1909905992

ISBN-13: 978-1909905993

ALSO BY JOHN WHITBOURN

A DANGEROUS ENERGY

POPES & PHANTOMS

TO BUILD JERUSALEM

THE BINSCOMBE TALES – Vol. 1. Sinister Saxon Stories

THE BINSCOMBE TALES – Vol. 2. Sinister Sutangli Stories

THE ROYAL CHANGELING

DOWNS-LORD DAWN

DOWNS-LORD DAY

DOWNS-LORD DOOMSDAY

FRANKENSTEIN'S LEGIONS

FORTHCOMING

BABYLONdon

AMY FAITH & THE STRONGHOLD

AMY FAITH & THE ENEMY OF CALM

PRAISE FOR JOHN WHITBOURN

A DANGEROUS ENERGY

John Whitbourn's first novel... is a humdinger. ... a terrifying story, marvellously inventive and written with great power and conviction.'

The Times.

'A work of brilliance. Never was a prize more richly deserved.'

Starburst magazine.

POPES & PHANTOMS

'Terrific, cynical fun.'

The Times.

THE ROYAL CHANGELING

'This is alternative history/fantasy at its very best – sort of C17th meets the X-Files... An excellent read, well-imagined, intriguingly constructed and extremely well written with a rich vein of underlying humour.'

Historical Novels Review.

'Alternative history pulled off with panache and no small amount of humour. Whitbourn's wit is both unforced and splendidly droll.'

The Daily Express.

'Gutsy, witty and time-twisting.'

The Daily Telegraph.

ABOUT THE AUTHOR

JOHN WHITBOURN has had ten novels published since winning the BBC Bookshelf & Victor Gollancz Ltd. 'Fantasy Novel Prize' with *'A Dangerous Energy'* in 1991. Most recently they include his *'Downs-Lord'* trilogy concerning the establishment of empire in an alternative, monster-ridden England; and *'Frankenstein's Legions'*, an extrapolation of Mary Shelley's classic gothic tale. Whitbourn's works have received favourable reviews in The Times, Telegraph, and Guardian, amongst others.

A rare press interview with Whitbourn in 2000 was revealingly entitled *'Confessions of a Counter-Reformation Green Anarcho-Jacobite'*.

ACKNOWLEDGMENTS

Honour and gratitude alike dictate that the author acknowledges his mountainous debts to the following:

Joan Whitbourn (1917-2000) and Albert Whitbourn (1912-2008).

'We kissed and parted. I humbly hope to meet again, and to part no more.'

(Samuel Johnson, 1767).

&

Dave & Roz Morris. Writers.

& two Doctors:

Dr Amy Faith Ludwin. For cardiology treatment.

Dr Smudge Whitbourn, PhD (London School of Economics, 2011, £25. *'Towards a Typology of Libyan Sticks & Squeaky Toys*, 1911-2011'). For physiotherapy treatment.

DEDICATION

This conclusion of *'The Pevensey Trilogy'* is dedicated to:

Miss Caroline Elizabeth Gale.

And Lucy too.

CONTENTS

JOHN WHITBOURN

****

****

PROLOGUE

FOR THE NEWCOMER:
'RANDOM HERALDS OF CHANGE'

****

****

****

A TRUE accounting of the order for the Reception & SOLEMN ANOINTING
of:

CHARLES STUART-OGLETHORPE, by Grace of G*D

CHARLES V

*KING of **UNITED ENGLAND**, and WALES, and CORNWALL;*
PROTECTOR of SCOTLAND-SECUNDA, DALRIADA & THE ISLES;
PROTECTOR OF MANNIN; PATRON OF THE JAFFA &
JERUSALEM CITADELS; DEFENDER OF THE FAITH.

St GUY'S CATHEDRAL, WESTMINSTER, St Dismas' Day, the
25th day of March, the year of our Salvation in Christ, 2014.
[*Published in both the Latin and English tongues, by Mr Daniel Soutar's Ephemeralia*
Press, Croydon, Wessex, England. 2½ d. Paper covers].

... the Papal Dragoons and Palatine Musketeers, preceding the King's
Own Troop of horse and Chosen Schiltron of Pikemen of the Corporation
of London.

... As His Majestye processes the nave, the choir will sing:
Rex et virtutum opifex, pastor bone in populo, sic plauisti Domino.

[O King doer of good deeds, O shepherd good to thy people, thus
hast thou pleased the Lord].

Accompaniment: *'Luther, lift thy eyes from torment.'* Trad. arranged Henry
Purcell. Schola Cantorum of Westminster and Caer-diff Cathedrals.

... Turning left the procession shall then make obeisance to the Blessed
Sacrament in the Chapel of Blessed Mary III *'Restorationist'*. The *familiares*,
sword-bearers, and Chamberlains of the Noble Secret Antechamber will
remain outside, beyond the grille.

... When all are in their places before the High Altar and have made
full prostration, the Cardinal-Archbishop shall arise and approach the

supine King. He will sing:

Protector noster aspice Deus. [O G*d, our protector behold].

Salvum fact servum tuum. [Save thy servant].

Deus meus sperantem in te. [Who hopeth in Thee, my G*d].

... [Cardinal-Archbishop]: Do you accept the proconsulship of G*d and His Holy Church, to rule under His direction, this land?

[King]: [**I do**].

[C-A]: Do you undertake and avowe before that same G*d and your people, to serve Him and them, to the oblivion of self?

[K]: [**I do**].

[C-A]: Do you spurn heresy and cleave to the narrow gate to salvation?

[K]: [**I do**].

[C-A]: How speak you of those here before: the Tudors-save-Mary?

[K]: [**I abominate their memory forever**].

[C-A]: Have you the power of thaumaturgy?

[K]: [**I have not**].

[C-A]: If such should descend on you, will you declare same and submit yourself to the will of the Church: Universal, Roman & Catholick?

[K]: [**I will**].

[C-A]: Do you renounce the guidance or counsel of sorcerers, save those in the service of Mother Church and licensed by proper authority?

[K]: [**I do**].

... the Cardinal-Archbishop will then be handed the fiery-flail, signifying the wrath of G*d, and dissemble the scourging of the King, to show his fate, in this world and the next, should he fail in duty or obedience.

... If the Cardinal-Archbishop consents then the King shall arise and a suitable crown shall be placed on his head. His Majestye may then leave the House of G*d...

****

****

From: *'THE BOOK OF CEREMONIAL MAGIC'*
By Sir Arthur Waite.
Published London, Auto-da-fé Press, 1911.

Chapter 36 : *'Social Etiquette for Sorcerers'*

'... in the stubborn souls of the uninstructed, suspicions of the grimmest sort attach still to those whom Almighty G*d has seen fit to gift with the thaumaturgic art. That certain minds are so strong, so capable of self-convincing, that they may mould reality, seems forever unacceptable to many. Vulgar prejudice, proof against all persuasion over the ages, prefers the idea that sorcerers derive their powers from dark forces, holding perpetual communion with them. Or else we are held a sinister brotherhood, biding our time, and conspiring to rule over mundane humanity.

From these fears came the early persecutions, the terrible murders and tortures, yea even the infanticide of innocent babes, which the great Charlemagne himself was unable to suppress. Happily, Mother Church, of her apostolic kindness, decreed in our favour and the more violent afflictions accordingly ceased. Gathering the angry and bewildered remnants to Rome, She succoured them, making a peace whose fruits we still enjoy. However, it remains my unshakeable opinion that only the sheltering wing of the Holy Catholick Church prevents the bonfires' return.

In England our cause was aided (after a fashion and in due course) by the reign of King Joseph I, *'the Wizard'*. Seen in retrospect, those lively and remarkable years achieved much: for religion, for England and for sweet toleration. And all this from a merry monarch who never departed from his avowed intent *'to enjoy life as much I d*mn well may - and then go to heaven.'* He most certainly fulfilled the first, and we may venture reasonable confidence on the second count. Even if he did *'worship the female form'* and *'cavort with elves and elementals'*, as mean-spirited detractors allege, surely our Merciful Father's anger is less roused by such lapses of the flesh, than the more cold-hearted and bloody sins?

But I digress, prompted by warm feelings for our great benefactor in these Isles. In essence, I say that even in these most favourable times, the Christian wizard should sigh and *resign* himself to life-long petty discriminations. He (or she) must accept it as mortification for the blessing granted them. Against the sidelong glance, the wounding remark, they can turn the other cheek and earn grace thereby. Knowledge of the deadly retribution available by curse or spell only makes our forbearance the more commendable....

A.W.
London, Bognor, Jaffa. 1902-10.

****

****

'On this field once stood 'THE TOWER OF LONDON', of hideous memory & a place of horror to all English-folk. Founded by William 'the Conqueror' as a stronghold & symbol of the Norman Yoke, successive monarchs herein incarcerated, tortured & murdered their enemies, oft-times innocent patriots or hapless barriers to their gross ambitions. Foremost in the catalogue of iniquities witnessed by this soil are Henry First-Tudor's infanticide of the young 'Princes in the Tower', & the numberless martyrdoms of the 'Reformation-Devastation' period. Waxen-mannequin cameos of these despicable deeds may be seen in the Chamber of Horrors attached to the 'Chapel of Perpetual Lamentation', Seething Lane.

Briefly taken and partly slighted, its myriad prisoners released, in the fleeting but glorious days of the *'Gunpowder Plot'*, The Tower was then the blood-drenched, beleaguered citadel of 'King Essex' and other crazed schismatics. Its entire razing was ordered by King James the True in 1688.

St Richard Challoner, Archbishop of Canterbury, decreed that no successor structure ever be erected on this site, so that it might be henceforth given over as silent witness to the wickedness of history-makers and the sure eventual triumph of G*D.

These beautiful grounds and gardens are maintained by the brothers of the Crutched Friars, Fenchurch Street, and a 300 day indulgence (usual conditions) is granted to anyone donating one quarter the contents of their loose change purse - as they may truly find it upon the notion - into the sealed box below.'

This plaque was unveiled in the presence of His Royal Highness, Guy, Prince of Wales, under the auspices of *ÐA ENGLSICAN GESIÐAS* Society.

The 23rd day of March, the year of our Deliverance 1958.

****

6

****

'Notes Towards an Inventory of the Collection of the Royal Stuart National Portrait Gallery: for the reference of scholars, and the enlightenment of visiting quality and the better-educated degree of yeomen.'

By Fr. Brian Sewell, O.S.B. Curator. 3rd edition. 2s/6d. 1981.

'... it is indeed salutary to note that not a single undefaced depiction of 'Henry VIII-and-last' survives in our possession. One, unmistakably of his porcine form, even has the visage of St Guy angrily daubed over the original head! The overall effect is unedifying and I hasten to forestall morbid curiosity by saying this quasi-laudable revenge is *not* for general view.

In the same manner, few likenesses of Elizabeth I remain without expressions of disgust, conveyed in paint or blade; potent reminders of the powerful emotions roused by her brief reign and the forces she unleashed - but proved unable to control.

At times, I survey these mutilated works of art, many of them sublime expressions aside from their rebarbative subjects, and ponder the wisdom of repair. Should, for instance, Holbein's or Van Dyke's *oeuvre* forever be impoverished by an unhappy choice of patron? Art, which is only the dimmest echo of G*d's whispering in our ears, answers *'surely not!'*

But then I recall history, and in my mind's eye see Abbott Whiting dragged on a hurdle to be hung, drawn and quartered on Glastonbury Tor; I hear the pleas of soon-to-be widows and orphans fall upon 'Black Betty's deaf ears; and smell roasted flesh from Edward's hecatombs at Smithfield. After which I turn again to the wounded pictures and tell them *'so shall ye stay'....'*

****

JOHN WHITBOURN

****

****

THE FIRST CONFESSION

'For I know that my redeemer liveth, and that he shall stand at the latter day upon the earth:
And though after worms destroy this body, yet in my flesh shall I see God.'

The Book of Job. Chapter 19, verses 25 - 26.

****

'Harden Not Your Hearts.'

Psalm 95.

****

****

****

****

THE YEAR OF OUR LORD 2037

****

****

CHAPTER 1

For several days there had been no messages; no invitations, threats or pleas. That was a mercy, a rare holiday from relentless pressure. He realised how hard his guardians strove, and at what cost, to block every approach and was duly grateful for it. Nor did he blame them for the frequent failures, knowing the enemy was implacable.

Then their agents must have found another way in, suborned a brother, forced illicit entry or else employed fresh sorcerous tricks. When he dragged himself from bed to early prayers in the chapel the old man found a scrawled note tucked into the pages of his missal. In seeking the *'proper of the day'* it was liberated from concealment and slipped to the floor. He was happy for it to stay there. His name adorned the front and that was sufficient. They generally wrote in blood (though not their own) and he'd no wish to soil himself with such sordidness. The words might vary but the general sentiments did not, and he knew all they had to say.

Sadly, his monk-bodyguards saw fit to retrieve and read the thing, and then pass it on with eloquent expressions of disgust. Unable to afford any lapse from virtue, courtesy obliged the old man to accept delivery.

'Come forth' it said, as always. *'Leave the old god's house and lead us!'*

So that was another opportunity for saving prayer lost. They'd succeeded in distracting him.

The letter was disposed of and in due course the brothers arrived for the service of prime. The old man said the responses but his attention was divided. Part of him considered the ravenous and watchful ones outside. They were probably close enough to hear the plainchant.

After breaking his fast, he sat alone in the library, too aged and feeble and threatened to join in with community labour in the priory's grounds. Basking in sunshine in a window seat he deluded himself he was studying St Richard Challoner's *'Lives of the Lewes Martyrs'*. Then it started to rain.

It began as heavy droplets, impacting against the diamond-pane glass. They came in slow but steady succession, like the drumming of impatient fingers. Gradually the pace increased, imparting more urgency to the sound. He was caused to look up and thus note this was no shower from heaven. Each incoming speck arrived with venom, akin to spittle flung into a hated face. Each expired in a puff of corroded glass. Within a minute or so the window was pockmarked with tiny craters.

The old man tottered over to the library rope-pull and raised the alarm. Soon a group of monks arrived to splash the panes with holy water and erect the specially prepared steel shutters. One of the team of Rome-wizards now permanently stationed at the priory supervised. He frowned at the attempted incursion, whilst reinforcing the warding spells round the window frames. All the chalk and wax symbols were painstakingly checked.

It was done in unhurried, seen-it-all-before, manner: as well it might, for this was a familiar drill. None of them spoke to or acknowledged the old man. Discouraged by their confident precautions the 'rain' ceased, its pitter-patter gradually dying away.

Then he was left all alone again, in the now darkened library. He was amazed to find himself weeping, only alerted to the fact by the fall of teardrops onto his robe.

Even as a boy and all through the too-long years he'd always refused to wave a white flag at life. Only once before had he weakened - and that was the day he lost *her*. But this was unconditional surrender. The tears became great heaving sobs torn from deep inside his shrivelled chest.

'Where did it go wrong?' he asked the echoing empty room. *'When did all this start?'*

****

The answer to that was: *long* before he thought.

In the beginning was the Power and the Power slept, and whilst it slept it dreamed.

Tired of activity since the start of time, it chose to rest and escape the torrent of sensation. There was a period of total repose, a blank black interlude from which no light or sign of life escaped. Then the dreams began.

Bubbles and whirlpools of activity boiled to the surface of that part in which it stored its memories and thoughts. A minute degree of wakefulness returned. Things had slipped since the sleep began and the Power's private universe had gone its own way. Without permission, tiny motes of matter had gathered and coalesced to form galaxies. Within them suns had exploded into being and spoilt the infinite night. Such gross insubordination!

The Power lazily considered these signs of rumbustious anarchy and then fed on the nearest spiral form, rending it apart into nourishment. The cleansing hand reached on towards all the others - but at the last moment was withheld. The Power restrained its momentary flare of anger. After long neglect a few cobwebs were only to be expected. It would let them live a little longer before visiting due punishment. Replete, the Power slept again.

One dream was persistent and intriguing. A current of sleep-castrated excitement slithered through the Power's expanse. It dreamt that a keyhole had opened up, through which one could peer into an altogether different universe. Yet that was unlikely, for such a thing was forbidden by the strictest and most eternal of rules. The Power, and its countless brothers and sisters, and even their cruel superiors ascending into infinite heights, were all of them barred from *travelling*, in anything else but thought. And even then any trip was by invitation only and bound with humiliating conditions. The Power ignored the implausible, unsettling, temptation for many millennia - but the dream persisted.

Its view seemed fixed; persistent, the tiny scene visible through the portal hard-edged and real. The Power might have presumed this a state of being that actually *was* - save that that was impossible. More likely was an unusually vivid intersection with another Power's personal creation. Which wasn't uncommon and supposedly the way the Powers bred.

Unable to resist, the small proportion of the Power not in wearied sleep, drifted towards the keyhole.

****

It looked through and saw that the scene was *true*. Rock barred the way but it being in molten state meant the Power could bore a tunnel through with just a look. The way was cleared.

Nothing occurred for a very long time, though the view itself was entrancing enough. Sometimes the Power surrendered to total sleep but when any portion was even half awake it kept its 'eye' pressed to the gap.

Then, much later, some activity presented itself. The Power's eye winked open and beheld life forms. It studied them and their past and future and it amused the Power to tell them the truth: namely that *'one day, through this portal, I will behold your Messiah....'*

They left, but soon returned with other 'people'. Over time, there came a small but steady stream of them. They were most attentive and polite. Therefore, in return, over the centuries when sufficiently awake and playful, the Power gave them the same good news.

****

****

THE YEAR OF OUR LORD 1994

****

****

CHAPTER 2

'Well, *damn* your eyes then!'

The cabby considered his passenger's verdict on the view. He'd been around and seen a thing or two. Two decades in the trade had left him no longer sure where 'normal' ended and 'strange' began. If someone wanted to stop and get out and curse, that was their business - and good business too, since they were paying for the lost time. Only idle curiosity prompted his enquiry about what so enraged his fare in the distant prospect of London.

The stocky young man span round, revealing a face in thrall to powerful emotions. Momentary concern made the cabby recall the cutlass tucked away beneath his perch.

'What?' said the young man. '*What?* What d'you want?'

The cabby whistled through his teeth.

'Blimey! I only asked. Don't jump in me face. All I asked was what's amiss?'

The horses required some quietening, long service allowing them to pick up on their master's alarm. Meanwhile, the passenger composed himself and turned back to the panorama of the metropolis.

'Now *there's* a tricky question,' he mused aloud, in bitter tones. 'Where shall I start?'

'Eh?' The cabman's interest in his human cargo had naturally dulled as the years went by, but he thought this one had the makings of a decent tavern-tale. It merited a little effort. 'I don't catch y'drift, sir.'

'You asked what I object to in *Babylondon*. Well, take your pick - select a steeple: I'm told there's a church for each day of the year!'

It hardly needed checking but they both looked. The evening-sunlit domes of St Paul's and St Guy's (sometimes still called Westminster Abbey) were only the centre of a great circle of spires, towers and steeples extending right to the City walls. Even the one breach in same, at London Bridge Station, was so blessed. A few constructions competed for size; some factory chimneys, the 'Parliament' and Royal Palace, the 'Exchange' and golden cupola of the Guildhall, pierced the smoke level; but in reality they knew their place. If any should still presume to challenge the supremacy of the spiritual there was the black bulk of the Papal Westminster Citadel to correct them. Watt's *The Defeat of Mammon* monument in the 'square mile', and St Peter's Column, recently restored, looming over Lepanto Square, made the same point in less intimidating manner. Lessons had been written in stone.

'More, probably,' agreed the cabby, harsh suspicion now entering his voice.

'I dare say,' the young man continued. 'And so there's fair reason for spitting on the place, if no other. And that's a happy choice of words! It's because of those places I'm *spat* out of London - and every-bloody-thing else. I wish a lightning bolt on each and every one!'

The cabman's voice became low and level. Preoccupied, his passenger didn't register the change.

'Are you expelled? Carrying a *dicta*, am I?'

The man shook his head.

'No, don't fret, you haven't broken canon law in 'aiding' me. I'm not under interdict or excommunicate. They dealt with me by *'administrative order'.*'

'Oh aye...?'

'Mind you, one feels much the same as the other.'

The cabby thought a while before responding: a departure amongst his swift-witted type, which should have swung alarum bells in itself. He twitched fretfully at the horses' reins.

'What's your grievance, mister?' he then asked, slow and deliberate. 'Are you apostate?'

His passenger turned again and shrugged.

'I *told* you: I'm not full 'bell, book and candle' if that's your worry. I've to go and *'pause and reflect'*. Only right now it's not having the effect they had in mind. *'Blessed are the poor'* is it? Not in my book they're not, and if their book says diff-..... Hey! What are you doing?'

The crash of a trunk down from the coach roof interrupted his bitter speech. His gear was being off-loaded with minimum respect.

'Bloody obvious I should have thought,' said the cabman.

'Hang fire - you can't dump me here!'

The cabby's laugh was malicious.

'Oh no? Bide and watch me. And don't think to interfere or you'll be earless as well as apostate.'

To illustrate the point he slid out just the hilt of the concealed cutlass.

The young man was furious – and also worried. But for the moment fury was foremost.

'I'd didn't say I was apost-....'

'Turk, Jew, Druid or atheist may ride with I and welcome,' interrupted the cabby. 'Drunks and fornicators I carry likewise - but not a turncoat: not at any price. I'm true Church me.'

His now ex-client dashed to stand in the road. He oughtn't to have been so surprised. For time out of mind, courtesy of Mother Church, St Christopher's Cab Guild had had the monopoly on London short-hauls: something to do with God's wish for full employment and similar nonsenses. Accordingly, cabbies could be prickly-pious.

'City of London law says you must accept any fare!'

Again there was that laugh.

'And how will you go to law after I've driven over you? Eh? A flat, dead, litigant with ruts in him? I don't think so. Clear the way or cop eight hoofs and four coach wheels!'

He was as good as his threat and whipped the team round and then forward. Only an undignified scramble to the roadside prevented a none too accidental accident.

'Think again, footslogger!' shouted the cabby as he passed, not even deigning to look at the person he'd recently called '*sir*'. 'Consider well as you tread the road to Hell!'

And then he was away, back down to his smoggy City.

There was silence, free even of birdsong, there being an absence of trees for them to roost in. All means of concealment were kept cleared well back from major thoroughfares.

The Great West Road was indeed like the path to perdition, being wide and easy going and yet joyless. The best the spring day could do failed to sweeten its features. Abandoned, the traveller looked about and, though trying hard, could find no encouragement in the sere surroundings. Ditched just two miles out of *Babylondon* - maybe less if that much detail could still be seen looking back - a long slog lay ahead. His destination, the fortified grimness of Heath Row Coach Park, straddled the twelfth milestone west. Worse still, he expected only cold comfort there: a maelstrom of transients and the sharks that preyed upon them.

For the most fleeting of moments he wished to just... lay down, to struggle no more, and peacefully find reunion with the dust. Then he recalled that dust was all he was, whatever all the others purported to believe, and that only darkness followed the final closing of the eyes. Being, however tedious, was better than un-being. He had to keep faith with that.

And therefore he had to eat what was put before him, feigning enjoyment of the present's tasteless offerings. The only way to the years ahead lay across Heath Row, all other routes being closed to him. Accordingly, its joys must be sampled and whining only served to poison the slog.

He reset his face into the belligerent smirk it was easiest with - and straightaway felt better for it. *'Down but not out,'* he repeated to himself, *'down but not out!'* That was the only manly attitude to take and he repented of any other, however momentarily maintained. Half carrying and half dragging the heavy trunk, and keeping a wary lookout for footpads, he resumed his journey.

There was the chance, albeit a poor one, of a late-running *'longrider coach'* at the Park or, second best, shelter at Colnbrook or one of the other hamlets which dotted the Waste. Failing that, one of the weird solitaries who chose this place as home might - after due inspection and reward - give refuge in their barricaded cottage. Push-come-to-shove he could even sit out the night in an abandoned dwelling, refusing to surrender to sleep or speculate how his refuge came to be blackened and tumbled.

'Down but not out'. If you determinedly sought it there was always hope: unfortunately not enough for optimism, but just sufficient, doled out in miser doses by life, to keep you persevering.

On the other hand, dusk was on its way, the time when those - human and otherwise - who drew a more predatory living from the Great Road came out to play. He'd heard of one band who saw fit to skin their victims and leave the pelt on the highway for next morning's wheels to trundle over. Others were said to hold human roasts to celebrate their robberies. Whilst safe behind London's walls he'd always scoffed and pronounced them 'smugglers' tales', designed to chill the blood and keep nosey-parkers indoors. Now, out on the heath and lonely, like a pea on a drum under the darkening sky, he was less sanguine.

With such cheerful thoughts as company, ancient habits reasserted themselves and he felt a powerful urge to pray. The temptation was - with effort - resisted. Instead he struck an inner bargain: that if he came through all this he'd wrench some benefit from it and learn his lesson. Misfortune was only opportunity in disgusting disguise. If he survived, ever after he'd keep his subversive opinions to himself.

Barred from the capital of his own nation, Samuel Melchizedek Trevan sweated his way into exile in the far West.

CHAPTER 3

He was set upon that road, quite unexpectedly, not two weeks before. Previously, all was well and every hope and plan in glorious ascendance. Then there arrived a series of visitors, each bearing fresh instalments of misfortune.

'I have just seen Hell!' said the first of them, a priest.

'No you haven't,' Samuel answered, 'not here anyway. I've been set up!'

He still had to raise his voice to be heard above the machines, even though they'd adjourned to the comparative peace of his office. The workplace noise inferno easily prevailed over London's street sounds outside. But he was of a mind to bawl anyway, whether in a Whitechapel factory or High Mass at the Vatican.

The Churchman swung round to confront Trevan's outrage, drawing close.

'Is that what you think?' he roared back, just as angry, though more in cold control. 'Is that *really* how you delude yourself?'

His companions shuffled forward, seeking conversation range.

Samuel spread wide his hands, a visible protestation of innocence.

'I just don't see what's *wrong*! It's been like this for ages. No one's complained!'

'Incorrect,' snapped a prim and disapproving curate, hitherto occupied making copious notes of all that the Church inspection party saw.

'Apart from them, I meant,' Samuel ranted, waving at the Labour Guilds observers, who weren't even bothering to conceal a festival of smirks and sneers. 'No one who works here's complained!'

'If you meet all opposition with such unreasoning fury,' replied the presiding priest, once again confident aloofness personified, 'I should imagine both labourers and artisans were too terrified to protest.'

'Fair point, Father,' chipped in one Guild man, a Turkic type clearly very proud of his parish-convenor's sash. 'All our tip-offs were anonymous.'

'Yes..., so you said.' To be fair, the priest seemed glad he had the plain evidence of his eyes to rely upon, rather than just the Guilds' testimony.

'Balls! Cack! Be quiet and give your arse a rest!'

Simple abuse silenced them when little else now would. Contrary to what they'd thought, it transpired Trevan had been restraining the bulk of his annoyance. All of the balance now came tumbling out to play and he was wild-eyed.

'I tell you people are *fighting* to work here,' he yelled. 'I'm turning them away all the time: no one pays better than me!'

The priest, a Cornishman by the sound of him, looked fit to strike Trevan at being spoken to thus. Internal engines of self-control, every bit as powerful as the lathes labouring all around, cut in to forestall such self-indulgence.

He stared at the factory owner and somehow aborted expression of first and best thoughts. The little group were hushed and expectant. Even some nearby machine tenders, who wouldn't normally dare to slacken or look up, stopped to await developments, imperfectly glimpsed through the office windows.

'And *don't* you just get your money's worth!' the priest said eventually, as soon as he could trust his tongue. 'Come with me!'

So saying he grasped Trevan by the shoulder and Samuel had no choice but to be born along. Left to themselves, force for force, Trevan might have made mincemeat of him. In reality, it being just one man, however blessed by nature, against a civilisation, the contest was forgone. The Guildsmen and sundry Church administrators tagged behind. They re-entered the workplace. Shouting became obligatory.

'Some things just seem to be invisible to you!' the priest told his captive, right in his ear. 'So let's see if I can't break the spell. Observe!' He pointed to a nearby crowded workbench. 'Now, are those children or what?'

'Yes, but-....'

'You don't maintain they're albino pygmies, I take it?'

Apparently not.

'It's only finishing work - no hot metal stuff. And their parents begged me to have them; the families need the money!'

'*Forbidden by law*, Trevan, as you well know - and likewise the strap your foremen employ to keep them at it.'

'How else do you make urchins concentrate?'

'What?'

Samuel repeated himself - still the soul of offended reason. Underwhelmed, the priest's lip curled.

'How indeed?' he roared back.

'But a schoolteacher'd treat 'em the same!'

'And speaking of which,' said the priest, 'where is the schoolroom obligatory for apprentice-employing establishments? Have I somehow missed it?'

'You know what space is like in London. Even for this pokey place I have to pay.... Hang on, who ordered...?'

The noise was dying. Someone had dared to damp down the great drive engine behind the far wall; an augury of things to come. The ranks of spindles it powered span more slowly. Thwarted lathes were being turned off.

'No schoolroom? *Forbidden*, Trevan: as are the hours these wretches' parents spend here.'

Samuel half-heartedly tried to wrench his shoulder free of the limpet grasp - and failed.

'We work the hours our clients need,' he said, 'and none longer than me. It's the Army and the Navy that urge us on: they've placed all this work here and it's them as screams when it's late. Why can't you cast an ear to that...?'

The priest's hesitation tacitly accepted a weakness in the indictment here. The source of funding that drove this sweatshop was the Achilles heel of the Church's otherwise unanswerable case. He pressed on, his prisoner with him.

'And I suppose this cheap crucifix on the wall is the statutory chapel facility?'

Actually, embarrassingly, it *was*: though the workers were generally too frantic to consider such things. Samuel could have repeated his protest about the space constraints but he was done with explanations now. For all his sleepless zeal he knew a lost cause when he saw one. A verdict had already been reached and the only thing available for salvage was his dignity.

'Righto,' he said, at last daring to bat the priest's guiding grip away, 'so that's it. We're finished here.'

The Industrial Inquisitor seemed relieved that the screamingly obvious was no longer in dispute. The impious assault on his hand was graciously overlooked, as religion dictated. He surveyed the myriad lines of tight-packed workbenches, the ant-like operatives and dangerously proximate lathes.

'Well, *you* are, certainly,' he agreed, in more reasonable tones than before, deciding this energetic rough diamond was owed the unadorned truth at least. 'In other hands *some* of this may remain, transformed into a more... civilised workplace.'

Trevan adjusted his work-stained frock coat and black beaver hat after the priest's rough handling. If he was to be dispossessed he didn't want to go looking like something the cat had played with.

'It's all yours then,' he said, in what he hoped were stoic tones, 'I'll leave it to you to administer the wind-down. And don't expect an abundance of blessings as you tell them they're sacked. There's families as'll starve because of this.'

'Better hunger than life as a blur of overwork,' countered the priest.

'Oh, you've convinced *me*, Father,' said Samuel. 'And good luck with persuading those who know what hunger really is. I do hope your ears don't burn when people say their prayers tonight - if they still bother....'

He was sailing close to the wind here and in an act of mercy the priest waved him to silence. The man was in trouble enough without courting blasphemy. That gesture, backed by an organisation that had authority over everything forever, was sufficient. Trevan stepped back from the precipice.

'Fair enough, Father,' he said. 'So on you go and fare ye well.'

The news was getting round the workforce, whispered from bench to bench. For the first time in the factory's history people dared to down tools and express an opinion. They now knew their master was going, though few fully understood why. The Church and Guilds had apparently spoken and, from the lowest oil-rag-monkey to best paid craftsman, it was appreciated there was no point in disputing with *them*.

Nevertheless, they could still comment.

As Samuel left for the last time, the rifle-makers affectionately applauded him on his way. The priest and his party shook their heads in sad disbelief.

At the door Trevan turned to acknowledge the fond farewell. He tipped his hat to them.

'Worry for yourselves, not me,' he said in reply, an unfelt smile occupying his slab face. 'Down I may be, but not out!'

And those of them who heard it, knowing what they did of the man, well believed him.

CHAPTER 4

When they wanted to, the wheels of Church administration could achieve a sprightly speed. Documentary confirmation of the decision reached Samuel just one week later. He was not hard to find, being self-confined to his rooms in the interval.

The Court's emissary discovered him 'at ease', unshaved and in shirtsleeves, a marked contrast to his own imposing gown of black slashed with papal-red. He arrived just as the empty brandy bottles were being cleared out. Their contents had been kind to a hitherto total-abstainer, blurring the first few days of dispossession. Samuel was still careful though, and declined to let that friendship blossom into love. Soon enough he'd pulled himself together and started writing letters.

There was the need to wind up one part of his life and then seek to explain all to those he hoped would still feature in what came next. That had proved hard work. The crumpled wreckage of those first, second and umpteenth drafts littered the floor of Trevan's furnished rooms, to be crunched underfoot as he paced up and down. Not one had yet reached finished form or been entrusted to a postal courier. Samuel was having trouble sanding down catastrophe into mere misfortune by dint of words.

'Come on in, don't be shy,' he said to his visitor. 'I've been expecting you.'

The officer-of-the-court noted the box of bottles.

'Evidently....'

He was wary, still seeking to gauge the situation. His host looked more like a prizefighter or churl-stock fairground wrestler than the *'industrialist'* he'd blithely expected. Worse still, his manner betrayed signs of uncertain temper and irregular opinions. A court-issue short-sword by the officer's side should have supplied comfort, but somehow did not. The less authorised brass *'knuckle-enhancers'* close to hand similarly failed to spark boldness. He was getting too old to roll round the floor with clients, especially when so close to retirement. Most likely this one could snap him in two, stealing all his golden years and pension. Pondering the wisdom of postponement and returning in force, he hesitated on the threshold.

'Mr Trevan? Mr Samuel Melchizedek Trevan?'

'None other. Why, who do you think I was? Mind your back.'

Samuel shoved the clinking box of dead-men through the door and out onto the landing. The house skivvies would clear them away later - probably. Meanwhile, let the other tenants see it and note the prodigious consumption. If he'd cared little enough before, there was even less cause for concern now. Meekly treading the path of 'respectability' hadn't exactly drowned him in acclaim, had it? He'd soon be on his way in any case.

Though he'd brushed past this elderly-but-erect caller brusquely enough, Trevan seized neither the opportunity to escape or the officer. So it seemed safe for him to proceed.

'This is for you.'

A thick parchment envelope sealed with the smoky red ribbon and wax seal of the ecclesiastical authorities was held out to Samuel.

'Oh, so I'm to be made a bishop at last, am I?'

Trevan's witticism was ignored whilst his right shoulder was anointed with the package.

'Official service,' said the officer. 'There's no going back now. You may open or dispose of it as you wish, young man. I strongly recommend the former.'

'Righto. Take a seat: I may have some questions.'

'That's why I'm here. Those things are always served by senior tipstaffs: to avoid confusion or ignorance of its terms.'

'Fair enough.'

Trevan crashed rearwards into the chair behind his desk and cracked the missive open. The officer meanwhile scooped some half-written letters out of a nearby horsehair chair, first checking for dust, before arranging himself and waiting patiently. A cheap boxwood mantelpiece clock ticked away the heavily pregnant minutes.

'Interesting...,' said Samuel, eventually, when he'd perused the quarto sheet within from close covered top to bottom. 'If you have to ruin a man's life I see there's ways of phrasing it nicely....'

'I may have to wish you good-day, Mr Trevan. It's queries I've bided here for, not sarcasm.'

'And don't for a moment think I'm not *gaspingly* grateful,' said Samuel. 'Yeah, there's a few things I'd like to ask.'

'Fire away.'

'Don't tempt me. London's out, I see.'

'Alas yes. Within seven days from service. Your name is infamous, your example unwelcome; you can never return.'

'On pain of?'

The officer's brow creased.

'Mediterranean galley service is the usual thing: though I've rarely seen the penalty imposed. I must tell you that the galley captains of the Hospitallers of St John are harsh masters, their enemies many. The ten year sentence is not often survived. Is London-life worth that risk?'

'Nope,' answered Trevan: swift and sure. 'It holds no intrinsic appeal and I'm a country boy for preference anyhow. Never fear, I'll be gone if required to. However, there's also mention of compensation; that sounds good: unexpected but good.'

The officer shook his snowy head.

'Mother Church does not steal, Mr Trevan. Always in these cases the market value of the business is assessed and refunded - less expenses and a deduction for any immoral enhancement of worth. The Archbishop's office will write to you with a - non-negotiable - offer. You may nominate a Hebrew goldsmith or Church Bank to hold it, or even take receipt in cash.'

Samuel mustered a gallows-grin.

'That'll make writing to my prospective father-in-law a sight easier. It was tricky trying to break the news he's gaining a beggar for a son.'

'You'll note there's restrictions on the money's use.'

'Yeah: no further *'enterprise or employment'*. For life?'

'*'In perpetuity'*; which is the same. Also the money is conditional.'

'Ah yes, that was my second major question: the confession business. What happens if I'm not given absolution?'

The officer leant back in the armchair. They had reached the point where Christian integrity forbade the slightest softening of edges. That stage was honoured with an expression of grave regret.

'Then,' he said slowly, inclining his hook nose in fatherly manner towards Trevan, dutifully anxious there be no grounds for mistake or doubt, 'forget money, marriage and all else. Exercise your rowing arm instead.'

'Ah....'

The officer stood up to go. He'd now stressed the one truly needful thing. In a neutral sort of way he wished this half-tamed ruffian well.

'If I may speak plain, young man, I suspect you've considerably advanced yourself in life. Your accent and manners still - just - reveal that. So, how sad it would be to end your - shortened - days criss-crossing the Middle Sea: below decks and in chains. Accept my counsel, which is, I assure you, disinterested and well meant. Repent handsomely, be shriven and complete your pilgrimage on earth as best you may. Why waste your one life and the troubles taken so far? You've come a long way Mr Trevan....'

He had indeed.

****

'And the King of Sodom went out to meet him after his return from the slaughter of Cherorlaomer, and of the kings that were with him, at the valley of Shaveh, which is the king's dale.

And Melchizedek king of Salem brought forth bread and wine: and he was the priest of the most high God.

And he blessed him, and said, Blessed be Abraham of the most high God, possessor of heaven and earth:

And blessed be the most high God, which hath delivered thine enemies into thy hand. And he gave him tithes of all.'

Genesis. Ch. 14, v. 18-20.

'... this Melchizedek, King of Salem, priest of the most high God, who met Abraham returning from the slaughter of the Kings, and blessed him;

To whom also Abraham gave a tenth part of all; first being by interpretation King of righteousness, and after that also King of Salem, which is, King of peace;

Without father, without mother, without descent, having neither beginning of days, nor end of life; but made like unto the Son of God; abideth a priest continually.

Now consider how great this man was, unto whom even the Patriarch Abraham gave the tenth of the spoils.'

St Paul's Epistle to the Hebrews. Ch. 7, v. 1-4.

'... Now, Melchizedek is a most interesting biblical personage; a mysterious, elusive and prophetic figure; a vehicle for all manner of symbolic portents, the significance of which are perhaps not fully unfolded and revealed to us even to this day. Though often referred to, for instance in the Psalms of David and by the apostle Paul, we meet him but once and then but briefly. The Patriarch Abraham has gained victory over the Kings

Amraphel, Arioch, Chedorlaomer and Tidal, who had kidnapped his son Lot when they prevailed over the doomed cities of Sodom and Gomorrah. The priest-king Melchizedek of Salem, an even then ancient name for Jerusalem, appears as from nowhere to approve the triumph. Our Father-in-faith, Abraham, defers to him, for reasons not vouchsafed to us, and accepts his blessing in the form of bread and wine. St Paul attests to Melchizedek's puzzling precedence by noting that 'that which is less is blessed by the better'. By contrast, the gratitude and gifts of the King of Sodom are disdained and rejected by Abraham.

We do not know the antecedents of Melchizedek, this primary monotheist, we do not learn his fate or hear one jot or tittle more of him. He draws back into the obscurity of the Bronze Age where, in this life, our curiosity cannot follow. Faith, however, allows us to be patient in our unknowing, whereas the pagan must be resigned to ignorance amidst his despair. The creed that has its roots in Melchizedek and Abraham inspires the quiet confidence that one day, for each and every one of us, all shall be revealed. Yes: just consider that for a moment: ALL!

Meanwhile, though this story's prefiguring of the Christian sacrifice of bread and wine is crystal clear, we are left to wonder what other revolutionary truths might be concealed within....'

'A Concordance to the Book of Genesis (together with a meditation on the significance of certain antediluvian animal relicts recovered in the County of Sussex).'

Cardinal Dave-Pierre Fairfax, Archbishop of New Wessex, Australasia. Fiat Lux World-wide Press Corporation, Brighton, England, the year of our Salvation 2420 AD.

****

CHAPTER 5

Samuel Melchizedek Trevan was born in the Downs Country. Or so he always maintained. When sufficiently off-guard to answer such questions, it suited him to say he came into being there. The assertion was broadly true, in the sense that his earliest recollections were set amidst those chalk-ranges of southern England. His custodians would neither confirm nor deny the notion, so he stuck with it. Certainly, Samuel carried nothing with him from any before-time.

So, when he first looked out upon the world (and remembered) the five year old Trevan saw rolling hills of close-cropped green, moulded by nature into voluptuous, feminine, form. Later, when innocence was past, he thought that might be the secret of their appeal to him, as surrogates for the mother he never knew. The theory was plausible, but no practical assistance, not to mention 'soft', and so he abandoned it.

There was no real 'first memory', but rather a collage of days. He was always atop a rise, briefly alone, the first, the most eager and energetic of the group, with the view to himself. All Sussex (the entire world then) was spread before and below him. The Downs air invigorated, the sunshine blessed him, and springy turf, close-cropped by the numberless sheep and colonised by rampion and rock roses, actively assisted his feet. *Tempus* didn't always *fugit* back then, at the beginning of Trevan-time, and it had no pretensions to tyranny. Mere minutes could seem like... as long as he liked.

Then Father Omar would loom over the brow of the hill, along with the rest of the children, and he would know he was safe and cared for, free to disobey mock-severe instructions, and rush on to fresh adventures.

Later images were more hard-edged and factual. Sights gained fixed names, like Lewes town, Firle Beacon and Mount Caburn. The mysterious *'Long Man'* dug into the hill at Wilmington, and Firle Place, home of the magnificent and holy Gage family, were pointed out to him. The 'New-Haven' and the glittering sea were just visible on the horizon, and it was even said there were lands beyond that! Samuel also heard whispers of less desirable things upon the Downs, of *disva*, of *downs-tigers*, and the inhuman Elf tribes, whose existence it was forbidden to acknowledge. Sometimes at night the orphans heard strange cries from the dark hills and trembled in their beds, but - in the south at least - mankind had the land well under control. Obedient children didn't need to worry.

In due course, Samuel learnt that the sheep were not toys, but useful things, called *Southdowns*, and it was they who kept the rolling hills open and treeless and as he wanted them to be for ever. It was also they who supplied orphan children with clothes for their back, and meat on Feast Days. Samuel was duly grateful and never more tormented them or chased them with sticks. One day, when he came across another, older, orphan-boy doing so, he broke his nose.

It was then he learnt another lesson: that Father Omar had an implacable side to him, and was willing to use his greater strength, just as Samuel had, to enforce justice. He'd struck both wrongdoers just once and each boxed ear immediately puffed and swelled. Samuel did not cry, although he dearly wanted to, because his... disappointment lent him resolve. Father Omar gravely observed that but, as was his way, never referred to the incident again.

As for the rest, it was all happiness, or at least all the happiness a cast adrift child should reasonably expect. The high-walled orphanage at Cliffe, industrial suburb of Lewes, had its fair share of bullies, cold-hearted staff and sordid secrets. Father Omar dealt with those he knew of as firmly as they might merit, and Samuel, already a sturdy boy in every sense, was equal to the unsuspected balance.

Even better, the children were daily instructed that the Universe was fundamentally *just*. Then it was proved for them one morning when they saw their giant presiding priest hurl a discovered-to-be-cruel tutor (with 'contacts' in the Town!) clean off Cliffe Bridge into the river Ouse. Father Omar Abdalhaqq ibn J'nna then tracked him along the bank, silently daring the half-drowned man to come ashore for further instruction. He didn't care for the challenge and struck out downstream to distant New-Haven. Receding frantic splashes were the orphanage's last sighting of him. He too was never mentioned again.

There was a coin for each child at Christmas, and sugar-sweets on their saint's-day. People quite often donated toys. Then, once a year on St Pancras' day, the nearby priory would entertain the entire orphanage, laying on a stupefying meal, with the solemn, silent monks waiting on the little children (for their own mortification and instruction). Afterwards, the gaunt old prior, a sorcerer of great repute, would entertain them with his art, causing stone gargoyles to caper in a jig, or great flames to spring from his fingertips and singe the lawn. They were terrified of him even as they admired him, and wondered why it was such an infinitely powerful man should dress so poorly, shave his head, and do as he was told, spending his life in prayer and service. Thus there was a lesson for them there too, even in that innocent occasion (though to be fair, a more or less unintended one). In adult life they'd discover that every (Christian) wizard was the creation and property of Mother Church - and they'd draw the proper conclusions from that.

So, all in all, it wasn't too bad a life; not the lap of luxury - far from it - but not grim endurance either. Father Omar, greater in height and bulk than any man in Lewes, expended himself and lined his face in warding off the worst the world could do to his charges. Whole decades passed and he was more or less successful.

Despite that benign regime, the young Trevan came to realise that the table set before him wasn't the standard menu. To start with, normal children had parents and, however rough and ready (a mere generation or two back for the peasantry), a family tree and context. Whereas he had none of those things. If Father Omar or the Orphanage trustees knew how and when he was entrusted to the *'St Philip Howard's Foundlings Refuge'*, they failed to enlighten him. Laying awake at night in the restless dormitory, Samuel's mind often circled round that fact, probing the void from which he apparently sprang. Strangely though, those ponderings failed to awaken much curiosity or sense of loss. He didn't pester Omar with questions on the subject, as other children often did. Separately, both he and the priest found that instructive.

Another difference sprang from the first, and was deepened by the self-containment just related. Samuel was driven by strong tides, but still retained complete control. From the very first, right from the initial anecdote retained in orphanage memory, Samuel *competed* - and nothing else but first and best would do. Even these victories, once achieved, were not celebrated but just shrugged at: transient stepping-stones on the way to greater things. Samuel Trevan never played childish games just for fun.

He was focused. Whatever he set himself to do expanded in size to eclipse the rest of the universe and, for the most part, whatever he required he obtained. Not overly blessed in academic skills, Samuel would sacrifice sunny holy days to wrestle with his books, his lips moving as he repeated the words till they made sense. Contrary to each successive tutor's expectations, he graduated from class to class. Whatever Father Omar and other priests told him about the ordering of the cosmos, he took in without challenge as in accord with his worldview. It just made sense that there be a no-nonsense Pope, and then God, to cap the hierarchy he saw about him. At sports and amidst his peers Samuel's width and strength made him unstoppable. It was not in him to be a bully or be bullied. From under heavy brows and from an already bulldog-ugly, intimidating face, Trevan looked out upon the world without fear.

And if any went in fear of *him*, it was only because they were up to fighting back, were in the way, and had been warned. He was very keen on 'justice', both received and meted out, and didn't see the need to be fairer than that.

In life therefore, as at orphanage mealtimes, Samuel ate every scrap set before him, without comment as to quality, and extracted maximum benefit from it.

For his part, Father Omar felt it almost a sin to cavil at such a success story. Some of his charges would perpetually lag in the game of life thanks to the poor initial hand dealt them. Samuel Melchizedek Trevan, by comparison, looked fit to cause *Life* problems, rather than the usual contrary. There was no good reason why so spirited a boy should cause his brow to furrow in projected concern. Yet he did.

Samuel's start in life comprised the first horse hitched to his cart: a spirited beast as it turned out, but not quite up to gallop speed alone. The second member of the team arrived by chance. Thereafter, with ambition as his fuel and a prize in sight, he required a lot of stopping.

****

****

On St Guy's Day Lewes came to a halt - or came to life, depending on your point of view. Business paused in despair and put up the shutters. Liberated from the mundane, most others were glad. Approving or not, every thought tended towards bonfire and anarchy.

Lewes Town had been rough-handled by the *'Reformation'* (or *'The Devastation'* as popular usage now termed it). Whereas Henry *'VIII-and-last'* ransacked a monastery or two, Edward, his son, closed churches, and Mary *'the Great'* burnt a few fanatics for reneging on the faith of their fathers, *'Black Betty'*, Elizabeth I, had visited the Downs and Weald country with a scourge of iron. For all that it had been sacked and burnt *after* smallpox called her to judgement, Lewes still bore scars from that reign. Later historians would note a centuries long absence of 'Elizabeths' from the Town's baptismal registers, a small token of their memory and appreciation.

Worse followed. Cecil's rebels briefly held Lewes, attempting a 'Protestant' utopia by fiery purging of 'ungodly' elements of the population. The unceasing sickly sweet pall over the Town provoked its besiegers to assault and massacre. Likewise, Spanish volunteers and the furious English amongst the royal army were not always able to distinguish between oppressors and oppressed. Fire broke out with no one minded to control it. Lewes almost died that day and surviving Lewesians, even the priests amongst them, wondered in their hearts if God slept.

Their waking nightmare continued, though with less intensity, through *'Armada'* and *'King Essex'* days. There were both good and bad years, but men were more inclined to repair town walls than their houses, and to stockpile arms rather than children. Lewes, in common with many places, grew grim.

Then Guy or 'Guido' Fawkes and his band of heroes blew the whole establishment asunder, beheading the state.

Headless nations may feign frantic activity, just like chickens in a similar predicament - but death is on its way all the same. After final paroxysms of violence born of fear, better times eventually returned - and the Church came with them so that the two appeared connected.

Lewes town had suffered more than most and keenly recalled the event that heralded liberation. On St Guy's Day, November the fifth, the daytime was therefore spent in holiday and pious remembrance. A sense of anticipation then grew as the hours passed and authority and propriety alike prepared for temporary withdrawal. Nightfall saw town-wide surrender to wild indulgence; to masked processions, bonfire and licence. Glass was broken and wild oats sowed, but nothing worse (generally). Good St Guy was toasted again and again and the *'Black Betty'* atop each towering bonfire damned to hell in chorus. The next day was an unofficial holiday, devoted to repairs and repentance.

Every parish in the town had its own bonfire confraternity, joined at birth and for eternity, thanks to the *obit* Masses they also arranged. In-between those two alpha and omega events, the organisation was always there to be turned to should poverty or sickness descend on any 'bonfire brother'. Over the centuries they acquired land from bequests and invested the means-tested subscriptions of the brethren, and thus came to prosperity. In Sussex County life they occupied a curious position; as institutions of great age and wealth and benevolence - yet still a league short of respectability, akin to a banker with both philanthropist and hooligan tendencies.

The Cliffe Bonfire Society chanced to own the land on which Samuel's orphanage stood, and had granted it in long, free, lease to the Church for that purpose. Accordingly, all the boys within were honorary members of 'Cliffe' and marched beneath its skull-and-crossbones black banner on the great and glorious day. It was also customary for each society to construct huge effigies (*'Black Bettys'* of course, but also others) to parade behind and confine to the fire. Every group vied to produce the biggest, most life-like, most insulting, figure, and pains were taken to ensure secrecy around it until unveiling. The walls of 'St Philip Howard's offered ideal concealment and for decades past the orphanage served their benefactors in this way. It was the merest return it might make, and if Father Omar didn't always approve of the grotesques constructed before his very eyes he was powerless against such a weight of tradition and indebtedness.

It was partly as a result of this, and chance, and - as with so many matters in his world, a certain Tudor King - that Samuel received his mission.

****

****

The idea was to get your figurine to the main procession's start without any other society catching sight. That way its impact was maximised by novelty. There were few things more gratifying to a true 'son-of-bonfire' than to hear gasps of acclamation, outrage and surprise greet the revealing of your labour of love. Since each grouping had the same task before it, the same urge to speed and discretion of delivery, it wasn't all that hard to achieve success. Everyone was too intent on their own project to much hinder or thwart another's. On the other hand, in honour of the day, a token amount of prying and mischief making was expected, as were exertions to evade it. By late afternoon the Town was swarming with conspiratorial parties. That was how Master Trevan came to the forefront and his fateful moment.

Lewes was strung through with short cuts, called *'twittens'* in local dialect, just as other places called them *'gates'* or *'passages'*. Survivals of the medieval street pattern, they'd once been run-offs between tenements, stretching down to the defensive walls. Now hallowed by time and formalised into pedestrian ways, cold-shouldered by and walled off from neighbouring houses, they ran for long distances, offering a discreet means between many an *A* and *B*.

'Church Twitten', with its high flint walls and overhanging trees, was perfect, albeit a tight squeeze, for Cliffe Bonfire's purpose. It stretched right from the river and priory up to the High Street. With partisans to guard either end, the effigies, all shrouded in tarpaulin, could be dragged along to commence a brief public life in relative privacy. This was the Society's favoured route, even though it entailed first pontooning the figures over the Ouse, and they'd have used it every year save that such lawyer-caution wasn't in the spirit of the feast.

The Orphanage was always entrusted (and honoured) with pulling one of the creations, and that year, 1988, it chanced to be the principal parody and main effort. By virtue of his size and spirit, Samuel was chosen captain of the selected boys. He ordered awaiting the chimes of five and serious dusk before sallying out. The cold nipped at faces and fingers but at least it was dry: perfect Bonfire weather.

Soon he and his team merged into the protective midst of the swarming, excited, Cliffe contingent; a multitude all too willing to offer assistance should youthful muscles flag. Then, with such an abundance of helping hands to haul the precious charge, Trevan felt free to press ahead, to scout the route and secure the twitten's further reaches against surprise. Two-score Cliffe rascals were with him, in ribbon-enlivened Sunday-best and war-painted faces. Each brandished the traditional *'Black Betty's fan'* (illegal on any other day): a stout hardwood club decorated with that dead queen's screaming face lapped by hellfire. As fully intended, they looked a desperate crew, merely half-feral at this decorous stage of proceedings, yet hungry to commune with the wilder-still heart of 'Bonfire'. Samuel felt fitted; part of the group and in his place. It wasn't in his mind to leave or change, and the years ahead seemed set to roll on pretty straightforward.

He shouldn't have presumed.

Two thirds along, Church Twitten took a right turn. Strolling around that corner came his future.

****

'Oh....'

'No passage here, miss,' said Samuel. 'Cliffe's coming through.'

'I'll go back.'

'Ain't offering much choice, am I?'

'No, not really.'

She was his age but educated: well spoken - very well spoken - though light on the haughtiness that usually rode tandem. Outside of the licence of Bonfire day Samuel might not have spoken so briskly to her. Then one of his bonfire-brothers felt free to push the boundaries even further.

'About turn and show us y'rear view, dolly-dumpling, 'fore we tread you in!'

Samuel had learnt the knack of shutting people up with just a look. He used it on his coarse friend.

'Walk with me,' he told the girl, who had blushed most arousingly. Issuing orders against the current of the class structure was presumption in itself, but there and then Trevan could pose as her protector and thus be excused. They drew clear of the slow oncoming mob.

Trevan escorted her back whence she came, to the junction with High Street. The expected gawpers were waiting and his companions got distracted in dispersing them with waves of the betty-fans. There was an opportunity for unpressured discourse. He wondered why he felt so tense.

'You'll have to wait till we pass. Where were you going?'

'Out.'

And so Samuel learnt she wasn't so soft or flustered as she looked. Nor did she feel obliged to elaborate. Samuel was... unsettled by his strong wish to learn more. There was a queasy feeling of ebbing control.

'Are you in charge?'

Her question was a killer, perfectly exploiting his sudden self-doubt. Could she detect it? Or was the girl simply up to turning the tide of interrogation?

She had to elevate her head to address Samuel eye to eye. That contact was fleeting but long enough for him to note the flash of cobalt blue under long lashes. He felt eight foot tall and clumsy with it.

Samuel looked down into the pale face and, quite unlike him, wanted to say the most impressive instead of truthful answer.

'Sort of.... Well, not really. Just of that one.'

He pointed behind. By application of brute force and ignorance, the star effigy was negotiating the twitten's corner. Beneath the covers the rough shape rocked and wobbled alarmingly.

'Is it any good?' the girl asked.

That was almost saucy, though he couldn't detect any mockery in her modestly evasive gaze. If Cliffe didn't think it was 'good' they'd not have entered it! There was a prize that went to the finest creation, and a full year of honour and boasting besides. Up to that moment Samuel would have said their 'Henry-Abomination-Tudor, VIII-and-last' was 'good'. He'd even been caused to grin at it as the monstrosity took shape. Certainly it was the best, a walk-away winner, and local patriotism would have had him say so even if it wasn't.

Strangely though, just then, he'd rather the girl wasn't about when it was unveiled, to associate it with *him*. Samuel knew how King Henry's codpiece swelled obscenely up to meet a drooping gut. The titanic arse they'd grafted on him would raise laughs - but also embarrassment. Then he recalled the naked maidens being devoured in Henry's bloody maw....

'You ought to go.'

He'd bluntly ignored her question, and she visibly registered that and the new rough edge of his tone. Directly repenting it, Samuel sought to explain.

'Only it's like... well, the Cliffe boys will speak ripe - and there'll be beer flowing and the flaming tar barrels.... Look, miss, ain't you got your own society to go to?'

She ought to, for every locality banded together to celebrate the day, and only the most prim and proper and unpopular stayed away.

As answer she just nodded. And left. Leaving Samuel unsure whether he'd upset or frightened her, or if she'd simply cut short an inconsequential exchange, forgetting him already. He found he didn't want any of those things to be true.

She was still visible for a little while, a pint-sized plump figure threading her way, not noticeably distressed or hurried, up the rapidly filling High Street. He tracked her with his eyes, a hard and hungry, single-minded stare that others spotted but thought better than to comment on. There was a final sight of her bonnet and hennaed hair, glimpsed in a gap between a decorated dray and the Martyrs' monument, and then no more. But Samuel wanted more.

After that he was occupied with things to do; with positioning King Henry and divesting him of ropes and sheets to be shown forth in all his sordid glory. The animal cheer that greeted the sight showed straightway this would a great day for Cliffe.

Samuel took full part in it, not stinting himself in anything, from procession, to Mass, through to pyrotechnic evening; right until Orphanage gate-time. Even under that last spoilsport restraint, he found time to taste beer and break glass, amply honouring Lewes' long ago deliverance. After that spell of weakness in Church Twitten, transfixed by the 'elf arrow' as the Downs shepherds would have called it, no one would have noticed anything different to him.

Yet, all the time, Samuel Trevan was thinking on. Thinking on a single thought.

He had to have her.

CHAPTER 6

It wasn't romantic 'love' or anything daft like that. Romance was not exalted in Samuel's world. There was 'lust' and 'friendship' and 'affection', but the only 'love' his civilisation recognised was as mentioned in its holy book - a very different concept. True, infatuation featured in some popular ballads but by and large it stayed there. Too close to the harsh facts of life to revere mere sentiment, Christendom (and everywhere else as best they knew) looked for better reasons in choosing a companion for one's pilgrimage on earth. Piety, inheritance or childbearing hips rated way above attraction.

Samuel knew all this - and accepted it. Even aged fifteen he could well distinguish between lechery and deeper longings. It was all the more strange therefore that, from that day on, without doubt or decrease, he was fired with a new ambition. Like a prophet heeding revelation, humbly accepting the new dispensation, he just got on with the unavoidable.

In all truth, as he soon found out, there was a steep mountain to climb. At the same time things became much more simple for him - in a complicated sort of way. *He had to have her* - and not just in the sexual sense, but have everything she represented too. That was the long and the short of it: a life's project capable of summary in five words. He had to have her. Whatever it took, that's what he'd spend his time doing. There was no point debating it.

Once again, Samuel Trevan uncomplainingly ate what was put before him. Only this time he was ravenous - and salivating: covetous of a feast intended for his betters.

****

She (for it was some time before enquiries grafted on a name) lived in comfort and Southover. Those two words went together like horse and cart. There were a few paupers' places over towards the priory grounds, drawn and protected by that institution, sustained by the charity it offered daily, but otherwise Southover held mostly *nice* houses. Samuel's heart dipped on hearing she emanated from *that* part of Lewes town.

He'd moved cautiously to learn what he wanted. There was no question of being so crass as to search her out himself. Neither could he employ anyone who might be curious about *his* curiosity. This was a weighty matter, too important for haste or hostages to fortune. In the few gaps in Orphanage routine he pondered little else. In the Chapel he sought guidance in prayer.

Providence then sent him an itinerant knife-grinder, a sad crippled veteran of the Welsh wars, who did business all over Lewes. From Snowdonia sniper days he'd learnt the art of careful observation - and the joys of silence. For his part, Samuel had contacts in the Orphanage kitchen and could arrange regular, much needed, business. There was a conversation, skirting round matters of mutual benefit, innocent of crude bargaining. Even then Samuel knew solicitude for other people's dignity, especially among the luckless, was half the battle. They easily came to an arrangement.

The old soldier plied the streets longer and more attentively than was usual. It didn't matter that his stump-leg rubbed raw and his good eye tired: he'd been *entrusted*, like in past days. Shortly after, the target entered his sights. He reported back - and got sufficient trade to drink himself to sleep every night for a week, easing both the inner and outer pain. Each blade in St Philip's, every metal tool capable of taking an edge, was honed like a barber's razor. Father Omar was caused to slice his thumb open when peeling an apple.

Samuel Trevan then took charge of the metaphoric musket. She was in his sights now - never to leave them again.

A few days later the orphans were granted a holiday, consequent on a great Crusader victory in Latvia - or possibly the Crimea: Samuel was too preoccupied to take in the details. He made straightaway to Southover.

The Town was ablaze with bright stars of tin or painted wood - or even paper in the poorer quarters - to mark the impending nativity. Man's weak imitation of God's night sky, they symbolised the coming of light into the world - or maybe the Star of Bethlehem: opinions varied. It was just another of those innovations brought back by the victorious Crusaders three centuries ago, and now as 'traditional' as the twice life-sized crib scene dominating the brow of High Street. Pious folk even cast stars up into the boughs of evergreens, acquitting the innocent trees of Baltic-pagan Yuletide associations.

Her home was in Keere Street, whose constellations were among the best; polished steel sunbursts from the Wealden forest foundries, or complex glass and wire lattices harbouring a lamp within. Apparently, she resided near the bottom of that steep and select cobbled road.

For one bad moment Samuel thought it was *Southover House*, the great edifice built of Caen-stone robbed from the first priory of St Pancras back in 'Reformation-Devastation' times. The Church, when it returned in victory, robbed it back so to speak, and bestowed the freehold on more faithful servants. That happened to be the Howards of Arundel, Earls of Sussex, advisors to Cardinals and Kings, and even Trevan's energies quailed before the notion of approaching *them*. He didn't dare consider what favoured tenant or retainer they'd installed within. Father Omar (a fanatic re local history) related how the Blessed Isaac Newton had conversed with the Creator in that very property, writing down verbatim the *'Aetheria Principia'*. The study in which the voice of God once resounded was now forever sealed; a shrine to Christendom's few dabblers in *'natural philosophy'*.

It was all too intimidating for Samuel to contemplate. Despair stood in the wings, poised to come on. Fortunately, his misapprehension soon became evident.

The correct address was not so unattainably grand, but a powerful mismatch all the same. The best destiny Samuel could reasonably aspire to was a trade apprenticeship in the Town - and even scrolling on a decade or two, once qualified and Guild-approved, no Lewes artisan, however assiduous or fortunate, would end up in such favoured accommodation. There was Caen-stone in those walls as well as good Wealden brick (though insufficient to merit Church repossession). The roof was capped by strong Horsham-stone, not thatch, and the wide windows were defined by fashionable '*mathematical*' tiles (peculiar to well-to-do Lewes and Brighton) in pink and red. In the small front garden there sat an ancient sundial. But best of all, the front gate bore a brass name-plate, boldly stating:

GALEN HOUSE
M. Farncombe Esq. MA (Wessex). Surgeon.

The house was old and yet preserved and improved all at the same time - and thus perfectly in keeping with the spirit of the age. Samuel stood before it and did homage.

There was no way of knowing, but he indulged himself and just assumed she was within. He thought of her at the - presumed - grand dining table, or seated before a harpsichord, or even, despite the hour, pink and naked tucked up in bed. They were all equally ravishing visions. He remained there a long while and barely noticed a brief shower of rain.

Perhaps Samuel's fervent thoughts called her forth, or maybe made the atmosphere inside humid and unbearable. Whatever the reason, like an answer to his prayers, she emerged.

The girl was arm in arm with her presumed father, a set-faced man in a stovepipe hat. He loomed over her, stiff and unaffectionate in Samuel's attuned judgement: though little enough time was wasted in studying *him*.

As for *her*, in cape and black crinoline and matching riding bonnet, she looked even grander than at their first encounter - and more glorious. The reality was plumper and paler than the image he'd treasured, but it was the reality, not illusion, he was after. False, enhanced, recollections were mercilessly jettisoned without regret in favour of the actual. His sincerity was vindicated.

Father and daughter noticed him at the same time. Myriad minor signs told them this was no pure and simple passer-by. Father glared - though unsure why. Daughter surveyed - although free to interpose her opened umbrella. She and Samuel fixed glances: for just one precious second.

'Ignore him, Melissa,' ordered Papa. 'Keep walking.'

'Melissa' obeyed. Then they were past the interloper.

It was an inconsequential encounter to all outward appearance. Superficially, there was nothing untoward about it. In a relatively unrushed world people often stood and stared. Yet, inwardly, each of them knew, even if presently only via a vague dislocation, that something life-long had been born.

****

'Your going is a cloud in the clear sky of our happiness. We require you to repent and reconsider.'

For all his years in Sussex, Father Omar retained the courtly and poetic form of speech peculiar to his homeland. What scholars called *'Jerusalem dialect'* beautifully mutated whichever tongue it employed.

'Ask anything else.' Samuel's bad conscience made him hard-faced and curt. Being a disobedient son left internal scars. 'You know the *one* thing that's impossible and then ask for it. That's not right.'

The autumn of life had come upon Father Omar swiftly. His spade beard, hair's final redoubt on his head, was grizzled. Those broad shoulders found it an effort not to slump. Both locks and vigour had fled away and now Samuel proposed to emulate them.

'Inform me,' said the priest, 'oh Samuel-of-the-single-mind, who first taught *you* of right and wrong? Who whispered the sublime notions in your infant ear? Do you now instruct *me*?'

'If need be!'

Samuel's eyes were porcine and uncharitable at the best of times: but, them being God-given, he couldn't be held responsible. However, in surrender to anger they became as hard and shiny as sea pebbles. Blame might be attached to that sight.

The priest accepted their ill will without demur - which only made the situation worse.

'You have answered me correctly, child,' said Omar, gently. 'A dawn breaks in our darkness. We have taught you well.'

Samuel sat back and closed those same eyes, pretending that summer sunshine slanting through the window pained them. Yet the scene persisted, printed upon the retina.

'I am an ungrateful sod,' he said. 'I know. I'm sorry: really sorry.'

Father Omar steepled his massive hands and looked out of his office at the river.

'No, son-of-chance, you are not one of these *sods*. You are driven. We pity you. We will never approve but we... sympathise.'

That surprised Samuel and he opened his eyes again. He realised he should have had faith. In consequence, and if it were possible, he felt even more unworthy.

'So, I go with your blessing?'

Father Omar smiled.

'Samuel Trevan, my blessings will never leave you. No child of these walls is ever threatened by mere conditional love. All I implore is that you do not tread a perilous path.'

Samuel looked down, burning a hole in the floor.

'I have to. Otherwise I'd stay, I'd take the apprenticeship and never leave. But... I'm not destined to be a barrel-maker.'

Omar disdainfully shook his head.

'There is no such thing as destiny, or what you English called *wyrd*. There are only decisions. Today you are fifteen years and 364 days old, and thus in our charge. Your '*destiny*' is still our remit. Tomorrow that changes. Decide well tomorrow, Samuel, but never for one moment think our care for you could be severed by a birthday.'

So that was it. All the family he'd even known or wanted had acquiesced to his radical plans. He'd steeled himself to do it but, thank God, there'd be no final rupture. Despond was replaced by elation.

'If you forgive me,' Trevan blurted out, 'then I have all I want!'

The priest frowned, unable to prevent it.

'Not *all*, surely?' he said quietly. 'You only go to London in hope of procuring what you do not have – and what a Lewes barrel-maker can never have.'

It needed no elaboration. He spoke unmistakably of Miss Melissa Farncombe. The past year had been dominated by Samuel's stormy courtship of her - and seared by the lightning it produced. Not that he had disgraced himself, instead proceeding like the gentleman he wasn't with 'chance' meetings and the most decorous of letters. Even so, the air between Cliffe and Southover turned sulphurous when Mr Farncombe found out. Father Omar had aborted talk of '*horsewhipping*' or the stocks: he had that much influence in the town. Nevertheless, the price of peace was a strict cordon separating Samuel and Southover.

Being a dutiful son of St Philip's - for a little longer - Trevan had complied with every term imposed. A promise to Father Omar was like a bargain with the Deity he represented. But both parties knew that this was just a cease-fire, a postponement of the struggle rather than defeat. The boy was quite open about it: the campaign would continue as soon as he was free and a man - and a freeman.

Samuel declined to discuss the painful subject. That ambition was forever bubbling up inside him, just below the surface, close to boiling over. Thoughts of it prompted his next question.

'So, do I get my file?'

It was the usual practice, though at their discretion, for the Orphanage to offer their parentage records (if any) to children leaving its custody. A surprising number spurned the chance, wisely passing up on the usual sad litany of accident, bastardy and abandonment. Unlike them, Samuel thought he could take it. And besides, there was always the outside chance of some favourable circumstance of birth - admittedly gone horribly wrong - being revealed. That might assist him in his great project.

Father Omar crushed the suggestion with finality absent from his previous strictures. The answer came out in unadorned English.

'No. You do not. It should not matter to you. Where you are going people are as careless of backgrounds as you have hitherto been. I shall pray that that remains the only similarity between Samuel Trevan and London life.'

CHAPTER 7

'... if you are reading these words and have not so far transformed yourself as to forget my instructions, I must assume that you have remained obdurate and are now in London. I send you greetings - and my fears. I fear that life has equipped you all too well to survive. Your strength of brawn and brain may tempt you to the straightest routes. Recall that straight routes are quickest but oft cross other persons' property. Do not trample that which is in the way merely because you can.

I am mindful that your leaving bounty is inadequate. In Lewes it would have been your start and sufficient; but in the big city where you are alone, £20 is a razor-breadth from poverty. I would not have you resort to crime. I have little enough but need even less. In my sinful selfishness I desired to retain sufficient to purchase my obit Masses for when I am gone from here. But no, you shall have it all and my remembrance shall be your duty. Herein is a promissory note drawn on an Arundel goldsmith, now amended in your favour. I believe you may redeem or invest it with a Hebrew merchant, of which, it is said, there are many in London Town. Alternatively, a Church Bank could safeguard this sum but you would not, of course, earn interest. Recall Matthew, 25:14, the parable of the talents.

My grandfather came from Egypt, the land, as you would recall if you paid attention to your geography lessons, of the Mameluke-Caliph. However, there were rulers there long, long before them, called 'Pharaohs'. They are mentioned in Scripture. This was right at the beginning of time, soon after Creation and the Fall; before Christ but after Babel. Consequently, their script is strange although scholars have translated some of it. Thus my father's father could tell me of a blessing of theirs that he saw, painted on a tomb wall even before Abraham left Ur at the command of the Almighty. It had lingered and waited patiently through all human history for me to repeat to you now – because I feel it is apposite to your situation:

'May G*d be between you and harm in all the empty places you walk.'

To the greater glory of G*d, from Omar Abdalhaqq ibn J'nna.
St Philip Howard's Foundlings Refuge, Cliffe, Lewes, Sussex.
The 23rd day of June, The Year of Our Salvation 1989.

One hundred and twenty-seven pounds! One hundred! And twenty-seven! Pounds!

It was a fortune - and yet not enough. He could buy his way into a decent Guild apprenticeship with it and look forward to a settled, fairly well-off, life. Employing hard haggling he might even acquire a little shop... or something.

Samuel was both glad - and not. This was the antidote to starvation - but at the same time his doom. The temptations to mediocrity and compromise were back again, powerfully reinforced. He'd retained a strong grasp on his ambitions, for all that fear and hunger were stamping on his fingertips. It helped that there was little alternative - but now....

'May the Lord keep *you*, Father Omar,' Samuel whispered, 'and also forgive my ingratitude.'

He was in the right place to say such things, having come into a church to read the letter. The workers' hostel which had been draining the last of his pennies was too much a madhouse of noise for serious reading or thought or anything.

The absence of a mother figure meant many of St Philip's inmates developed a strong devotion to Mary. Samuel didn't go so far as some, but neither was he immune. Sighting a 'Our Lady of Flowers' image, ablaze in candlelight, he was reminded. He offered up to her his sore feet, dirty clothes and empty belly - and a vow.

'It's like *this*!' Samuel stated, setting the Universe straight. 'When Omar goes, I'll see to his obit Masses: the high altar, Lewes Cathedral: every year. It's my business now. That's how it'll be.'

In his amateur opinion he doubted Father Omar would be long in purgatory anyway - but that wasn't for him to judge.

'Also, sweet lady,' he added, 'give me strength.'

And She - or someone - apparently did.

****

'Now, are you *sure?*'

'Completely.'

'Young man, I wish there to be no doubt. Your signature entrusts this money for five long years. Otherwise you gain no interest. This way the rate is good but meanwhile you cannot dip within free of penalty.'

'Bloody hell, Christ-killer! How many *more* times?'

The Hebrew thought and then decided. He smiled to reduce the tension and pushed the tally book forward. Samuel took up the offered inkstick and added his name to the form of words.

'I hope you will forgive some further observations...,' said the goldsmith-cum-banker.

'Depends what they are,' answered Trevan.

'It is merely that you seem... young to possess such a note. Yet the name in Arundel is good with me; the making over to yourself faultless....'

Samuel saved the man some trouble.

'But I look like I've been through a hedge backwards, right?'

The Hebrew shrugged, a disarming *it's-your-life* gesture. The tassels on his prayer shawl repeated it at waist level. He could afford to be relaxed. Given the nature of his trade there was security aplenty to hand: a stiletto beneath the shop counter, three hefty sons out the back. Even so, there was something innate to this young Christian that impelled the seeking out of his right side. And if his professional life had taught the Hebrew anything it was that instinct knew best. He decided to go with it.

'When you said you wished to invest, my initial misgivings disappeared. The fraudulent desire only immediate gold in their hands. Thus I am satisfied. Would you care for refreshments whilst your certificate is drawn up?'

The tally book was already passed to an elderly clerk perched on a high desk. He began to unroll a piece of vellum on which to inscribe the transaction.

Samuel was ravenous but he'd heard disturbing things about the Jewish way with food - something about saving or removing blood. Whether true or false he still feared falling on whatever was provided and *devouring* every crumb. Which wasn't on: not here. It must serve as another

51

test of resolve.

'No thanks,' he said. 'I'll call later and collect it.'

'But you'll have no receipt till then,' the Hebrew protested. 'It is a substantial sum....'

'I trust you. You wouldn't cheat me.'

There were two aspects of truth to that. Firstly, it suited Christendom to tolerate some usury in its midst - but any fraud allowed expression of a backlog of disapproval. Justice wasn't often tempered by mercy in such cases; and punishments had been known to get a touch indiscriminate - even communal. The Hebrews, mindful of this, operated their own draconian system of control. Legend had it that throats were slit and wrongs put right long before the Christians got wind of them.

Secondly, Samuel was discovering that he'd brought more than luggage up from Sussex. The caution he inspired at Cliffe survived the transfer to London's wider stage. For all that he was on the way to being ragged, something within him made people... careful, and solicitous of his good opinion. Aside from the sum he'd just stored out of reach for five years it was his only asset. Aware of that, he was constantly testing its extent.

'You're right,' agreed the Hebrew, keeping any inflection from his voice. 'I wouldn't cheat you. Because God is watching.'

Trevan followed the Hebrew's upward gaze – and made clear he saw only ceiling. He even waved at the nothing. The transaction failed to end in handshakes.

Outside the fortified shop, Samuel punched the air in triumph. He stared down a passing group of black-clad clerks who'd looked at him.

'*Yes!*' he said, to no one and everyone.

Yes: he'd won another victory over self. That was another temptation gone. With such a record of defeat his weaker impulses ought to soon give up the fight and depart. The sooner the better: they're weren't welcome on the voyage he intended.

Samuel strode off down Lower Thames Street into the future, stomach rumbling plaintively.

CHAPTER 8

'Get him!'

'Oi, shit-a-bed! Come 'ere!'

Samuel had no intention of doing any such thing: Middlesex Street market must see him no more – unless/until he got hungry again. Meanwhile, this pilfered round of bread was rightly his by virtue of the Trade Guilds shutting him out from every honest employment. If he was forever damned as a *'straw-head Sussex foreigner'* everywhere he went then he'd bloody well behave like one.

What he lacked in speed he made up for in bulk. People that might have impeded a swifter but thinner man thought it higher wisdom to get out of Samuel's way. Thus he made good time through the crowded market place. Sanctuary or concealment were hard by: Crutched Friars or Pepys Park respectively. With luck he ought to make it.

Unfortunately, the path he cleared was of equal use to the Watchmen and stallholder. Some of them had longer legs than he. There was also the question of them tiring of the chase and seeking a clean shot. His back, broad enough as it was, felt a mile wide and getting wider.

As if it weren't enough that he should chose to turn thief just as a Watch patrol passed by, fate saw fit to throw in a moral dilemma. Samuel could just have trampled the toddler: she would have survived. Her mother had shamelessly failed the test and drawn back from impact, but the child was not so agile. Trevan could not go round her; his pace too headlong, the way blocked by stalls. As with life itself, the choice was either to proceed or concede. Much as it might be desired, there was no option to step aside for

53

a while, to rest and soberly review.

Given his background, it wasn't open to Samuel to be ruthless regarding an abandoned child. He halted and turned to face the hunt.

There were four main actors besides himself, plus a swarm of bit-players who might saunter on stage when the plot was clarified. The officer of the Watch stood back, dimly glimpsed behind his men and of no present account. Samuel calmly rested the stolen cartwheel loaf on a handy barrow.

'Righty-*ho!*'

They hadn't expected him to speak first. Nor was it playing the game to not surrender.

'Righty-ho to you too, you basta-....'

The portly Watchman, all puffed out and florid, hadn't thought to be drawn forward by the muzzle of his own musket. He'd been waving it in the general direction of the criminal's chest. That should have been deterrent enough. Meeting Samuel's fist ended his brief and petulant thoughts on the subject.

Then an elbow jab and an agonising boot to the vulnerable shin area greatly reduced the interest of two more guardians of market law. Finally, since it didn't seem fair (as the injured party) to likewise anoint the bread stall man, Samuel dismissed him with a *'Boo!'* to his frightened face. And that seemed that.

He was armed now with the fallen Watchman's gun, but made no move to use it. The field was his to quit. Around him the circling mob drew back. There was even some applause. Samuel looked at the grinning faces and realised his mistake. He'd hadn't come to London to earn this sort of approval. He imagined other faces - and two in particular - observing.

'On second thoughts,' Trevan told his adversaries, both sleeping and shrinking variants, 'I'll keep my dignity: you keep your bread. I'd sooner starve.'

The loaf was spun at its former owner and thudded into his chest, causing him to step back - his favoured direction at the moment.

'And... sorry.'

So saying, Samuel dropped the musket, having first disabled it by wrenching out the lighted cord. He turned to go.

'I don't *think* so.'

It was the Watch-officer's first utterance and had horrible confidence about it. Whether he was doubting Samuel's apology or departure or both was unclear. What was certain and relevant was his pistol aimed at Samuel's head.

He was a drinker, his face told that much: but presently in passable control. He might even be a jolly man when not borrowing the Grim Reaper's eyes, as now.

'Oh *yes*, certainly,' the man laughed, perceiving and answering his target's unspoken question. It was kind of him to confirm he would shoot. Samuel looked and believed.

'For mettlesome gentlemen such as yourself,' said the officer, his business arm never wavering, 'we go that extra mile. *Special* care. So that you can go extra miles for us….'

The worst elements in the crowd guffawed and started to make rowing motions.

****

'Look on, boy: store that sight in your mind to tell y' grandchildren.'

There was only one person Samuel wished to sire descendants from, and here, mired in this slough of fortune, he didn't thank people for reminders of her. So the rickety old soldier's attempt at conversation went unanswered. Unfortunately, the man's lonely home-life led him to persevere.

'Still, a well-set-up bruiser like you, I s'pose you'd rather be out there in the thick of it.'

Further failure to reply would be downright insulting. Samuel forced himself to think, studying the view.

He knew that, over to the west, Reading was ablaze. It had been a smoke-pall against the sunset and now a faint glow by night. Lesser lights orbited it as nearby villages went up. Guard duty on London's walls provided a nicely distant view of the Leveller insurrection dying in flames.

'I don't know so much,' Samuel answered eventually. 'Not having killed anything more than a rabbit it might not be to my taste. Besides, death himself is striding round out there: it's not all one way. I can't be doing with too much danger: I've plans to fulfil first.'

The old man was obviously impressed, taken aback by an honest reply.

That wasn't too common in the not exactly elite City Watch, especially now its better elements were drawn off into the Thames Valley Crusade. Samuel would have joined them but for the ten year term binding him. That had been the price demanded for escaping a galley rowing-bench; the local commander's way of retaining a few handy types at his disposal. *'Set a thief to... well, you know the saying'*, was the way he put it as Samuel put his signature to the contract. It was a bargain and a kindness really. Mediterranean galley slaves rarely outlived their sentence.

'You've a good heart, Trevan,' his companion informed him, still staring out at the holocaust that would end the campaign. 'Don't lose it. Carry on just as you are. I've raised men up and laid men low in my time, and I've no doubt which's better.'

Samuel turned about. The sentry duty was dragging, and nothing was going to happen anyway. The fiery horizon told him that: the rebels were beaten, and he only had the squalid Watch barracks to go 'home' to. He was overdue some human contact.

'I didn't know you had family, Walter. Someone said you were all alone.'

'I am. I lost 'em in a shipwreck off Morwenstow - that's down Cornwall way, I'm told - back in '63. The wife and all my little 'uns perished.'

'I'm sorry.' Samuel hefted his heavy musket and shifted footing on the parapet.

'So was I. People said wreckers done it, holding out Judas-lights to draw 'em in. I know they do do that down there, but not to a troopship I reckon. Where's the sense in that? A mountain of risk for a mole-hill of gain: that's the way I reasoned. Leastways, I never went looking for revenge.'

'Probably wise, Walter.'

'They were coming out to join me, see; so for a while I held me-self responsible. I went a bit mad I think, looking back.'

Samuel could have left it there, employing the distraction of cannon fire from behind the wall. The great bombardment of Reading's defences, titanic but too far off to be heard, had ended at dawn that morning. Then came the assault. Therefore this must be the Westminster Citadel's salute to victory. Although London had contributed men and ordnance to the fray the stay-at-home remainder had felt left out and so now let rip with zeal.

Street revellers in Whitechapel cheered each cannonade. It all merited an easy comment about rear echelons' lust for blood, but Samuel left it unsaid - and thus changed his entire life.

'I might have stayed in the Bosphorus, if they'd made it there.' Walter hadn't even heard the gunfire; all his attention was long ago and far away. 'But they didn't. So I came back home.'

Samuel had heard of the place, courtesy of Father Omar. It was mission territory, as exotic and obscure as Australasia.

'You're a dark horse, Walter. I didn't think you'd set foot outside London.'

Beside him his colleague swelled with pride, though his eyes were still beholding lost faces.

'Me? I did two tours with the Knights of Rhodes, boy: just as an auxiliary, of course. One more and I'd have got my plot of land. In another world I'm tilling the Bosphorus soil, not stuck here. One of me sons - well, grandson maybe - might have made knight!'

Samuel had no more expected this than to be paired with a Mameluke. Here was opportunity. Having burst beyond his own first horizons he now saw no reason to ever limit them again. If knowledge beckoned from nearby he'd seize it, since there was always the chance it might be profitable.

He little dreamed then how well chosen that word was, or how profitable their idle time-killing might be.

'So, what's it like out there then?' he asked.

Walter tried to recollect. It took a while.

'Good wheat country, if you're left alone to grow it. And there's plenty room: lots of ruined places. They say Saxons fled there after Hastings, so maybe the castles were theirs. We repaired some – had to. 'Cause you're alright near the coast or beside one of the citadels: the best and earliest grants of land are there. Further in you learn to plough with one hand.'

'A?'

'The other has to hold a musket, boy: or a rifle if you can afford it. That's what the Crimeans hand out to the Tartars, so they can raid and pick us off from afar without us so much as seeing 'em. 'Course, them Crimeans, they're clever: advanced like, for all they're pagan - good with cannon and rifles and such. They churn out more than we can from their wicked *factories*. And their women bed with other women and the men drink, only meeting to breed - or so they say. I never saw none: they always paid the

Tartars to fight us.'

There was something in that speech that fixed grappling hooks in Trevan's mind, refusing to go away. At first he thought it was the intriguing allegations about Crimean social life, but those images soon palled. Not even a massive explosion from Reading-way; a powder store or rebel bastion perhaps, could distract him from the nagging thought that he'd just heard something... important.

Finally, when they were checking in their weaponry at duty change it came to him. He'd doggedly teased out the one useful thread in a blanket of moth-eaten memories.

'Walter,' Samuel asked swiftly, ''fore you go: what is it that's so special about these... *rifles?*'

****

'... therefore plain duty and Christian prudence, if not inclination, requires that I mention, as concisely as may be, of the transmogrifying process applied to the common arquebus or musket, named 'rifling' by those few artisans who can perform it - hence 'rifles'.

I have not troubled my chivalric sensibilities in undue probing of this regrettable innovation, but am made resolute by the sad recognition that what is learnt cannot be <u>unlearnt</u>. The gentleman studying the warlike arts may meet this ignoble weapon and ought to be aware of it even as he deplores its being.

Evidently, a screw or spiral precisely milled within the projectile tube imparts additional vigour to the deadly missile. The gun may therefore be shortened and lightened. It can even be reloaded whilst the shooter is prone on his belly like a serpent. These are the facts, as I myself have witnessed, and they must therefore be accepted as G*d's inexplicable will.

The trick has been known since Reformation-Devastation times in Christendom, and in the dual Caliphates soon after. In the hands of game-keepers and huntsmen (who have excuse to wound from afar) 'rifles' have long been employed in the control of beasts and vermin - of both the two and four legged variety. To that extent no cavil may be raised.

The more 'progressive' minded commander may mock me but I stand firm with the great generals of old in deprecating the distant kill. If life must be taken it should be at eye-to-eye and breath-to-breath length so that the magnitude of the deed is clear. I concede that the time-hallowed bow and javelin thus also stand condemned, but stoutly maintain that the gunpowder devil speaks loud as an evil of a different magnitude. The longbow and the spear require healthy brawn and acquired skill in their use, whereas any ill-bred runt may strike down a far-off better with a musket. This 'rifling' development permits a still more cowardly strike and is Satan's shoulder following his cloven foot thrust in the door of our turpitude.

Fortunately, Christendom, save at its crusading edges, has been at peace for two centuries. Likewise, our musselman cousins, sharers at least in the Abrahamic monotheistic faith, are at an understanding with us and pose no threat. The European armies are thus well up to their needful tasks without recourse to a sinful 'arms race'.

These 'riflemen' are therefore thankfully few and resort to sniping at unwary enemies from craven concealment. Should one be captured the traditional expression of disapproval of their black art is the removal of both hands. They may then go a-begging

for the remainders of their miserable lives, and thus reform others by example.'
And as for cannon....'

'At the Altar of both Mars and Christ - being an instruction in the ethical pursuit of war: required preliminary reading for gentlemen volunteers of sundry Christian nations in the service of His Most Excellent Highness, The Holy and Roman Emperor Joseph IV.'

By Pascal Gudarian. By grace of G*D, Imperial Commander of the Varangian Guard, the convert Turks and Croat hussars.

Belisarius Press. Constantinople. The year of our Salvation 1933.

****

CHAPTER 9

When the first prisoners were delivered the officer of the Watch was drunk. He usually was well gone by midday, but Samuel ensured it by baiting the guardroom with a bottle of brandy. It was snatched up, beheaded and gargled down in short order. Soon enough, the shift commander had discovered the secret of the universe and was trying to enlighten his men. Then, worn out by that exertion, he departed to dreamland.

Samuel dutifully took the reins. In fact he insisted on it and no one dared argue. It had all the appearance of keenness, selflessly volunteering to handle the headachy business of the Reading survivors. Few, if any, had been looking forward to this grim departure from the leisurely routine. Up on the ramparts they observed them coming from afar, despairing human cattle drawn out of the still burning city. Their regular army and Crusader escorts were not gentle and careless of what London thought of them. Several times Samuel saw a slow or troublesome captive dispatched. One whole group was blasted with blue flame by a sorcerer priest and danced for what seemed like ages before they died. Samuel had the privilege of introduction to that scarred, hot-eyed 'Father Oakley' at the handover, and got to shake the hand that had killed. Afterwards, he took a break to scrub his fingers raw.

They were all en route to the Port of London and a new life ploughing the Mediterranean; the 'lucky' pick of those spared. London Wall and a change of captors was just a respite on their long road down. They squatted on their heels or lay flat out as the formalities were performed, reflecting silently on utter defeat.

All the names and ages and professions had to be recorded; the more disabling wounds seen to. Likewise, even heretics and galley-fodder required a certain basic feeding and watering and voiding. Some wanted to recant and be shriven, so statements needed to be noted and a priest fetched. Meanwhile, one upped and died on them. He got 'conditional absolution' and then the communal pit.

There were, in short, all manner of things to do. Samuel saw to the lot of them. He saw to everything.

First and foremost he saw that the skilled craftsmen were put to one side. He interrogated them - and none too gently either, with cuffs and cudgel taps. It struck him as important - even as he struck them - that they should start as he meant to go on. He found three adaptable to his needs and set them discreetly by.

They, like the others, were in a state of shock, unreconciled to survival of battle and the rout which followed. There was a certain base level of gladness at just being alive, and growing realisation that there might be more days for them. However, selection for galley service wasn't something you could celebrate for long. When rational thought returned notions of a quick death might grow in appeal. Fortunately, Trevan had caught them at just the right moment, dictating terms in a seller's market. Any argument or pleading being answered by a musket-butt, negotiations went very smoothly.

Samuel spent a guinea he couldn't afford arranging a colleague's blind eye at the right moment. Devotion to duty suddenly forgotten, he then left early with his catch.

Renting the workshop in the most sordid part of Whitechapel (which was saying something), and buying just the bare minimum of tools and raw materials, had taken everything Samuel could scrape together or borrow. Father Omar's invested gift was used as security for loans. The rates of interest arranged were monstrous, leaving little margin in which to sink or swim. He had nothing spare, not even enough to buy tomorrow's breakfast, but didn't mind in the least. Tomorrow would have to sort itself out: Samuel Trevan was arranging the longer term.

He shoved the former - and future - musket-makers into their new home.

'This is where you'll work,' he told them.

They looked at the Spartan benches - and the leg-irons and coils of chain attached.

'Hard,' Trevan added. Needlessly.

CHAPTER 10

To: *Samuel Trevan Esq. Proprietor.*
C/O St Philip Howard Firearms and Munitions Manufactory.
Whitechapel.
The eastern part of London.
In the County of Middlesex.

From: *Mr Melville Farncombe. Surgeon and medical practitioner.*
Galen House.
Keere Street.
Lewes.
In the County of Sussex.
Dispatched this Wednesday, the 23rd day of March, the year of our Lord 1994.

My dearest Samuel.

Your recent sojourn in Lewes and attendance on my family was, as always, most welcome. My lady wife directs that I convey her effusive thanks for the bolt of Cathay silk and Kernow rose plants. Both will add to the adornment of the Farncombe household very shortly I am sure.

I also write to communicate the intelligence that, two weeks hence (Deo volente), Mrs Farncombe and I will celebrate the 25th anniversary of our nuptial day. Accordingly, mindful of G*d's blessings, we intend to mark the occasion with a Mass at St Pancras Priory Church, followed by a small social gathering 'at home' for family and close friends. It would add to the pleasure of our day if you should find time to be present.

In fact, I shall speak plain. We have, I feel, danced long enough around a <u>certain</u>

matter which is, I am now satisfied, the closest to your heart. What, therefore, could be a more timely and auspicious moment than a commemoration of the sacrament of marriage to resolve said *matter*?

It is, of course, for you to speak first, but you may entertain a degree of confidence in obtaining a sympathetic hearing from me.

My daughter Melissa is at Lyme visiting her maternal aunt and taking the seawater cure. Were she here I have not the slightest doubt she would send you her warm regards. As do I.

I have the honour to remain, young man, your good friend:

Melville Farncombe
Surgeon of the Ancient and Proficient College of St Luke, Winchester.

****

'So, Samuel, what is it that is so special about these... *rifles?*'

Mr Farncombe didn't really want to know that: he was actually enquiring where Trevan's wealth came from. That was just his nature - and also fair enough. The man was thinking of investing his only daughter, so any contract had first to be exhaustively quizzed. The fruits of Samuel's wealth: the clothes, the confidence, were only too evident; but, it being such a suspiciously swift grown thing, the roots needed a little probing.

'The answer is, sir, that they cost more!'

In company, Samuel was careful to speak slowly. His elocution tutor said a modicum of care should soon mop up the stubborn churl tones and earthier bits of vocabulary. This caution with words gave him an air of profundity, and married to the ever sparkling innate force, it was a great success - just like Samuel himself. People listened to him. Even Lewes people listened to him. They hadn't been there to witness Samuel scouring the ruins of Reading for salvageable gun-stuff; him going hungry whilst hiring and terrifying Whitechapel's lowest of the low - the poorest Hebrews, stateless Moriscos, and Croats fresh off the boat. They hadn't seen him scrabble around sinking his teeth into those first, elusive, £s, just to keep things going and buy himself out of the Watch.

'And,' he added humbly, 'so long as people will pay more for quality, then both sides prosper and I'm content.'

The little group around him nodded and smiled at so much wisdom atop such young shoulders. Business and tradesmen of the higher sort, they well appreciated the joy of pricing high to an avid market.

'The *explanation*,' Samuel continued, when the approbation ceased, 'is that they shoot better. One doesn't pretend to understand it though. I dare say my newest apprentice knows more than me - leastways he'd better if he wants to keep his position! No, gentlemen, I merely sell the finished item. One gets by....'

So they'd heard. Again they signalled approval. A bit of humility from this youngster was very welcome. Rumour said he was a man of account in his own world, an employer of hundreds and worth all his audience put together. There was the potential for older, less lucky, noses to be put out of joint by that. For a few decades it would still be open for the ill-disposed to say *'at least they knew where they came from - and it wasn't from some orphanage or the ranks of the London Watch either.'* Samuel was painstaking in not giving any cause for that. The first few steps of the social ladder were the least forgiving of slips.

'I'm told,' he said, seeing the audience were still waiting for more, 'that there's something to putting seven three-quarter turns down the barrel. The bullet flies further and more true by virtue of the spin imparted. Though quite why that should be so....'

Mr Farncombe prided himself on his keen local patriotism and knowledge of Lewes' more famous sons. Samuel had feigned ignorance with that in mind.

'The blessed Isaac Newton pursued that puzzle whilst resident at Southover,' Farncombe informed them. 'I recall some treatment of it in his *'The Atmospheric Mechanism'* - it's little read now of course, overshadowed by his works of revelation.'

No one was in a position to dispute it. With 'magic' readily to hand (or for hire) few inquiring minds - and none of the more practically inclined - took much note of 'the lower sciences'. Interest in them was associated with the well-to-do with nothing better to do. Even the wide ranging intellect of the great Newton himself, once informed of the *'Universal Ether'* in which all things moved and were interconnected, had speedily abandoned study of the merely material world.

Ever after, his 'discovery' was taught, however sketchily, in every sort of school, and all but the shepherding classes had heard of it. Accordingly, vaguely remembered notions of a seamless robe of being, an unbroken linkage between man and the Deity itself, arrived to dampen conversation. They were being listened to, their words recorded, and thus it didn't do to be too worldly-wise.

In the lull, a hired-for-the-day footman accosted the group with a tray of Sussex white wine. Samuel declined, as was his invariable custom. The only alcohol ever to cross his lips was that dispensed at Mass. At all other times he was a strict abstainer. Mr Farncombe noted it approvingly. Life in '*Babylondon*', where temptation beckoned night and day, and all things went to pot, had left no - visible - stain on Trevan's good character.

'One hears,' resumed the owner of the *'Lewes Times & Pious Intelligencer'*, 'that you are well in with the military. Guaranteed trade with big spenders, eh?'

'I have my contacts,' Samuel confirmed, politely enough but not willing to give the man claw-purchase on a 'story'. 'They spread as word spreads....'

'Really?' asked another man. 'How so?'

They wanted more and wouldn't be satisfied otherwise. And Samuel was happy to oblige them - in non-specific fashion - till the cows came home.

'Well, to give an example: a colonel of Foot recently expended his own cash to rifle arm his best company, and achieved great results, so he tells me, in the Welsh bandit country. Similarly, a ship's captain who equipped his marines from me cleared the rigging of a Greenland privateer before it even got to musket range. These people talk amongst themselves of course, and, if you're liberal with discounts, they can be loyal friends to a businessman.'

'Like keeping the Trade Guilds off your back, I dare say!' chortled the holder of the local salt monopoly - who had no such problems.

That was a sore point, and doubtless chosen as such. A lot of Samuel's profits went into that particular noisome pit. He'd learnt that even supposedly respectable organisations, half a millennium old and Church approved, could be as rapacious as any blackmailer.

'What's a Trade Guild?' he riposted cheerfully - and got a laugh out of it.

The select gathering in Galen House's suntrap orangery had gotten to be most convivial. Midway between the pieties of Mass in the vast priory church (bigger than Chichester Cathedral itself!) and anticipation of a happy announcement to come, people were enticed into edging - just slightly - out of their protective shells. There was ideal spring weather, a bearable number of industrious bees, and unstinted refreshments. This was a *good* spell, a stable era, conducive to trade, accumulation and long perspectives. They were happily unaware that Charles IV's long reign would end in the *'Commotion Times'*. For them, at present, all was well.

'*Love* the gig-and-two, by the way,' said a portly man, a speculator in horse stock from over Glynde way. 'Always look out for it when you're visiting. Very flash.'

Samuel saw the chiding, protective glance that comment earned from Farncombe. Clearly he didn't like the familiar tone. Samuel rejoiced. It showed he was *in*.

'Not *too* much, though,' the man swiftly added, mending fences. 'Befits your new station - lets Lewes folk know the score - like it a lot!'

'Aha!'

Mr Farncombe had spied a new arrival in the room and suddenly became hyperactive host and circus ringmaster rolled into one.

'Right! Now, gentlemen, have I shown you all my latest purchase? A square of Roman mosaic pavement lately uncovered at... where was it, Samuel?'

In his campaign to woo the whole family, Trevan had noted Mr Farncombe's antiquarian interests and diligently made himself knowledgeable in the field. In the smarter circles it was becoming almost expected for a gentleman to pursue a non-remunerative hobby. This one suited Samuel as well as any other.

'Fishbourne, sir,' he answered, tonelessly. 'Near Selsey.' His attention was unmistakably elsewhere.

'Young Trevan authenticated it for me,' said Farncombe. 'Alas, these dealers can be such fakers and rogues. The pattern is near complete over the space of a yard! I intend to mount it on my study wall. Come....'

His cronies and contacts obediently followed, though the horse-trader lingered for a final friendly word with Samuel.

'I'd sooner look at *your* latest acquisition,' he confided softly. The man was known to be a voluptuary; his house as well stocked with human fillies as his stables were with the equine sort. But it was delivered in a fatherly rather than salacious fashion and acceptable as such. Fortunately, he judged his audience enough to forego the intended follow-up about *'which he'd sooner mount as well....'*

Then Samuel and Melissa Farncombe were alone - for only the second time ever. A lot had happened since that first encounter in Church Twitten – and all of it directly related. There was a promising symmetry about now risking everything on a sequel.

Previous visits to Galen House had been closely chaperoned, not to mention minutely monitored (as was only proper). It genuinely hadn't occurred to Samuel to attempt anything more venturesome. Whatever his ways in the snakepit of 'business', this was one asset where nothing less than proper title would do.

She was in a summer dress of yellow and blue. Her bonnet matched. He found it hard to meet her glacier coloured eyes. If he did there was the danger of imagining her spread-eagled on his bed - or the floor of the orangery, or anywhere at all *right now* - in front of him. He couldn't afford that distraction. Otherwise though, so long as lust did not intrude, he was all single-minded and steely. He just wished the erection would go away.

'Well then....,' she said. Her voice was deep, always provoking mild surprise.

Samuel couldn't be doing with small talk: he wasn't up to it. Never had been and never less than now. He'd primed himself for this, rehearsed to the point of weariness and polished words till they wore out. Rejecting them accordingly, he'd then hit on pretending he was negotiating a trade deal of infinite import. Somewhere in his London office there was now a decision-tree drawn up, a tangly thicket of contract-breaker evasion detours and multiple fallback positions. He'd not needed to bring it with him: long acquaintance had burnt every tightrope line deep into his brain.

In short, none of Trevan's rifles had ever been so carefully loaded. And now he instantly forgot the lot.

'Has he spoken to you?' he asked her. His tenseness made him sound blunt.

'Has who?'

'Your father,' Samuel snapped. 'Who d'you think?'

'Yes. Of course.'

So now they were almost at the precipice; the real deal. One step more and the consequences went on forever. Samuel didn't waver, but strode boldly to the very edge.

'And?' he asked.

Melissa shrugged her shoulders.

'What else can I say? I'm a dutiful daughter.'

She almost never maintained a stare; her wicked eyes usually flitted to and fro. People often grievously mistook her for a nervous type. But not now. She and Samuel locked glances. They couldn't disengage without one or the other somehow losing... something. His insides were knots of ice.

'That's not enough,' he said.

The tone was commendably strong - and a fraud. He'd forced himself to speak. There was no need for it; he'd won what he wanted. Yet he also wanted more. Just this one time, in this one case, he desired free agreement rather than a conquest. That wish was overpowering. He'd offered his throat to fate's razor the once and survived. Now there had to be a second pass. Utter ruin started its run-up.

'Isn't it?' she shot back. He didn't know if that was a real question or if she was playing with him - whilst she still could. He'd have his revenge, he swore it.

'No, not enough,' he said. 'Not for me. Not in... this instance.'

Melissa nodded gravely and looked down, breaking the confrontation. Samuel felt like a bull with a musket, or some thick-fingered giant fumbling with delicate clock innards. The pit was calling to him and he imagined what life-long descent into its blackness might be like. Falling for ever and ever. Into absolute cold. A tomb before the tomb.

Melissa was looking at him again, but this time he couldn't meet her gaze.

'I assumed you knew, Samuel.'

He shook his head: it occupied years.

'Obviously not. Humour me.'

Melissa smiled.

'I fully intend to, from now on and forever. You're for me, Samuel: I'm for you. Father pushed at an open door. I'd far rather have a gentle man than any *gentleman*....'

He felt... nothing, surprisingly - but was confident the full carnival and fireworks would arrive in due course, once feelings fought off the paralysis of fear.

'I... I shall always be *careful*,' he said, reaching out to take her small hand. She consented to it. 'And *kind*. I shall always be kind - to you.'

****

He'd added those final two words because he was in many ways an honest soul. Samuel knew full well he couldn't promise to be kind to everyone. That hadn't always been possible in the last few years: nor was it the way of the world, whatever its Creator might command. It would be enough - and more than most ever attempted - to be continually kind to one beloved at least.

He drove back to London at the crack of dawn. The April day rose especially golden, to Samuel's eyes anyway. It wouldn't last, this suffusing of the world with glee, but he made the most of it. At East Grinstead, en route, pausing to dine, he gave a ragged Walsingham pilgrim a guinea. Enough to get him there in lordly style!

In Whitechapel that free and generous spirit had to be put back in the box to await more suitable surroundings for an outing. There were production targets to be checked and slacking to be sniffed out. He'd hired some good foremen but things only went at their best when everyone felt the terror of his breath on their necks.

That night, though it was late and he was drained, he celebrated in his usual manner since coming into both London and money. Selecting two choice painted whores from Seething Lane, he had them in the factory office, monstering their privy parts with especial zeal and zest. Then, afterwards, his secret gladness inspired him to tip them lavishly for their time and trouble and soreness, so that even they should - unknowingly - share his joy.

****

****

From: *'THE LEWES TIMES & PIOUS INTELLIGENCER'.*
The 22nd of April 1994 AD.

'... Mr and Mrs Melville FARNCOMBE are pleased to announce the commencement of bans of marriage between their only daughter, MELISSA FAITH, spinster of the Parish of St Michael-in-Lewes; and SAMUEL MELCHIZEDEK TREVAN, late of Cliffe, Lewes; bachelor of the Parish of St Simon-the-zealot, Whitechapel, London, in the County of Middlesex.

Deo volente, a High Mass and ceremony of marriage will be celebrated at St Michael-in-Lewes at midday, the 20th May 1994 concelebrated by Fr. Oliver Rounday, incumbent of St Michael's and Fr. Omar Ibn J'nna, of Cliffe and the Jerusalem Citadel.

CHAPTER 11

Samuel passed by his factory - the factory he used to own - at just the wrong moment. A priest was sealing the great iron gates with a flimsy papal ribbon, sealing the knot with papal-red wax. The nameplate - *his* nameplate - that used to be there had been roughly torn off. He could see the corners of it still screwed in place.

Samuel wanted to cross over to the priest and *smash his face in* – then tear the man to bits like they had his sign. It would have been so lovely. However, there was a papal dragoon dancing in attendance. Foresight had been shown, putting the delicious indulgence out of the question. The foreigner would be no toy soldier, and all too keen to do his duty.

The dragoon looked bored, staring lazily down from his horse. To him it was just a mild holiday from routine, a trip out from the grim Westminster Citadel. To Samuel Trevan he was nemesis.

Samuel walked on and neither priest nor soldier knew he'd passed.

Whitechapel natives and peddlers out from the Ghetto alike made way for him, but still received the evil eye. Nothing and no one could do right. Even the smile on the bronze Pepys, *'England's Neptune'*, outside Trinity House, hitherto humane, today mocked the fallen Trevan. The world scowled and he replied in kind.

How had it come to this? He'd been fairly *sprinting* up the mountain; never dreaming you could overshoot the summit and plummet down the other side. That was the only way Samuel could describe it to himself. He'd thought himself a comet, an adornment to the sky, getting brighter and brighter till the time came to move on to a new life out in the dark.

However, it turned out he was just a firework, a momentary flash of glory and then nothing. No - worse than nothing: a piece of rubbish falling back to earth where it belonged.

He couldn't work out what Providence was playing at. Up to now he'd *trusted* - as he'd been told to - and never doubted. For all that life dealt him a rough first hand he hadn't whinged or borne a grudge. He'd got on with things and this was the thanks he got. Well, it wouldn't do. It wasn't plain dealing!

Brick by brick, Samuel had built himself a cathedral of achievement. It had looked as solid as the stone sort which graced London. He'd assumed it would be there for future generations to look at. And yet, and yet... just one or two surprise visitors and it all came tumbling down. Because they didn't like his building methods. Never mind the grandeur of the sight, the pains taken or exalted vision: no, they just didn't care for the masons' hours. Yeah, right.... Had St Paul's or St Guy's - or St Peter's Basilica - been raised to strict Trade Guild rules? The hypocrites!

Samuel brooded on the power of unexpected visitors all the way back to his lodgings. There he found another one - the last and worst - waiting for him. The one illusion he had left to be ripped away was that fate wouldn't demand abject surrender. He'd blithely assumed that at least his cathedral's foundations would be left intact.

Wrong again.

****

Father Omar had let himself in. He'd always had a facility with locks and bolts, so there was no mystery to it.

'Your forgiveness, Samuel-of-the-disgrace, I did not relish waiting on the landing.'

Samuel threw his topcoat on the bed. The place was in disorder, the result of several abandoned bouts of packing.

'Don't mention,' he said. 'My home's been liberty hall to lots of churchmen lately.' He grimaced, hating it when his brimful pail of bitterness slopped over to splash the undeserving. 'And anyway, it's good to see you....'

The horsehair seat, fine for normal frames, was far too close a fit for the priest. He shifted round seeking elusive comfort. Perhaps it was that that put edge on his bass tones.

'I shall not let you linger in that opinion, child. Matthew 10, 34: *'I came not to send peace, but a sword.'* A sword thrust cannot be made palatable with platitudes or prevarication.'

'*Et tu, Brute*?' said Samuel.

Omar smiled, displaying brown peg teeth. Along with the Church he belonged to, he'd always venerated the Saint from Stratford who had done so much to re-convert England. It was news however that any line from that sublime pen had lodged in this pupil.

'No, not I, Samuel-of-the-telling-quote. *'Et tu, Farncombe'*, you should rather say. Here.' Omar retrieved and held out an ominously thin letter. 'There is no honey that may be poured on it. Take and read.'

Samuel balanced the missive on three spread fingertips, killing it with a look.

'No need,' he said. 'I can guess.' He flicked it into an inaccessible corner.

Father Omar watched it go: a welcome pause in distasteful duties.

'Neither does Lewes wish you back,' he said eventually. 'Mine was the sole dissenting voice on the Town panel. Exile is your lot and the Town Governor, who is a pious man - so he repeatedly assured us - thirsts to enforce the ban against you. Should I say at this juncture that I am sorry?'

Samuel crossed to the bed, evicted his coat, and lay down, hands behind his head.

'If you like; yes please.'

Omar obliged. 'Then know that I am a vessel of regrets; for my failures and for yours - and for *their* mean spirits.'

Samuel signalled he'd heard.

'So, where am I to go then? Is Beachy Head what they're hinting at?'

'Perhaps - but that is not *my* sentiment. I have come this weary and unpleasant distance precisely to command the contrary.'

Samuel expelled a sigh through his teeth.

'Well, I've been getting a fair number of commands just lately, Father - as you may know. Arguably, a *sickening* amount....'

Omar nodded.

'I have been in London a full day before I came to you, Samuel-of-

74

despair. Not being entirely deprived of what are called 'contacts', I have spent my time exploring the extent of sanctions against you. Accordingly, my commands - my *council*, if that probes your wounds less roughly - are well informed. When we first met, I could - and did - hold you in the crook of one arm. That is no longer possible, but my wishes remain equally protective.'

Trevan wearily turned his head.

'Proof against the hardening of the heart are you? Wish you'd tell me your secret.'

In a trice, Omar's voice was all harshness and reproof.

'I never ceased to expound it in every lesson and conversation, my boy. It is you who have chosen to forget: just as you chose to spend my life savings on... rifles.'

That struck home, though Samuel strived not to show it. He was glad the priest's chair wasn't in direct line of sight.

'But you didn't forbid it either. So why not now tell me plain: how was what I did so *bad?*'

Omar had always been a patient teacher; patient to a fault. Remaining so was now a visible trial.

'You were *temptation*, Samuel-out-of-depth, to others who could not resist. A cold-eyed man out of Rome clearly expounded your sins during my appointment in the Westminster Citadel. He was gracious enough to receive me because I bore a bishop's recommendation, and because I had been in the Holy Land, as had he. By the by, I suspect his time there was less innocent than mine, even though I had occasion to fight at Aleppo and in the Druze Country. I admit that I was frightened of him: I who have no fear of death! But even that was eclipsed by learning of your oh-so narrow escape.'

As with Farncombe's letter, Samuel could guess. *Roman* visitors often arrived in nations to deal in deaths - of people and places and institutions. The thought of insignificant him attracting their fish-like stare was a real bowel-churner.

'I see...,' he said.

'Oh, how I doubt that, Trevan-of-fools-rushing-in. Your money-lust, which I concede was driven by another, more laudable, lust - if such a thing can be — was making waves in much bigger pools. Seas and oceans even. Listen and learn, foolish child: learn that cheaper and better and more abundant... rifles may well earn the pennies of generals and Kings, but, thank God, they are not to every taste. The Roman said you may have ended as a Duke or Earl, if permitted to continue. But by then England would be well-armed and expansive; and Scotland and Ireland and France would have to take heed. Shortly, the Empire would require rifle armies - and so therefore would the Turks and Mamelukes - and thus the Benin Horse-tribes and Zimbabwe and Cathay and... eventually *everyone*. You had become Mars' ambassador on Earth! Can you believe it, Samuel? A midget horseman of the Apocalypse riding out of Lewes! And the Archbishop of London, perhaps even the Holy Father himself, has heard your name!'

With that charge sheet there was no point in pretending unconcern. Samuel had to search around for words.

'I... thought it was the Trade Guilds - and the Church commercial rules, that... you know....'

'Them as well, Samuel; though I presume you bought off the first and hid from the second. No, they merely served as pretext to bring you down. If you had selected another trade in which to prosper, perchance you might have continued much longer in your exploitations. Not for ever, naturally, but long enough for your one great need.'

Samuel reeled that in and, overcoming his repulsion, dined on it. It tasted bitter and he doubted the flavour would ever leave his mouth. He got up. It wasn't clear to him how long the pause in conversation had lasted.

'Oh well,' he said (though it was just something to say), 'thanks for that. Now at least I know....'

'And from knowledge I pray there may grow wisdom. Your life is spared, Samuel; there will even be a small pension to sustain it, but – and mark this well - no more *business*. No more employment. And, I shudder to say, no more freedom.'

Trevan was still digesting the discovery that there was an order of magnitude above catastrophe, and depths to fall into below the abyss. It was a wider, more grown-up, world than he'd credited.

Omar hammered the point home.

'You will always be under scrutiny, always suspect. Tread with care, Samuel; take the one route mercifully left open to you.'

'Right. Which is to where, incidentally?'

'Where you first came from, in the far West. Here is your file, child.'

Omar retrieved another item from his scrip, a slim, faded, paper folder tied with a grey band. Trevan didn't move to accept it.

'You did not need it before, Samuel; all your mind was on the future, not the past. Also, there is little enough within, alas. However, the Church required of me a place where you might find sanctuary and merit forgiveness. Since Lewes will not have you, I could think of no other. I shall pray that there are people there who still recall you.'

'Well, you do that, Father.' Samuel was grim faced and took the file in a grip which flaked its dry paper. 'But I'm none too sure I *want* people right now.'

Father Omar shrugged. 'I had hoped there might be at least one person you would stay constant to - two if you include myself. But let that pass. Your present condition reminds me of my other purpose here and the remaining obligation on you.'

'They want *more* flesh?'

'No, not flesh but spirit, Samuel. It is required that you obtain absolution after full confession. If that is not confirmed to the Archbishop's staff they will not release you. What your fate would be then I cannot say. Save that it would not be good. I and Lewes and England would not see you again I think. Therefore ponder hard on it, I beseech. As you are at present, knowing your stubborn resolve, where would you find a priest lax enough to absolve you? Whereas only I in all this mighty City knows the real Samuel Trevan and that he would not truly persevere in evil.'

Samuel briefly glanced within and saw it was so. Yet he still couldn't control his sense of betrayal for longer than two words.

'Whereas you alone,' he half-accused the only parent he'd ever known, 'would absolve my insincere confession.'

'That choice of phrase is yours, Samuel. I see things differently. Take the opportunity offered.'

Trevan's face was set. He had come to the very end of (open) rebellion against fate.

'Oh, don't worry: I *shall*,' he said - and straightaway knelt down on the threadbare carpet.

'Forgive me, Father,' he recited through gritted teeth, 'for I have sinned: thorough my fault, my own fault, my own most *grievous* fault....'

CHAPTER 12

'... *your gross deceptions as to your true character, which have brought such embarrassment to this family, render you unfit to bear the name of a Christian, let alone a Christian gentleman. The last service that you may render to me and mine, and the very least that is owed to us, is that you obliterate any recollection or trace of this most regrettable association. To think that my dearest daughter....*

...

... any attempt to renew our lamentable acquaintance will be met by the severest consequences that Temporal and Spiritual law permit.

I am, sir,
Mr M Farncombe'

Samuel crumbled the single sheet such that, though compressed, it made not the slightest show of straightening out. He noticed Farncombe had used the cheapest of his two types of stationary.

The envelope would have gone the same way but for an anomalous red circle around one corner of the reverse. It struck a chord, being of the exact shade ink that Father Omar used to mark the orphanage's schoolbooks. He examined closer.

It proved to contain some minute writing, a mere couple of words to look at, but whole volumes of meaning to Samuel Trevan. He recognised that crabbed feminine script. *'Acts, 18, 21'* it said, in as small as space as possible.

Samuel had to rush out and borrow a Bible because he'd flung his own into the Thames.

****

****

'The Acts of the Apostles'. Chapter 18, verse 21:

'... but I will return again unto you, if God will.'

CHAPTER 13

For a generation now, the power had been blessing them more frequently, visiting the world two or three times a year. Occasionally it even spoke in a tongue they could understand and then prophesied to them. At other times, losing control or in an act of chastisement, gobbets of flame spat from the portal like an ejaculation. Many devotees were grievously burned - but thought themselves fortunate to intercept the god-seed.

As the process accelerated and the unknown climax drew near, so the sacrifices were increased, to show proper gratitude and force the pace. Dozens of the lost and abducted went down into the unnatural light. Even one elderly member of the inner council volunteered to end one life and start the next in that way. Perhaps it was this great gift that so pleased the power.

Whatever the reason, soon after the signs were manifested with especial vigour. It seemed clear something spectacular was in train. Accordingly, the sisters and brethren made extra effort to ensure the next gathering would be a fitting response.

They took a priest, stolen from sufficiently far away to shake off suspicion or pursuit. He was ferried down from his Cumbrian parish, blindfolded and befuddled with drugs, from isolated farm to farm, and barn to barn, along the chain of believers.

The appointed night came and he was roused and made sensible with counter-potions. A flurry of grey-shrouded guards conveyed him underground. Then, after the customary '*degradations*' and '*educations*', when his vows were broken and his faith flayed - that is to say much later - he was offered to the power.

And yet he was not taken straight away, as had always been the case before, time out of mind. Instead, he was held on the portal's lip and *possessed*. It was a signal honour both to him and those who gave him. The devotees shrieked with joy.

Whether it was still him or not they could not say, but the human resemblance remained as he turned back to the throng and spoke with the power's voice.

'He comes!' said the thunderstorm tones, ravaging the inadequate-to-the-task human vocal chords. 'He comes! The promise is true!'

And at that news, if there had been frenzy before, it was as nothing to the abandon shown after.

At the very end, some snippet of knowledge was drawn aloud from the dying mind. Or perhaps the priest's intellect, feeling itself devoured, rallied at the last. He or the power spoke again.

'Verily I say unto you,' said the wavering puppet, quoting from scripture, 'this generation shall not pass away, till all be fulfilled!'

Then he was sucked away into the tunnel, to his unguessable fate.

CHAPTER 14

'Meea navidna cowza sawsneck.'

Samuel nodded sadly - and then employed his strong right arm to lift the man right out of his seat. He was carried thus across the bar-room and pinned by the throat against the wall. The rough arrival there knocked the breath out of him, with no prospect of re-supply.

'Call me suspicious if you like,' Trevan told him, in a cool tone out of keeping with his expression, 'but I reckon you do *cowsa* some *sawsneck*. Let's try again. What is the time please?'

Weight was applied to his claw grip. The prisoner's feet scrabbled desperately for the floor two inches away.

Trevan's free hand drew the man's fob watch out of its waistcoat pocket home. It was held before the owner's purpling face.

'Ten - past – five.'

Those retching words were his last gasp. Merciful oblivion was almost knocking at the door when Samuel let him go. He gulped in air like a landed fish, his neck bearing livid purple souvenirs of the incident. They looked fit to live a long life.

Trevan wrenched the watch from its fastening, bringing half the waistcoat with it. He checked the reported time with exaggerated care.

'Goodness me, so it is. My appointment is late. Morwenstow manners: as piss-poor as its welcome!'

The timepiece was politely returned. Samuel resumed his seat by the inglenook fireside and sipped, without relish, at the cordial he'd bought three quarters of an hour back. If the atmosphere had been chilly when he first entered the alehouse, it was past glacial now: an ice-age ambience. The conversational buzz of the other middling sort of gentlemen in the saloon-parlour was as angry as the marks left on their countryman. It was all in Cornish of course: every word had been since Samuel crossed the threshold - though he knew full well it was all English up to then. He'd heard the dying away of comprehensible language at first sight of him.

Ordinarily that wouldn't have worried Samuel: the less contact with humanity the better was his attitude nowadays. The reception here seemed a good metaphor for the whole world's response to his being around. But this '*meea navidna...*' thing: the *'I can't - or **won't** - speak English'* business, he'd heard it once too often. There were even villages over the English side of the border that took that attitude and it had started to rankle. He'd mischanced to leave his watch at what passed for 'home' and just wanted to know how long he'd been kept waiting - and so the local got jostled a bit for his ignorance and rudeness. Serve him right.

Samuel half wanted the Cornish clientele to work themselves up to do something about it - he'd almost welcome some good honest open hostility - but knew they never would. It was only black looks and whispered curses as usual, even from the injured party. So Samuel spat on the fire and made it sizzle - and the landlord tut. He stood on the very verge of having fun – but suspected fate wouldn't permit Samuel Trevan that.

He was right. The parlour door opened and more bad news strode in.

****

There was a well-worn path for them to confer on, pilgrim defined, along the clifftop pasture. It led eventually to the Blessed Robert Hawker's driftwood hut. A century past, that rustic holy man would sit within to observe the storms and write opium-fuelled sonnets with swan-feather quills. Charles III, *'Cheerful Charlie'* himself, had sought Hawker out, seeking theological approval for his 'regal-polygamy' initiative; only to receive a dusty answer for his pains and the long trek west.

Hawker survived the encounter and successor hermits followed in post to this day, but Samuel had no mind to consult anyone but the old body hobbling beside him. Far below, the tide whispered ebbing adieu, laying bare the black, twisted, rock strata that comprised Morwenstow beach.

'Right then, Father Jago: thanks for coming: better late than never.'

The elderly priest looked sidelong at his companion, and in so doing almost stumbled.

'Damn! What? Oh, we *are* tartar-ish, aren't we?' It was a comment rather than a reproach. 'I can see you're a Trevan alright.'

It became Samuel's turn to crack a wry smile.

'Well, that's my first question settled. I hope the others are as easily solved.'

'Probably. It's a short - though none too sweet - tale. Look, do you mind slowing down a portion? I can't walk so fast as when I first met your clan.'

Samuel actually stopped and let the old man catch his breath. The blustery wind off the sea ordered their hair aloft, though the priest could only contribute remnant white rats-tails to the dance.

'Fair enough,' said Trevan. 'We both know you set the speed tonight: in walking and everything else.'

The priest's face hardened.

'Well then, Samuel, I'd better hasten to tell all so you can stop resenting my 'advantage'. Save us, boy, you've got such sharp edges on you you'll end up cutting yourself! Calm down.'

'I am calm.'

'No, you're not. You don't fool me. A happy man doesn't antagonise an alehouse of strangers. Nor refuse to meet a priest in Church....'

'It stems from courtesy. I've outgrown your certainties; I didn't want to enter what you call a house of God when I know it's all a load-....'

Trevan faltered, even *his* courage failing him and realising he'd gone too far.

Father Jago kindly let it go and continued.

'... and thus insult his calling; and impose a journey on him, and then chide him for being late. No: even if I'd not yet seen the fire in your eyes I'd still have known you for what you are.'

The trap was thus set for Trevan to ask *'which is what...?'* It was easily stepped round. He'd had a gut-full of people anxious after his spiritual welfare.

'Sorcerers detect what mere mortals can't.' Samuel nodded towards the band of silver stars stitched round one arm of the priest's cassock. 'Though

I don't recognise the school....'

'Liverpool.'

'I didn't know there was a-....'

Father Jago jumped in, self-deprecating, to save time.

'It's not renowned. My talent is marginal and periodic. The demi-academy there specialised in my type.'

Samuel gave him a sideways 'oh-I-*see*' look.

'Which explains how a wizard-priest comes to be buried alive in this hole. I'll admit I did puzzle about that.'

Deserved or not, Morwenstow had an evil reputation. Samuel recalled old Walter the London Watchman had spoken of it: had suffered through it.

From time out of mind ships had come to grief on this hazardous coast, and a peculiarity of the tides usually deposited the victims on Morwenstow beach, where sharp rocks and birds finished what sea and fish had started. Although everyone, even anonymous body parts, was supposed to get a decent Christian burial, sometimes the numbers or trouble or expense were too much, and then they were just put under the sand. Therefore, people shunned the beach even on the sunniest of days. Not only that, but the inhabitants were accused of assisting Neptune's grosser moods, luring ships in with lights and then murdering those who made it ashore. It was always said suspiciously few mariners survived a shipwreck off Morwenstow.

Father Jago overlooked the gibe and implications. Magicians were used to unsolicited hostility from normal humanity.

'I'd no need of sorcery to read you straight off, young man. All priests acquire the skill, *talent* or no.'

'Whatever you say, Father.'

'Oh, is that so?' They set off again, at a more stately pace. 'Right then, master Trevan, what *I* say is go back home and leave the past in peace. It would be better, trust me.'

Samuel shook his head, a sharp, jerky action, killing off further argument.

'Whatever you say: except *'leave well alone'* or *'trust me'*. And another thing: I have no home.'

'No welcome in Welcombe, eh?'

'The place is misnamed. A rabid dog would have got a warmer

greeting. My so-called family are fearful of me.'

The priest compressed his lips, an expression of some or other disapproval.

'That is a... shame, Mr Trevan.'

Real sympathy or not, Samuel didn't need it.

'Don't waste your concern. It's nothing personal. They're two generations out of churl class and worried I might be after my property rights. Land's everything to them; even cack land like here. My Church problems are just something they've seized on. Believe me, I don't covet their little fields, but you try telling them that.'

'So, what precisely *do* you want?'

'I want what they won't tell me, even after I kicked a door down. Not even after I put them out of pocket. *'Cost half a guinea to fix 'er it will'*, boo hoo. What is it that's worth *money* for them to keep dark? Trouble is, you see, Father, I find myself at a bit of a loose end in life at the moment. Which makes me minded to trace my story back to its beginning even as I ponder its end. Good enough?'

'Did the family put you on to me?'

'Nope. I never beg for favours twice. One refusal serves for all time. Henceforth I wouldn't ask them to piss on me if I was afire - please excuse the peasant-speak. No, it was my own discovery, and simply made. You were the incumbent at Welcombe round about when I appeared. Mother Church never loses track of its shepherds. I enquired and there you were, just up the coast, albeit in another country. *What* a happy chance!'

'Another country no longer, Trevan: Kernow is Cornwall now.'

Jago had turned abruptly vehement on this point, and Samuel had to signal his lack of objection. Presumably, the priest endured daily trials as a foreigner in a restive land. To Trevan's eyes *'Kernow'*, as was, seemed to have blithely ignored its absorption into United England in the 20's. The gory 'Sack of Truro', the marriage of the last of the Ducal line to an English King, were inconvenient facts that had trickled away into the sands of passing time. When Samuel walked the half mile from Welcombe, Devon, England, into Cornwall, Cornish militiamen in the Ducal livery had demanded what his business might be.

Trevan's patriotic feelings were just part of the avalanche of previous opinions now slipping away from him. His present indifference to the Kernow question knew no bounds.

'Whatever, Father. Now, as to the favour I was asking...?'

The priest turned to face him. He looked tired and disinclined to much raise his voice over the noise of the waves.

'The truth will do you no favours, boy - but I see you are implacable and won't settle otherwise. I'd long put this story to rest. I don't thank you for digging it up.'

'Better a bad memory than no memory.'

Father Jago laughed out loud.

'You'll learn different if you're spared. A priest gets to hear all manner of things and gets no choice in selecting. The sheep come all mixed up with goats: horribly deformed goats sometimes. I tell you truthfully, my mind's well furnished with grotesque items I'd cheerfully swap for blanks.'

'Snap. So what?'

'Well, if you won't be told, you must learn. It's God's will. Yes, I knew your mother. I baptised her and I buried her.'

'You missed out her first communion.'

'No I didn't. She had no call for it. She was an *innocent*.'

Samuel flinched; for a second his face broke free of control. This was a blow he hadn't prepared for.

'Don't be ashamed for her, Trevan: for that is an evil way of thought. She understood all that the Almighty fitted her for, and went through this world unstained by it.'

Samuel had to turn aside. He didn't want his distress to be seen.

'Her kind have a virtue all their own, Trevan. They are like little children and Satan is powerless against them. Their years on earth are never long and they're here for us to lavish love upon.'

Samuel regained composure, but still declined to turn round.

'Was... was she the full type, or just partial?'

'She had all the marks, if that is your meaning.'

'Slant eyes? Slack face? Everything?'

'Yes.' Jago's reply was blunt. 'And she was beautiful according to her type and in God's eyes. Now guard your words, for she looks down upon you from heaven.'

Samuel snorted dissent.

'Best place for her: that's what the family would have said, isn't it?'

Again, the priest could not compromise with the truth.

'Probably. They have their fair share of narrow-souled members. One or two I recall had it in mind to expose her at birth, but word got to me and I *spoke* to them. The Church crusades against that old practice, but in these wild areas....'

'I suppose I should thank you, else I'd not be here.'

'Yes, you should, but I'll overlook it if you don't.'

A thought then landed on Samuel, which grew and grew in both size and malignity - like a hideous black spider swarming over him. He swung round.

'But if she was an innocent, then who... how...?'

Father Jago looked up at Trevan with such compassion as he could muster.

'It was never discovered. She liked to wander the woods, to gather ferns and flowers. She used to make posies of them and hand them out as presents. I usually got one when I visited to check the family weren't working her. It must have happened one day in the woods.'

'... Never... discovered....'

'Some vile and wicked person, probably long since gone to their reward. Don't rend your heart, Trevan. Your 'father', such as he was, has not escaped giving full account of himself. To the one and only honest judge. Who delivers faultless justice. And due sentence. And as to your mother, she didn't understand. When you arrived you were taken straight from her. The family had arranged everything well before. I found the refuge in Sussex for you.'

'"*Melchizedek*': the man with no father or mother.'

'You did have a mother, Samuel.'

'Whose idea was the name? It's a clever little joke, but do you know, strangely enough, I'm not all that amused. Fancy sending me on my way - far away - with a jest.... How droll. The culprit, please.'

'One of the family. I don't know who. I wouldn't tell you if I did, not in your present mind.'

'But tell me, did dear 'Father' come back for more? Have I got any brother or sister Melchizedeks?'

Father Jago was glad to be able to close off that route.

'No. A magician-priest came from Exeter and gave her the '*mercy*' spell. I couldn't do it; my gift's too weak. Sterilisation requires a bishop's dispensation, but in view of her... condition afterwards: I mean, knowing what she now did but not understanding, it was felt....'

'It was felt right.'

'And your family were threatening to keep her prisoner indoors otherwise.'

'And they were right as well.'

'She never mentioned it, Samuel. I honestly believe she didn't even realise. Your mother had some more years of happiness.'

'I envy her. One other thing before you go: do you recall where you buried her?'

CHAPTER 15

'A Brief guide to St NECTAN's Church, WELCOMBE, DEVON, for the edification of visiting worshippers, enquirers after wisdom and salvation, and trippers.'

'Welcombe Church started its long life as one of the chapels attached to Hartland Abbey - founded in the 11th century - and was confirmed by name in a Royal Charter of 1189. The font dates from those early days. St Nectan, patron of the parish, was a Cymric hermit who came to Hartland in the 6th century. He was attacked by robbers who cut off his head, but, unperturbed, picked it up and walked to the well at Hartland Point which now bears his name. Wherever his blood dropped on the way foxgloves sprang from the ground. The well has never since failed and all Nectan's twenty-three brothers and sisters were inspired to become holy hermits by the miracle.

... the rood screen comes from the 14th century, a prime example of a great Devonian art whose sublimest creation famously adorns the Chapel of St George in Constantinople. Over it is a beautiful early 16th century cornice, perhaps by the same craftsman as the screen at Stoke. There are traces of gilding on the vine trail, and of brilliant red, blue and gold on the main beam, sad remnants of the glory eradicated by the Commissioners of Henry VIII-and-last or his bastard son.

We know that the screen originally stood nearer the centre of the church because of the fine carved roof bosses, and the wall-plates representing the fruitful vine and the barren fig tree. These - alone in Devon, apart from Exeter Cathedral - retain their original colouring. This work was intended as a canopy of honour over the Crucifix which stood on the screen. It too was desecrated to ruin during the despoilings of the 16th and 17th centuries.

The other roof bosses include emblems of the Five Wounds of Christ, roughly carved in hard wood.

During the 'Reformation' some of the 15th century pew ends were stuck to the screen. The old pews had unusual 'poppy-head' tops but they have disappeared, presumably also at that time. The reading desk survives on a Jacobean-style base.

The window-sill in the south transept is the original altar-stone; one of the consecration-crosses can still be seen. Below is a memorial brass (the name alas erased by subsequent 'Protestant' vandals) of a Spanish gentleman-volunteer martyred in battle during the reign of Mary the Great.

In 1508 Welcombe was made an independent parish, and the church was *'fittingly rebuilt'* - transepts were added and possibly a new chancel - and consecrated along with its graveyard. On the wall may be seen a copy of the Deed of 1532 (the very eve of tragedy!) whereby the parishioners agreed to provide a priest, and the Abbey to pay £5 a year towards his wages. The dedication was kept on the Sunday after Michaelmas, but it is now on the Sunday nearest St Nectan's Day - the 17th of June, when children and maidens in procession bear foxgloves to the church.

The 16th century pulpit originally had a sounding board.

The tower contains 6 bells. An inscription on the tenor reads: *'A Gooding cast us all fower for this new builded tower 1731'.*

In the 17th century there was a gallery across the back of the church, and on the porch was a sundial dated 1735 and inscribed *Fugit Irreparabile Tempus.*

The naive but charming reredos paintings of the Good Shepherd and St Mary Magdalene are the work of the Blessed Bridget Butt, a hermitress (and skilled water-colourist) briefly attached to St Nectan's in the 20th century. Her powers of prophecy and ecstatic visions led to her 'invitation' to Rome and eventual beatification, as well as artistic immortality via Bacon's controversial *'Screaming Saint'* (sic) triptych.

The bold Creed, Lord's Prayer and Commandments, are typical late 'Pure-Stuart', from the reign of Joseph I when orthodoxy harboured unnecessary concerns and churches were required to display them over the Altar.

The three stained glass windows are in different styles, each portraying an aspect of Our Lord's existence. The light is a feature of this Church, ranging from clear daylight to depth and mystery around the Altar.

The graveyard contains a tapsel gate, more usually associated with Sussex, and a clearly marked mass-grave pit from 'Counter-Reformation' days....'

****

'One, two, three, four....'

Samuel stopped and looked down at the low mound before him. The intervening years had caused it to weather and settle; in a short while it would be flush with the ground: invisible. He had come just in time.

He reconsulted his notes. The fourth grave from the Salway sepulchre, *'ten or so paces'* behind St Nectan's Chancel wall, in line and to the left of a yew sapling. Samuel checked. That *'sapling'* was now a tree, but it and all the other clues were present and correct. There was no marker to assist him - though other Trevans in the family plot had merited a memorial stone. He was entirely reliant on Father Jago's memory. The priest had said he remembered this one well, out of the many hundreds he'd seen on their way. He'd even recalled his words at the time, that *'she was as good as the rest now, their equal at last, if only in death.'*

Samuel wondered. It would be a fitting end, and the best joke of all, if he was now before some stranger's grave, mistaken and deluded for ever. However, he was left with no choice but to trust. He had to make a decision and so made it. This was the one.

The light was fading swiftly. Samuel squinted up at St Nectan's square flint tower, and it was not only the declining sun that misted his vision. It was a quiet place this, a sheltered dip amidst steep green hills, separated even from the little village of Welcombe it served. Samuel was glad of that.

He'd gathered some woodland flowers and ferns, fashioning a rough arrangement of them with clumsy fingers. If anyone should have seen him at work in long and careful selection, in doing the best he could to make a posy; if they'd laughed at him, a great grown man thus engaged - and there were no other witnesses - he might have killed them.

Samuel gently placed his offering on the raised turf.

It would have been... nice to say a prayer - but he couldn't do that now. There were only useless words, a cold comfort to him, and nothing at all to *her*. She couldn't hear him. But he spoke anyway.

'Hello Mum…. Goodbye Mum.'

CHAPTER 16

'What do *you* want?'

'Some courtesy for a start. What do *you* want: another broken door?'

'I'll get Dad.'

'I should.'

Uninvited, unsuspected, Samuel followed the youth into the house. Around the great kitchen table the farmhands were having their cider and fat-bacon breakfast. No one commented. They knew his form from last time and carried on eating.

The youth bellowed into empty air.

''Ere, da! That blow-in's back. 'Er looks like trouble!'

A gruff voice answered from upstairs, though its tone was less robust than the choice of words.

'Then 'e'll surely find it. Bind him there while I get me gun.'

Samuel brushed past the stocky boy, who'd been unaware he had close company.

'Oi! You can't just barge-....'

But by then Trevan was past him and heading up the narrow stairs. Significantly, he wasn't followed or hindered, though there was ample opportunity.

Faced with a selection of doors on the landing, he headed for the one muffling frantic sounds of distress. It opened wide at the prompting of his boot.

His beloved cousin was still in his nightshirt, though milking was at least an hour past. Roused up before schedule, he was sitting on the bed, revealing acres of hairy flesh and equal trepidation. Perhaps it was the unusual circumstances, but a fumbling meal was being made of loading a plain and simple fowling piece.

The farmer's wife was beside him, still tucked up. She saw Samuel first and, just for an instant, he got the impression she'd not object to finding him there more regularly, in place of what she'd got. That was a notion, a bit of leverage, a potential ploy, to be pondered on later. Meanwhile, the lady recalled propriety and screamed.

One of Samuel's hands permitted the farmer to see stars in the morning; the other took the gun from him and smashed it against the bedside cabinet. Neither weapon nor furniture survived their introduction. Then the stunned man was heaved off the bed and stood shakily upright. Samuel kept hold of a bunched handful of nightshirt and shook a bit more awareness into him. He smiled close into his captive's face.

'*Walkies!*' Samuel told him.

****

'That's about the shape of it. I don't know no more.'

Samuel indicated that, however reluctantly, he believed him.

'Very well. Yeah, it ties in with what I've been told. But things would have been easier on everyone if I hadn't had to prise the story out.'

Cousin Trevan judged it was safe to let some of the exasperation he felt out to play.

'I was a boy when it all happened. No one weren't proud of it. You reckon it was a tale we swapped round the Yule log? No, you just heard rumours and passing comments. Aunt Lucy never said a mite that made sense anyhow. And normal folk don't have much time for innocents. She were getting on when I knew her and sat by the cooking range all day. They let her turn and baste things. That's all I recollect of 'er. We never 'eard hide nor hair of you till you ships up here, and I call on God to witness I've kept nothing back.'

'After a little prompting, cousin.'

'And that's another thing. You had no call. You made I look a right Tudor in front of all. How I gonna stand up in front of wife and workers to exercise authority after what you done?'

Samuel seemed abstracted, his thoughts elsewhere.

'I couldn't say. I don't care. Time's a great healer in these things I'm told. People soon forget.'

'Not round 'ere they don't. You've done I an ill service.'

Samuel came to a decision and returned his full attention to the exchange.

'Then we're all square now, the Trevans and me. We can start afresh.'

The farmer warily shook his head. Pound for pound and unarmed he might be no match for this family-foreigner, but he had brothers and cousins and friends, and together they might....

'I'm not so sure of that, mister. We can't reckon out exactly what you might be after.'

'Nothing. I want nothing of value off you. That's how we can be at peace. If you want, I'll sign a document renouncing every interest. Go into Bideford or Bude and get a lawyer to draw one up. Then I'll sign it.'

Cousin Trevan's interest was aroused. If the kin thought it was he who 'drove' the cuckoo out there might be a powerful lot of credit in it for him. Still, he had to beware of a trap; in this hard, harsh world it wasn't natural, not *reasonable*, to exchange something for nothing.

'That might work...,' he said hesitantly.

'And all I ask of you in return,' Samuel continued, relishing both the disappointment and pleasure warring over the man's face, his hopes punctured even as his prejudices were confirmed, 'is one thing.'

Cousin Trevan resumed his normal, bristling, 'us against the world' self.

'I thought as much! And what might her be?'

'A day of your time.'

'Don't muck I about. It's cruel.'

Samuel caught his shifty gaze.

'No, *really*. Since I'm stuck here in this last-place-God-made, I may as well know it well. I want a guide, I want a tour.'

The man's eyes widened. He made a final inspection for mockery or fraud but found none.

'Done!' he said.

A hand was upturned, spat upon, then held out.

Such a sweet deal was never going to be walked away from, no matter what the slight. But excess hesitation might sour the 'family moment'.

Samuel fastidiously brushed the proffered palm and thus broke with yet another past.

****

They sealed their farmyard treaty with a quart of beer in 'The Forge Inn' at Welcombe. This was where Samuel was lodging, in the absence of hospitality from his wide-ranging family. The owner knew and feared him, concerned about the upshot of those long brooding sessions at his fireside, and only Trevan's ready money and prompt payments made him a tolerable guest.

Consequently, they got good service, full tankards and a breakfast platter to set them up for the day. Samuel spoke little and paid for all.

His relative warmed to the new role and a day's break from cursing at the churls. He soon so far forgot himself as speak to Samuel like a fellow human being from Devon. They strolled out into the rolling landscape and Samuel took what he needed from the accumulated wisdom of centuries.

'The road branches 'ere but both ways lead down to the sea. 'Er's the quickest but the foreshore there has an evil spirit so don't tread 'er after dark. The other beach has a Lady Shrine carved in the cliff so she's clean and safe to use.'

'Stratton's down that way and she's fine if you want the simpler things, especially on the first Thursday market. Anything rarer or made-to-order you gotta head for Bideford. There's no two ways about it. Her market is on the Tuesday every week and if you go to the Joiners Arms you'll get a special market luncheon that'll half kill yer. Proper job!'

'That land's sour. What? No, I don't know how come but 'er is, take my word for it. If you're a blow-in with money sooner or later you'll be offered some. Steer clear.'

'Look over there and you might see Lundy. Steepholm's that way too but she's not often visible. Evil places! Avoid they however gracious the invitation. The Lord of Lundy is a pirate, famous poet or no. I've seen empty drifting boats with blood all in 'em with

my own eyes. That's their work, or some of their Irish brethren. Go armed if you put out in a little craft, or else stick close in unless there's a King's ship nearby. They sweep down from Bristol periodic-like. Any privateer they take they hang 'em from their bowsprit and leave 'em on as a trophy, like crows on a fence. I've seen that sight too'

*'And don't buy of **their** produce. There's a plague-pit hard by, though they'll swear blind otherwise. They can only sell to uplanders or the Welsh slave plantations.'*

'Cider? No, you'll derive no money there. Each farm makes its own. The first draw goes to the family and the churls 'as the scrumpy. My advice is don't touch it. It blows up the veins in yer nose and can put a fighting frenzy on yer, if enough's taken. Mass production? What's that? No - who'd buy it? The gentry wouldn't be seen dead with cider, and you'll not make a farmer pay coin for what he can brew in a barrel hisself. You've got some funny ideas, mister, I'll give you that.'

*'Mebbe two hundred souls in all, more at harvest time, and most of 'em as poor as Protestants. I'll recount to you the Welcombe families that matter... and if you get the cod-itch there's Joanna Polway or Morwenna Zenn who'll oblige you for next to nothing.... Father McGlashan, he's not so bad but 'e's a **stickler**; you daren't confess one half the truth to him or you'd pray a hole in your breeches 'fore penance was done.'*

'This'll take corn, but it's stubborn like. A wise husbander will leave it sweet-meadow and graze it to death before a fallow time.'

*'**Course** the Cornish still raid over the border. Their friends the Welshies are not above joining in on occasion either. Why else do you reckon places round here are still fortified and barred up? You won't find that up country; people there can make their homes all comfortable like. And it's 'cause the Cornish get up to their tricks that you've got the demi-demon problems biding roundabouts. Those vermin love places as ain't safe or tamed: it's easier for 'em to hide and get their meat there. I tell yer, if it weren't for the sodjers permanent in Bideford and their horse patrols, this land would be worse than Cumbria. It's one-hand ploughing up there they say.*

*Do we raid back? **Course** we do. Sometimes it's unofficial; a few lads after the inn's chucked out. Other days the Governor at Bideford proclaims the Posse Comitatus and we get paid for lending our horses. Men from East Devon come to help. Me? Oh yeah, I've bin on a couple of 'trips over' as we call 'em. It's more or less expected of a young blade; it shows his mettle for the marrying stakes. Bit long in the tooth now but*

I've showed the Trevan flag in my time, don't you worry. Best day was when it were eye-for-an-eye for a manor house over Woolfardisworthy way. I shot a yeoman type point blank, and then had his wife upstairs 'fore we fired the lot. Typical Kernow girl she were: buttermilk skin and black natural ringlets - above and below, if you take me meaning. Lord, but I gave 'er a lapful....'

'Morwenstow's safe enough. They'll trade and talk with you there. It's the traditional truce spot....'

'Glastonbury? I've heard of 'er. Somerset way ain't she? I don't know so much about those parts. No one does.'

'And mind extra careful when you're walking in this portion round here. It's dotted with the old miners' shafts. Some say they're bottomless but I don't see how that can be. There's standing water in 'em and water don't stay where there's no base. That's my experience. Either way, go down one and that's the end of yer.'

Samuel had listened to and absorbed everything else without judging. It was necessary he learn about the landscape he was chained to. The natives presumably knew best. But this last, almost throwaway, snippet, he rebelled against.

'Mines?' he boggled aloud. 'No, I don't think so.'

His cousin was unconcerned. Things which weren't useable, edible, drinkable or swivable didn't feature greatly in his thoughts. They weren't on his land: so long as he didn't trip over them, that sufficed.

'Well, what else then?' he asked, growing daring. 'Giant rabbits? No, people say they was mines.'

Samuel repented of his open outbreak of disbelief. Despite all that had happened to him, his inner gaze had never ceased to search the landscape for *advantage*. Therein lay the only path back.

So he said no more. But to himself he thought *'well, I reckon people say wrong....'*

CHAPTER 17

'My dearest Melissa

I am well. I hope you are likewise. You are always in my thoughts - except when I am at business. No, on reflection, even then, for what else are all my struggles and conspiring but the means to regain you? Accordingly, I find that you are never out of mind, one way or the other.

I have not heard from you. I have no way to tell if Father Omar delivers my letters. It may be that you cannot reply. I will understand if you have given an undertaking to your father not to correspond. If, however, you are free in honour to write, I ask that you do so. Even one word - or a sign - would cheer me. It is dispiriting to labour alone in a hostile world.'

Samuel paused and brushed away the frantic crane-flies drawn to his candle. He wasn't sure about that last line. Were the sentiments too craven? Would a woman *respect* a man who - occasionally - faltered? Chewing the end of the ink-stick, he thought on and decided to let the phrase stand. What he'd written was the truth, and Melissa would get nothing else but that from him.

'My so-called family are no more hospitable than before; nor ever likely to be. They are an inward looking and clenched fist crowd and we are well shot of them. One deigned - after hard bargaining - to show me the district yesterday. I learnt one or two things of interest.

I have registered my presence in these parts, as required, in the nearest place of any consequence: an Abbey in a secluded place called Hartland, which is north of here. They

100

have been entrusted with my 'case'. Every Saturday I must travel there to report my doings and swear I have commenced no enterprise nor employed any person. In return I receive my 'pension'. You see, I am become a gentleman of leisure now. The sum is more than adequate for a simple life and I shall accumulate respectable savings. It pleases me to bank the un-needed portion with the very people who dole it out.

However, it is a long walk to Hartland, and steep going besides, so I may soon take mercy on my blisters and buy a horse.

The whispering old monk-cum-clerk that I see tries to tempt me to their evening Mass, which would fulfil the Sunday obligation. I do not succumb. He thinks me a neo-Druid, of which there are no shortage round here.

This is a stark place, not like Sussex. The Law is far away and enemies close at hand. Across the water, in Wales, there are the Irish plantations, and their troubles spill over. The Red Dragon fighters hide and train here, so it's said. And every man with a boat bigger than a coracle turns pirate if money's tight. Thus, people pray on their knees and prey on their neighbours. That way the country is poor and always will be. Even Hartland Abbey is fortified; its walls thick and windowless, save for loopholes. But it is better now than formerly. Each village has a tower from the old times, before the Navy came, before 'Kernow' was subdued. They are still kept in good repair.

Near to Welcombe is a valley where nobody will go because it is haunted by the spirit of Damned Drake - he who sold his soul in hope of thwarting the Holy Armada, only to be doubly betrayed. They say that when his 'Golden Hind' blew asunder Drake's broken body was hurled all the way here from Plymouth Sound. Nor is that the worst nonsense I have heard. There are few schools, as you may guess. I go and sit in that silent valley when I wish for solitude and freedom from mankind's silly chatter - and that is often now.

But be entirely confident, and never doubt, that I shall always hunger and thirst for your company. Its absence, through others' actions, is like a toothache to me. A word from you will dull the pain.

I will write again. Till then, I am your

SAMUEL TREVAN

Samuel consulted his pocket watch. It had taken the best part of an evening to haul this letter out from the torrent of what he'd actually like to say. He didn't begrudge the time however, for there was nothing better to do.

So, now he had two communications to entrust to the postal courier tomorrow. Even though it meant a tedious trip all the way to Hartland to the nearest acceptance point, Samuel reckoned the commitment as time well spent. For all that the first had taken far less effort to compose, he had hopes, or perhaps a premonition, it might prove just as important as the outpouring to his lady-love. Tonight and tomorrow's efforts would push matters forward somewhat. Whether it be a lot or a little wasn't in his hands.

He went to take a drink from his long-cold posset night-cap, only to find a variety of bugs had left this life by drowning in it. Both insect-enriched liquid and pottery mug went out of the window.

It only remained to sign, seal and address his handiwork, and doing so brought it home to Samuel how low he'd sunk. Both letters had to go under some or other subterfuge.

One he'd need to send 'care of' St Philip Howard's Orphanage and rely on Father Omar's reluctant indulgence. To do otherwise was as good as chucking it on the fire himself.

The second could be sent direct for sure, and even the return address was the true one. But in writing to *'The Holy and Supervisory College of Mercantile Trade, Sub-school: Resources: Chapter of Minerals and Mining'*, at the Church's Westminster Citadel, he judged it wisest not to use his real name.

Samuel took up the inkstick again and chuckled wryly as he signed himself *'J'* [for Judas] *Farncombe'*.

CHAPTER 18

'But your name ain't this...,' said the Landlord.

'Farncombe's my mother's maiden name. I use it for business purposes.'

'No it weren't. I knew your mother, bless her.'

The look Landlord got gave birth to fears greater than his misgivings. He allowed Samuel to snatch the letter from his doubting hand.

'Trust me,' Samuel growled.

'Oh don't mind I,' the man complained, 'I just run this place: the place where you live - for the moment.'

Trevan hadn't heard him. He was already half way back to his room. Fragments of a papal-red wax seal were left on the stairway.

He didn't even sit down to read it. There was that feeling of premonition again, of a high path foretold and destined.

'Dear Mr Farncombe', it read.

Ad Majorum Dei Gloriam

We acknowledge your enquiry of the 23rd inst. The Prior of the Minerals and Mining minor-chapter requires that I advise you of the following intelligence:

It is inconceivable that there might be, or ever has been, mineral extraction of any size or consequence in the region described. Reference to the most recent All-England survey (1978) by the Holy and Supervisory College's prospecting staff shows that the rock strata thereabouts are a barren womb as regards useful deposits.

For your further elucidation, I can add that the Earth's mantle in this area (among the first substance brought into being by the Deity) has been wonderfully conjured into extravagant forms by later convulsions attending the Creation. Such much-mutated antediluvian layers are rarely found to be of utility.

Thus, whilst this region's coast and exposed areas may attract remark and specialist study by cause of the twisted rock forms revealed, it has never featured prominently - or indeed at all - in the annals of mining endeavour.'

I trust that the above will assist (or enable you to <u>desist</u>) your enquiries.

I remain, sir, your brother in G*d

Samuel didn't bother with the signature or the pre-printed prayer to St Piran (patron of Miners) beneath. He had no desire to be indebted to any individual, least of all to some scholar-monk lackey of the Church. Nor had he anything to say to a saint. More importantly, his thoughts were racing ahead, unwilling to be detained by civility's pedestrian pace.

'Gotcha!' he exhaled, and throttled the letter in his hand.

****

They were well spaced out, and often concealed by years (centuries?) of neglect. Stunted trees, impenetrable gorse and the impoverished stumpy grass of the area blurred the rims. All the same, thirty minutes none too hard search revealed three shafts plummeting into the earth. He strongly suspected there were others further off or less easily approachable.

Samuel stood on the very edge of the last one discovered and peered within. There were even shrubs-grown-to-saplings which had lodged and survived in the crumbling shaft-walls. Desperate for life they lunged steeply for the sun, away from starvation and the blackness below.

He tested the depths with a stone. Long seconds went by before its impact tokened water. Echoes sounded far below him and lingered unpleasantly overlong.

Projected into the murk he had a sudden image of *her* face, of *her* flesh, and all her collective deliciousness. It was marvellously vivid. This he also took as a sign; that he should see her so clear in this place. The route to what he wanted started here. The way to one lay through the other.

'Never fear,' Samuel told the dark interior, and perhaps Melissa Farncombe also, 'I'll get to the bottom of you.'

CHAPTER 19

'Go on, fill 'er up an' kill me orf!'

The Landlord took the old man's leathern tankard to the racked barrels behind the bar, but put an edge of protest on compliance.

'You've a thirst on you tonight, Dead-yet, my friend. Mind you leave some pennies for food this week.'

'You sound like my old girl, rest her soul. Sing another song, boy. I shall drink as I please. In-comer Trevan pays my tally tonight.'

'Oh, does he now?' That was both a relief and puzzle, for the Landlord had never noticed his guest be either sociable or generous before. However, he didn't care to look up, for fear he and Trevan should lock glances in challenge. 'Well, that's nice. Though I notice he's too tired to come fetch it for you.'

'I ain't dead yet! Don't you worry about me. I can still walk.'

Indeed he could - at a shuffling pace, hindered by creaking joints and the weight of years. His tankard required both shaky claws to ferry it safe back to the bar parlour.

Samuel was waiting for him: impatiently.

'What have you been doing? Brewing it?'

'I ain't so fleet on me pins as former. I gets where I want soon enough. I ain't dead yet.'

'So you keep saying. Sit down and carry on.'

It was a labour for the ancient to set his drink down and lever himself back into the high-backed chair. He wasn't used to *this* corner, though he'd been coming to the *Forge* all his life. Samuel's character had altered such that it never occurred to him to help.

'Carry on what, mister?'

Trevan closed his eyes on the scene for a second.

'Save us but this is hard work!'

'And so he shall save us, the Lord Jesus,' the old man chose to misconstrue. 'That is our sure and certain hope. The priest told I at school and I keep that by my 'eart. But I don't see where hard work comes into-....'

'The mines, Mr Dead-yet: you were telling me about the *mines*.'

'That's my nickname, child: you can't put mister in front of her. And those mines, I've told you all I know.'

'Which isn't a lot, it transpires.'

'If you find anyone 'oo knows more, you go buy them ale. But you won't find a soul. I've outlived all. All them who were boys with I are gorn. *Long* gorn.'

Something about that achievement, a sense of triumph or perspective perhaps, made the old man laugh into his beer. The head of froth bubbled accordingly.

'Fair enough.' Samuel liked to hear things put starkly. 'So you're sure about the gold bit then?'

The tankard was slowly, carefully, lowered to the table.

'So my father told me; and he span no yarns. But it were from before his time. Gold mine or gold store, there were stories saying both: I don't judge 'tween 'em. All I recall is about the gold, and that a flood came - of foul waters: each said that - and drown-ded all.'

Samuel barely tolerated the pause as the old man took more refreshment, but it was worth the wait. 'Dead-yet' stopped drinking as a fresh notion occurred to him.

'I suppose,' he said slowly, 'it must still be down there with 'em. I marvel the story don't get round more; that people don't go looking for it....'

Samuel's face was a mask of innocence.

'Yes, odd, isn't it,' he agreed. 'Have another drink.'

****

****

From that night on, from some unknown source, old 'Dead-yet' seemed to have come into money. Suddenly, the adequate, though hardly ample, basic Church pension was no longer a ball and chain on his way of life.

Being a man of limited ambitions, he simply chose to indulge his thirst to the full, without hindrance, without counting the cost; to the exclusion of all else. No one was over-shocked: he'd always been inclined that way, when funds permitted.

Soon his ruddy face turned purple; he moved and said less and less. What he did say was slurred and made no sense. His decline was rapid. Within a surprisingly short while, some years ahead of time, old 'Dead-Yet' was.

CHAPTER 20

'To Whom It May Concern.

The bearer, Mr Samuel Melchizedek Trevan, is an 'excluded person', under my supervision. Whilst, obviously, I can therefore offer no assurances as to his piety or character, I am desirous that he should find a wholesome outlet for his undoubted energies. He has expressed an interest in the history of his birthplace, which I state to be the village of Welcombe in Devonshire.

So long as his researches are restricted to such innocuous matters, I would be grateful if every assistance could be extended to him - and thereby to me.

Your servant in Christ
+ Richard, Abbott of St Nectan's Abbey, Hartland, Devon, England.

'It's a letter of recommendation,' said Samuel, smiling down upon the librarian-brother, 'sort of.' He accepted the parchment scroll back. Its contents were well known to him: he was past taking offence.

'As you say,' the monk replied, neither face nor tone passing judgement. 'Are you familiar with books?'

That did manage to slide painfully under Samuel's skin. Was it malicious? He couldn't tell. Monks were notoriously light on social niceties; Samuel had come across that before. Supposedly, their best attentions were focused elsewhere. Sense should have favoured giving the benefit of the doubt.

'What do you mean by that?' The growl was part and parcel of his reply.

'Exactly what I said, Mr Trevan. Are you an practised scholar and researcher?'

'Do I look like one?'

'No.'

'Well then.'

The monk took up Samuel's hard gaze, held it - and shoved it back at him. Trevan was impressed and warmed to the man. Apparently he hadn't sheltered *all* his life amongst bookshelves.

'*Well then,*' the brother returned the words also, 'in that case, I shall be happy to guide you.'

And so he did, beckoning the visitor out of the administrative antechamber, through guarded double-doors and into the presence of more books than an abashed Samuel Trevan had ever seen before.

****

The famous painted dome helped enforce quiet, for it emphasised and repeated every sound, every footstep. People stepped gently and spoke in reverential whispers. Thus the atmosphere in Exeter Cathedral Library was every bit as church-like, and maybe even more serious minded, than the ancient house of God to which it was joined. The characters depicted in Lely's renowned '*Day of Judgement*' looked down upon the scholars and gave them additional food for thought. Several times Samuel caught himself gawping round like some Scot in the Vatican. He forced himself to be more blasé, but it was difficult. Happily, there was distraction in being schooled.

'... and each volume is indexed sequentially within the year of receipt - not publication - which can lead to some confusion for neophytes or in the case of offerings from remoter parts. I suggest consultation of the index for two adjacent years to the suspected publication date, but if perplexity persists then a duty-brother is always available to render aid. No book should ever elude you, for otherwise we have failed in our duty and vows. Some texts are proscribed or restricted and in the latter case can only be consulted under supervision. Too frequent requests for such books will merit interview with a senior brother: you have been warned. Please do not mutter as you read, trace the words with a fingertip or turn down page corners....'

Samuel couldn't dive into this beckoning sea straight away. First, he must be assessed for allocation to a suitable *'orientation acolyte'*. Regrettably, Trevan's precise position in the social hierarchy not being crystal clear, they got it wrong. For a whole morning a young brother of the Library order instructed him in the ordering of books, the filling in of request chits, and use of the elephantine catalogues. The necessity for grease-free fingers, the prohibition on spitting and partaking of victuals whilst reading, the availability of limitless scrap paper, were explained in words of one syllable whilst Samuel bit his tongue. This was another indignity, cruelly imposed on him by a... thoughtless Church; that he - *he* - should be requested to have a handkerchief about him - and make use of it, not his sleeve or the floor, when necessary! The few others with him, prodigy churls rescued from obscurity by Mother Church, or servant types indulged by their masters, solemnly took it all in and were grateful.

But when he was finally set free, and the Master Librarian he'd first spoken to returned, Samuel's spirit soared. There was... everything here, and thus, by implication, the one thing he sought. It was somewhere nearby, up in the high galleries or the reserve stores below, waiting for him. All he had to do was hunt it down.

The monk apparently recognised that intoxication, even if he couldn't suspect its source and end. He again asked for and consulted the Abbot of Hartland's letter, and thought on for a worrying while. For that space Samuel feared another last minute disaster. It would be in keeping. He held his breath.

Finally, the Librarian stored the scroll away and, raising a thin arm, indicated one quadrant of the massive circuit.

'Welcome to the Great Western House of Wisdom,' he said, unafraid to speak at normal volume. 'History and Geography are yours, Mr Trevan. So long as you do not stray from them, you will remain welcome. So long as you are welcome I shall be your guide.'

****

****

It was a requirement, right from the Tudors' dying days, that every publishing house, of every size, should lodge copies of their publications with the senior cathedral churches. When Elizabeth I (*'Black Betty'* to be) was frantically casting round for ways to endear people - anybody - to her regime, it had seemed like a good idea. Some bolstering flattery to a national, 'Protestant', Church dying on its feet from lack of conviction and bad conscience could only help. Unfortunately, a lot of the books being churned out in those fervid, anticipatory times were far from acceptable to the *'Church of England by law established'*. The increasingly confident underground 'papist' presses took great glee in supplying copies of their (untraceable) efforts. In the end the usurped cathedrals were burning as many books as they accepted. It was a major distraction during the short slice of history allotted them, just sorting the literary wheat from chaff. Then, soon enough, they and all England were otherwise occupied with more serious bonfires.

Thus, it was not until the great changes were at last put behind the nation, when people could be sure what was Holy and what was not, when they'd had a civil war, and London was burnt and rebuilt, and people traded instead of raided again, that the law was re-enforced. The efforts of later, settled, times went some way to filling in the 'Reformation-Devastation' gaps, but scholars had to accept that the record would never be complete. Historians considered this not the least shame of that... inexplicable era when even the devout queried the Almighty's stayed hand.

From then on everything English presses had to say, for good or ill, was gathered in and preserved. Other nations saw the sense in it, or at least couldn't bear to be left behind. By 1750 Scotland followed suit and Ireland soon after. After decades of stately consideration, Rome (deciding it approved) ordered an *'All Christendom'* library to be constructed. One centre in each country was obliged to surrender its stock and see it safe to the Vatican.

High King Calvach of Ireland, a fanatical bibliophile, refused to part with his pride and joy, the *'Bibliotheca Fuath-na-Gall'* at Skibbereen, and was promptly deposed (and cut in two) by his pious people, even before the Papal interdict arrived. A new ruler, with more realistic priorities (and

Ireland's first ever Over-Queen), was in place ready to greet and placate the Roman Legate when his warship sailed into Dublin harbour.

Otherwise all went swimmingly, and the titanic *'Campion Library'* (named, in pointed recognition of its inspirer, after one of Elizabeth's victims) took shape in the north-east corner of Rome, replacing all twenty-seven acres of the still spectacular ruins of Emperor Diocletian's Public Baths. Amongst the fair minded of either civilisation it vied with the Damascus-Caliph's *'Allah's Garden'* library as recognised successor to Antiquity's Royal Library of Alexandria.

Exeter, a prosperous though hardly first rank city, situated in a region where Englishness started to... thin, couldn't aspire to such heights, but it did its best. Samuel Trevan was quietly confident that it was up to serving him.

CHAPTER 21

It had snowed the day before but failed to settle. Now the sun made recompense by soaking up the remaining damp. Samuel welcomed her kiss and undid his coat. Someone dared to speak to him.

'What d'ye make of that then, mister? Her's an Iroquois ship!'

'Really? And there's me thinking she was out of Swansea....'

Samuel heard himself say it, and wondered at the need for such sarcasm. The Devon dockside-loafer agreed.

'Miss Mass this morning did we?' the man asked. 'Should 'ave gone I reckon; it might have sweetened y' temper.'

Trevan could have taken that further: in fact was half minded to. Thereagain, there ought to be proper cause for falling out. He had to guard against this growing sourness. The locals were only making conversation - and besides, there was no shortage of them. They'd band together, no questions asked, against a rough-tongued uplander. He moved on further up the quay.

The tea-clipper was indeed a fine sight, as big and well constructed as anything that put in to New-haven, let alone Lewes, but made wild looking in the Americas style. The sides were festooned with Blessed Virgin totems and each sail bore a lively pictogram of the owning tribe. Even the cannon were cast ornately, with extravagant curlicues and demon faces bizarre to English eyes. Depending on who you believed, the gun ports depicted gaping mouths or vaginas.

Samuel recalled reading that it was the Jesuits who'd taught the native 'Americans' shipbuilding, along with many other useful skills including the modern way of war. If so, they'd long outstripped their tutors, and not only survived but prospered. The Iroquois League, a vindication of the Papal 'nativisation' policy and by no means the least nation of expanding Christendom, now dealt with the east coast colonies as equals.

The mariners certainly looked confident enough, though far from their home continent. They swarmed lithely over the rigging, securing the gaudy sails, or else packed the deck, preparing to dock. For the moment they were in standard, practical, seaman gear, but on dry land they'd resume proper dress and the famous lone feather for the traditional dance of thanks to the *'Great Spirit-and-his-Christ-son'* for safe deliverance. Only then would it be right to think about off-loading or stowing supplies for the return run - or a night on the town.

The Devon dockers and merchants stood politely back awaiting the seemly time for business. Only a few port-wives, recognising their lovers, broke the respectful quiet to whoop hellos from the quay.

Apparently, the dance was quite a sight but Samuel had other calls on his time. He forced himself to forego that pleasure. The purpose of this walk was meant to be the marshalling of his thoughts, prior to another day of directed effort. He was not in Exeter to kill time or please himself, but to continue his crusade against fate. There was no excuse for idle moments.

Samuel was in the right place to frame no-nonsense thoughts. Few people came to Exeter and the West for frivolous reasons. It was a hard place and hard-working, where gains were valued and held on to, or else shipped east for safekeeping. Back in the previous century, *'United England'* enthusiasts had come west to fight and conspire, but that struggle was now largely won and the movement become respectable and orthodox, even staid. The dwindling band of zealots who came on pilgrimage to the famous *'Three Liberators'* monument outside the western 'Kernow' gate now had all they wanted (save Scotland under its unchallengeable Papal guarantee), and were as content as they'd ever be. There also arrived monastic orders and hermits and seekers-after-God attracted by the sparseness of settlement and many mortifications. Otherwise, visitors were all like Samuel: passing through; out for what they could get.

In fact, he'd acquired a great deal during his stay in the city, though for the present without appreciating it. If his great objective remained elusive, there'd been other gains. Way back, in another life, he'd studied the antiquarian arts the better to endear himself to Mr Farncombe. Then, what started as just a short cut to the man's daughter had grown into genuine interest. He'd since devoured books with pleasure and actually worried away at the mysteries of pre and post Flood days. In merely seeking to dupe Farncombe Samuel surprised himself with disinterested curiosity. Now, set loose amidst the Lewes-dwarfing riches of Exeter learning, those forgotten feelings revived.

Whilst drawing a blank about gold in Welcombe he'd been obliged to read about other things. If records of the old days said nothing about treasure there then he had to weigh up the things they *did* say. Whereas to start with he skimmed impatiently though hard reading about matters dead and gone, soon enough he found he was paying proper attention. There was no strict call for him to line-by-line read some dry essay about 'cromlechs' and stone circles. There was certainly no reason for him to recollect it over dinner and wonder why and when men built them. He had no cause to lay awake in his lodgings and consider how come there was only *one* known Roman villa in the far west. And as for the question of the giant 'dragons' bones' that sometimes turned up in cliff faces or rockfalls, what manner of creatures could they have been...?

His pace of study slowed, its quality deepened, and though he should have controlled himself (as he did in everything else), he... chose not to.

There'd never been a mine at Welcombe: he knew that much now: nor a castle or rich palace, or anything of that kind. There was no legend attached to the place he could get his teeth - or spade - into, other than half-baked country-slowness tales about headless coachmen and hell-hounds. It seemed like the area had always been what it still was; not even a footnote in history.

On the other hand it *did* have the mossy and sweet-tasting well by the Church, miraculously brought into life by St Nectan himself. Samuel had drunk from it on numerous occasions and spent an afternoon likewise absorbing a tome about that and all the other holy wells in the west.

Trevan repented of it after, as though he'd been indulging in something shameful. For penance he hurtled through a vast pile of Bideford assize records, ignoring intriguing tales of blasphemy, heresy and sodomy, in vain search for fabulous wealth lost, hidden or stolen over Welcombe way. There were none – nor anything even like it.

Right now, the Library wasn't open yet, or leastways the psalms and pointless prayers that started its day would still be going on. And, fine as it was, he didn't care to idle in the ancient Cathedral Green awaiting some priest's pleasure. There was ample time to stroll on, pitting himself against Exeter's steep climbs and develop a fine headache chasing 'will she?/won't she?' enlightenment. For Trevan's problem was stubborn persistence in thinking there must be some fresh approach to be found, if only he could batter his brain enough to see it.

And yet... and yet, it was such a well-chewed bone there might actually be no meat left on it. God knew (if he existed or cared) Samuel had gnawed away in search long enough. This wasn't like some child's jigsaw, or a wander in a maze, where there was certainty of a complete picture or a way out, even if you yourself couldn't find it. He'd been in the city – what? - a fortnight? Soon enough it would be Lady Day, when Christian women dressed all in blue and white and their menfolk abstained from them and gave them flowers. He hadn't thought to still be here to behold that. It would pain him. He'd always loved that day in Lewes, making special devotions in preparation, and saving his pennies for blooms to lay before the Orphanage's plain but beloved plaster Virgin. Last year he'd had funds and opportunity and the desire to bestow expensive hothouse roses on both Mary and Melissa. Now, for different reasons, he'd be neglecting both women. So Samuel didn't want to be still in Exeter then, to have the measure of his defeats held before him.

But others... they were quite happy to transfer his humiliating 'pension', that insultingly sufficient dole, from St Nectan's to the Cathedral bursar for ever. It *'kept him out of mischief'*: Samuel could almost hear the Abbot saying it. By keeping on, by having faith, he could well be co-operating with them neutering him. Best betrayal of all, his cussedness might their chief ally, delivering him, legs apart, to the castrating knife.

Arriving at the west-gate, Trevan looked at the incoming people going about their pressing business - and he wished with all his heart to get into powerful *'mischief'*. All he had ever wanted was one or two little things, but apparently that was too much to ask. Other people didn't get mucked around like that: witness the untroubled mugs all around. So, either he could join them - as was only fair - or maybe they should try a taste of his world....

Above the city-wall Samuel saw the marble crowned heads of the 'Three Liberators', supposedly the largest depictions of the human form in England, bar St Joseph atop Glastonbury Tor. Incongruous amidst Exeter's industrial area, they loomed over the workshops and mill-leats, high above the serried cloth-drying racks extending out to Shilhay Island. A falconer paid by the Joint Guilds Council strove ceaselessly to save those from the gulls' visiting cards, and as a by-product prevented the statues turning white too.

Unbesmirched therefore, Athelstan, Edward I and Oliver Cromwell shared an artificial hill and stared challengingly out towards Cornwall. They'd each prevailed in their time, pushing England's frontier further west and rescuing Saxons from a harsh yoke, until the third named won lasting victory. The Cornish were expelled out of Exeter and back over the Tamar, setting the border for good. The ambitions of the independent Cornish 'Dukes', hitherto intent on reviving '*Dumnonia*', were refashioned into hopes of mere survival. Accordingly, the 'Lord Protector' was much revered in these parts and even the returning Church Universal chose not to quarrel with that. Over the centuries She had acquired the wisdom of when to leave well alone and the confidence to treat local cults with generous spirit. So, though She might have had her quarrels with the man himself (before his conversion), it was reasoned that true Christians suffered less from his rule than under many a true-anointed King. Thus, when at the fervent height of their crusade the 'United Englanders' wished to honour him, no objection was raised. Cromwell rose again after two centuries absence, and took his place beside other heroes of the English.

Such wise moderation, this calculated meekness, bound the Church to the people, allowing it to sink in and meld to the very sinews of the society it served. It could not removed again without fatal surgery.

Samuel approved of the monument and what it symbolised. There was no hint of conciliation here, but a bold statement of dispute. That was the way to do things, instead of shrouding them in false compromise. It was right to step straight up to the enemy and tell them what was what.

'The enemy'? *The enemy!* A noun leading to a notion, a corner portion in the jigsaw, a half glimpse of a door opening in the maze.

'Now, *there's* a thought!' Trevan told the puzzled crowd.

CHAPTER 22

'Original documents appertaining to the Reformation-Devastation in the South-west peninsula' - compiled, together with a cross-referencing index and full notes and commentary, by Monsignor Anthony Rawlinson S.J., Seminary of St Charles Lwanga Press, Plymouth, Wessex, England. 1888.

Great Western House of Wisdom, Exeter. Ref: 4102/89. Vol. 23, Folio 97.

'A true and perfect accompte of items taken by y G*dly arm of His majestie from y sundry parishes of Bradworthy, Clovelly, Welcoome and Hartlande, for the putting away of the popish mass and suppression of feigned miracles, idolatry and superstition. Being namely a certifcat and extract of any golde and precious stuffe from the anciente tainted drosse other-wyse utterly disposed and sundered or putte to flames.

Sworn in the name of Jesus Christ our saviour without mediation, by Thomas Polwerran, Knight and Commissioner-Extraordinary under the authority of our most Holy and Protestant King Edward y VI.

ITEM : 2nd and 3rd chalices of silver without adornment, from the impious chantry-hyse formerly at Darnehole Point.

ITEM : 1 pyx and 1 monstrance of plated golde from the church at Stoke, Hartlande that was burnt in the cleansing of it.

ITEM : 2 silver cruets like-wise, one loaned from All Saints, Clovelly.

ITEM : A holy water bockett fr y so-called our Ladye help of Christians chappel at Markadon. Like-wise one each of a censer, chrismatory, communion spoon and paten all of silver. I state that this hse was a most profitable hse and well worthy of being reformed, for it escaped earlier visitations by its obscuritye and armed hostility of y deluded

119

congregation. His Majestie's Allemagne soldiery did disperse them but are suspect of also secreting some choice pieces. We are few and reliant and so cannot alltimes restrain their bloody arrogance. The Church is nowe bare and seemly.

ITEM : A processional cross set with good gems, and also a chasulbe thicke with thread-of-golde, taken from papist hiding at a private house in Wembsworthy.

ITEM : A chalice of flemmisch glass and chassed-golde, disguised as a profane goblet from y Church of St Nectan (saint that never was) Welcoome.

Y Gospell of John, 2, 10 - 'the best wine is kept till last': ITEM : a chalice, well anciente, of thick and softe old golde, kept privilly by the stubborn abbotte of y dissolved monk-ish hse of St Nectan, Hartlande, (who spente five fingernails and gained racke-inches in his wicked wishe to keepe it). It has four good gems sunk within and a golde placke of new-make attached, whereon the latin verse, I now render into good plain englyshhe:

> Sole sad survivor am I
> rescued from the suddeyn fall of night.
> In sharing bread and wine
> pray for all my lost brethren.

I opinion it came from underground, from the olde, lost, St Nectan-sub-terra monk-ish hse, at Welcoome, famed in priestly legend, that fell to satan (who full knows his owne) long ago. If such were its riches it should bee re-sought, for lately the papist temples here are poor pickings so zealous have we beene. If His most Holy and Protestant majestie so decree I will search it out, be it never so forgotten. This one mere token, all I have come acrosst, augers much I saye, and alone, melted and made into honest coin, will funde a battell of soldiers to combat the enemy within and withoute. But I must have men to do itte for the G*dly are besieged hereabouts. Matthew 9, 37, 'the harvest is plenteous, but the labourers are few'.

Meanwhile, Majestie, I ever remain your strong right arm in y west. This twenty-fifth day of the twelfth month, the year of our reformed Salvation 1552.

Thomas Polwerran, Knight.

Restraining all reaction, Samuel consulted Rawlinson's more modern commentary at the back of the book.

'... Polwerran, Thomas, Sir, (? - 1553)... a vicious heretic and persecutor, the

methodical despoiler of churches and Holy places throughout north Devon, and held accountable for the entire absence of ancient road-side shrines and market crosses in the region. He was born in Liverpool....

... a dramatic, indeed Damascene, re-conversion to the true faith on Mary's accession failed to convince, and various tales have him torn limb from limb in Clovelly or hurled from Hartland Point after appearing in public adorned with rosary beads. His younger (and estranged) son, Cardinal Bede Polwerran, made spectacular amends by....'

He'd had no time! Chameleon Sir Thomas, that is. They'd got him before he could do anything! Centuries too late Samuel cheered on the angry mob and thanked them. He thanked the remiss Church librarians too. They hadn't thought to purge the vanquished *enemy's* records. They might clear or hide every reference from their own sources, but revulsion had made them slack, their efforts at concealment incomplete. He'd found a hole in their perfection. Arch-Protestant Polwerran now had belated revenge for his high jump off the cliffs.

Samuel had read everything about St Nectan's Abbey; that had been one of his earliest ports of calls. There was no mention of an earlier house or preceding foundation; not the faintest glimmer of anything at Welcombe. Thinking on, he recollected that the early stuff was pretty sketchy: thin almost, though not so much as to wake suspicion. A lot of Church institutions gave the appearance of just always having been there. Until, that is, you had cause to question their beginnings....

He'd had no inkling - nor ever would have if he'd ploughed on in *their* furrow. There was a lesson in that. Yet he had to give Mother Church credit: she was good at teaching things and good at keeping things secret too. Somehow they'd nigh killed off any local memory of what had been. They'd done a thorough job: almost. But he'd had faith as strong as theirs - and so faith was not a weakness after all. Far from it. He'd believed. He believed that if Samuel Trevan looked hard enough there'd be a way though - because that was the way he wanted it to be.

Once again he saw that if Samuel Trevan struggled sufficiently, the world - however much it might whine - would eventually go his way.

CHAPTER 23

To: The Abbot-Registrar.
  The All-England Register of Land, Titles and Rights.
  The Monastery of St George-of-the-Mark.
  Gosport.
  Hampshire.
  Wessex.
    England.
The 25th day of March, the year of our Salvation 1995.

'Sirs.

Since it is land belonging only to Almighty G*d and to no other, and whereof it is bad ground uncropped or brought to benefit mankind since time immemorial, I request your lightest terms for the reclamation, draining and making sweet of the virgin site detailed hereafter:

Welcombe. Devonshire. England. From St Nectan's Church, west-nor-west, four-fifths of one mile, adjacent to Foxhold; through Knaps Longpeak, Shag Rock and to Newthorne Beach, being one-half of one mile south-sou-west of South Hole hamlet, bounded by the climbing slope of Strawberry Water and Watergap, unto the cliff tops, for the distance of 900 yards from the Mary cairn beside The Hermitage cross-roads to 175 yards from....

... yours in faith.
Benjamin Jethro Trevan
From: Trevan Farm.

Bideford Road.
Welcombe.
Devonshire.
Wessex.
England.

Samuel folded the letter and sealed it. As ever, it galled him to appeal to *them* for permission for anything, but since the whole earth was the Lord's His sole representatives held all the paperwork. They were easy-going landlords for sure, and ready enough to permit improvements or overlook ground-rents in hard times, but it *did* permit them stick their nose in Trevan business once again. He'd also seen their more intransigent, obstructive, side in such matters, when seeking leave to expand his London workshops outside the city wall. The humiliating rebuff then had been swift and thundering - as all the worldly-wisemen had predicted. For some reason the Church wasn't keen on big cities and liked to preserve green fields right up to their walls. If that meant cramming people in, building upwards and throttling business, then so be it was their attitude. The more go-ahead (quietly) cursed about it, but there was no point arguing.

Samuel was optimistic this time round. On the surface - and he chuckled wryly at the pun there - there was no harm proposed; no inconvenience to anyone; only the chance of some good. Every unlikely field wrenched from Nature's more disobliging moods made winter famine less likely - or shorter and less severe. The Church had even been known to sponsor some of the more up-hill projects with grants of cash or seed or oxen: witness the implausible bounty wrenched from the edges of Dartmoor. Samuel laughed again. Now, that *would* be funny, should his proxy-proposal touch Mother Church's heart and cause her to lob funding his way. He'd have to keep out of the way when the help arrived for fear of wetting himself laughing.

Come to that, he had to keep out of the way full stop. Hence the need for involving his beloved cousin. *He'd* been easily drawn in, on the promise of half any profits for the mere loan of his name. There was nothing on paper though, so when the time came just let him try to collect....

That was another amusing vision - the evening was turning unexpectedly cheerful. Drinkers in the *Forge* had never seen Samuel smirk so much, and rightly jumped to conclusions in seeing no good in it.

Strictly speaking there was no need for subterfuge. So long as he did not employ or produce, the terms of Samuel's 'exclusion' left him free to use his pension as he wished. A spot of land speculation, particularly with the reclamation element, would probably be smiled upon: a sign of useful occupation. All the same, it was wise to err towards caution. This wasn't just any old bit of land, nor was he just any old person. The Church might harbour special memories about either. Thereagain, its centuries long concealment of what had been might have draped even her own land registry in ignorance. That was devoutly to be hoped. If she *had* been too clever for her own good, it would make drawing her (gold) teeth extra sweet.

But there was no point speculating about it, he just had to wait.

Samuel went to see if 'Dead-yet's tankard needed filling.

****

It was the length of the wait that should have warned him. Since the Registry was also a religious house, the monks saw swift reply to mountains of mail as part of their vows - and a valuable mortification. Yet Samuel waited and waited and heard nothing. Until:

To: Mr Samuel Melchizedek Trevan.
C/O The Forge Inn.
Welcombe.
Devonshire.
Wessex.
England. 10th day of June, the year of our Salvation 1995.

Dear Mr Trevan.
Thank you for your (proxy) letter of the 25th March. Our reply is as follows:

NO.

Your servant in Christ.
Philip Grimes. Senior Brother: Wessex: Stacks 17 - 23 inc.

From: The All-England Register of Land, Titles and Rights.
  The Monastery of St George-of-the-Mark.
    Gosport.
      Hampshire.
        Wessex.
          England.'

To illuminate that 'NO', to spend time on it with fine pens and coloured inks, and twirl its finials into fantastic shapes, that was pure insult. Gratuitous mockery. Likewise the passing over of his deceit without comment. They knew who'd written and they'd winged it back to him like a slap in the face.

He tried to think of a proper response, but words weren't really adequate. Then, for once, inspiration struck when it was needed. He *would* derive value from their reply.

Cruelly torturing the letter in his hand, Samuel headed for the privy.

****

The Librarian at Exeter was briefly informed of developments. There'd been a similar occurrence back in his predecessor-but-two's time. Another searcher had stumbled on the Polwerran text and also promptly quit the library he'd striven so hard to join. He too had been *written to*, and ever after ate his heart out, wondering how could they have *known?*

The policy of trailing just one loose thread, one vague clue, was again vindicated. Either enquirers never found it and enquired in vain till patience gave out; or else, whether by luck or judgement, entered the baited trap. Any request for that one record was flagged up and investigated and monitored. Other departments of Church and State (the Land Registry the very least amongst them) were told. To date it had never failed.

As a true scholar the Librarian could hardly rejoice to see curiosity thwarted, but neither did he like his books being ransacked for mere material gain. That struck him as misuse. Likewise, he'd long ago learnt that not all knowledge was wholesome, or pleasing adornment to the mind. There were many books in his custody that he wished he'd never read.

Therefore he'd come to believe that it was partly his job - and a kindness - to conceal as well as reveal. The Librarian was sure that one day (though perhaps not till the life-to-come) this Mr Trevan would bless him for what he'd done.

CHAPTER 24

It was the quiet that told him something was wrong. Nowadays Samuel lay in bed till all hours of the morning, the least of the bad habits drifted into during almost two years of indolence.

Great events had come and gone; the 'Commotion Times' attending the death of Charles IV, the 'Agrarian Crusade' that struck down England's rising industrialist, land-enclosing, classes: they all passed Trevan by. Still marooned in obscurity at Welcombe, Samuel knew none of all the busy-ness was his business. He kept himself occupied and he kept aloof. But even books and learning eventually pall and now he mostly studied ceilings. It would be drink next without a doubt.

On the other hand he'd acquired mastery of the local routine. There was nothing he didn't know about it - alas. *So*, though a gentleman of leisure himself, he expected the sounds of other people going to work. Today however, there was no labourers' chatter along the road, no cart clatter, no tokens of animals being ferried about. The absences accumulated into something noticeable; the hush which should have lulled him woke Samuel up.

Normal noise from downstairs, a grate being cleared and plates going into the sink, confirmed the strangeness must still be outside. Samuel rolled from bed to go and have a look at it.

'*It*' was there, bold as brass, waiting for a look at *him*. The soldier, leaning on the garden fence and enjoying the sunshine, grinned and waved at Samuel. He was playing a game: it amused him.

Alerted, his comrades in a circle round the *Forge* moved in.

The domestic sounds below were replaced by crashes and screams. In all too short a space they were replaced by the thunder of heavy boots on the stairs.

Still in his nightshirt, not given time to meet... whatever more fittingly attired, Samuel addressed the door. Somewhere he had a *seax*, the handy single-blade knife Common Law permitted all Englishmen to bear, but he didn't go in search of it. The visitors - and perhaps story's end - would be upon him momentarily. Better to meet them face-to-face than arse-up scrabbling about through your possessions.

They *did* knock - and then stood back: which said a lot about the company they kept. When no shot came from inside the caller returned to pressing the door, introducing a sabre into the gap to lift the latch. Suddenly, Samuel had lots of company.

'Post!' mocked the foremost, a grim giant whose whole face and tone was cruelty - and flicked a letter at him. Samuel was so surprised that he caught it.

The bluecoats didn't seem inclined to mayhem, for all that it looked their stock in trade. They entered in but did no harm, content for the moment just to have him safe. One began to sort through his clothes, selecting a mismatched ensemble.

'Well, read it then!' ordered the one blocking the open door.

Samuel had calculated the odds on resistance or escape, and come to an answer close to nil. Therefore he complied and cracked the seal. It was blue wax: the army's colour.

Inside were copyists' versions of his correspondence, both his letter to the Land Registry, and the reply to it. Someone else had scratched out their sarcastic 'NO'. It now read, in a careless, hasty, script:

'Perhaps'.

'R.S.V.P.,' said the spokesman soldier. 'Come with us.'

****

****

The island was full of hanged men. Their bodies lay, broken necked or purple-faced, in piles. A final few were still on the gibbet when Samuel arrived and he couldn't prise his gaze from their jerky dance.

It made no sense to drag him across the Bristol Channel just to hang him; but Samuel knew better than to expect sense from the world. He thought on it as they approached the village from the jetty, but found no great regrets or fond farewells welling up from inside. What did trouble him was something he'd heard whilst in the London Watch. Supposedly, hung men became erect or fouled themselves. That final indignity would be... regrettable.

It was dusk when the army yacht reached Lundy. The landing beach was chock full of military craft and soldiers standing guard over the islanders' boats. Further in, there was a vast bonfire in Settlement Square, casting shadows against the lighthouse and Castle walls. A four-man gibbet, fully occupied, stood stark before it. If notions of escape still lingered now was the last chance to try. Samuel might heave the nearest soldier off the path, or seize a sword or gun to make a show. But then where would he go? Bolting off into the oncoming dark would only postpone matters: there was no escape from this bit of rock. Taking a few with him would be in character, but still a mere gesture. No one would know. So Samuel decided to save such indulgence till the last moment. Then there might be an officer to set violent hands on.

Even now he wasn't exactly a prisoner - but only because he obeyed. They'd barely had a word for him all the way to Clovelly to take ship, or on the twelve or so miles over the water; but neither was he bound or frogmarched at all. Samuel soon gained the impression that these weren't ordinary bluecoats, a few years off the plough. They were taciturn and used to wilder lands and getting their own way. The rough stuff at the *Forge* wasn't affectation but habit. When he attempted conversation he was ignored. Samuel knew the professional military castes called his kind '*usurers*' and '*Mammon-slaves*', despising those whose life revolved round pounds and pence.

He also knew a bit about Lundy, even before his cousin condemned both place and people. He'd considered it when casting round for business opportunities. The island was made of serviceable granite and, a few centuries back, King Joseph the Wizard had pockmarked it with quarries, seeking stone to rebuild London. The slabs which now embanked the Thames from Tower Gardens to Catesby Station came from here, and Samuel had thus, so to speak, walked on Lundy before.

That, however, had been the limit of his dealings, for he'd caught all the stories. Everyone agreed about the natives; that they were inbred and clannish, being sprung from one lineage - and that a bad one. Kings of England might be up to trading with Lundy-men but Samuel Trevan didn't own such resources. It was too risky to strike deals with those who were businessmen and pirates by turn just as it suited them. He'd left Lundy well alone and now desired more than ever to continue that policy.

Someone had had dealings with them though: they'd dealt with them and *dealt* with them. That much became clear as he was marched across Settlement Square. The Castle had been rough-handled and some outlying farmsteads were alight. Samuel saw no shortage of females and little ones bewailing their fate, but Lundy's menfolk were all lifeless and longer-necked than hitherto. Samuel acknowledged he was in the presence of a uncompromising initiative.

Its source sat in the commandeered church. Trevan's guardians stood back, pushing him into its porch, leaving him to make his own way inside. He found a trestle-table set up beside the font, blocking progress up the nave. Samuel presented himself to the busy throng around it. Eventually he was noticed.

'Another?' asked a dapper but pocket-sized moustachioed soldier occupying the only chair; perhaps a decade older than Trevan: young to be senior. 'You don't need to ask about each one. Hang him.'

Samuel thus identified the seat of power here, for soldiers a foot taller and twice the bulk of the little man fairly hurtled forward to obey his order. Though he had other things to think about, Trevan noted the awe or fear inspiring them. It was a puzzle but one he'd have to set aside. Strong hands started to bear him away.

'Possibly not,' said another voice; not loud but equally commanding. The pinions round Samuel instantly fell away. He was able to turn and face his - temporary - saviour.

He'd met the occasional Negro before. St John's-sub-Castro in Lewes boasted a '*son-of-Ham*' priest for a while, and London had a fair few Africans scattered about. Nevertheless, they were still rare in Northern Christendom and country people would touch them for luck. To find one on Lundy was remarkable in itself: that he should be a *sicarii* was an event of blue-moon proportions.

Samuel didn't cavil: anyone would do to rescue him.

'Hello.' The Vatican agent addressed Trevan with a smile. What nation he once came from was now impossible to tell – by design. All sicarii were from Rome, of Rome and *were* Rome – and nothing and nowhere else.

Though odd to hear entirely unaccented English, it was otherwise perfect. The sound came from a face stamped with sunny cheerfulness. Samuel even felt up to responding.

'Hello…,' he said.

'Are you the would-be miner?' The Sicarii peered closely, as if scrutiny alone might tell.

Samuel wasn't sure. But if that person wasn't to be hanged he'd be him.

'That he is, sir,' confirmed his former acquaintances at the church door.

'Who?' asked the small, seated, soldier; puzzled, but not in any irritated way. He seemed genuinely solicitous to know.

The Sicarii leant down to whisper in the soldier's ear, and enlightenment dawned.

'I remember now,' said the little man, gladly. 'No, we don't want to hang *you*: we want to help you!'

And with that he came round the paper-strewn table and shook hands most courteously with Samuel, as if they were old friends. Trevan mustered a strong grip from somewhere. His tormentor really was tiny: not actually dwarfish but well into the lower range of Anglo-Saxon physique. Samuel wasn't aware the army took soldiers that petite: not even the militia or the Watch would've had him. It was curious.

He didn't seem to mind Trevan looming high over his head - merely pleased to meet him.

'Are you hungry - or thirsty? Have you been looked after? Let me get you refreshments. Colour Sergeant, see to it. Will chicken do? Do you *like* chicken? And cider? That's what the people here seem to have lived on.'

'Um, fine,' said Samuel, 'but I'm not all that-….'

It was too late; already a bluecoat had rushed off. The small soldier frowned.

'You appear troubled: don't be. You are amongst potential friends. I have the potential to be a very *good* friend.'

The Sicarii glided over. He seemed permanently teetering on the edge of amusement, though well content to just balance there.

'The problem is,' he confided quietly, 'that our miner doesn't know who you are.'

'Few people do,' agreed the soldier, unfazed. 'Yet. Though I warrant when he does he'll have heard of me.'

'Doubtless,' agreed the Negro, starting up a slick but unappealing double-act: two crocodiles agreeing to share their prey. 'And then he'll realise just how good a friend....'

'Or bad a foe,' said the soldier.

'... you....'

'... or we....'

'... can be.'

'Allow me to cut the knot and introduce myself,' said the small man, still holding on to Samuel's reluctant hand. 'I am General Mott.'

Trevan's jaw did, alas, sag a fraction before he regained control.

'That's right,' the soldier added brightly, noting the involuntary reaction, '*The Beast of Llanarth*'?

From behind an impassive front he was later proud of, Samuel gingerly greeted the third most powerful man in the England.

****

ARCHBISHOP OF LONDON'S LIBRARY - WHITEHALL CITADEL.

'ENCYCLOPAEDIA BRITANNICA' 2020 EDITION.

'SICARII: from the Latin. Literally 'knife-man'. Originally a terrorist assassin group murderously active in 1st century Judea. See Josephus' *'The Jewish War'* passim. In modern parlance applied (initially jocularly) jointly and severally - in defiance of correct Latin usage - to the elite legion maintained by his Holiness. Established 1828. Volunteered by pious parents in tender youth or liberated from heathen slavery; selected against the most stringent of criteria and raised in long years of seclusion at the famous Ravenna Monastery of St Peter-of-the-Sword, there emerges a soldier free of family ties or national feeling, zealous only in the service of the true faith. The Legion's proud boast is that they have never experienced defeat in the field. Notable battle honours include Sparta, 1858; the recapture of Constantinople, 1900; and the Iroquois-League 'Prairie War', 1980-85. Their giant battle banner is notable for being emblazoned with objectives to be removed when achieved. Athens and Constantinople are now duly unpicked; Cairo and Mecca yet remain. However, in more recent times the Sicarii have also acquired a less overtly militaristic role, in keeping with Christendom's largely peaceful condition. [See, for example, in connection with the events in England 1995-96: ENCLOSURE CRUSADE, THE]. They are now most often employed as individual emissaries and agents of political policy....'

****

Extract from: *'Advice and admonitions to my successor, G*d preserve him'* Found amongst the effects of Ariel ben Yisrael, Pope Simon-Dismas, 1979 - 2002. First generally published in *'Wisdom of the Holy Fathers'*. 12 volumes, Ed. Cardinal Frank Holdsworth, Archbishop of Ankara, Fiat Lux World-wide Press Corporation, Rome, the year of our Salvation 2402 AD.

'A word regarding sicarii. The world is as it is and how Almighty G*d made it, but we can still deplore the wicked necessity to so pervert a G*d-given life by breeding these human attack-dogs. Alas, there is need of such men to thwart the malevolence of other men. But I feel in my bones that each successor to St Peter will be hard put in the tribunal of the afterlife to excuse it. However, we know that G*d is love and mercy, and that His son and the Blessed Virgin will be there to intercede for us. There are always grounds for hope.

But that hope must be earned. I earnestly implore you to visit 'St Peter of the Sword' at Ravenna, where sicarii are made out of mere boys. Witness their birth and acknowledge fatherhood. I have done so as reparation and penance every year since taking up the cross and yoke of the papacy. Whereof I say to you most solemnly, that I found precious little love and mercy there....

... But they exist. That melancholy fact being so, be advised that the sicarii, our well-named 'daggermen', represent a sharp tool ready to hand: so very sharp however that it is quite possible to cut oneself by mistake. There is the temptation to reach for them at every opportunity, knowing that they are equal to all tasks. Yet this is a mistake. Do farmers cull rabbits with cannons? Do barbers trim bunions with broadswords? No indeed. Both, I grant, will do the trick but they are too <u>much</u>. What is the gain in success that leaves behind a blasted landscape? No, use your sicarii to pluck just one choice fruit high in the tree, not gather in the whole harvest.

I will give you an example of the required restraint. When England was ruled by the boy king Guy, and every faction in that restless nation writhed and strived, ambitious for the regency, I sent them a sicarii. He, a Nubian, attached himself to a notorious man of blood, an English soldier named Mott....'

****

ARCHBISHOP OF LONDON'S LIBRARY - WHITEHALL CITADEL.

'THE DICTIONARY OF NATIONAL BIOGRAPHY'
Published Stalybridge. Auto-da-fé Press. 2098.

MOTT, Alexander Scipio. 1967 - 2050. English general and statesman.
'... origin is obscure in every sense. Such indications as survive suggest

that he was born of what was then administratively termed '*Saxon*' and '*churl*' stock in a Surrey-Hills hamlet called Binscombe, (near Guildford, the county town). However, even these bare facts exist in only one contemporary reference: namely a (mischievously inspired?) pencilled note by the artist Miss Mary ('Pat') Freeman on the reverse of Mott's official portrait for the National Gallery. This presumably escaped the General's attention and life-long policy of mystification. The single-source attribution acquires some credibility via Mott's death-bed decision to take the title 'Lord Binscombe' upon his controversial and much belated ennoblement.'

...

'... the Welsh so-called 'free-state' had long troubled the Kings of United England until Mott's brilliant lightning campaign in the summer and autumn of 1995. Its success, culminating in the unconditional surrender of Caernarfon on Christmas Day, owed as much to Mott's painstaking preparations in the preceding two years as to his martial skills in the field and repeatedly proven personal bravery. A blight was however cast on his achievement by the treatment meted out to an unresisting, albeit less than friendly, area in mid Wales at the start of operations. This seems to have been a quite deliberate act of policy on Mott's part. The village of Llanarth, together with its every inhabitant, regardless of sex or age, was swept from the face of the earth amidst horrific scenes of massacre and rapine. Nothing remains of it to this very day. Even now, in some parts of Wales he is burnt in effigy on the anniversary of the event and dubbed 'The Beast of Llanarth' - an epithet coined at the time and in no way discouraged by Mott, who relished fame or notoriety alike. Conversely, Mott's apologists, of whom there were no shortage, stated that the war was shortened thereby, citing the list of rebel towns who straightaway capitulated at the news, thus saving them and the English/South Walesian army from the rigours and waste of combat. This is arguably so. Certainly, Mott established a lasting settlement in the former 'Cymric' areas which had eluded others for centuries past. Nor was he thereby debarred from aspiring to the most glittering prizes offered by the English state....'

****

CHAPTER 25

Samuel was then dismissed and locked up. Far from being aggrieved, he was glad of it, having not just food for thought but a whole gargantuan banquet of the stuff.

They chose a small house near to the Castle to hold him in. A few hours back it was probably home to a prosperous fisherman-cum-trader-cum-pirate; someone of close lineage to the Lord of Lundy. It had been a nice home too - once - that much was clear, worth sacrificing much to hold on to.

Having sacrificed all, the presumed former owner sat in its parlour, shot to death. Black beard resting on his chest, he looked just drunk or asleep, fit to rise again and resume ownership. The body was still warm. Nearby, a spray of blood up a wall recalled someone else's vain resistance. Yet only the dead man remained out of all who had lived here, the last vestige of what had been until this day. Now the house was very still, waiting for a new beginning. Samuel knew he was not part of it and had no place there. He found a seat beyond sight of the instructive tokens. From outside there still wafted the distant wails of women being loaded onto ships like cattle.

Along with 'refreshments' came a file, a collection of papers bound in blue card. The soldier who delivered them told him to *'eat!'* and *'drink!'* and *'read!'*, as he set each down, making no distinction between the commands. Even without such compelling advice Samuel was happy to comply. It provided a welcome distraction.

The promised chicken didn't show. Instead came a jar of brawn and an inappropriate, ornate, dessertspoon to fetch it out with. Samuel studied the coarse jelly in the glass and realised that he was indeed hungry. Appetite had been suspended whilst thinking of final things and mastering terror. Now, in accepting there might be days to come, there was occasion to refuel.

Slow to start with, but speeding up, heaped spoonfuls of the stuff were enjoyed, washed down with scrumpy from the jug. Gradually, Samuel felt strength return.

With it came the will to plunge into the file. Since its source was Mott he assumed there would be scant comfort within, but as the same source ordered him to it he had little choice. His best hope was for some explanation of his plight before the fate they'd already decided on was dumped in his lap - or drawn across his throat.

Samuel should have been more himself: less defeatist. What they'd given him was actually the very secret he'd been hunting. By two pages in that was clear. Trevan also learnt - if further proof were needed - he was dealing with short-cut taking, trespass-careless, people. These documents hadn't been acquired in the regular manner, but rough-torn from books and records just as it suited them.

Some ancient leaves threatened to crumble in his hands and their script was often beyond his scholarship, but usually a modern transcript was provided, scrawled in any old spare space. Which was thoughtful.

Food forgotten, lured by the promise of great things - at great risk - Samuel read on.

****

'Fr: THE WESTERN ANNALS AND EASTER TABLES, supposedly from the time of Saxon kings to the reign of James the True - but greatly incomplete and damaged and replete with inconsistencies. In seven ancient volumes at Exeter Chapter House and in variant form, five volumes, in custody of the Mayoralty of Bristol, as per custom, time out of mind. Folio 1145, detached by authority of M. Pothecary, gent. Officer, first company, The Queen's Own Guards Regiment. Transcript by same, where possible, with assistance from Mrs Joyce Preston, M.A., a scholarly lady and discreet, by virtue of her husband being of my command.

'... ye year of our glorious salvation by the sacrifice of God's only son, Christ Jesus [which pious preamble, being constantly repeated, is henceforth omitted, but only for brevity's sake. JP] *1480. Wherein certain Bristol merchantmen and fish-venturers* [? JP] *returned from the new-founde-land with strange pelts and vittals and recountings. Item: to subscription* [? JP] *of listing of those poor persons, hale in body and the women good for child bearing, to go to said land to make their way and regain their fortune, whilst spreading the word of almighty God.*

1482: Wherein the old dark prevailed and finally, at ye unfortunate and cursed St Nectan's-sub-terra house. Few but the gate-brothers emerged with what poor little of the great glory and riches within (which same proved vain guardians) they might gather with trembling hands. [illegible. JP] *glad reports and tokens of a valiant struggle within. Of the rest, full many, we despair save that those who perish against fallen angels are gathered straight to the bosom of Christ Jesus. Sealed is the pit until d*[indecipherable - presumably 'Doomsday' JP]. *Earl Talbot mounted guard until one month past Candlemass but no sign was from within.*

1485. Henry, called Tudor, strove in battle at Bosworth field....

****

EXTRACT. Westminster Citadel Dragoons' Regimental Diary - enciphered secret section:

'Twelfth day of July 1702. The pit being breached sufficient by our pioneers, a descent was made, the Legate and Roman troops and Mendip miners preceding.

Thirteenth day of July 1702. No sign or sound. Two troopers distracted by the evil breath of the open pit, fit only to be sent away. Cornet Fitzgerald, likewise afflicted but being stubborn in blasphemy, was hung. T'was contracted that messengers be sent back by now, but none come.

Fourteenth day of July 1702. The sentinels (who can abide no more than half of one hour at the mouth of the pit) report musketry and cries from in the deep. Colonel Cadwallon, though fetched, heard none of it for t'was short lived.

Fifteenth day of July 1702. Nothing and no one.

Sixteenth day of July 1702. Nothing.

Seventeenth day of July 1702. Nothing.

Eighteenth day of July 1702. The Colonel ordered a Holy Mass at the entrance. Satan made no audible protest. Flaming bushels and tar-barrels were cast down and the foremost props sundered. The pit burns. Nothing.

Nineteenth day of July 1702. The pit was sealed forever.

Twentieth day of July 1702. We marched to Bideford, little loathe, but sullied and with heavy hearts. The King's orders direct us to the Kentish coalfields where Anabaptists and Levellers....'

CHAPTER 26

'I've suddenly realised,' said Mott, abruptly all charm and solicitousness, 'this must all seem rather strange to you.'

There was a fine view of dawn over Lundy from the top of the Castle keep, heralding a perfect spring morning. The general had moved his base of operations there. Blazing torches around the battlements made the scene look like the court of Attila. Fixed forever in a gape of surprise, the head of the former lord of the property, a knight of the realm no less, adorned the flagstaff. Another lesson.

'The feeling passes,' said Samuel, dryly. There was no clue as to which particular bit of madness the General was referring, but that reply covered all.

'Good man. Stout stuff. Wish we had more robust types like you.'

The General may have approved but Samuel couldn't read the faces of his entourage; the various aides, bodyguards, intelligence officers and, of course, the Sicarii. They looked at him like not-especially hungry men would survey a lamb they might - or might not - dine on. Apparently, the great man Mott had been alone for hours past, communing with the sky and his thoughts - or something. Now, by contrast, he seemed almost chatty.

'Lundy was a nuisance, you see,' the general explained, lolling back in his chair. 'It has been for generations. You can't have people being pirates one day and honest seamen the next, can you? They ought to have made their mind up long ago. So I made it up for them. Problem *is* – was - you can't distinguish 'tween good and bad by sight. Only God Almighty can separate sheep from goats; that's not given to us down here. So we hung the lot - the men I mean - and transported the totties and brats. Shame, but there it is. Also a demonstration for their Irish brethren, else I'll be across the sea to teach them likewise. Besides, Lundy can be restocked. I'll hoick some beggars out of Bristol and bring them over. I think I ordered a few elderly natives kept alive to teach newcomers the ropes....'

He turned to his staff to check this was so and got half a dozen swift confirmations.

'There you are then. Intrinsically, Lundy's quite a nice place, so I'm told. St Patrick got rid of all the snakes - like he did in Ireland. Not only that, but apparently there's seals over by the western cliffs. I might go and have a look at them: I like seals. Do you like seals? Have you ever *seen* seals?'

Samuel didn't want to commit himself. This was no normal conversation: innocent sounding subjects might mask lethal metaphors. So he lied and shook his head. Mott seemed excessively disappointed but soon recovered.

'Oh dear. Never mind: you may do one day. Come back here when it's all settled. Though really it's all settled now, isn't it, come to think? Despite all the unpleasantness. Good can come out of ill, eh? Sweetness from strength – Samson and the lion sort of thing: do you see? Leastways, that's the way *I* see it.'

Then his tone, his expression, everything; all changed without warning; the avuncular manner snuffed out like a light.

'His majesty's given me complete authority in the West,' said Mott. 'Mark that. I serve him and the right as I see fit.'

He wasn't boasting but stating a fact, seeing if, taken unawares, anyone had problems with that.

Samuel didn't because he'd purposefully stunned all his cussedness to rest. He wanted to get off this island. Nor was he alone in treading that path of wisdom. Mott's staff, though each twice his size and each as hard as a lawyer's heart, all looked like men on thin ice, living in mortal fear of him. The one exception was the Sicarii - who was trained not to be read and also child of an invincible patron.

Then, like slipping on a familiar, comfortable, coat, the General was his old-friend-well-met self again.

'So you see that I have ambitions just like you: on a different scale of course, but recognisably the same species. You're a businessman, or would wish to be one once more. I'm in business too: the business of acquiring renown. Free Wales is no more: I did that! I also dealt with Liverpool in the Agrarian Crusade. Now I'm an everlasting chapter in Lundy's history. I shall get on top of this piracy nonsense and bring peace to the West country. If Kernow should lift its eyes from the dust it will meet my gaze. I am making myself *useful* wherever I can, tying up all manner of loose ends. This lost monastery mystery is another such, albeit very minor. Mother Church's perspective spans millennia and her memory isn't lulled by passing years, not like mere nations and dynasties. I've learnt that she still wonders what's down there in... in....'

'St Nectan's-under-the-earth,' prompted the Sicarii - because no one else seemed to dare.

'The same,' confirmed Mott, gratefully. 'She also ponders the fate of the - you've read my file of pilfered piffle, I take it? - Eighteenth century de-consecrating expedition. Did they succeed we all wonder? Yet technically there is an interdict against molestation of the site; against any revival of awareness of it. Now, I tell you most solemnly, the Church's concerns are mine also; I'd no more go against it than I would my beloved parents. Where I am heading I cannot be seen to grapple with this issue. Yet you, dear man, have no such constraints: you are halfway to outlaw already! You, Samuel Trevan, are a desperate but most resourceful man. *You* wish to plunder the reputed abandoned treasure; Mother Church and *I* would like to resolve a puzzle. All sorts of interests, high and low, converge. Do you not see the happy pattern?'

Samuel restrained himself to a simple nod. Mott waited for it all the same before continuing.

'So, here's how it is: you keep any valuables, bar holy relics naturally. That's only fair: what you can take you keep. But first find out what we want to know. That's your top priority. Because we don't like the thought of the sacred in unclean hands. *I* don't like it. It's not *nice*. So find out. Get rich if you can and want but find out first. I shall have to be strict with you about that. Afterwards, you're away and free. Leave us to sort out the aftermath....'

Mott actually licked his lips at the prospect: an involuntary action – and would have sworn on oath he hadn't.

'In fact,' he concluded, 'it's a neat deal. I can assist you, with *'volunteers'* and funds, but I can also deny you if things go wrong; forgive me for speaking so plain....'

There was no point in being just a yes-man, Samuel saw that now. It wouldn't be accepted as sufficient.

'Don't apologise, general,' he said, butting in, 'I like plain talk.'

Mott enjoyed sturdy replies less than he pretended, but surfed the resultant wave of irritation without falling off. Just.

'Then you shall have all you want of it,' he said. 'But, more importantly: are you in?'

Samuel hesitated – but only for strategy's sake. It wouldn't do for Mott to realise they were made from the same mould.

'What if I'm not?' he asked. 'In that case am I 'out'?' Samuel indicated the battlements and the long drop to the rocks.

The General mimicked horror at the very idea. He might have convinced some. Some toddlers perhaps.

'No, no, Mr Trevan; worse still! You go back to obscurity; to a *little* life: safe but... little.'

There'd never been need for thought. Samuel held out his hand. Mott honoured a fellow intrepid spirit by rising to shake it.

CHAPTER 27

'So, you're a 'plain talk' man, are you?'

The side with the whip-hand had celebrated their new spirit of partnership by locking Samuel up again. Back he went into the homestead-plus-deceased-ex-owner, with just his thoughts and a bearded corpse for company.

Even so, and despite the lack of distraction, he heard no turning or forcing of the lock, no indication of an impending visitor. The Sicarii just... appeared beside him without warning.

Samuel would rather not have jumped, not have flinched, but there was too much death nearby to expect perfect control.

'Shite!' he exclaimed. 'Don't do that!'

The Sicarii smiled. His teeth were perfect and shiny-white.

'Shall if I want,' he said, 'if I can. You did well against Mott: better than most. I like you. So I say again: plain talk is it?'

Trevan sat down. There was nothing he could do against such a prodigy, nor any point in vigilance. He stretched out and made himself comfortable. Although a spare chair beckoned the Sicarii chose to prowl instead, attempting to wear a path in the reed rug.

'Plain talk for preference,' Samuel confirmed. 'But I doubt my wishes count for much.'

'No,' chuckled the Negro. 'Still, we can pretend. Listen: General Mott has plans; you stand in relation to them as a garnish does a banquet: desirable but by no means essential. That is both opportunity and peril for you. Prosper, be a sparkle on the shine of Mott's reputation, and you may clutch on to his coat-tails as he ascends. Fail and he will say *'who?'* It is far from heart-warming but that is the way people must behave when they *aspire*. Do not comfort yourself with moral superiority. You are no different in your own little way. We know the manner of your leaving London.'

'I'm astounded you can bring yourself to talk to me.'

The Sicarii stopped his pacing. It transpired there *was* a core of prim seriousness to him.

'I talk *down* to you,' he said, convinced and convincing. 'A standing man to one slumped in a chair. A servant of God to a slave of sordid Mammon. I speak thus to Mott, a creature of blood and passions. I've been shown the full picture; I've looked in the face of Truth. We're just energy given form by God. Nothing matters once you know that. *So*, it's given to me, by training and wisdom and authority, to speak my mind to people you would faint in front of.'

'Don't bet on it.'

Samuel spoke levelly enough, but within he was resigned to a spell of unconsciousness at least. Sicarii were reputed to be able to stun or kill with the merest finger-tap.

Instead, the Negro smiled approvingly from above his high military collar, back in amiable mode.

'Right answer. I'm glad I saved you. You have kingly spirit in a humble husk.'

The sheer relief of continued wakefulness made Samuel conciliatory.

'Don't worry,' he said in jest, 'I don't aim *that* high.'

But the Sicarii took it at face value.

'Good. Wise move. Nor does Mott, fortunately. He limits himself to hopes of the regency: merely the *second* man in England. At present, Lord Onslow of Guildford holds that post; an honourable and pious soul, held in great esteem by most parties that matter, thus requiring great effort to displace. Hence the General's urgent thirst for glory. I am here to encourage Mott - a little. To guide and perhaps restrain his energies. Impatience or frustration in such a man can be so... dramatic. Not to mention ruinous for ordinary people. As ever, the Church acts only for the common good. And, no, I don't mind if you tell him all this. He is by no means silly or blinded. Do not underestimate Mott: he is bigger – far bigger - than the frame God gave him: he might well seize the prize he wants. Then of course, he must consider if it was worth all the sacrifice and sin - but that is another question. We have other experts available who will help him with that.

Meanwhile....'

'Meanwhile, you can help me....'

The Sicarii nodded.

'You steal the very words from my mouth, miner-man. But there is no need for you to steal any more. Because, yes, I can help you.'

'I'll draw up a list.'

'Send it to me - and *only* send things to me. My reputation is proof against contaminants or scandal. Ask and you shall receive. Though how you might succeed where Rome soldiers and Rome wizards could not I don't quite see. I suspect our correspondence may be short. Would you like Masses said for you if we must reseal the pit?'

'No.'

'I shall arrange them anyway. Foolish infidel: how dare you tug at death's shirtsleeves so? Is your 'worst case' mere eternal sleep? Ha! Consider scripture: Hebrews chapter nine, verse twenty-seven: *'But after this, the judgement'*.' Then he spoilt the high sentiments with a grin.

'I dare because I shall win,' stated Samuel, 'and come back. And I'll come back because I've got things to do. Important things. And that's the difference 'tween me and other tries.'

The Sicarii almost looked impressed, but there was no real way of telling.

'Do you know what?' he said, amused. 'You're half-way plausible.'

He stood to one side, clearing the way to the unlocked door and the wider world - and freedom. Mock theatrically, he waved Samuel on.

'So go forth, doubting-one; away you go to resolve the believers' doubts!'

Trevan knew he'd fallen amongst capricious people, and so took the chance whilst he had it. Only when actually through the door did he pause and turn back.

'I'll be in touch then,' he said.

The Sicarii nodded and smiled warmly at him: a horrible, chilling, sight.

****

****

To: The Officer of the Vatican Inner Cabinet of Temporal Affairs, commonly
'THE SICARII', attached to:
The Commander and Staff.
The Military Encampment.
Llanthony
Near Brecon.
West England.

Sir (for I do not know the proper form of address to your kind)

I acknowledge safe receipt and proper employment of the generous funds already supplied, for which find the exact accounting on the separate sheet attached. Communications by the swiftest means is sought with some of my former mechanicals in London, the best and most discreet experts in the harnessing of steam, and contracts enforcing confidentiality are drawn up ready. If they accompany the engines purchased in the Crutched Friars City Foundry last week, I am confident of draining operations before the month is out. To this end, the 'volunteer' pioneers and sappers mentioned will be required at your earliest convenience. Likewise the bonded Cymric labourers available, as you say, from the Hibernian farming collectives in your immediate vicinity. Also some English-speaking slavemasters, from the same source, for the workers' proper ordering and discipline.

Then, since you ask for a full and complete listing of my foremost requirements, I append as follows:

Item: Gabion baskets, 4 score of.

Item: 300 cubits of standard-beam seasoned mining timber.

Item: 50 cubits of cast iron tram track - for appearance's sake.

Item: One sturdy dolly-tub and winch.

Item: 12 cut-off carbines, of the new flintlock mechanism, thus fit and safe for employment underground.

Item: 12 brace of pistols, similar.

Item: 1 brace of shotguns, similar - but truncated.

Item: Canvas tenting sufficient to house...

...

Item:...

Samuel hesitated over making the last entry in two close-written pages of demands. His ink-stick came off the page, he postponed matters by taking another sip of cold coffee. All instinct argued against revealing the slightest weakness to these people. On the other hand, when again would he be offered every wish by miracle-workers? Did faery-godmothers revisit those who spurned them?

Answer: no, probably not. This chance would never return. So, it all depended just how much he wanted the thing. Was it worth the risk?

Samuel thought - for less time than it took for his pen to fall. It *was* worth it. It was the only thing on the whole list he really wanted.

Item: Removal of all barriers to matrimony between myself and Miss Melissa Farncombe, only daughter of Mrs and Mrs Melville Farncombe, Lewes, East Sussex, England.

Awaiting your prompt and kind reply, I remain, sir-sicarii, your obedient servant.

Samuel Melchizedek Trevan

This day of Our Lord, 12th May 1997
at the Forge Inn, Welcombe, Devonshire.

****

In business matters the Sicarii was a man of few words. Samuel's letter was returned by military courier with just a cover note attached. It bore the terse message: *'Agreed'*.

Suspending breath, Samuel double-checked - and then kissed the paper. His every request, including the last, was ticked without comment.

CHAPTER 28

'Two ratchets!'

Samuel's order was distorted as it echoed up the shaft, but the surface team got the gist. The craft lurched downwards twice more.

'That should do us.'

Trevan leant over the side and buried a halberd blade, grappling-hook style, into the side-tunnel wall. Assisted by the ham-like arms of a miner, he pulled the passenger tub closer to the opening. 'Close enough?' he grunted, the weight of half a dozen, not exactly sylph-like, men straining even his powers.

'Sooner a drop than a jump,' said the mining engineer, quoting some professional axiom. He was entirely at home in such dark, watery and God-forsaken places - and proved it by vaulting over the side. There was a pause, and then they heard his boots thump onto the tunnel floor opposite. Candlelight from his helmet reflected off the walls, mimicking a swift tour of inspection.

'She's sweet,' he said finally, a disembodied voice from out of the black. 'You can come over.'

You could if you were agile and brave or disinclined to be thought timid. The tub swayed over the unplumbed drop, ten or twelve feet above the new flood level. Their torches barely reached that far, revealing only uninviting inky waters. It required fine judgement and faith to time your swing out of the tub into the side passage.

Samuel was last out, just to be awkward, and minus its human ballast the carry-tub swung like a pendulum. He left without grace, travelled without style, and arrived like ten sacks of potatoes - but made it.

'Right,' he said, re-asserting himself by having the first word, 'if we've come down a ventilation shaft, what's this then?'

'My words were *mebbe* a ventilation shaft,' answered the engineer, who was not to be imposed upon by any mere employer. 'No ladder or pulley fitments *can* mean that, but not always. 'Specially in old time diggings. Let's hold judgement a space, if it's all the same to you.'

Duly told off Samuel shut up. This was a fraught enough project without him sparking discord at the start. All kinds of sensitive souls were being brought together, not all of them knowing the truth of the matter. There'd be occasion for a time of reckoning when the true objective was achieved.

'And mind your footing,' the engineer ordered. 'It's wet and treacherous here and like to get worse.'

Samuel saw the man's final dubious look before setting off. New to the company, he couldn't place half these people currently with him. The engineer didn't see how they had any business down a reclaimed digging. And, if they weren't miners or drainers or investors, then what were they?

Trusted men was the answer but Samuel wasn't about to divulge that. He'd written to London and brought various useful types west. Two of those with him now had jollied up his slower debtors back in the old days, in-between keeping Guild stewards quiet. Up above, the steam-engine artificer had been rescued from taking service with the Cairo Caliph, plucked off the very ship at Tilbury, just about to sail. Mr Jimmy Smith had worked wonders for Trevan before, setting up a munitions works from next to nothing, back when they'd not two pennies to rub together and everything was credit. Now the little cockney had readily forsaken taming the Nile floods in favour of reforging the old team. It was a sort of tribute: Trevan paid well, kept his word and was only semi-civilised. With him it was weariness, never boredom, that made waking up a torture. Trevan magicked mere business into adventure. That and a brand new '*Easton & Amos Drainage Engine*', the renowned '*Drain-ace Mark II*', to play with, were worth missing the pyramids for.

That response was repeated time and again. Few turned him down - for he'd rarely employed pious types. Even the arid (but honest) old bookkeeper who now kept the 'mine' accounts had hastened west when the call came.

And if that exodus rang alarm bells with those who monitored

Samuel's every move, he now had a patron to tranquillise their prying. They'd not dare move against Mott's covert blessing.

Another cause for the engineer's disquiet was all the weapons. He saw no need for blades and guns where they were going, and he tried to put his foot down about firearms under-earth, for fear of sparks or flame amidst foul air. But his Master wouldn't harken. There was compromise as far as 'just' flintlock pistols, not match-burning guns, but no further. True, tin levels weren't known for detonation-gas, but it still went against all practice. The engineer weighed up the risk against reflections on his most generous contract - and ate his next words. But he now brandished a caged songbird before him with especial vigilance.

'Mr Trevan, step forward if you please.'

Samuel carefully brushed past the others to join the engineer at the front. His nail-shod boots failed to grip securely on the slick floor. There was the constant temptation to veer to the sidewall for support, though once there it was no great help. The surfaces were smooth and finger-grip free.

'What is it?' he asked.

'Happen you were right, sir. It's a queer do this place. Here's too broad and fair for a ventilation way. I don't see sense in making such a shallow audit neither, but there it is. She dips down, but so slight you'd barely notice 'less you're attuned. This is a way *forward*.'

Samuel was glad of it. He hadn't looked for such good fortune so early on. Some of Mott's 'volunteers' had accused him of over-subtlety in looking for a less obvious start than opening the main entrance. That had been found early on, but previous generations had shut it so snug you'd wake the dead in undoing their work. Samuel sarcastically suggested they blast their way in with cannon fire, and then see what came up to greet them. Then, whilst the soldiers silently chewed on that he put forward his own plans - which were now vindicated.

'So let's go then,' he said, and gestured the engineer forward.

'No point, Mr Trevan: not yet. We'll not get far. You can see the water level in the main shaft. We're only a few yards above it. Like I said, this here walkway dips. There'll be water ahead till you drain more.'

'Prove it.'

'Right. I see. As you wish.'

They shuffled forward, advancing the feeble pool of light shed by helmet candle and 'glass-bubble' tar-torch. Samuel sensed the engineer's discomfort as his prediction was postponed step by step.

'There's *been* water here - till our pumps started,' he restated. 'You can feel it underfoot and on the walls.'

'It's damper in my tent,' joked one of Samuel's former enforcers. He was known for ill-timed humour and the engineer was in no mood for it. This was *his* world down here and it wasn't behaving.

'Well, happen you shouldn't piss in it then,' he retorted. 'You shall have all the water you want soon enough: up to your damned neck and beyon-.... Oh....'

'What is it?' snapped Samuel, diving in on the hesitation just as he was about to silence the stupid banter. He discreetly drew his seax knife.

The engineer was slightly ahead and over by the tunnel wall. He was frantically exploring it with outstretched hands. Trevan joined him and merged their private spheres of light. He could see nothing untoward.

'I *said*,' he repeated, 'what is....'

'Dry!' whispered the engineer, puzzled and upset - and more to himself than in reply. 'Dry as a bone! You feel....'

Samuel did. It was.

'I don't get it,' the engineer murmured on. 'Something's held the water out, but I don't see-....'

'You don't need to,' cut in one of Mott's men who had come forward. A charmless and sour-faced soldier, he gave the impression of having been around, seen a lot, and immunity against surprise. 'You won't be able to see: but you can feel.'

He held his wiry arm out ahead.

'Go on,' he instructed, 'feel!'

Both Samuel and the engineer gingerly extended their hands into the dark - and then snatched them back as if burnt. Their hair rose, their skin crawled, as they recognised the touch of sorcery.

****

Whilst things went weird underground, the proverbial bricks came through the upstairs window as well. Samuel assumed the two were associated and acted accordingly.

When some stored spares for the steam pump were destroyed - with painstaking malice - Samuel put their replacements out on tempting show. Concealed snipers watched day and night but no one came to claim the bullet they'd won.

One weekly payroll en route from the goldsmith's at Bideford disappeared off the face of the earth: coin, courier, guards, horses and all. Churls in an isolated roadside hamlet claimed to have heard gunfire and cries about the right time, but hadn't cared to investigate. Samuel recognised he'd been robbed but not, he thought, betrayed by his own. Strings were pulled and Royal Dragoons combed the surrounding area till civilian life ceased for a while. Plenty of crime was uncovered: smuggling, fornication and witchcraft were brought to light, and some people accordingly went galley-wards. But of Trevan's former property no sign ever emerged. He had to make good the shortfall from his own pocket and henceforth had the chore of accompanying the convoy.

Then the Cymric bonded-labourers claimed to have seen ghosts flitting through the camp and in the tunnels. A portion of them were so frightened as to strike. Their Irish masters had rough ways with rebellion and took some tongues out, but for once it did no good. Generations of slavery to the Hibernian 'Joint Stock Farming Companies' had cowed but not broken the poor native Welshmen. So, Samuel took over and quoted scripture at them, decrying revolt against proper authority and the vain illusions of Satan. Then he hurled handfuls of silver sixpences over their heads and stood clear of the resulting scramble.

They were not used to either argument or kindness and so Trevan prevailed where pincers did not. Work resumed, the miners protected by as many saints' medals and charms as they cared to take from the crate-load Samuel placed by the shafthead.

Those were just the highlights of a series of cowpats dropped in the project's path. Things went missing when needed, people acted out of character and misfortune was permanently on duty. Samuel didn't lose his temper, not even when all the tent canvas inexplicably began to rot. Instead, he sat down to think and tot his troubles up. Reviewing each mishap, set down in cold black and white, a structure to them hoved coyly into sight. For a brief moment he thought he discerned a pattern in the chaos, for all that it was elusive: a shadow glimpsed at the end of a corridor. He could almost credit these things as *clever* nuisances, nicely contrived to dismay. If so, it was a question of finding the common thread - and tracing it back to the spinner to supply payment in kind.

Then the army wizard arrived and every other distraction had to be put aside.

****

'... *The soldier-thaumaturge is an unnatural hybrid, neither one thing nor the other; welcomed by neither profession. This class of man, this career, is like unto the <u>mule</u>, a similar aberration; useful perchance as a living tool but an unfit vehicle for a gentleman. Recall that our blessed Lord and Saviour, Jesus Christ, who entertained the most wretched and debased of creatures, chose a <u>donkey</u> on which to enter Jerusalem. Even He, infinite in love and forgiveness, forswore carriage on that which is against nature.*

To expand: when a soldier kills he does so with blade or bow or bullet: things which, though fell, are known and natural. But when a wizard slays who knows from whence the means comes - or to where his poor victim goes? I myself have seen both foemen and comrade alike crisped in blue flames that give no heat, or turned inside out by invisible forces, or in other ways die horribly without explanation. This I say boldly is not war but coward killing by strange forces. The true gentleman warrior strives with like against like, but that can never be the thaumaturge's way.

Fortunately, these precious charges, these rare products of long training, fall prey to plain sword or gun just like any other man. Accordingly, they are usually cosseted and sheltered from the lottery of battle, kept safe from harm in the general's pavilion. There they may consult with occult powers or wrench the truth from unhappy prisoners under an honest soldier's supervision. Such is their only proper place (if indeed one may apply that term to them) in the chivalrous tournament of war.

It is also true to say that martial wizards are often degraded wretches, barred from their usual softer and more lucrative employ by past crimes and infamy of character. My experience is that most are fugitives from the justice of G*d or man. For example, when I had the honour to command the Burgundians occupying Latvia in 1923....'

'*At the Altar of both Mars and Christ - being an instruction in the ethical pursuit of war: required preliminary reading for gentlemen volunteers of sundry Christian nations in the service of His Most Excellent Highness, The Holy and Roman Emperor Joseph IV.*'

By Pascal Gudarian. By grace of G*D, Imperial Commander of the Varangian Guard, the convert Turks and Croat hussars.

Belisarius Press. Constantinople. The year of our Salvation 1933.

****

155

CHAPTER 29

'It's alive.'

'Alive?' queried Samuel. He peered at what could not be seen but barred the way. 'Not magic?'

'That too: but mostly alive. They all are. Sort of…'

Trevan studied the wizard's face as best two-candle-power permitted. It was no sweeter a sight in below-ground gloom than sunlit above. The plump visage of florid curves offered nothing to interpret or supplement its owner's words. He seemed a preoccupied man; his attention focused long ago and far away. There *was* information to be had from him but it was like drawing teeth.

'Listen to me,' snapped Samuel, 'are you going to co-operate or-….'

Vaunted 'straight-talk' bounced off the magician like a sheep's growl. The man suddenly turned.

'How's your headache?' he asked, sounding solicitous.

Samuel shrugged.

'Much the same but - hang on, how did you know I…?'

'I didn't – but do now. It comes as no surprise: everyone I've spoken to here gets them. Real shockers. Coincidence, do you think? Then think again. And harder. And better. They're exercising influence against you – subtly influencing you away.'

"*They*? Who's '*they*?'

The Wizard smiled.

'Haven't the foggiest. Not yet. But it's them, you may be sure.'

Without asking for permission, the Wizard touched Trevan's forehead. It felt more like a spark or gnat than a fingertip. Instantly, the brain-pain cleared – and then just as promptly returned, crashing back with momentum, when the fat hand withdrew.

'See?' asked the Wizard. 'It went, didn't it?'

'It did,' said Samuel, 'but only for that second. Couldn't you make the relief more lasting?'

'Yes,' answered the Wizard: but made no move.

'*But...*,' said Samuel, rather than give him the pleasure.

'But it would involve effort,' confirmed the Wizard. 'And everyone would want it. You must carry that particular cross, Mr Trevan. Accept it as flattery. At least someone takes account of you...'

The Wizard had a way of turning his back which signalled he no longer even recalled the conversation just ended, let alone might return to it. You just had to study his broad rear view and lump it.

'*Lumpit*' was Trevan's least favourite food. It made him retch. But for the moment it had to be got down.

'Tell me more about the barriers,' he asked, trying to salvage something. 'Are they all identical?'

No answer came. The Wizard waddled past Trevan as though nothing had been said - and leapt out into the vertical shaft.

In the course of a laborious morning they'd visited all of the 'dry tunnels' now revealed by the labours of the steam pump. The Wizard had studied the invisible barrier blocking each, muttered, looked concerned, fiddled with his sparse rat's-tail locks - and then said nothing. The carry-tub had been up and down the now enlarged and pinioned main shaft - *'like a whore's drawers'*, as Samuel put it when his temper ran out - until the midday sun shone directly overhead. Come lunchtime, Trevan was still none the wiser and impatience got put into words.

He couldn't emulate the Wizard and just levitate down to the next port of call. Mere mortals had to board the tub and order its descent, jerking gracelessly ratchet by ratchet till his companion's helmet-candle came back into view. The man was standing on thin air, his great bulk making it seem all the more incongruous, beside the lip of another transverse tunnel.

'You didn't need to do that,' Samuel reproved him, in the gentlest manner he knew. 'You could have come down with me.'

'I *'come down'* enough in your company as it is.' The Wizard wasn't really regarding Trevan or his question, but musing dreamily to himself. 'You depress my spirits, maggot of Mammon, forever snuffling around after gain. What *is* the Army thinking of in servicing you? How apt it is you must writhe maggot-style round these tunnels pursuing mere gold.'

Being used to abuse on these grounds made it easier for Samuel to hold his tongue. All the stuff about *'and you - and your mother!'* was said only in the privacy of thought.

'Is there a blockage here too?' he asked instead.

The Wizard looked into the black mouth of the tunnel and tilted his head as though seeking a scent.

'There is. One more of the same. Alive - as I said before. I will show you.'

He trod on nothingness till it was exchanged for the firmer support of the tunnel floor. Samuel jumped across to join him. Halfway there he wondered if, should he fall, the Wizard would swoop to catch him. It seemed doubtful.

'Twenty paces on,' the Wizard confided, again twitching his nostrils as he plucked knowledge from the dark. 'The dampness ceases and there is something perverse.'

'Then you and it belong together' thought Samuel - but said nothing. He followed in the Wizard's confident footsteps.

'Here.' He signalled that Trevan should halt. 'Right here. Even your gross sensitivities should be able to detect it.'

Samuel ignored that insult also. Even if he were as attuned as a brick his eyes would still have marked the sudden change, candlelight or no. Damp, slick walls became dry-as-bone rock. Something had long held the waters at bay from that sharply delineated line.

But that was not all. Close to, the air was both charged and sluggish, resistant to any passage through. A meaty aroma oozed out when the vicinity was disturbed by their arrival.

'Yes, I perceive it,' Samuel told him. 'Now you explain it to me.'

The Wizard looked at him - or rather through him to some further and more interesting point. Trevan had observed before the famous lack of focus in magicians' eyes. He found it more disconcerting than any straightforward intimidation. Always, at the back of your mind, there was the persistent tale that wizards read men thoughts like open books. Samuel tested the theory with heartfelt murderous notions but the magician showed no signs of perception.

'It is alive...,' the man repeated.

'Yeah, we've had that already.'

'... though more as an... idea than a being. It is... pervasive and half awake.'

'Lovely. What shall we do about it?'

'I don't...,' - he'd been going to say '*care*', Samuel was sure of it - '...know. Isn't that up to you?'

'Your advice is sought. That is why you were brought from-....'

'Llanthony; yes,' said the Wizard. 'I saw bad things there. Mott had me torture people, even though I protested it was illegal. No, here is preferable even if you are nearby. I prefer to linger in this place. Yes, I'll advise you. What do you propose to do?'

Samuel looked down the tunnel into the lack of light or welcome.

'Press on.'

'Surprise, surprise. Then I will rupture the membrane for you. I know I can penetrate or destroy it.'

'It's weak then?' Samuel liked that: both a necessary question and retaliation for all the insults. The Wizard didn't even notice.

'Not weak but old; old and neglected and never tested. This is an ancient cobweb drained of its youthful virility.'

'And if it's alive like you say, will the breach be noticed?'

'Probably. I think it sees us even now.'

Samuel didn't appreciate that thought - as entirely intended. He wasn't able to prevent the resulting nervous glance.

'We'll proceed even so,' he said. Then: 'No! Not yet!'

He had to shout that, for the magician had already stretched out his arm to probe the mystery.

'Patience, Wizard, patience. We'll do it when we're prepared and fitted.'

The chubby arm was slowly, reluctantly, withdrawn.

'As you wish, businessman. What you say goes....'

They walked back together, the Wizard without a second glance, Samuel with more than half his attention to the unguarded rear.

'Look!'

He'd skilfully got Trevan to such a pitch that the urgent suggestion made even him jump to comply. Magicians had ways of introducing 'mundanes' to the borderlands of their own uncanny world, thereby to master them.

'What? What is it?'

The Wizard pointed.

'There is old-life here - in the rock. Your money-grubbing has stumbled over beauty. See?'

There were indeed non-random forms within the wall. Samuel looked and thought he recognised some curled shell-shape protruding its back.

'Pre-Flood demons,' he said. He knew of, if not about, them. Mr Farncombe had one as a paperweight on his desk, a present from a relative in Lyme Regis.

'Antediluvian, but not demonic,' the Wizard corrected him, more gently than hitherto. 'They are innocent beasts frozen into stone by the drip, drip, drip of time. Sometimes one finds the remains of dragons; huge monsters' bones and terrifying teeth. Hedgerow spell-casters prize and powder them for their potions.'

'Fascinating.'

'Actually it *is*, Mr Trevan; but you rightly discern there is no sordid *profit* in them. Some afflicted men are oblivious to the marvels strewn by God for our delectation. As the prophet Jeremiah and other sundry scripture reminds us: there are none so blind as those who *will* not see. Meanwhile, let us return to the light.'

Samuel wasn't going to argue with that, but he'd had enough of the man and his contempt. The tally between them was still lamentably one-sided.

'What, so soon?' he mocked. 'I thought you were mad keen to forge ahead?'

Once again the Wizard 'honoured' him by actually turning his head to speak. The toes of his huge army boots protruded over the tunnel's lip and the abyss below.

'Oh, but I am. It will be wonderful. You don't know the half of what I have sensed here.'

Trevan bristled. 'Do I not, sorcerer?'

'No. My soul feels in places you do not have. What awaits us is like a long hung pheasant.'

That was about the last simile Samuel had been expecting. His clever retort aborted before it could be born. Only straightforward enquiry was left to him.

'How so?'

'Because,' said the Wizard, licking his lips, 'it is old, and rotten, and rank - and *delicious*.'

CHAPTER 30

'The most that I'm proposing,' said the very relaxed man, 'is an arrangement to our mutual benefit.'

'I can sort of see that,' agreed Samuel. He would have been unrecognisable to those who knew him: mild, accommodating, almost apologetic for having the temerity to be alive. The visitor, knowing no different, was taken in. 'But I must admit, Mr...?'

'Glendower,' said the red-haired thug lolling in Trevan's own armchair. 'Owain Glendower.'

So, he was arrogant with it, as well as overconfident. Why did they assume that no one but them knew any Welsh history?

'I must admit, Mr Glendower, I *was* getting worried about security....'

He couldn't have come at a better time. Samuel had just emerged from the mine, fresh from his interview with the Wizard; enraged, clue-less and blinking at the light. To find the source of at least some of his troubles showing its face in his cabin was just what the doctor ordered. All other tasks were postponed for the duration. Now he was both enjoying himself *and* sorting things at the same time. It was sweet, sweet, sweet.

'Your concerns are past, Mr Trevan,' said the visitor. 'From now on you can concentrate on what you do best. Extract whatever precious bounty you may from Mother Earth's entrails whilst others, better suited, fend off the evil-eye of this wild country. If we have your well-being as our charge, you might depend no more payrolls will go astray. No, don't gasp, we know about that. It is our business to be well informed, just as it is yours to direct the tides of commerce. Is there any more of this rather fine apple brandy?'

There certainly was. Samuel would have this unctuous land-pirate as chatty as he cared to get. He jumped up like a skivvy and poured as he imagined a nervous man might. The visitor accepted without thanks and drank without style, knocking the tumbler back drunkard fashion. So there was the explanation for the red tracery on his cheeks.

'Choice! Better than a wench - well, an English one anyway: no disrespect to you, Mr Trevan. Now, like I said, my associates have extensive interests in this vicinity, for all it might not be our homeland, but rather the back garden of our bitter enemy. No matter, the profit extracted is all the most tasty, plus tiny recompense for the lashing you've - present company excepted, sir - dished out to dear Cymru. Most sensible enterprises round here oblige us with donations, so don't think you're unfairly singled out. No indeed. We even have *bases* here, see; safe from the maelstrom made of our nation. In short, the Dragons are in a position to do you much good, as well as - just speculatively speaking, of course - the contrary.'

'As with the pump spares, I suppose.' Samuel thought his pre-emptive cringe was not at all bad.

'... Just so, Mr Trevan.'

Now, that hesitation *was* interesting. Either this terrorist's pimp was badly briefed or else not all Samuel's recent misfortunes were their doing.

'I don't suppose I have much option, do I, Mr Glendower?'

'Not if you tread the path of reason, Mr Trevan; and I've heard nothing this afternoon to indicate that's not your way. Our premiums are modest, as you've heard. Take a route *around* trouble if one's offered, that's my counsel.'

Clearly well satisfied, 'Glendower' prepared to go, drawing his green oilcoat from the back of the chair. It dislodged the antimacassar Melissa had embroidered.

'*Pick* that up, taffy!' shouted Samuel.

From sheep to roaring lion in an instant. Stupid! Bad, indulgent, mistake! The sudden change of tune might undo all.

Trevan needn't have worried. The Welsh racketeer put his puzzlement down to mishearing or the brandy.

'Pardon, Mr Trevan?'

'Nothing. It's just... I wondered.... Are you sure the demands won't go up and up? I've heard of such things.'

The visitor smiled down on him. 'Not with us, boy. We're an old firm -

had time to learn. Geese and golden eggs and all that.'

'Oh good.'

'If you *do* have problems, we may be contacted at the *'Arthur'* in Newport, just across the water. We are patriots, not blackmailers, Trevan-*Seasneg*. Value for money will be given if necessary. The rent can go to the same address. Do you understand? I don't want to have and come and see you again. You *will* be in touch, won't you?'

Samuel's reply could at last contain plain truth, though he had to address the floor in order to mask his grin.

'Oh yes, Mr Glendower,' he said meekly, all the while trying to prevent his shoulders from shaking, 'you may depend on it.'

****

ARCHBISHOP OF LONDON'S LIBRARY - WHITEHALL CITADEL.
RESTRICTED
'A BRIEF GUIDE TO SOCIALLY-HOSTILE, IRRELIGIOUS OR
IMPIOUS GROUPINGS.

(For the perusal of officers new to his Majesty's Secret Service or fresh arrived in United England from elsewhere in Christendom. Thoroughly revised November, the year of our Lord 2020 AD).

[on cover, in hand-script]
To: The Dean-Temporal's Librarian and Remembrancer's department - and such others as may be interested.
From: The Dean Temporal's National Intelligence Department. 19/01/21.

Dear Helmut.
Do we want this on file? They send it to me every year. Our own stuff is much better informed. Happy New Year by the way.
Yours in Christ (and haste)
Alfred

[below, in another hand]
Dear Alfred.
We may as well I suppose. Copies made and distributed. Thanks. How are Persephone and the children? God bless....
Yours
Helmut. 06/02/21

... **RED DRAGONS**: the collective term, formally in use since the 18th century, for the armed protagonists of that section of WEST ENGLAND aspiring to independence and statehood. The title is drawn from the formless chaos of early 'Welsh' legend wherein such a mythical beast is taken to symbolise the (equally mythical) nation.

Initially applied to the regular forces of infantry and some light cavalry maintained by the Caernarfon statelet, and then, after its final extinction in the Christmas campaign of 1995, to the irregulars and terrorists who dispute that settlement. Fleeing their pacified 'homeland', the latter came to wield some influence in the southern commercial towns such as Cardiff, Swansea and Newport, as well as extending tentacles further afield. The Hibernian agricultural joint-stock companies were also much disrupted by their activities amongst the bonded workforce. See, for instance, files available on the 1980's 'Gower Rising' and resultant 'Father Oakley's Campaign'.

However, in a dispiritingly short time they then acquired the manner of a criminal conspiracy, and the material wealth that always flows to men unfettered by compassion or fear of Divine judgement. Political activity, aside from the purely rhetorical, waned in favour of the pursuit of profit. Accordingly, for present purposes they are a grouping more of interest to constabulary forces than ourselves.

Nevertheless, a minority faction still adheres in more than just sentiment to *'the armed struggle'*: sponsoring assassinations and gunpowder-outrages [q.v. The Fishguard Assizes atrocity 2008]. It strives in occasionally bloody feud against the business-orientated majority. If their fortunes perchance improve so as to merit attention, his Majesty's agents then ferment strife amongst them by sowing suspicions of treachery or feigning fraud. By these means our work is generally done for us, and in the directest manner, by knife and by garrotte.

Therefore, it should rarely be necessary to make arrests amongst the 'Dragons' but, if so, be aware that speakers of their own tongue will be required, both for the interrogation and in applying inducements. The names, ages and habitations of all their *'High Council of the Round Table'* [our own agents and informants flagged either † or ‡ respectively] are as follows....

****

EXTRACT. The 'DAY DIARY' of The Wisbech and Spalding Regiment of Foot.

... no sign of the boots left for repair with the cobbler ABBOTT in BLANDFORD FORUM and promised faithfully for today. Cornet

GRIFFITHS ordered forth to pursue same. ITEM: re hire of pack-horse and provision of bread and beef for GRIFFITHS - £0/10/6d.

Friday 1st August 1997. Embarked on College of Temporal Trade Privateer 'HABAKKUK' and her 2 sister transports to CAER-DIFF / CARDIFF. Rest and then evening's forced march.

Saturday 2nd August 1997. We continued to NEWPORT, arriving privily at 0600 hours, demanding the town gate be surrendered. As General MOTT directed, destroyed entirely were:

ITEM: 1 public house. 'The 'ARTHUR'. Hung from the Inn sign: 1 publican and 2 impertinent customers.

ITEM: 1 Fire engine. That the townspeople may have even more cause to rue our return.

ITEM: 1 Town fishing fleet, save one boat which hastily set sail and anchored beyond cannonshot.

ITEM: 1 Town cannon, whose crew meanwhile refused to fire on said boat, and who lost an eye each in consequence.

ITEM: Sundry fishing nets, lobster pots and oyster-draggers.

ITEM: The town powder supply, employed upon:

ITEM: 1 Stone and timber Quay. Brand-new built and thus sundered much to the lamentation of the townsfolk.

N.B. The zeal of the attached civilian advisor, TREVAN, was with difficulty restrained. He was for the drowning of the obstinate cannoners, claiming the General's authority. Our Colonel BRAGG countermanded him.

N.B. The separately listed 'DRAGONS' or sympathisers, to the number of one score, were all taken in their beds or seeking escape in night-clothes. They now accompany the Regiment in the provost-marshal's wheeled cage.

Sunday 3rd August 1997. En route to LLANTHONY Camp. Cornet GRIFFITHS rejoined us without the boots....

CHAPTER 31

20/07/97. Galen House. Lewes. Sussex.

My dearest, gentle Samuel.

I will not hide from you that Father's rage is unabated. If he should discover our sporadic, covert, correspondence, I would have to box with him to save my hide from his riding crop. At least Father Omar is no longer implicated in our intercourse, for I have a new channel to you. Our scullery-maid (who terms herself a 'romantic' and thus my ally!) now takes these missives to the post in South Malling where she nightly returns home. I should not mock her simple presumptions, for she risks her position and reference on our behalf. When things are aright again we must see her well rewarded....

... the deceptions and now outright lies I must employ against father rend me, Samuel, for I would have you believe that he is at heart a kind man, and by nature the source of half of what I am - which you ever tell me you so admire. He now proposes alternative matches, which I must, of course, decline. That little sweetens him to your memory, for he hears, second-hand, the gibes against me of 'old maid'. But let such sour souls flap their tongues: I shall not be the one to break our understanding. Be assured I nightly fall to my knees and pray for some miracle to change minds and circumstances. If only you would unclench your heart to copy my example, it might be that our joint prayers would be answered.

... Father Omar has been unwell, for even a giant must submit to the afflictions of age. But rest easy since he is now recovered and almost fully himself. The orphanage gateman, who well recalls you, says he will still continue to hold your letters to me for my collection. And since I speak of those, I must charge you that of late your news is sparse. I gain no idea of what you do or how you fill the hours. Be sure to keep busy (innocently so) lest idleness tempts you into bitter and angry thoughts. Write more often and tell me

what you do.

> *I await your obedience to my command.*
> *Your faithful love, Melissa*

****

The weather had held for him; it was a lovely day to be on the beach.

Samuel hacked at the quay with zest, imagining the faces of his enemies below each pickaxe blow. Red Dragons, Mr Farncombe, His Holiness the Pope, and a host of others all got it in the mush as the hole grew wide enough to take a barrel of powder.

He was just one of many such workers in a line down Newport beach, right to the water's edge. Invisible but very audible teams mirrored the work over on the other side of the great stone structure. Though not strictly his place to lend a hand, it was all part and parcel of entering into the spirit of the day. He'd had a wonderful time so far, dishing it out for once, rather than the usual opposite.

The plaintive wails and pleas of locals lining the front competed with the thud-crack-thud of the picks. Smoke drifting from the inferno of the '*Arthur*' varied the music with a few coughs. The multitude had been gathered up to witness their quay, that fruit of years of scrimping and public subscriptions, the sure foundation of the Town's livelihood, ascend to heaven in fragments. For General Mott required that all the stories he span end in an abundantly clear moral, told to the widest possible audience.

A renewed keening of distress greeted the arrival of the powder barrels, borne on slings between pairs of bluecoats, and each trailing a prepared fuse. Much the same noise had preceded the destruction of the fishing boats and nets: to just as much avail.

Samuel's request to the Sicarii had caused much consulting of files. What they read only confirmed state suspicions. Even if Newport was no 'Dragon town' it had tolerated their presence. It would do as an exemplar. Traitorous indifference to the eternal struggle between Crown and subversion must be seen to bring only poverty and woe as its reward.

Samuel exercised his self-discipline muscles by not stopping to see the harbour and quay go up. That was scheduled for twilight and thus maximum visual effect. He decided there were better things to do, and besides, the explosion would only worsen his perpetual headache. He'd had his holiday and revenge, his grand getting-it-off-your-chest session. Enough was as good as a feast. His heart felt the better for it even if his head didn't.

He left the foreshore-strand and climbed the not-long-for-this-world harbour steps to where a bluecoat was holding his horse. He felt tiger-ish and on top of things: once again there was no limit to what he might achieve, so long as he put his mind to it.

For starters, there was an important letter to reply to. That shouldered its way to the top of the list. Samuel gave it serious thought.

Dusk should see him at the chartered yacht moored off Chepstow. Then, with a fair wind and using the spur once ashore, he could be back, bright and early, for work tomorrow. That would surprise those relishing a holiday from his all-seeing eye. If he also resisted sleep during the crossing..., yes, he reckoned on having time and energy enough to answer Melissa's loving enquiries.

****

Though he'd searched Newport most assiduously for 'Owain Glendower' Samuel never found him. He had to be content with leaving a note, prominently addressed and nailed to the market cross. It read simply:

'Dear Mr Glendower and Red Dragon associates.

St Paul's letter to the Galatians, ch. 6 vs. 17:
'I want no more trouble from anybody after this.'

> *Yours, pointedly.*
> *Samuel Trevan Esq.'*

Nor was there; not from them.

CHAPTER 32

'So, who *did* do it then? The Elves?'

The mining engineer fazed Samuel by taking the suggestion seriously. Down in the West Country they had less grounds for flippancy about mankind's secret cousins.

'Could be, Mr Trevan, could be. The old miners always said they heard the 'knockers' working in hidden tunnels alongside them.'

Samuel passed a hand over his furrowed brow. Then he looked again at the vellum map of the drained levels they'd revealed. The other team leaders and main players gathered in the works cabin wondered what inspiration he'd find in all that blocked progress.

Time and close contact had grafted a name onto the engineer. Trevan thought he'd venture the personal approach.

'Well, don't think I'm not grateful, Wulfstan; but how much further does that theory carry us? In your vast experience have these 'knockers' ever come out to play?'

His ebbing patience was again depleted by the engineer making a meal out of mere sarcasm.

'Not face to face as such,' came the eventual reply. 'But thereagain I've seen some hellish funny things below ground - like when-....'

Samuel's dinner-plate hand stopped the flow.

'No. No, you'll oblige me by skipping the anecdotes. Let's keep our finger-grip on specifics for once. Have you ever known anything foul a pump like that?'

'Nope!'

Wulfstan the engineer didn't appreciate having his wealth of stories disparaged. They were the ornaments to a long career and evidence of his steep climb out of churl-status. Slow-burning anger made him taciturn. The next stage, though still a way off, would be berserk fury and Samuel knew enough to be wary. That was the trouble with educating pure-blood Saxons....

'Nor me,' chipped in Jimmy Smith, Trevan's old artisan-lieutenant from Whitechapel days, 'and I shan't be choked if I don't see the like again. The engine's buggered well and truly. You can't even get people near enough long enough to clear it!'

'Then what's to be done, Jim-boy?' Samuel didn't mind putting himself in the experts' hands so long as they kept it short - and cheap. He was to be disappointed in one respect.

'Give up on it,' said Smith, surprising all. 'Give up and 'eave 'er down the shaft: *Easton and Amos* or no. Stuff the expense. You'll never get the cack and taint off her. I spewed my guts after just a few minutes having a go. It's disgusting: not natural. Pitch it down and put in another.'

Samuel frowned. That was a way out, not a solution. They were no nearer solving how their below-ground pump had come to be clogged with what appeared and smelt and felt like Satan's spittle. Parts of the machine had obscenely folded in on itself like (in both looks and usefulness) a wax frying pan.

He didn't so much mind providing a new secondary pump - Mott and the Exchequer were providing, after all - but it went against the grain to move on without first holding the duff item to account. It felt weak and... wasteful. He hadn't had his full two-penneth out of the old engine yet.

'But then have the replacement guarded,' added Jimmy, who knew his master well. 'Let's not lose that one too.'

'Hmmn,' 'agreed' Samuel. It was as much a growl of resignation as affirmation, but the nearest they were going to get. 'See to it then.'

'Sorted,' Jimmy informed the meeting, narrow competence personified. 'I'll away to Bideford then. I warehoused the makings of one there against such a turn-up.'

'Pity you didn't foresee it then,' was all the thanks he got from Samuel. General opinion said Trevan was getting sourer by the day.

'Still getting the headaches are you?' asked Jimmy, brightly, unoffended. He had leeway that other employees didn't - but was pushing it even so.

'Only when I talk to you. Sod off to Bideford before I repent of my generosity.'

Jimmy did so, sadly shaking his head once out of sight. All the redeeming humour was gone out of the boss: the man was becoming *mean* as well as tough. For a moment it had looked like he'd order another useless go at restoring the befouled engine, just for devilment and because he could. Jimmy pondered on that. In the old days Trevan & Co. was like being on the gash, but now…. Maybe serving the Sultan and a decko at the Sphinx would have been his best bet after all.

Back in the conference, Samuel forced himself to consult the fat wizard. The man had been daydreaming the distasteful meeting away, doodling pentagrams and desired dinners with his inkstick.

'If we might presume to shake you awake, Mr magician? What's your opinion?'

'About what, Mr Trevan?'

It was deliberate, all this casual disdain. Samuel's only response to it so far was lost tooth enamel, ground off in biting back replies - but the Wizard should have seen the letter to Mott awaiting launch in Trevan's office safe.

'Concerning the vile and corrosive guck adorning our secondary pump, if you please.'

'Oh, *that*. You should specify.'

To his credit, the Wizard had been one of the first down the shaft when the discovery was made. He'd probed and tested the substance closer than anyone, and been sicker in consequence.

'I can't say,' he concluded, 'never having encountered its like before, either in life or in reference. Stomach bile from Mother Earth perhaps?'

'Then I reckon she spits it dead accurate,' scoffed Wulfstan. The rest of them didn't know what to make of that fair point. There was the undying rumour that some Saxons still had secret regard for *Nerthus*, their original 'Earth Mother' goddess.

'Maybe she does,' agreed the Wizard. 'Who knows? I only make the suggestion because there is nothing sorcerous to the substance. It is, hard as it may be to believe, natural - in a rebarbative, unnatural, way.'

Trevan's fist clenched on empty air. If he hadn't needed to speak his teeth would have done likewise.

'And just happens to drape itself in and over my pump and nowhere else, eh?'

'*Exactly,*' nodded the Wizard, firmly, as though Samuel were a slow pupil who'd at long last got there. 'And before you ask, I did indeed delve amongst the shadows of the recent past in the vicinity. There were only the echoes of our footsteps and hard work.'

That also hit home - as intended. They certainly had worked hard, which made this recompense all the more gruelling. Things had been going really well. The main shaft was now widened, safe, lit and laddered. They'd lost no one: not had so much as an injury (save what the overseers deliberately inflicted). It was a measure of their success that the second, auxiliary, pump had gone below so soon. After that the black waters were really on the run and long drowned levels were being reclaimed all over. True, they were all blocked by sorcery but you couldn't have everything. Come the time for penetration they'd be spoilt for choice of routes.

Samuel uneasily recalled these thoughts and choice of words when the Wizard continued. Maybe his freak-type really *could* trespass unperceived in normal men's minds. Maybe the mob was right back in Dark Age days when wizards went to the bonfire directly they revealed themselves. The Church had forbidden that but Trevan could well believe *she* was mistaken.

'As for the membranes obstructing our desires,' the fat man informed them, 'their virginity is intact. I have checked each one. The magic is old and dusty and undisturbed in a manner I cannot adequately explain to you... non-practitioners.'

Those present looked from one to the other as they considered what less flattering description he'd applied to them in the privacy of his head.

'They remain unpenetrated from either direction, I assure you. Every bit as *virgo intacta* as the... husband,' he gestured languidly with a heavily be-ringed hand at Samuel, 'of this project-cum-bride would wish.'

If he actually did read thoughts the Wizard ought to have then paled or fled. Samuel was constructing shortened futures for him.

However, there was no outward sign of it and Trevan spoke in a reasoned, reasonable tone. Most were not deceived, any more than they still believed this was 'just' a mine. The monkeys had chattered whilst the organ-grinder listened. Now he'd decree how it was going to be.

'I'm very pleased to hear that,' said Samuel. 'Because for as long as possible we should let sleeping dogs - or whatever they are - lie. So: install the new pump when Jimmy returns with it. Have it perpetually watched by two - no, three - armed men: non-nervous types. Get the water down further. Keep the miners occupied: have them tidy the camp or whitewash coal if need be. The rest of you get ready. Because the time is approaching, gentlemen, for us to go further in. But first I want to find an unguarded way. You see, call me over-sensitive if you like, but I get the distinct impression we're unwelcome here. Accordingly, let us also be *unexpected*....'

CHAPTER 33

'Gone? Gone where?'

'To a better place, Master Trevan. One's already set off, the second's departing shortly. Dunno 'bout the third. You best come quick.'

This oldster's job was to deliver the workers their dinner or *'bait'* of pasties, not supply crucial assessments. Therefore, Samuel considered he'd done well - but shouldered him aside all the same.

Samuel also agreed on the need for haste, but not so much of it as to prevent him fetching pistols first. On the way he also gathered some security types. They were still drowsy and thinking breakfast thoughts but his bellow roused them.

'You and you.' Two of the soldier 'volunteers' from Llanthony were gestured into the descent tub. 'Fast as safety allows,' Samuel instructed the taciturn Welshman who oversaw the shafthead gear, 'and then send three more. Count off thirty minutes: if you've heard damn all after that then seal the pit.' Then Trevan jumped into the craft himself and left the upper world behind.

Because he was feared rather than loved, his orders received close attention. They dropped like a stone and knuckles whitened as they clenched on the cold iron of the tub. Swinging wildly on the supporting chain, the caged canary piped its alarm.

They were entirely in the hands of the Welsh 'top-boy' above, but he'd spent a whole lonely lifetime tending winches and cages, seeing people down and awaiting their return. That's how he'd got out of the habit of talking. Samuel paid him well and was now well rewarded in turn. The man knew just the depth they wanted, right to the last ratchet, and delivered them there safe, if shaken.

There was still light at the pump station, which was good news. They could lay aside the giant lucifer-flares brought for emergency and rely on the safer mine lanterns. Samuel studied the scene, read the story, and found no other grounds for cheer.

The requirement for leaps into the dark was past. A plank jetty now extended from the tunnel mouth into the shaft, making getting to and fro far more civilised. Samuel went first, seax and pistol foremost. Behind him he heard the tub bell rung to order its return, and then the wary tread of boots in his support. Out in the chasm the great chain groaned and protested and they felt rather than saw the tub leave, stranding them there. It provoked the pang of regret that Samuel was told never quite left miners, however long in service.

His perceptions were now so skewed that the main thing he noticed was the pump. Yet more trouble and expense. It was just like its predecessor, all leprous and besmirched. Samuel could even see into the guts of the machine through holes oozed deep into the interior. It would never work again. Only then did he look at the people. They were in similar shape.

One was well gone, his face and abdomen and loins erased by the same stuff that afflicted the pump. But for a distinctive neckerchief Trevan would never have recognised him. Then he noticed some kind of mushroom growths flourishing within the ex-man's new cavities and could examine him no more. The pervading aroma - sweat meets sewage meets cloying sweetness - was now reaching them all and they were glad that the alert had cancelled breakfast.

The second of the engine guards was still with them but plainly on his way. You didn't need to be a surgeon to see it. The substance was bubbling away at his legs, still virulent and vital, releasing little gouts of vapour as it triumphed over portions of flesh. The man now concluded in a spreading pool. Samuel had to command his own stomach contents back down.

'Finish him. Use your knife,' he told the soldier behind, and then pressed further on, weapons poised. There proved to be not far to go and nothing more to see. The barrier remained in place, detectable in invisible fingers caressing the skin plus a whiff of corrupting spice. Samuel backed off from it. Of the third guard he knew to have been posted there was no trace.

The dying man was still dying; the selected soldier, blade idly in hand, still standing over him.

'I told you to-...,' said Trevan.

'No,' said the soldier. The refusal was flat and unalterable. 'He still sees, still speaks. You want cold murder: butcher's work.'

Samuel didn't argue. This was a scene and place that could breed mutiny.

'Move forward,' he ordered his companions. 'Watch the tunnel.' They were happy to comply.

He forced himself to kneel by the fallen guard. Close to him, or perhaps just more concentrated near the floor, the stench was worse. Samuel felt its active ingredients sizzling in his nostrils. To his surprise he saw the milk-sop soldier's scruples had some grounding in fact: the guard's eyes came in and out of focus; he was mumbling. Trevan remembered him now: a great gangly Surrey-hills hillbilly boy: all *'o-aaa*'s and *'I be*'s and rustic innocence: not long in the infantry.

Samuel sought for some appropriate behaviour, dredging back into the days when he was still a Christian.

'What do you want? Shall I get a priest?'

That woke him up. His eyelids shot open, his voice returned. Samuel marvelled at it: a whole swathe of him was already vaporised.

'Yes! But... no! NO!' The man ought not to have been able to muster a shout, let alone grip Samuel's lapel. The stout material tore. 'No priest!' said the dying youth.

'Alright, alright,' Trevan calmed him. 'Suits me....'

'I carn't....'

Samuel gently disengaged the clawed hand and set it back down.

'Can't what?'

'I.... No heaven now, not for I. Oh God!'

It was better than Trevan had hoped. He was speaking clear enough to derive some advantage from. The show of charity was set aside.

'You're going anyway. Tell me what happened.'

Annoyingly, the youth could only think of himself.

'I couldn't help... so pretty... so ripe. She... he... oh, I be *shamed!*'

Trevan forced himself closer.

'Come on, man; you're running out of time: spit it out.'

'Oh no! It can't be shriven. That one cries-out-to-heaven, don't it? T'ain't my fault. They *tempted* I.'

Samuel was also now subject to temptation; a desire to hoick the whinger up and wring words out of him. Against that course of action was the realisation that the man had two armed allies nearby, and that down here in this forsaken place they were all decoupled from the normal world. There was no back-up to his authority but himself, no deference but what he could command.

So Samuel chose discretion: analysis rather than action. Weren't there four - or maybe seven - unforgivable so-called sins the Catechism said *'cried out to heaven for vengeance'*? Hadn't Father Omar once delicately recounted them? Had that been one of the days he'd paid attention?

Samuel was distracted by the sound of the tub descending. The requested reinforcements would be with them within minutes. His options were further curtailed.

'Come on, come on!' he said. With luck the soldiers would think he was urging on the tub.

'Mum?' said the youth - and then solved Samuel's dilemma by leaving the world behind.

'Hell-bloody-fire!' spat Trevan in exasperation. The uneducated soldiers obliged him by misunderstanding.

'Aye,' said one. 'Too true. That's what were 'ere. That's what he was feared of.'

Then they both crossed themselves. For form's sake, Samuel deceitfully joined in.

****

By the time they got the bodies to the top, gingerly wrapped in thick shrouds of canvas, word had got around. Work was at a standstill and an audience gathered at the shafthead. Even the Cymric bonded-labourers were craning their necks over the wattle walls of their corral. Trevan's expression discouraged direct enquiry but the foremost could see for themselves that the dead men... weren't the right shape.

Samuel scowled at the low buzz of speculation and realised he was losing control of it all. Thoughts of '*it all*' made him scan the whole mining camp and appreciate just how much he'd undertaken. All these men, all this gear, all these efforts, and to what end?

The end of two, maybe three, lives - so far - came the inner answer; not that he'd lose much sleep about them. All via pursuing the end of General Mott's ambitions, and the end of some ancient niggle of the Church and... the end of love for one woman (and her *end* too, being honest). That was ultimately where all this came from: clearing his way to her *end*: love and lust in unspecified proportions. Was just *that* worth all *this*?

He wouldn't always have conceived it in those crude terms. He could have any number of women, for money or the asking. So, did it absolutely have to be *that* one? Did he really still feel the same way?

It was a crushingly dangerous question to pose, but one quality Samuel still retained was his courage. He was willing to abide by whatever the response. So he asked - and received confirmation. Not one faint-heart brain cell failed to step forward screaming '*yes!*'

Though fresh returned into daylight, Trevan's first few moments above ground had been dark. He now shrugged off the bad memory and moved on. Yes, all this *was* all worth it; and by comparison there was nothing else to worry about.

Except possibly.... His survey of what he had wrought expanded to take in the setting and surrounding hills.

'Who are *they?*'

His staff had been keenly anticipating his first words, hopeful of all-compassing explanation. Their grudging faith was misplaced in every respect. They followed his pointing finger.

'Just some idlers, Mr Trevan.'

'Been there all morning,' added one of the tally-clerks, a known window-gawper.

Samuel had learnt to prefer instinct over dull-dog reason every time, and instinct told him that the distant knot of figures staring down on them were not well-wishers. And both ways of thinking equally disapproved of their formation and their standing too still.

'Reach out to them, Wizard,' he ordered briskly. 'Tell me what they want.'

The magician had to screw up his piggy eyes to even behold them at all.

'Too far,' he said, dismissively. 'Magic, yes - miracles, no.'

For his part Samuel couldn't see a distinction, but declined to argue.

'If you say so. Then go below and test if the sorcerous membrane by the pump station has been ruptured. Perhaps our missing man went through there.'

'And perhaps the stench and goo will wipe the smirk off your chops,' he thought to himself.

Samuel let him waddle off a few paces before shouting:

'But travel in the tub on your own: we don't want the chain breaking!'

He had the satisfaction of seeing the man's shoulders clench.

'And you,' he addressed the security staff as though they'd failed him, 'go fetch those nosy *'idlers'* up there. I'm told the devil finds work for idle hands: so let's save some souls from Satan!'

****

'A CATECHISM OF CHRISTIAN DOCTRINE'
or
'THE HA'PENNY CATECHISM'

First published (in English as well as Latin) Winchester 1745.

Imprimatur: + Richard Challoner, Archbishop of Canterbury.

Revised and reprinted from time to time. This edition 1996. Total printing over 30 million copies.

Approved by the archbishops and bishops of United England, and directed to be used in all the parishes thereof and appertaining thereto.

1. Q: **Who made you?**
    A: God made me.
2. Q: **Why did God make you?** ...

...

327. Q: **Which are the four sins crying out to heaven for vengeance?**
    A: The four sins crying out to heaven for vengeance are:

1) Wilful murder. [Genesis 4]
2) The sin of Sodom. [Genesis 18]
3) Oppression of the poor. [Exodus 2]
4) Defrauding labourers of their wages. [James 5]

****

CHAPTER 34

'Too late, I reckon.'

'For what?' said Samuel.

'For saving his soul – like you said: from Sa-....'

'Yeah, yeah, I know what I said. More to the point, what about the rest of them?'

'Gone, Master Trevan,' exclaimed the soldier. 'Vanished off the face of the earth. Don't see how, but they were all gone 'cept matey here.'

Samuel wasn't happy. He'd been through all this '*gone*' business shortly before and it had turned into trauma. How come all bar one of the group on the hill evaded detection by his swarm of horsemen? On the other hand, they'd at least solved one mystery - at the cost of posing another.

'Has he said anything yet?'

'Nothing as makes sense,' replied the captain of the pursuit. 'He just stood there grinning and awaiting us. We had no trouble out of him: not as such....'

Samuel didn't swallow that trailing hook-line. He'd make his own judgement.

They'd confined '*matey*', the once missing, now found, third mine guard in the site office. Everyone who'd had contact with him was dropping hints that all was not well. Samuel had got the message a dozen times over but refused to entertain them by running with it.

'And how could he have got right up there?' he challenged the searchers, taking a different tack from the one they wanted. 'He hadn't been gone long. Did you see any open shafts that might connect with the mine?'

They shook their heads. Trevan's scowl deepened.

'Why not just rejoice?' asked the Wizard, who was standing alongside.

'I beg your pardon?'

'That is what the Good Book advises, Mr Trevan. Matthew, chapter 18: *'If a man have a hundred sheep and one of them be gone astray, doth he not leave the ninety and nine, and goeth into the mountains, and seeketh that which is gone astray?'*'

'Yes, thank you, Wizard, for the scriptural comfor-....'

'"And if so be that he find it, he rejoiceth more of that sheep, than of the ninety and nine which went not astray.' Need more be said?'

The Wizard had recently re-emerged to confirm that the unseen barrier by the pump-station had indeed been breached, but was now closed firm against them once more. His session below had not dismayed him, nor inverted his grin. Samuel knew he shouldn't let himself be goaded but he was striving against an expert. Retaliation was irresistible.

'On reflection, Mr thaumaturge, I now see you're absolutely right. So come with me and rejoice over this lost sheep. Tell me what you make of him.'

The Wizard, otherwise occupied, hadn't heard all that Trevan had. He accompanied the little group to the site-cabin free of trepidation. Even the two sentinels posted by its door didn't alert him.

Fortunately, Samuel knew a little of the lost-and-found guard's prior state: because he couldn't judge the present without knowing what went before. This was a local man, beyond the first flush of youth; almost of yeoman status, though not above accepting wages to supplement his farming. A captain in the militia, a family man and churchwarden; well respected in the area. He was a natural choice for a supervisor and general help. Trevan had spoken to him once or twice, though what about wasn't recalled. He'd given the impression of a pillar-of-society sort.

Such people don't normally flash lascivious smiles or manipulate their parts, or leastways not before an audience. The arrival of Trevan's party didn't stop or abash him. He had no '*hello's*' for them, or any words at all. His freshly bloodied nose seemed no bother.

The soldier they'd left in charge was full of protest and explanation.

'I had to clock him,' he told them. 'He was scrabbling at my breeches. Bastard mollyfrock!'

'I doubt that,' Samuel contradicted. 'He has a wife and children.'

'So did King James the Scot...,' came the muttered reply. An educated soldier, no less. This really was a day of perverse wonders.

However, the 'lost sheep's look at Samuel, the way his eyes shone, added weight to his guardian's testimony. The prisoner was cruising way offshore 'normal'.

'Hold him in the chair,' Samuel told two of the security staff.

The man writhed and smiled under their grip. They held him, though with difficulty and strange expressions of distaste.

'What's the matter now?' Trevan barked at them.

They looked from one to another, not wishing to be the first to speak. The older's nerve broke first.

'It's just... well, he don't feel... like, *clean.*'

'He's all sort of... cacky,' said the other, 'only you can't see it.'

Samuel dismissed their nonsense with an impatient shake of the head.

'Where-did-you-go-to?' he asked the man, as though addressing a child. There was no answer. He seemed absorbed in a world of his own, more interesting than the one before him. It was also pretty clear what was going on in that world.

By dint of much shifting about Trevan caught his gaze and held it.

'Talk to me or I'll have your hands bound.'

That got through. Fearful of losing the means to pleasure himself, he desisted and paid attention. His captors were bathed with a rapturous look.

'Sorry,' he said. 'I don't know what came over me.'

'Really? No idea at all?' said Trevan.

'My mind's a... blank,' the man answered - and seemed particularly pleased with the choice of words.

'See if it is,' Samuel told the Wizard.

The magician lurched forward and applied his outstretched fingers against the man's brow. Futile attempts were made to lick them.

'It seems normal enough,' came the verdict, 'I sense only dull stuff. Deeper in there might be... aaaaaa!'

The Wizard hurtled back against the cabin wall. The wood protested. He held his arm tight against him, as though the funny-bone was jarred. His face was twisted with disbelief.

'*Yuks!*' The magician's pink tongue protruded from a grimace. He looked like he'd tasted something unutterably vile.

'I was in the dark,' the prisoner told them, quite softly, speaking sensibly. 'I embraced the dark. I *love* the dark....'

****

He got out in the night, somehow clawing and chewing his way though all the bonds *and* the thick planks of the cabin. There was blood and fingernails left where he'd worked away like a wild animal.

The first they knew of it was his return at dawn, wrapped in coils of rope and chain, dragged behind a group of horsemen. The riders were cold-furious and armed. Yet *he* was still smiling, though both mouth and fingers were mere red ruins. Samuel was roused out of bed to meet them.

'We want justice!' said their leader - and they meant to have it as well. The air crackled with imminent violence. Trevan's men closed ranks behind him

'What for?' Samuel asked - though he could guess. The prisoner was naked and marked by passage through mud and briar. He seemed proud of it.

'For my niece's buggering!'

'And my serving-girl the same!'

There was a babel of similar complaint from about half the houses in Welcombe. The escapee had had a busy night.

'And this window-creeping monster's says he's one of yours,' added their leader, dumping all in Trevan's lap. Silence awaited Samuel's acceptance of delivery.

It might have gone either way at that point. All sorts of taboos had been broken and third-party dignities rubbed raw. They wanted satisfaction every bit as badly as their prisoner obviously had. A lynching was one way of achieving it, as was shaking someone else into action. For a few seconds yet they had a narrow preference for the latter. Samuel saw the sense of that. Better this should go no further or get out of hand.

'And so he is,' he said, openly, unresisting. 'Or was. We sorrow with you - and we shall deal with him before your eyes, this very day.'

Trevan was taking a great deal on himself. Even the caught-red-handed were meant to go to the assizes and through due process of law. And sodomy was no longer a capital crime, not for decades now, for all that they never got reprieved. Strictly speaking, the man should end up bridegroom to an oar.

For the moment though, it did the trick. Fingers relaxed from hilt and trigger. They released the captive into Trevan's care. To reassure them, he had the man battered around a bit. He appeared to enjoy it.

Whispered orders were given for the drinks store to be unlocked and a generous breakfast prepared. Within an hour the powder-keg was defused and an almost jovial atmosphere prevailed.

'It's not like she lost her maidenhead,' confided one huge and florid farmer, speaking of his niece, cider-flask in one hand and cutlet in the other. 'A sore bum's no grounds for breaking off her betrothal. She can still marry.'

And then to round off festivities - and to bind them into his illegality - Samuel had them stand witness as the rapist was kicked headfirst (and radiantly cheerful) down the mineshaft. Though geared up to applying the final boot over the edge himself, in the end he delegated the task to the nearest soldier. So far in his quest Trevan hadn't killed; though doubtless that would come. He was ready and willing - but this just seemed a poor place to start.

'Helen of Troy,' he thought, 'and Melissa of Lewes. The things love makes us do....'

They heard the man impact against the sides two or three times, prior to a long delayed splash. Justice was appeased. They had sent him back to his Maker - and his makers.

****

The pigeon flew from the camp like an arrow, free at last from imprisonment and then Samuel's ungentle hands.

Animal seconds can be endless, unsullied by spoilsport past or future. It enjoyed the faithful power of huge breast muscles, the warm bath of the sun and the glitter of the distant Bristol Channel. Those pleasures were experienced for an equivalence of eternity. Likewise, alas, the subsequent insertion of talons and the stab-pause-stab of the hawk's beak. Pain and terror also went on like forever, and then so did death.

The bird of prey knew fear in one limited respect only: via the displeasure of its rearer. Therefore it did not directly rend and feed, but took the cooling dead-food back to base. 'Base' was one particular black gauntlet; protection for the feeble flesh of 'rearer'. Rearer gave pain and praise and permission to obey instinct. Rearer was both the beginning and end of life; each was in his power.

The pigeon's leg - and the message attached to it - were torn off and then hawk had the rest. She had done well and every strip of meat peeled away tasted the better for it.

It took some while but Samuel's code was eventually broken. Interested parties noted that *'the time was too soon'* and *'the unknown too great'* for him to proceed. They smiled.

Then what hawk didn't want was gathered and reassembled, re-united with leg and message, and magically raised to un-life. Fleshed out by other bird donors it would last long enough to deceive and complete its interrupted mission. For necromancer-magicians had discovered that, however small the animal residue they worked with, the primal urge (like homing instincts) always remained. Which just went to prove the old country adage: *'what's bred in the bone, comes out in the meat'.* Which in turn surely supported some even higher wisdom – but sorcerers were rarely theologians and vice versa. So, the correct, staring-you-in-the-face, conclusions had not been drawn yet.

Meanwhile, mind a relaxed and wiped blank-slate, the avian Lazarus was released to resume its journey.

****

Trevan never knew the full ins and outs of it, but he'd expected something similar. He'd given the pigeon mock last rites before setting it free.

His true message to the Sicarii; an expression of readiness authenticated by pre-arranged mark, was all this time wending its uncunning (and thus so very cunning) way to Llanthony by ordinary post.

CHAPTER 35

'One day and one hour: that is all. Then the cap goes on. Recall that your purpose is limited. Was deconsecration achieved? Discern that and be content. Smooth the path for others better fitted to follow. Do not think that because you carry arms-....'

'We've been through all this,' Samuel told the Sicarii. Had anyone ever interrupted him before he wondered? Possibly not, judging by the resulting rare twitch of the lips. That persona of lightheartedness was wafer thin.

'This is as much for me as you, Trevan. I shall be able to say you were instructed to the last.'

'Then I don't actually need to be around to hear it, do I? Lower away.'

The priest that accompanied the Sicarii said a blessing. Some of the men in the tub with Samuel crossed themselves.

In fact, it was the unacknowledged air of finality that fuelled his daring. If this was to be his last glimpse of the light he wished that look to be his usual stroppy one. It was only fitting.

The winding gear dropped them down, its cacophony drowning any other farewell. Samuel stared up at the dwindling circle of dusk above and said his own provisional goodbye. It comprised, he recognised with some shock, more curses than thank you's.

There were twelve of them in total, split into tub batches. Some had even been honoured with the truth, though none now remained deluded that this was just normal mine work. Wulfstan said he'd known all along. Allegedly, Trevan's generous wages had sedated his and others' suspicions.

Samuel's tub was the last down. Those who'd gone before were waiting bunched up in the small space available at the former pump station. With that engine's demise the water level had risen again and now almost

189

lapped the tunnel's edge. Samuel didn't mind: he'd despaired of finding an unguarded delving, even if they drained down to the earth's core. There were grounds for confidence that others had already obligingly cleared a dry-shod path.

The Wizard was with them, taking up more space than he ought. Samuel had taken pleasure in ensuring that and in seeing the Sicarii crush the man's mutiny with a single word. Wulfstan and an assistant were also present to advise and map their progress. The rest were just muscle and light-shedders: familiar faces from London or strangers from Llanthony, all mixed up. Mere orders had put the soldiers down below but Samuel's employees required dousing with coin. Then, to prevent trouble and forge a team, he'd had to treat the military likewise. It grieved Trevan's heart to be so spendthrift and the coffers were almost empty now. Thinking of it, he was semi-reconciled to not returning.

There was no room in the tunnel. This last group of four had to wait on the plank jetty. Even the short carbines and half-pikes were getting in the way in such confinement.

'Come on then, Wizard, I shouldn't have to tell you.' They had indeed rehearsed it to exhaustion. Trevan wanted to minimise the need for noise and orders.

'We were waiting for *you*,' the man wheezed back, but left it at that, though more was plainly said in his head. Already to the fore, he stepped up to the unseen barrier and drew out a set of pince-nez to study it more closely.

'Wonderful work,' he said admiringly, to both everyone and no one. 'It's geometry of being is perfectly flush with our world's prosaic atoms. You'd never see it.'

Absence of response told him his appreciation wasn't appreciated. He moved on.

Rolling up his sleeve right to the starry armband denoting his magical school, the Wizard slowly extended a thick right arm, palm outstretched.

'God is great!' he reassured himself - and then dived his hand in.

The up to now unseen was flushed out and agitated into frenzy. What appeared to be a wall built of slurry began, first sluggishly, then with baffling speed, to turn; spiralling in on the Wizard's arm. A vile smell emerged, like the opening up of a long-sealed slaughterhouse. They all gagged on it.

Eyes clenched tight, the Wizard was sweating from the hairline down. The barrier was draining up *into* his arm, causing the flesh there to bubble and swell, attempting escape from the bone. He sought solace in description of the experience.

'A cesspit...,' he told them, 'full of fat scorpions.... Be quick, please....'

As soon as there was a gap between the barrier and tunnel wall they slipped through, shrinking away from the spinning edge. In his desperation, the Wizard urged them past with sweeps of his foot. 'Go! Oh God! Go....'

He couldn't wait for the last one to be fully past, but spun himself round the gap, shoving the man forward with his bulk. He came to rest, chest heaving, against the wall and vomited the absorbed material back out. It left his arm at furious speed, re-seeking its proper place. The spiral formed again, filling the tunnel, then slowed, then vanished.

'Realignment,' puffed the Wizard, and hawked some nasty taste from his mouth. 'If we can't see it then it went back just right.'

'Terrific,' said Trevan, sarcastically. He couldn't enthuse about having *that* between them and home. It was the agreed plan but even so....

'We go,' he told them, and led the way.

The glass-bubble tar-torches slow roasting the back of his head shed light about five paces into the future. Held perfectly still by bearers with both hands free, they might just have been adequate. As it was, Samuel had entrusted them to men with other duties as well. There was room for two to walk abreast. Wulfstan was beside Trevan, making close study of their path and assessing its safety. He made frequent reference to a handheld compass. Behind them were two torchmen with pistols at the ready. The Wizard followed on alongside Wulfstan's assistant who traced their progress on special waxed paper - human memory being too fallible to trust with recalling the way back through a labyrinth. Behind them were the soldiery and more torches. Samuel had drilled all to move in slow steps, treading softly.

They didn't need a mining expert to discern that the tunnel sloped down. The water level should soon have been there to meet them, but dusty dryness persisted. Samuel didn't query that particular unanswerable, but he did wonder about the nature of their route. Why the smoothness of the walls? How come the lack of props? Wulfstan detected the silent question in Trevan's expression.

'Not man-made,' he whispered. 'Melted, not cut.'

Before Samuel could decide if that was good news or not, facts came along to contradict it. The tunnel took a hard right turn. They edged cautiously round it and arrived at a junction with a more grandiose downward route. The torchlight picked out shaped stone and brickwork succeeding the bland curves, reuniting them with the work of human hands. A single glance identified it as both old and church-style. They'd found what they were looking for - or at least the start of it. Samuel punched the unoffending air in glee. No one else seemed so pleased.

Dutifully they took the descending option. Their footing was no longer as easy; rocks and pitfalls dotted the floor. There was abundant dust; so much that it stiffened the already soupy atmosphere. Wulfstan held forth the caged bird and observed its unaltered despond.

'The air's still sweet,' he hissed, and smiled for once. Samuel presumed this to be some highly specialised use of the word. To him it smelt like history – minus the happy moments.

Then there were stone steps, broad and ancient, worn down in places by the passage of feet. The engineer directed torchlight at one particular point.

'See? Repairs.'

That was certainly what they looked like. Where fragments had fallen away on the edges of some steps, crude hard-core-and-pebbles had been rammed in to make good. This careless work appeared far more recent. Wulfstan overlooked that to run appreciative fingers over the original sides.

'Fire your pop-guns as you may,' he told them, in a voice touched by awe. It was obviously a point that had been preying on him. 'Shoot 'em all but this won't come down. 'Er's fine: solid: proper job!'

The reassurance was noted in silence. Samuel counted fifty steps down and then shied from tall figures revealed by the advancing pool of light. Behind him two pistols came up to the aim position.

Fortunately, there was no need to deafen Trevan by firing from right beside his ear. The objects of alarm were not at all hostile - quite the contrary. The steel beams sunk into floor and roof were passive in intention, merely an incomplete barrier against entry - or perhaps exit.

Samuel went up to them. Each column was as thick as a man's leg and the space between likewise. Save for a slim central gap, only a rat would be able to squeeze past. They were fixed into pools of Portland cement - which was revealing in itself. That was only made or sold by archbishop's licence, because of its instant-castle-making potential. Therefore this project had had 'friends-in-high-places'. Samuel was duly advised and regarded it with new respect - until the engineer showed it up as a failure.

'Look,' he said. 'They never finished.'

Over in the darkness by the tunnel wall was a final beam lying prone. About it were the tools and buckets and jacks to accomplish its erection. There were even some stacked bags of cement dust, their smoky-red papal seals still intact.

'The 1702 lot,' said Samuel, speaking his judgement aloud. No one dissented.

'They got close,' added Wulfstan's assistant, pointing to embryo-excavations in the central gap. The intention had clearly been to seal this way forever. So, either the workmen had left in a hurry - or maybe never left at all.

Well, that was sad for them but salvation as far as Samuel was concerned. Even with the right gear it would be a day's work cutting through just one of the columns. Save for the providential gap they'd be heading back now.

'Single file,' he commanded - albeit quietly. 'Twelve steps on and then halt to reform.'

In the event their path dictated that anyway. A dozen steps were all that remained after they edged past the bars. The stairs and descent ended in a wide vestibule whose edges were beyond the torches' reach.

'Circle. Then to the centre. My lead.'

This was another long-practised formation. The soldiers formed an outer ring round the two engineers and the Wizard. Samuel was at '12 o'clock' and others at '3', '6' and '9' could be deputised to lead the way at need.

They soon discovered myriad small objects underfoot, making each step treacherous. Samuel called a halt, and torches directed floorwards revealed they were walking on coins; a patchy, scattered layer of minted gold. Some looked fairly modern, others ancient indeed.

'Don't even think about it,' Trevan ordered, in wearied tones. Several of the gun-toters had developed stooping shoulder syndrome. It was rather disappointing really: he'd had hopes such a careful selection process might have sifted out those enslaved to instinct. But, thinking on, it was really more his failing than theirs. His fault in forgetting, even temporarily, the reliable shabbiness of human nature. Shame on him.

A few paces on and a grinning face lurched into sight. Fortunately it was dead - long dead - and detached from its former body and covering flesh.

The skull had been impaled on a rough-hewn stake, which was itself driven deep into the floor slabs.

Trevan drew close to his cheerful new friend and looked him (or her) in the eye. He learnt nothing. An exploratory tap to the brow dislodged a gentle fall of dust.

'Human,' he announced.

'Deceased,' added the Wizard.

Samuel span on him and served an evidently eloquent *'not here, stupid!'* expression which shut the man up. Indeed, it almost shocked him into apology - almost.

There were other occupied poles dimly visible now and Trevan ordered all torches held aloft. The chamber's outer limits came into rough and ready view. It proved to be ideal: he'd been looking for somewhere safe and small-ish to wean them off bunching together against the dark.

'1, 4, 7 and 11 o'clock to the room corners. Then torches high.'

It was gratifying and a tribute to him or his training that they went right away, no slacking; scrunching and sliding over the coinage carpet.

The rest of them waited in a constricted circle for the artificial dawn.. It duly came - and, like the real one, revealed a landscape of mixed blessings.

They were alone and unthreatened; the way ahead was fairly clear: a tunnel at the room's far end, like the one they'd just quit. Meanwhile, the making of moderate prosperity was all around, there for the taking. On the other hand, there were... discouragements. It was not a happy place.

Quite apart from the heads and body-parts thrust onto spikes, rearing up at eye-level from the floor, even a poor light showed the garish colour scheme that was surely no monastic choice. Brown and pink washes raged for supremacy on walls and floors and ceiling, in coats of varying thickness and age. The overall effect was claustrophobic, like being inside a joint of beef.

Samuel queried it with a look to the Wizard. He shrugged back his lack of comprehension.

'That's a mystery too,' the magician added, pointing at the nearest wall.

Samuel looked - and then peered harder. Could sorcerers enhance their sight as well as all the other unfair advantages? He tried again and then grasped the elusive images. A shape or symbol, innumerable inverted and impaled *m*'s or seagulls thus: **ω**, was daubed in mad, overlapping, lack of order on every flat surface. Soot or charcoal had been employed for some, but most were suspicious-red or faecal brown.

'I think,' said Wulfstan, transcending the decor to give a dispassionate opinion, 'that this was the vestibule; the way in.'

His assistant, a pale and intense youth, consulted his drawing.

'We've met the primary avenue,' he agreed. 'It should lead back to the main gate blocked in 1702.'

'Only now there's a new way out,' butted in one of the corner men. He was an old London acquaintance of Trevan's and thus felt up to joining their counsels.

Samuel went to look. The man was right but not thanked for it. What looked like a giant animal burrow clawed its way upwards at the junction of two walls. Though hardly fresh-made it was a lot younger than anything else here. Trevan knelt to investigate and thought he caught the ghost, far away above, of blessed fresh air. There wasn't space for a man to stand upright within but a crouched ascent might be just about possible. So, someone or something here cared to interact with the wider world. If you considered carefully there was comfort in that. Things that need routes for feet also had tongues to make talk and bodies to skewer.

'Doors here, sir.'

The low call came from the other side of the hall. Samuel crossed from one shadow zone to the other, threading his way through the stake display. Four decayed but still standing doors were pointed out to him. This was something else they'd anticipated and rehearsed.

'Threes,' he ordered. 'In and hold.'

A team of three addressed the first door. At Trevan's signal, one soldier booted it aside (and asunder) and stood back. Another piled in with torch and pistol; the third stood by, aiming, ready to supply back-up or revenge.

'Clear!' The process and call was repeated four times without incident. Samuel then went on a tour of inspection. They were all small side-rooms, functional adjuncts (once) to the entry hall. Taking a torch himself, he made swift inventory:

One: spare stakes, some flint knives (adeptly knapped); two stone bowls, a new-cut rowan branch. Dust and dirt.

Two: a part consumed man, long set aside and mummified by age. A clerical collar hung around his thin chewed neck.

Three: an armoury - of sorts. Two old muskets, not matched; a brace of pistols likewise; four spears, flint or glass topped; more flint knives and two human hands.

Four: nothing - but in the corner was another burrow, leading far away into dark. A faint, warm, animal odour trickled down it. Trevan sensed life but not intelligence. He disdained to explore. They were after bigger game.

'Not for us,' he told the Wizard on re-emerging. 'Others can apply cleansing fire and sword. Form column! Far tunnel!'

They assembled commendably quickly and advanced. The passage was broad and fair going and they no longer walked on human money. Wulfstan's whisper numbered their steps for his assistant to note. At fifty they were stopped again.

Once more, at outer torch limit, their encounter had the semblance of life, but closer to they were reassured - if not much. The effigy was crude, even allowing that they weren't sure what was depicted. Stone and gravel, dirt and bone, were compacted in some unknown matrix to make a shape. It had two arms and two legs, plus two breasts and a head: so it could be said to be man-*like*. But even assuming a spectacularly bad sculptor, Samuel did not think a human likeness was intended.

The Wizard came front-wards and examined it like a connoisseur pondering an acquisition.

'I'd say a demi-demon,' he said, in his own good time, 'of obscure breed. *Disva* perhaps? A *padfoot*? But no, note the pendulous udders and huge lashed eyes. I confess myself uncertain, Mr Trevan. There is infinite variety of these scum from nature's bath-tub.'

So Samuel had heard, though the Lord's favoured creation had exterminated many and driven the rest into the margins of the world. His interest lay more in learning this sorts' mettle than a precise taxonomic placing.

'But note the repetition of the vestibule motif,' said the magician, eager, for once, to supply helpful information. He pointed to the large 'impaled m' painted with incongruous care on the thing's bulging loins.

'And you note these,' Trevan replied, indicating the vestigially moist intestines coiled bandoleer-style round its shoulders. Tokens of contemporary life were mounting up.

'I had,' said the Wizard, without inflection.

There were doors to left and right but Samuel ignored them. He'd got the tone of the place now and didn't need to bother with side issues. The column parted around the tribute to something-or-other and moved on.

Another fifty paces forward and they saw light ahead to greet them. It was no torch flare and certainly not the sun's rays, but rather more of a dismal glow. Samuel wondered at the ancient instincts within that made any light at all welcome.

The corridor ended and they entered a colossal space, vastly beyond their powers of illumination. The light source was somewhere out in the middle of that expanse and they felt dwarfed and vulnerable in the sudden immensity. Wulfstan's assistant's dull-dog focus saved them by supplying location.

'This must be the cloisters,' he said, apparently uninhibited by the brooding silence. 'I reckon they've followed standard layout. There'll be a walkway round and all sorts of rooms off it. If I'm right, the *'refectory'* should be over to the west.'

'Speak plain,' snapped Samuel, 'Or do you see sun and stars to guide us?'

'Sorry, I mean the left. The kitchens and eating room and sleeping quarters should all be to the left. Y'see, there was an underground monastery in Estonia once - before it was overrun. I got hold of a plan. So far this is like it: not exact, but good enough.'

Trevan was impressed, though he didn't show it. He foresaw a big bonus for this boy should they both survive.

Wulfstan didn't want to feel left out.

'I picked him myself,' he confided. 'He'll go far.'

'I know,' agreed Samuel. 'He'll go to this 'refectory' and prove his theory.'

He turned back to the assistant. 'Refresh my memory: name?'

'Winston: Winston Cook.'

'Right, Winston; take four blokes and check it out. Oh, and 'fore you go, what should be over there where that glow is?'

The youth tried to nonchalantly ride the surprise extra delivery of fear. He almost managed it, hiding reaction in a hasty flick through papers attached to his clipboard.

'A central feature: to aid contemplation sort of thing. A statue? Or maybe a fountain.'

'Thanks. Cheerio.'

Young Winston departed like a dog to a bath but had to hurry lest the soldiers left him behind. They disappeared into the black, a diminishing cluster of fireflies.

'Let the boy earn his spurs,' Trevan told the rest. 'Meanwhile, we'll wander in cloistered calm'

'Peter 2, chapter 1, verse 19,' intoned the Wizard. *'Ye do well that ye take heed, as unto a light that shineth in a dark place'.'*

'Yeah, that as well,' said Samuel. He'd meant his levity to settle the troops, not incite the magician to scripture. 'Let's go look at this light.'

It was a bit of a wrench to leave the 'safety' of the corridor and issue out into the void. The torches' best efforts fell far short of the roof, and the clack of their heels, magnified and repeated, spawned the desire to mince along like a troupe of burly ballerinas. Dignity prevailed in that particular struggle but resolve weakened just a notch.

'*Boy'* Winston was soon proved to be doubly, even trebly, right. Slaves to the founding template, the monastery builders had put a sloping roof over the cloister-walk, even when there was no sun or rain to guard against. Then, in the centre of the presumed square, they saw there had been a statue *and* a fountain - once.

The original stone figure - a saint or church-father - was more than mutilated: it had been perverted a universe away from initial intentions. A monstrous stone prick had been grafted on, and the pelvic parts of a skeleton impaled on that. Where once there'd been a human head and piety depicted, a monster's face now sat in grinning triumph. Its skinny arms were likewise raised in acclaim.

Below, in the dry bowl of the ornate fountain, there were rag bundles; torso-shaped and carelessly piled high. Fortunately, they had an excuse not to enquire about them, for that would have meant treading upon the mushroom fields.

Ordinary fungi don't glow, and so that alone would have marked them out from the norm. However, their leprous light was only one of the incentives against consumption. Samuel was a country boy and had often gone mushroom gathering at dawn to enliven the orphanage menu. Even so, he'd never seen anything like these gooey, bulging, pink things, nor would he be distraught never to see the like again. They gave the impression that the slightest brush would trip some internal pressure, setting off a bomb of spores.

Yet someone must have relished them, for these were definitely fields of cultivation. All around the fountain, almost to the cloisters' edge, the monks' paving slabs were levered up to make way for a dark layer of humus. Some areas had been harvested of mature specimens, and reed baskets ditched to one side made their utility crystal clear.

Samuel doubted it was pure imagination to detect gentle movement amidst the crop. It was like observing an obscene phalli farm.

'What d'you reckon?' he asked the Wizard. 'Food or poison?'

'Tricky, Mr Trevan: as you know, one man's meat is another man's-....'

'Forget it! Circle. Follow me!'

He took them back to the deathly-still cloister route, near to where they'd entered. Its token outer wall and pointless tile roof supplied illusory comfort.

'Look!'

It was one of the local hirelings who spoke. A gamekeeper by trade, he was very far from anything remotely sympathetic to him. His voice conveyed urgency so Samuel stopped and complied.

'Look at what?'

'Nothing,' said the man.

'One annoying cunt is enough: not you as well!'

'I *meant* no dust: there should be even dust all over. Not here in the middle path there 'ain't.'

Trevan checked and saw it was so.

'Others walk here,' the gamekeeper concluded, 'and regular-like.'

'Perhaps some of the original monks got left behind?' said a sadly familiar voice.

Samuel suddenly found it easier to transcend the Wizard's 'wit'. His day of reckoning *would* come.

'Thank you, keeper. Good work. Move on.'

At last they hit the corner of the huge chamber and could turn north along its second, 'eastern', side. Now there were doors varying the plainness of the wall, but they were hardly inviting. Samuel sought excuse for ignoring them and found it in not wanting a barrier between themselves and the detached party.

Wulfstan had taken over mapping duties and his pen tapped two hundred paces before the opportunity arrived to turn again. They then hugged the wall along the third side, a constellation of puny lights in orbit round a cold fungoid sun.

The doors had stopped: which was a relief - until Trevan admitted to himself that exploration without event shouldn't be regarded as a blessing. They'd - he'd - let himself be *lulled.* '*First entrance - we go in,*' he resolved.

The great scriptwriter himself must have been listening, for straightaway an enormous doorway came step by step into torch range. As best Samuel could judge it was half way along the cloisters' northern wall, opposite the corridor that had brought them here.

'Double door. Team of five,' he decreed; then stepped up to be one of them.

Neither the proposal nor variation flustered anyone - which was good grounds for carrying through. Trevan felt justified in saying '*Go!*'

Two men slammed the solid barriers back and retired. Samuel and two others stepped in.

The lack of response or anyone to meet them allowed space to consider the implications. Wood of medieval vintage should long ago have rotted and weakened, even in this arid place. Likewise, centuries of disuse ought to have welded hinges into stubborn blobs of rust. The way these doors were so ready to serve spoke volumes. Samuel observed the signs of present occupation slowly dawning on even the dullest of the team but, visibly at least, no one wavered.

It was another big room, not as cavern-like as the one they'd left, but still above torch range. Its function leapt out at them, even if nothing else did. Those parts they could see were lined with shelves. Books and bits of books were everywhere, some stacked neatly while others, grossly tortured, lay wounded on the ground. Samuel edged forward under the cover of guns to sample the wares.

The worst treated were the oldest: he found only loose bindings and stray pages of those. He didn't trouble his scant Latin to discern precisely what they'd been. Some of them were likely original monastery stock, like the beautifully illuminated capital he found actually nailed to the floor. Another, more recent, tome, a translation of Herodotus, looked like it had been shot through; probably *after* the addition of childish obscenities.

Someone had spent hours drawing crude (in every sense) stick figures on every page. Samuel was about to hurl it from him when he recalled their location. The travesty was gently – and silently - replaced.

Yet, for all the wild anarchy wreaked on some of the stock, Trevan found other sections to be fastidiously arranged. He examined one such and discovered every work one could wish for (and more) on ornithology. Another gathered together all that Jane Austen had ever written, including editions only a few years old. They looked well thumbed.

Samuel had been brought up to revere the printed word, and that remained with him even now when much else was lost. All the same, the wantonness of this assembly, its tedium and perversity repelled him. He felt the urge to burn it, preferably along with its owner. Which, for once, was no vain daydream. In present circumstances, he might actually get to indulge the desire.

'Someone's buggered a good library,' he told his team, and left it - and the 'library' - at that.

Across its expanse, in the corner of the northern wall, there was a smaller door. A 'team-of-two' was sufficient to hit that and reveal a small office, recently vacated. The disorder there was more personal, though not so great as in the library. A selection of volumes on a desk looked intended for reading, not violation. There were pens and ink and candles. On a nearby trestle table was set an array of flasks and glassware and botanical specimens standing ready in pestles. An enquiring mind had clearly lingered here not so long ago.

Glances were exchanged at this definitive proof of company, even as the fact was swallowed. Samuel allowed himself a certain gladness that that hurdle was finally crossed.

He obliged himself to finger through the selected books. He found pornography and theology in equal measures. Neither appealed. All the stationary - old, heavy, cream paper - was blank.

The persona of the missing tenant loomed closer when Trevan observed his soldiers' distraction. On one wall were framed prints of Zeus enjoying gross indecencies with stableboys. Samuel marvelled at his men's priorities and relentless basic tastes.

'Never mind that. Team of two: the cupboard.'

They dealt with said small side door. Something flew out and a soldier shot it. The explosion sounded like the voice of God, its echo travelling out of the room to reverberate all round the cloister-cavern.

Though only *self*-trained to speed and commitment, Samuel's response almost got him in on the act. He had to give conscious orders to his gun arm to stand down, his trigger finger to relax.

'Team of three, outer door. Wizard, to me.'

For once the magician just obeyed. He and Samuel stood over the now dead thing. The soldier's reflex-action pistol shot had opened up its chest.

'Is... was it a man?' Trevan realised his lip was curling in un-authorised disgust. He regretted the concealing powder smoke's swift dispersal.

'No.' The Wizard was cheerfully confident. 'Men have faces.'

It was an unanswerable point. This creature, otherwise plainly human in its nakedness, had nothing but a bland stretch of skin where features ought to be.

'An altered man then?'

Again, the Wizard shook his heavy head.

'Nope. Demi-demon. This type is known, though rare. Domesticated, they can serve as guardians.' He tested the chain and collar round the thing's bull-neck. The silver link led back into the 'cupboard', its former home.

'What?' Samuel queried. 'With no eyes, no ears?'

'They manage somehow. No one knows how. Its kind are rarely caught to make autopsy of. They kill and kill for delight, like foxes in a chicken-run. Those fingers can penetrate a steel helmet - and the skull beneath. I don't recall an English sighting for decades, but the Druze country is currently plagued with them apparently.'

Samuel intended to explore its den but first glimpse of rag-clad bones and middens of the creature's filth served to dissuade.

'Footsteps! Half a dozen - approaching.'

The rearguard's call was appreciated but hardly necessary. A thunder of heavy boots from beyond the door was audible to all. It at least killed what seemed like endless echoes of the pistol shot.

'And fire: torches,' another sentinel added, more calmly.

'Stand and prepare,' Trevan told the men at the outer door. 'Remainder: half circle! Fire at clear targets on my order only.'

For men up against the unknown, in the dark and under threat, they were all laudably smooth. True, all the noise was enough to waken the dead, removing any element of surprise they might have had: but Samuel had an inkling they'd lost that some while back. Any discouragement was counter-balanced by the vindication of his team. Like Gideon he'd chosen few but better. There was justification in them pressing on and down - if they were spared.

'In sight - just,' said the furthest man, balancing his pistol over a steady forearm. 'It's men – or men-shaped. Moving fast. I *could* get one about... now.'

'Hold fire,' Samuel maintained.

'Wise move, boss,' said one of the old London hands. 'They're ours.'

'Who else would it be?' said Trevan, dismissively. 'If it is, let 'em in.'

Apprentice-engineer Cook and his minders got a welcome back and were visibly glad to be there. Hearing the gunshot had set the seal on their loneliness and they'd hastened to assist - or at least share the general fate.

Trevan briefly let them satisfy their curiosity. The dead thing was leered over and prodded. Then he cut through their whispered chinwag.

'And?'

Cook rose to the challenge. He could imitate the sound (if not substance) of command.

'Yes,' he confirmed. 'This place is the same layout; or near enough. We can use my plan.'

'The refectory?'

'Right, yes, we found that; amongst other things.'

'So?'

'A mess: centuries of cannibal feasts by the looks: bones and clothes and mouldy stuff they couldn't finish. And there was a burrow up from one corner: animal work, with a live smell coming down it. Sort of sweaty pork. We... didn't really have time to investigate that....'

'Good,' said Samuel, covering their discomfort. 'I think we've already met it. You did the right thing.'

'Mention the wall,' interjected a soldier - who wasn't going to have some boy sounding like his officer.

'Oh yeah,' said Cook, 'that too. Someone's decorated a whole big wall there: like a mural.'

'Of?'

'Um... one of those things there was a statue of in the corridor....'

'Giant, crowned, triumphant: striding over a landscape.' The soldier had butted in again. Samuel remembered this man now: the dark-horse educated one from the interview with their *'lost sheep'*. 'Looked like Devon to me,' he went on. 'The demi-demon was leading an army and blackening the land.'

'Humanity in retreat?' Trevan suggested. 'The rout of Christendom?' He could well guess.

'Pretty much. Superb detail. There's been a fine artist down here somewhen: total contrast to the surrounding squalor. Oh - and he had that symbol business on his crown: a human skull and bull's horns plus that symbol.'

'He?' Samuel asked. Above-ground would want every detail. There arrived an uncalled-for image of the Sicarii sinking his teeth into any gap.

'Definitely!' said the soldier. 'Huge cocker rampant! And there was a great orange egg-shell cracking-....'

'And an eye and teardrop,' said Cook, trying to elbow his way back into the de-brief. 'And toppled crosses and-....'

Religion, religion, religion - ever the bane of Samuel's life. He suspected that here had never ceased to be a religious house - of one sort or another.

'Right,' he said, cutting across it all before everyone wanted a go. 'I get the picture: if you'll excuse the pun. Leaving the decor aside, what more do we know? The plan's standard you say?'

'I think so,' answered Cook.

'So the heart of the place will be where?'

'Down - and tending west-wards. That's where the main parts will sit.'

'Like?'

'Well, um... the high altar, the quire, maybe the abbot's quarters and....'

'And the way there?'

Trevan was keeping up the pace, but meanwhile Wulfstan was a whisker off incandescent at being so marginalized.

'You don't need no book-study to tell you that!' he said. 'I scent a down-draught: outside and west-ways: I mean to say: left-ward. *That's* our path.'

'Yep,' Cook chipped in, liking his new prominence after years of dogsbody-dom. 'We saw a deeper black outside on our way here: only we were hurrying and didn't-....'

'Don't tread on my heels, boy,' snapped Wulfstan. 'I mentioned her first.'

The slave's rebellion was crushed and the senior engineer present redeemed himself by being spot on when they checked.

The stairs were broad and gracious - once upon a time. Now they were old and blemished by slapdash repairs. Their careless inheritors had stained them in numberless ways and the party weaved round various pools and packages, declining to enquire. The sordid descent continued for fifty steps.

They then arrived at the edge of a square landing, just small enough to be declared empty by their torches. Corridors bisected the other three walls. Samuel had them form circle whilst the two engineer factions argued the way ahead.

Wulfstan and Cook engaged in bitter whispers about which avenue to take, thus proclaiming neither was really sure.

'Forward in column,' Trevan ordered - since that happened to be the direction he was facing.

It led on for a fair while through dust and dinge. Sometimes the way broadened into vacant rooms; other times they had to squeeze close, shoulder to shoulder. Samuel had Wulfstan as his partner. The Saxon was now grimly focused on being right and Trevan noted it for future reference. Injured pride seemed to be a marvellous motivator.

'I think maybe we should have gone-....' Wulfstan started to express doubts but then bit the words to death as their random path was rewarded.

The corridor ended in an enormous chamber, though not quite so high and cavernous as the cloister cave. It was also far more elongated. One side wall comprised a long row of narrow doors.

'The dormitories, or '*dorter*',' said Cook, from some way back. 'Where the monks slept. There'll be a little cell behind each door.'

Well, it was always good to learn new words, but the schooling could stop there. With a shock, Samuel found that his natural curiosity had withered, leaving only a boundless indifference about how Time had treated the monks' rooms. Doubtless they had new occupants and uses but he could live without finding out. He hoped that that was just caution, not cowardice....

Either way, maybe the wobble was detected for, just as Samuel framed the thought and surprised himself, a fixture of the accommodation came out to say hello. Sort of.

She must have been standing very still out in the darkness, listening to them, or perhaps watching with acclimatised eyes. When she did move her

Judas chain instantly betrayed her presence.

The girl ought to have been grateful not to be shot; a pale, clanking figure suddenly staggering into the light. But thereagain, given her plight, perhaps that would have been welcomed.

The soldiers initially found grounds to hold fire in her gender and nakedness. Then it became clear she was more a subject for pity than fear.

'Can you speak, my love?' asked one of the softer-hearted men.

She could and did. Sing-song words came from the beautiful but slack face, tumbling out of a meaningless radiant smile. They listened carefully but could not understand.

'Welsh, I think,' said Wulfstan. 'Or maybe Kernoack.'

'Anyone speak that?' asked Trevan. This was unforeseen. Given his past experiences he'd demanded only fluent English speakers for this trip.

'No,' said the Wizard, not troubling to disguise his top-to-toe appraisal of the potentially pretty form. 'But I misdoubt discourse would profit us in any case. Listen again.'

They did. The chorus continued and soon became samey.

'It's just repeated phrases,' the Wizard confirmed. 'A song or poem I reckon. Poor gorgeous raven-hair is no really longer with us, are you sweetie?'

She looked through, round or over his direct question.

'I thought not,' he answered himself, and began a circle of inspection of the girl. 'She's seen too much - or are you a devotee? Or else - oh, I say!'

Samuel hesitated, but then looked as directed. A bright red and blue target was painted - or perhaps tattooed - over the cheeks of her backside. The soldiers forgot dignity and compassion and orders to scramble for a goggle.

'And who keeps you in such servitude I wonder?' asked the Wizard, not expecting any reply. He lifted the delicate silver coils of her chain with two fingers. It trailed back from her elegant neck-collar to some fixing point in the dark.

She seemed to register his presence for the first time, and then lithely assumed the position of her calling.

Discipline might have fallen apart there: for wildly varying reasons, but Samuel was equal to the moment.

'Form column - to her left! Eyes front. Advance!'

Trevan was last away and looked round at the young woman

dwindling back into the murk. She hadn't even noticed their going.

'Surely,' said the Wizard, calling back to Samuel, 'we can't leave her behind - ho ho! *'Behind'* - get it?'

That little *bon mot* sealed his fate. Trevan decided then and there the magician wasn't coming out of the labyrinth. He always knew his quest would demand blood sacrifice - and here was a worthy volunteer for the altar.

What he thought was *'oh yes, you'll get it alright'*, but what he *said* - in tones of silk - was:

'She left long ago. Only the body remains.'

'But *what* a body!' the Wizard persisted. 'Our Christian duty surely dictates that we-....'

Trevan levelled his gun at the man's pumpkin head. Only the magician's backward glance beheld.

'Be quiet please,' Samuel told him.

'You wouldn't!' The Wizard looked again. 'You would.' His tongue was stilled.

Fortunately, their march-for-marching's sake also took them somewhere, so there wasn't the need to backtrack. A good-as-anywhere corridor led out of the *dorter* area and Trevan had them take it. He shouldered his way to the front.

'Down and west, you say?' Care was exercised to airily address both competing guides.

'So I reckon,' answered Cook, quickest off the mark. 'We're looking for some stairs.'

In lieu of that direct route they had the diversion of some rooms. Every so often and in the twisting and turning of the way, the corridor broadened out into chambers or whole interconnecting suites. Some were marked with the 'symbol' or sprayed with fetid colour; one or two even held dusty parcels of disconcerting shape - but principally they were void. The expedition was now accustomed to the prevailing decor and passed without prying.

Until, that is, the Wizard just *stopped* beside one door. His sheer bulk blocked those following. One ringed forefinger was held aloft as though he was gauging the wind in this stagnant place.

'There is... history here,' he pronounced. Then, seeing his audience were unimpressed: 'Past things of relevance to us.'

Samuel trusted the man's thaumaturgic judgement, if little else.

'Right: front three: corridor ahead. Team of three to the door. Wizard and engineers to me. Rest: about face: corridor behind.'

The door responded smartly to rough treatment and the delegated man rushed in. Since he then continued to live and breathe, Samuel and the Wizard followed.

First impressions were of an armoury, but second thoughts deemed it a museum. Military technology didn't exactly race along in a world free of major wars for centuries past, but trends and improvements did come and go. The most casual glance could tell these stacks of muskets and side arms were archaic.

'I think we've found the 1702 boys.'

'Or the booty from 'em.'

Samuel realised he hadn't been party to this exchange. The two soldiers who spoke were having a military-only chat and appraisal. Up with that he would not put.

'Amounts to the same thing,' he said, butting in. 'What good's a soldier without weapons?'

They didn't like it - but didn't rise to it. Accordingly, he felt able to throw them a bone.

'In your judgement: how many? And were they reused?'

The two did a quick audit.

'Arms for four-score, I reckon,' said one.

The other bent down and selected a gun at random. A dust-flood and flakes of old rust fell from it.

'And that answers your second question,' he said.

'So,' Samuel asked, 'this accounts for all of them?'

'Near enough. Except it don't tell us how far they got: just how they fared at the end.'

'But there's no bodies...,' Trevan's cavil was half-hearted and easily shot down.

One of the soldiers stepped into the role of spokesman.

'These were papal troops,' he said. 'So this stuff came off 'em *after* death. No other way: not with them. Somewhere there should be a mountain of those they slew beforehand.'

He turned out to be a prophet. Mere minutes and a few more turns of the corridor separated them from the aftermath of battle.

'*Hell* of a do!' said spokesman soldier, smiling in appreciation.

Samuel was no expert but saw what was meant. Events had literally brought the house down. The corridor had always widened into chamber-size here, but great gashes in the walls extended it further. There'd been a bad roof-fall and the rubble from that now formed a compacted mound. Everywhere there was bones; scattered about or in groups. Some protruded from the collapse material. A small percentage were still covered in cloth of faded red.

Courtesy of a little thought and some wandering round, Trevan reckoned he could even see the flow of things. They'd fought their way back here; a rearguard had tried and failed to hold the far corridor. Then they'd been assailed by vast numbers; as many as would pack into the confined space - and more. Their perimeter shrank steadily: Samuel noted the tidemarks of resistance in tightening circles of dead. Finally, there was a last stand - and the defiant suicidal discharge of a powder barrel or some such. Judging by its effects on solid rock, that had swept the place clean of either side.

Then, after the thunder of the roof's descent, there must have been silence: a victory of sorts for those who would never know. Samuel idly wondered if that triumph only existed now there were witnesses to it. Try as he might, he couldn't deny a swell of pride in his plucky species.

For this hadn't been a purely inter-human struggle: the adversary bones were plainly... other. They might well be akin; roughly the same stature, feigning similarity by flickering torchlight, but they weren't the real deal. Also, those who'd come after had visited their race-hatred on the human dead, nailing bodies to the wall in demeaning postures. Vestigial smoky-red tunics still hung there, but the owners had long since escaped, liberated in skeletal form to the floor.

Samuel was returned to the present by the sounds of muttered prayer. Some of the soldiers were on their knees, commending the souls of the fallen (or leastways some of them) to eternal rest. The Wizard was with them. Wulfstan and Cook, in agreement for a change, both stood aloof. Engineers and suchlike lowly mechanicals were widely reputed to be infected with scepticism.

'Alright, settle down,' said Trevan, just loud enough to interrupt. 'That's enough of that....' He couldn't really afford to cause offence but there was a time and place for piety.

Gradually – though finishing what they'd started - everyone got back on their feet. Samuel had his box of soldiers again.

'So, they were coming back from down there,' he went on, pointing. 'They might have already achieved their aim. We're no longer wandering blind: we can follow and see.'

That passed for good news in the present context and the column reformed with slightly enhanced zeal. Samuel wanted them too occupied for wondering how they might prevail where elite troops hadn't. The march recommenced, scrunching on skeletons.

Ones and twos of the long dead dotted the succeeding corridor, some still tangled in now eternal combat, but within sixty paces they petered out. Then the only sounds were muffled boots and the tap-tap-tap of Cook's inkstick keeping count.

Finally, there was another aspirant-cavern like the one they'd just left. Death was there also, but in a manageable single dose. One of the *demi-demons* they kept meeting in effigy form was here in the – recently live - flesh. The corpse was nailed to a cross and inappropriate scriptural analogies occurred to most present.

It was therefore a relief to look beyond that and see a set of broad steps commence their descent in the far corner. Alongside were more of the upward snaking burrows, complete with hot pork aroma, but they barely detracted from the discovery. There seemed no other exit from the chamber and thus their way forward was clear.

It remained clear for all of five seconds. Then the burrows excreted a tumbling mass of problems. Troublesome choice returned.

The creatures arrived in silence, providing scant notice by the scrabbling of claws. It was when they hit the floor and boiled forward that the screaming began. Every circular mouth, brimful of needle-teeth, emitted the same piping sound and the human party was deafened. Fortunately, there were no orders to drown out just yet, for Samuel was thinking.

They were a rabble, landing in knots of skinny limbs - and undisciplined as well, fighting each other to arise and get at the enemy. However, they had numbers - the burrow shafts continued to discharge them in a torrent - and animal speed besides. They soon filled the ground with milk-white bodies and reaching hands, blocking the way to the stairs.

Samuel had seconds to decide whether to fall back or fight through. For the moment his men stood, although shocked, but that might not last.

Whatever the case, the hell-chorus was too loud for complicated instructions; he had to lead by example.

The corridor they'd just traversed looked empty, even inviting. It might just lead back to daylight via a fighting retreat into the days to come. Ahead were opposition and the unknown. It wasn't hard to choose. Trevan charged forward.

'To me!' he shouted, but might as well have saved his breath. No one could hear him. Though they could hardly miss his advance or the flash of his gun.

The bullet caught one creature square in the chest, throwing it back and knocking those behind down like skittles. That dissuaded them for a space, even carving out a brief interlude of quiet. Then the shooter followed his shot, stabbing with a seax. Two who felt it liked sharp steel as little as the rest of God's creation and went off to reconsider. Amidst his preoccupations, Samuel got the notion these things had grown unused to stout resistance.

True or not, they were up to seeing one man off, and soon sprung back. He was at the extremity of torchlight and so saw everything distorted by shadow. Whereas their saucer-eyes, fringed by incongruous long lashes, surely harvested every drop of light and beheld him clear. Also, Samuel was alone and they were legion.

Trevan's comrades watched him drop the first few; they noted the pause and then the recovery. Each had their own inner debate. For a brittle second it might have gone either way, but then they formed column and forged in his wake.

A whole volley of shots shoved the beasts aside like the strong arm of Jehovah. Something akin to that same limb, though the Wizard's own creation, pinched off two heads. The victims ran around awhile, spraying their fellows with orangey-green ichor – though without provoking undue dismay. Samuel found space to wonder what other sights had so inured them to horror. Gunfire increased the mad noise to pain level as powder smoke obscured the scene.

There was the narrowest window of opportunity to pass. The soldiers' blades dealt with dazed survivors in their way and then the path to the stairway was clear. Samuel shepherded the column along, startling himself by his officer-quality behaviour. They had to shift fast. A new breed were coming down the burrows now: the same shape but visibly more mettlesome. These had an orange tint to their hide and carried flint knives. They looked at Trevan and gibbered their hatred.

'Team of two,' he told the rearmost men. 'Hold the stairhead.'

To his amazement they obeyed him, not even protesting when he slipped past.

'Cheerio,' he thought. Army-bred blind obedience did have its uses.

Their sacrifice gained the rest a whole minute - maybe two. Samuel practically pushed the column down the steps. From behind he heard pistol discharges, then tumult, then quiet. It lasted long enough to inspire high hopes but then was spoilt by the distant rattle of clawed feet. They were coming.

At that low point Samuel realised he'd been mistaken: that they didn't *really* know the way. A downward route had just been their provisional objective. Happily, there was no time to lament.

The stairs ended in another landing. It extended way out into darkness, hinting at vast expanse. The right-hand wall was studded with little stone-built cubicles, most likely the confessionals where monks had come to admit their clutching-at-straws sins. They would have made good cover from which to ambush their pursuers, but for some obscure reason Trevan didn't want to take refuge there.

A corridor bisected the row of boxes and Samuel led the way to that. He thought it was probably the course of greater wisdom to just keep moving. An ambush might mow down the first few waves now hammering down the stairs after them, but there was no way of knowing how many more came in their wake. Samuel had a vision of infinite reinforcements pouring from the burrows like ants.

In any case, it transpired that the 'confessionals' were already occupied. Some demi-demon offspring, little spindly creatures on tottery legs, came out to inspect the visitors. Their presumed nurses, obese and myriad-breasted variants of the males already seen, waddled after them. Any remotely in the way were slashed aside with knife or sword.

They were moving at a jog now, a perilous pace on an ill-lit unknown route. Several times men fell and half stunned themselves. They were granted a few seconds to revive, failing which, as Samuel put it, it was *'best o'luck'* time. That incentive seemed to aid recovery. There was also need to ignite new torches as the originals now guttered low. In that pause and brief absence of the sound of their own feet and laboured breath, they heard heightened screams from the pursuit. They had discovered their dead children.

The *lucifers* flared and replacement torches burst into life. Samuel had them throw the old ones back up the corridor. Combined, they made a decent, if obviously failing, barrier of flame. Trevan recalled reading that wild animals didn't like fire. On the other hand brute-beasts didn't fabricate and carry knives either - but it was worth a try.

Quite how much so was proven seconds later when a oversized example of the foe leapt undaunted over the blaze. Fortunately, it proved to be alone. The rearward soldier shot it full in the face and the dead or dying creature toppled back onto the likewise expiring torches. It sizzled briefly, and then ignited in a *whooof* of noxious gas.

Philosophers had long speculated that the demi-demon races predated Man and were examples of God's earlier, less loving, handiwork. Certainly, this type seemed to be more inflated sausage-skins of life than close-knit muscle and sinew. There were (feeble) aspects of cheer in that.

In the absence of any other encouragement, Samuel seized upon it. They had spare torches for just one more renewing of the light and were emptying their brace-of-pistols-each too fast. Plus they were unlikely to be granted a respite for leisurely reloading.

'They die easy, lads,' he told all, when echoes and smoke permitted. 'Save your bullets: use blades.'

That was easy said but even he didn't relish letting the things get closer than need be.

They pushed on at increased rate and the corridor enlarged into another library – kind of. Someone had nailed the monastery Bibles, works of great art and age, higgledy-piggledy to the walls. Everyone noted it but there was no time for either rage or rescue. Nevertheless, the message got through.

Next came eruption into an even greater hall. The centrepiece was a huge throne which looked secreted rather than made. Bright orange pelts (Samuel spared a second to ponder those...) and rough cuts of meat were spread before it. The 'symbol' was everywhere, in every medium.

'The *'scriptorium'*, I think,' puffed Cook, who really was earning his keep. ''Tis usually found near the abbot's rooms.'

A squeal of elation banished such scholarly thoughts. At the doorway one of the orangey warrior breeds had caught up.

One soldier returned and screwed a seax deep into it. The squeal produced was soon drowned by some internal flood. Then, from out of view, a stone hammer descended to shatter both human hand and knife. Fortunately, help was nearby to put a shot through the doorway and deal with the offstage threat.

'Away!' said Samuel. 'Column to me.'

The injured man, clutching his jellied paw, rightly expected no allowances to be made. Stoically quiet, if deathly pale, he rejoined the ranks as Trevan took them off at reckless pace. They sprinted round the empty throne and offerings, up to the end of the hall and, mercifully, straight to a way out. Behind, in the returned darkness, they heard the arrival of the hunt.

'Abbot's office,' said Cook, again locating them. Even in these circumstances he couldn't subdue the tone of professional pride. It was then Trevan decided who had definitively won the contest and was top-dog engineer. Wulfstan failed to muster even a dismissive sneer.

In a presumed spirit of mockery they'd retained the abbot's desk, and then re-employed its fine surface to sacrifice things on or use as a latrine. Sandwiched between those layers of cack and gore and coin Samuel noted the familiar Bible-nailing statement again and, what was extra interesting, some mistreated maps.

Still more fascinating than those though, were the shots directed at the column. Two of them, quite distinct, more like musket-fire than pistols. Both missed, but not by much. Trevan's first thought was to speed away, his second that demi-demons did not use firearms. The third spiralled him straight back to his first: namely that bunched torch-bearers in the dark made a lovely target.

'About turn,' he shouted. 'Skirmish order. *Crab's claws.* Fire at will.'

It was untried formation but worked well. Strung out in line they presented less of a barn door to aim at. Also, the extreme left and right soldiers, at the very fringe of illumination, could edge along the walls and maybe deal out unexpected blows.

So it proved. Three more shots followed in their direction and junior-engineer Cook, so full of promise, became also full of lead, dying silently. Yet it would have been worse were they still grouped close. Samuel was then pleased to note his side's reply via powder flashes from either side of the chamber. A grunt and thud from beyond the doorway tokened reward.

Best of all, Trevan found he'd *had it* with being chased about. True to form, he decided to seize the moment.

'Forward!' he said. 'Kill!' It sounded *good*.

It also took the opposition by surprise. Samuel heard a panicky debate (with lines for both man and beast) from just out of sight. The toss was still being argued when the human wave hit them.

Samuel was first through and used his remaining pistol on the rank orange body he blundered into. Accordingly it went away . Then, stumbling over one of its fellows and treading into the squishy body, his outstretched knife encountered resistance which shrieked and flinched. He was dimly aware of others hacking wildly to either side. Two more shots were fired nearby. Samuel looked up and saw a corresponding number of monsters lifted up and flung away in ruin. Then the chain of reflex actions was jarringly broken. Suddenly there was nothing pressing to do: they had won. Five bewildering seconds of flurry had gained them the door.

Trevan wondered if the more practised soldiers experienced it thus, or whether they could impose sequence and sense? Nevertheless, he still felt he'd done well enough for a first outing, all things considered. However, fresh challenges now arose: like seeing an enemy stream away from you in flight. That was an intoxicating sight and temptation to rashness.

'Hold fire,' Samuel ordered, trying to sieve the excitement out of his voice. 'Except... except for that one.'

He pointed to an apparently man-shaped musketeer scampering off into the gloom of the 'scriptorium'. By now the rest of the party had arrived, improving visibility with their steady torches. A soldier took advantage of it and shot the fugitive in the back. The target went down and skidded forward with strange grace before coming to final rest. His gun did even better, skimming some extra yards along the floor.

'He had pals,' said the injured soldier, indicating with his good hand one of the corpses by their feet. A boot turned it over. The deceased had fallen atop his musket.

'Certainly looks human,' said Wulfstan. 'Looks Devon, come to that.'

First and foremost, Samuel reckoned he looked a mess, courtesy of the bullet in him, but otherwise the engineer's description was sound.

'Do you mean to *say*,' said the Wizard at his most disdainful, observing their surprise, 'that you thought this was just demi-demon stuff? Haven't you been waiting for their officer corps to come onstage?'

Plainly they hadn't.

'Save us,' they heard him mutter, 'the people I have to work with....'

There was no time to frame a reply, for the Wizard was immediately obliged with fresh corroboration. Commotion signalled new arrivals who cared nothing for discretion. In a new development, these carried their own torches, shedding a fitful, greenish, light.

'You four,' Samuel stabbed his finger at the designated men. 'Reload. The rest: stand until we see their numbers.'

The newcomers sounded numerous and angry. At the very edge of earshot Samuel thought he could hear human - and other - voices in conference.

'Be quick about it,' he added, needlessly. Those he'd instructed were fairly tearing at their impotent guns: even the injured man was lending what help he could.

Between the two zones of light there was a patch of twilight spanning much of the 'throne room'. The Wizard wandered off into it before anyone could stop him. He'd evidently seen something no one else could. His speaking loud and clear made Samuel wince. Surely they'd just shoot him down like a dog?

'Mr Brannigan?' called the Wizard. 'Stop skulking. Come out and face me.'

There was no reply, although the screaming of the demi-demons increased in volume and pitch.

'Brannigan! I'm talking to you, you pathetic bum-stroker! What's the problem? Are you a man or-....'

'There is no call for abuse,' replied a bulky figure, detaching itself from the dimly seen throng, 'however factual. In fact, I hunger and thirst to meet you....'

The figure strolled closer and they saw that his dress matched his voice and demeanour. A Piccadilly dance-hall dandy, albeit more fleshy than the norm, was somehow transported into the bowels of the earth. Ditto the tones of London genteel society.

Samuel felt sorely tempted to blast them both but, fascinated, for the moment held his hand.

The pair were within yards of each other now. The dandy exaggeratedly quizzed the Wizard, not troubling to hide mounting disgust.

'I don't believe I've had the pleasure,' he said. 'Though such billows of meat surely preclude much *pleasure* in any case. I wouldn't be surprised if you were as virginal as a-....'

The Wizard snapped up his right arm and formed a fist surrounded by crackling light. 'Brannigan' matched it and thus revealed a similar talent. The two hands approached, their auras met and merged. Within seconds all amusement drained from Brannigan's face.

'I don't...,' he stuttered; reluctant but obliged to speak. 'I don't... understand.'

'You wouldn't,' the Wizard crowed. 'Mott smuggled me in from Rome. I'm his secret weapon - or one of them.'

He seemed to exert additional force. Brannigan winced.

'Good, aren't I?' said the Wizard, perkiness personified. There was no reply.

The lively light was now seeping back up Brannigan's arm. His carefully coiffured hair was beginning to stand aloft, strand by oiled strand. Stitches from his embroidered frockcoat were coming unpicked.

'Stoke high the fires of Hell!' laughed the Wizard - and made a final effort: a head-butt that stopped short of impact.

Holes melted in his enemy's silken garments and red seeped from eyes and ears. Brannigan gave one small cry, a whimper of submission, and then fell backwards like a toppled statue. Samuel could not decide if he was imagining the wisps of smoke.

The Wizard returned as though from a particularly scrumptious lunch.

'He didn't merit his standing,' he told Trevan. 'Renegades are often over-rated, however infamous. I suggest you shoot now: whilst they're still in shock. And incidentally, I am *not* a virgin.'

Samuel preferred not to think about that, but he did see that the opposition were shaken - and more to the point, bunched and lit up.

'Fire!'

Eight shots followed, in two volleys of four. The enemy ranks became gratifyingly gap-toothed. The Wizard joined in with a lobbed projectile of thought. It landed amidst them, producing screams. A single shot came back but did no harm.

The Wizard raised his hand to stem Trevan's likely questions - and laughed at the resulting cringe.

'Don't worry: you're safe from me. And you shall have your dull-dog explanation, albeit in haste. We knew of him, but not till today the *where* of him. The manner of his defection caused a certain scandal – but it and he are now quelled. And yes, a magician's thoughts are like his calling card: detectable to his fellows from some distance. And no, he wasn't entirely without talent, considering. Satisfied?'

'Is he dead?' asked Samuel.

'Worse. I saw him glimpse the gates of Hell and heard his eternal howl commence. One was tempted to freeze him then, at the extremity of pain and fear, so that he might know the state longer. I resisted: Christian charity and all that.'

'What now?' Samuel was shocked to hear himself relinquish exclusive command, but couldn't help it. '*Mundanes*' were often undermined by their first encounter with tooth-and-claw sorcery.

'Now? Well, *now*–...,' The Wizard's superior tone was drowned out by an all-pervading roar from nearby. That first keening was joined by a second and then a third. It was pure savagery and hunger and Samuel had never heard the like. The Wizard apparently had. His ruddy face turned ashen, his smile became resigned.

'Now?' he whispered, once the sounds abated. 'Now we die....'

Trevan tracked the direction of his gaze. A group of larger shapes had lumbered into the far chamber: lumpen figures like two fat men melted together. They were surrounded by a cloud of smaller forms, implausibly skinny, their stick-limbs clicking a brisk drumbeat against the stone floor. After them came a group of human musketeers, though these now seemed an almost negligible problem. A glimpse of orange reinforcements in the background merely restated the bad news.

Ignorance could sometimes be an advantage in matters magical. It was now the Wizard's turn to be at a loss, whereas Samuel merely saw more targets.

'Reload,' he ordered.

'No.' The Wizard's countermand was so soft yet so final as to demand a hearing. 'No point. But let's spin it out. We go.'

Whereupon the magician abandoned all restraint and his companions too, swiftly shifting for himself along the directest route away from the foe. Authority was abdicated back into Samuel's hands and he felt the return of will. The party were turning widened eyes towards *him*, not the Wizard's broad back.

'Follow,' he ordered. 'For the moment.'

They turned in good order and raced back, flowing through the alleged 'abbot's office'. The Wizard was awaiting them at the far door. From rearward came the sound of stamping, tapping and booted pursuit.

The next room was much like the one before, if less thoroughly ravaged.

'The abbot's chapel,' said Wulfstan, self-indulgently usurping the deceased Cook's role.

He was probably even correct, though they had little enough time to check that. Nearby was a double bed, newly vacated by the looks of it, with silken - though obscenely fouled - sheets. A marble dildo, likewise stained, lay on the pillow. At the far end was an altar, now drowned in innumerable layers of thick black and red gloop. Atop was a fine, gold, 'Whore-of-Babylon'; the naked lady herself astride a six-headed, cock-studded, steed. At any other time it alone would have been an answer to Samuel's dreams, once melted down and resold. Now it was just a taunting part of the furniture, useless even as a barricade.

'Close the door,' ordered the Wizard, who now seemed just amused by it all, 'and I'll weld it shut.'

Trevan was chuffed to note nobody move.

'Do it,' he seconded. 'Let him.' They obeyed.

The Wizard was too far gone to register the slight. As soon as the barrier was swung in place he span his podgy hands in faster and faster motion round where a lock ought to be. Singing rapid gibberish to himself he then tied an invisible knot.

It was a solid door and muffled the sounds from beyond. They could just about hear the approach of heavy strides. Then silence fell.

Suddenly the door blazed white. There was the smell of flash-fried meat. The previously heard 'famished roar' was repeated, carrying on further up the scales to convey agony.

The Wizard's smile failed to convince himself, let alone anyone else..

'It'll take two, maybe three, goes from a *padfoot*,' he admitted. 'But no more....'

'A what?' asked Samuel, feigning mere curiosity.

The Wizard didn't/wouldn't hear.

'And they've raised up *marook*: those'll sneak in somehow.'

'I *said* '*what*'...,' Samuel repeated.

'Constructed men,' the magician spat, impatiently. 'Indestructible. And a Padfoot's only part this-world. If you're taken they say it-....'

'Enough!' ordered Trevan - and the Wizard complied. They had sufficient problems to hand without inciting imagination to make more. 'So, we move on?'

'I should.' His old adversary no longer sounded much interested. He'd obviously made his own calculations. Samuel added that to the charge list: he'd no patience with despair.

'Column: to my lead,' Trevan commanded. 'Stragglers: you're on your own.'

That was only fair enough and they set off with morale brittle but intact. It even survived a second thunder-crack and glow of light from the door behind. This time the yowl of pain was less prolonged.

'Strike two. One to go!' said the Wizard (in-between puffs), in mock-merry voice.

Praise be, there was an inviting avenue of escape, a corridor opposite the sealed but buckling door. They took it and pelted down the ensuing route. It curved back and forth like a serpent and was paved with mummified body parts. They trod them into dust underfoot.

There was no notice of the door's surrender, only the return of the pursuers' song. They were clearly both fleet and familiar with the way, for soon acclamation celebrated each sighting of their prey. The corridor's convolutions made the glimpses brief, but they were gaining and grasped every chance. A lucky first shot took a soldier away from all his present woes. Another stumbled over him and had to be left behind.

They could have saved themselves the shame of such callousness. Wulfstan was no longer keeping count but around four-score gasping paces on, harsh geography brought the curtain down on their writhings for life. The path passed through a high arch and then ended, protruding a few pointless feet over an abyss. Samuel - just - skidded to a stop.

'Cack!'

His heartfelt comment on fate journeyed into the void - and was met with laughter. Down below flared into abundant light.

Trevan had been to the opera - once. It was in London, with Mr Farncombe, back in the days when Samuel was still trying to impress. He recalled little of the ordeal save being in the dark, perched high above the action, wondering how on earth he'd come to this.

That memory now returned.

Beneath him, a great audience had gathered for this final act and every face was turned towards Samuel Trevan.

CHAPTER 36

One soldier, nobler than any of them, said '*Oh, sod it!*', fired his last pistol into the crowd, and then followed that up with his body. Both struck home, both caused injury, but produced only hilarity from the unafflicted. They then applauded him as he lay broken and expiring on the hard ground.

Meanwhile, above, the rest of the invaders allowed themselves to be taken - at the very moment their mission was fulfilled.

The 1702 expedition *had* been successful. Spectacularly so. Nothing remained of the area where the high altar once stood, save for a smooth scoop out of the floor to mark the cleansing explosion. Deep and matching scars in the walls and high ceiling testified to its force. Those who came after had been obliged to build anew rather than pervert the old.

Trevan and co. were hauled back from the ledge by humans: ordinary looking West-country folk bar their hot eyes. The weirder members of the hunt were drawn off by rough orders, to cavort and howl their frustration in the background. Samuel was thankful for that if nothing else.

He'd considered a last stand and all the clichés about selling life rather than giving it away, but the moment passed. They'd seen how far that got their predecessors. When it came to it Trevan found he preferred little hope over none.

The others were taking their lead from him again and so went along with being abused and bound in ropes that shone with grease and other things. The Wizard had some kind of amulet put round his bull-neck and instantly an indefinable part of him was snuffed out. The threat of sorcery being put to rest, the enemy visibly relaxed. Then those captives saying their prayers were particularly battered.

There transpired to be a quick way down to the underground cathedral; a concealed door just a short space back along the corridor. They stumbled or slid down the ramp thus revealed, arriving a third of the way along the chamber's length; a tangled, undignified heap to be booted upright and into order.

Those hot eyes - above hungry smiles - were *the* common feature, even more so than the uniforms. Otherwise, the hundreds present looked drawn from every place and calling. Samuel spotted the full gamut from workman's cords to silken dresses peeping out from beneath the universal grey gowns.

Their previous captors had not followed them down but there were new volunteers in plenty to rush forward and hold them fast. Their hands caressed even as they pinched and gripped.

That brief glimpse from above assisted Trevan to make sense of the scene - and being trussed so firmly there was little else for him to do. Towering above all, high into the vaulted roof space, was the mound of rubble erected where the altar once stood. A mixture of rocks and carved work, held in a secreted matrix, it rose to a narrow point four or five times man height. Resting precariously atop was a huge quartz-stone, fashioned into the semblance of an eye. Directly behind, the same ovoid shape but much magnified, formed the entrance to a cave hollowed high in the far wall. Straining his vision, Samuel reckoned he could see the brackets for the former altar-screen all around it. The blank eye now stared out from where saints and Christ-in-glory once faced the congregation.

In fact, saints were conspicuous by their absence. Either they'd been 'rescued' by the explosion or else expelled afterwards. Ditto the rood screen and choir stalls and almost every other pious feature. New figures now occupied the wall niches: animals and men or mixtures of the two, rendered in some black substance, engaged in equally black acts. A few, the more honoured in position and execution, did not indulge but stood in attitudes of serene detachment, extending their arms. Their truncated arms.

Samuel was naturally fearful of his circumstances: held in multiple grips like a pig on its last walk, and buffeted with anti-blessings. Yet he retained control till spotting the broken crosses. The central monument bristled with them but many others, just as mutilated, randomly adorned the walls until lost into the murk above. He'd not seen that symbol treated thus before, not ever, and though it shouldn't mean anything to him any more it did. It took that to bring home how far these people had travelled from normality. More than a lifetime's journey.

It had been a mighty church once - and still was for a new confession; a veritable underground Exeter cathedral. The star-map of torches and tar-pots all along its sides and walls barely lit its extent, leaving only the central candelabras descending on thick chains to spread a zone of perfect illumination. Samuel pondered how all had been ignited at once to greet him, and reluctantly danced around the answer of sorcery.

Confirmation of that came when, with one accord, the wall of people in front parted as though compelled by magic. Gliding down the avenue thus cleared there approached a stately party of both sexes. They trod the air inches *above* the floor, the pale bare feet not troubling it for support. Calm gazes and beatific smiles regarded the prisoners all the while, quite unlike the humid yearning of the mob. They differed also in their gowns of blander grey, and in their want of hair and hands.

A few others, wearing smoked glasses, apparently lacked sight instead and were led by the rest – as best their own affliction allowed. These bore before them the orbs through which they'd once seen.

The foremost and oldest, a skeletal man, glided straight to Trevan. He gazed into his prisoner's eyes and within seconds Samuel submitted. He couldn't stand against such impossible serenity. It was also unpleasant to note the shrivelled things strung round the man's neck and recognise them as amputated fists. Most of the new arrivals wore them. Trevan's head needed to be forced back to eyes-front.

The old man raised one smooth stump and gently stroked the captive face. He seemed more loving than hostile.

'Undiscouraged one,' he said, in tones of pure Somerset. 'Sooner than expected one; uninvited but welcome guest. We are here for you. Come to wisdom!'

'Wisdom,' confided another, coming closer, 'is sweeter than life.' She might have been a beautiful young girl once, before she was starved and mutilated.

'*Bogomils!*' boomed a familiar sarcastic voice from along the line. 'I know you - and you are *Bogomils!*'

The old man's smile did not falter at all. He travelled sideways to hover inches from the Wizard's face.

'Correct,' he said, as though delighted with a pupil's leap of reasoning. 'Just so. Loving followers of Brother Bogomil: or '*buggers*' as you see fit to term us.'

'For such you are.' The Wizard was steady and defiant. Samuel didn't think he had it in him.

'For such we are,' agreed the old man, not in the least offended. 'Or at least those of us who are not yet *perfecti*. We eschew the flesh of the other god and sow our seed in barren soil. The cycle is thus broken. It is warming that you know so much of us.'

'I ought to,' said the Wizard. 'For I've *warmed* many of you. In Rome I had the honour to be a Palatine inquisitor. We burnt you in batches!'

Samuel fully expected that would do the trick and send them on by the shortest route. He'd almost welcome it, for this recent news had puked all over his last spark of hope. He knew of this sort, recalling Father Omar speaking about them (in decently vague description). They were life-haters and numbered amongst the *dualists* (whatever that meant, but it was something bad - though not people who fought duels). They were kin to the Cathars, who'd thought this world had no good in it (and so were done a favour when crusaders sent them all to the next one). The classification and family tree didn't bode well.

Samuel tried to wonder what Melissa might be doing right that moment, so that his final thought might be of her. There were tales of messages being passed that way in dire extremity....

Meanwhile, the handless man didn't mind at all. None of the floating ones did, nor any of the congregation in earshot. They merely smirked or mouthed quiet prayers.

'Doubtless they died thanking you,' countered the old man. 'Forgiving you and blessing you for their release. Is that not so?'

The Wizard's silence admitted the uncomfortable fact better than words. Then, one foe vanquished, the old man air-walked back to Trevan.

'We preach Christ-uncrucified,' he told him. 'We serve the one-of-two gods whose domain is pure spirit.'

'Whereas you,' said the emaciated girl, 'are slaves of the meat god. Therefore, out of our love for you and all, we desire to give liberation.'

That sounded quite promising but the Wizard spoilt things – albeit with more cause than usual.

'She means kill us, in case you haven't twigged,' he said. 'You're kindly offering to free us from the material world, aren't you?'

The girl's eyes didn't shift from Samuel, though they shone brighter and her smile widened, as if offering her sweetest favours.

'Where you can sin no more,' the old man confirmed. 'For doubtless your sins are already great. *Happy* cattle-humans, we give you the chance to curtail your wickedness!'

'Sleep and sin no more!' chanted some of the front row, in what was clearly a familiar worship phrase.

The less stoic among the captives began to struggle, but to no avail and at the expense of dignity. Main speaker looked a little disappointed at the lack of thanks.

'Compose your last words,' he said, in a harsh voice that sounded more like his everyday manner. 'Bring 'em forward.'

The relative quiet ceased, replaced by an insect buzz of anticipation. Cacophony was added at the fringes by admittance of a tide of demi-demons, flooding in through burrows as well as more conventional entrances. They swarmed on the edges of the assembly, a white and green and orange surround to the sea of grey; pushy but careful to keep a respectful distance from acknowledged racial superiors. Their scent preceded them.

Trevan and colleagues were dragged along a Red-Sea-style pathway, and all along hands competed to touch and fondle them, particularly their behinds and parts. At the very least it was an undignified way to go. Wulfstan spat great gobs of retribution but that only seemed to further excite them.

'Sin no more! Life breeds sin!' was repeatedly hurled at them - with apparent good intentions.

'Two-godders!' someone shouted back. 'Cross-snappers!'

Samuel admired the Wizard's nerve in trying to goad, but it had the same small effect as the engineer's spittle: a few grimaces, one or two frowns, but nothing more. He was bundled forward just like the others.

The gunpowder scoop around the monument was full of dead things and bits even the demi-demonry couldn't stomach. Fortunately therefore, being made to bow low on its edge, honouring the white quartz eye, proved just a pause in the procession when they feared being pitched in. The congregation of hundreds followed on, shuffling in their wake.

There was a ramp of packed stone leading up to the sister-eye in the wall. Around it waited groupings segregated from the generality. A few were further handless ones, too weak to move and laid out on stretchers, but others were a contrast and challenge to all else on view. Samuel caught brief sight of flamboyant silk attire, and found irrational consolation in it. Even worn and muddied colour was seized upon in the present context: proof of a warmer world continuing elsewhere.

Then closer proximity snatched even that fig-leaf of comfort away. The wearers were unnaturally tall, and their milk-skinned faces regarded him through unkind eyes of gold.

'*Soul*-less! *Soul*-less!' taunted the Wizard, employing childish singsong tones. It nevertheless seemed appropriate. The Church discouraged belief in Elves, or even mention of them in anything else than nursery rhymes.

Moreover, he'd at last found a route under the skin of his captors, for they seemed wary of offence against these guests. The Wizard's chant was curtailed by slamming his face into the dust of the ramp. A knee then pinned it there, diverting all his energies into acquiring breath.

His comrades soon joined him in the same position, though more gently. Samuel was permitted to abase himself at his own speed. From that low position he saw a pair of uncared-for, uncherished feet float by and proceed further up the ramp.

'God-of-spirit,' their owner intoned, 'equal but better, we-....'

It seemed that they weren't used to any swift response. When the darkness beyond the 'eye' dramatically burst into life the assembly voiced both joy and surprise. Samuel used their distraction to raise his head and blinked against the yellow light and furnace wind. Sweat raced facewards to do its job and got thanked with instant evaporation. The skin of his brow felt stretched thin, permitting the sudden heat easier access inside his head. Beyond visions of steam rising from his brain thought became difficult.

If Samuel had it bad then the air-borne 'Bogomil' five paces forward suffered worse. He clutched (as best a handless man may) at the place where his heart sheltered below displayed-for-view ribs. Plainly struggling, he gulped in air like a landed fish.

'Lord... mercy! Be moderate... to... us.'

He may have been heard, for the problem abated. 'One-yard-from-a-bonfire' became a nice sunny day. The old man staggered back but regained his poise. The annoying smile returned.

'We are-....'

Whatever it was didn't think much of him, for he was rudely interrupted again. An end-of-the-world scale noise came forth from the eye, streaming back hair (if applicable) and raising hands (if available) to ears. The floating ones, being both hairless and handless, had no such recourse and were much afflicted. Samuel was glad to note thin rivulets of red emerge from the foremost speaker's ears.

The sound then lessened and resolved into voices, albeit a choir with inhuman range, speed-screaming up and down the octaves. There were words within but Samuel couldn't make them out. Even when the babble slowed and merged into a single tongue there was still no sense to it.

The congregation thought different. Trevan twisted his head left and right and saw that they were greeting the message with simple glee. The floating skeletons in particular had lifted their stumps in worship and allowed tears to flow.

Then the tirade ended in something even Trevan could understand. Plain English words concluded a long speech in... something else. *'Sweetest quarry...,'* he heard. *'Sweetest quarry. Hello!'*

The air before the eye throbbed with the aftermath of greeting and expectation of more, but mere quiet followed. Only occasional ecstatic sobs from the assembly marred the silence.

Belying age and condition, all fired up with zeal, the foremost speaker threw himself down and lay outstretched – but still inches off the floor.

'We have,' he said, 'oh one-of-two, we *have* your favoured titbits. Out of selfless love we bring you succulent delicacies. Forgive our subservience to your eternal enemy and the urges of this wretched *meat!'*

Samuel could not see it, but behind him the flock mortified the flesh, scratching and pinching their bodies till blood came. The more pious or impatient achieved the same end with little knives. Meanwhile, the prayer continued.

'Accept our repentance and virtuous disgust with Creation. Accept, we beg, words from vile mouths and likewise meditations from gory hearts. May they be acceptable to you till we rise again to cleaner life in heaven.'

The searing heat came again, but only for a second. It was taken as a blessing and approval. The old man floated erect.

'These came,' he gestured at the flattened captives, 'to poke and pry for their Church of Christ-crucified. Bestial stumblers from the world of beasts. Take them up, we beseech you, that they may be saved and enlightened!'

The mad sounds returned, even wilder than before, and then ended in sighs of contentment. Samuel could only see part way into the eye but it was clearly seething with light and life; the outer lip of a waking volcano.

'The Anabaptists and Unitarians may now wish to withdraw,' said their master of ceremonies. 'Our worship shall be rich and full!'

Some sober-suited figures around the ramp, edgy delegates from other denominations, took the hint and took their leave. Trevan recognised one as the Mayor of Bideford. Even chewier food for thought was the fear in their faces and haste of their feet. Samuel's fate was something they'd seen before and didn't care to relive.

'Come feed! Come feed!' exhorted the floating old man. 'Relish your enemy's children!'

The eye saw and heard and obliged, flaring with fresh energy. An invisible thing, hot and horrible, fell on Samuel's head. Even in the midst of fighting it he perceived all his companions were similarly assaulted. They thrashed and writhed against their restraints.

Now a spider made of burning coals was inside his skull, treading lightly over the brain; inspecting every Samuel Trevan experience; doing a stock-take and making an inventory – or menu. Horror or resistance were equally ignored.

It lasted for both seconds and centuries and then the thing leapt away. An inner Samuel was amused to note pure happiness arrive to celebrate release. Unlike the 'spider', he was able to brush the silly instinctual emotion off.

The rank and file were less fortunate. However unfairly, they'd had been judged one of a kind and were devoured in bulk. Trevan felt their thoughts fly by: the gamekeeper, his London men, the soldiers; catching the slipstream of each life-story as it was sucked out. He 'saw' fleeting images: first childhood and its terrors and consolations, then holy-days and hard work, love and loathing, wives and whores. Even the recent injury to one's hand was relived. Samuel caught resonances of the stone hammer descending and all that followed. Both the pain and fear were lingered over and savoured - and then taken.

Not everything met with approval. Much that might be called fine was left alone or spat out. The feeder did not want to know about the men's families or affection for them. It passed over marital kindness or words of honour kept at cost. Flashes of religious faith caused it to gag as though chewing gristle.

Samuel didn't know how he could be sensing this; merely that he did. All that they had ever seen and been was passing by in review and the receding tide sometimes splashed him. Only some unflattering references to himself made the ordeal more bearable.

The first speaker presumed to stand (or float) right in the flow of memories and was lost to ecstasy.

When it was done, the victims were left soft and sheep-like, purged of anything remotely abrasive. They smiled into the ground and were freed from understanding. Men came to lift them up and lead them by the hand, like trusting infants, to the eye in the wall. Then, one by one, their unresisting throats were slit and the bodies thrown forward to vanish beyond. The crowd acclaimed each death.

Samuel's opinion of Wulfstan soared when, seeing the lie of the land, he opted to buck the schedule. Leaking memories of tough training and the humiliations of churl-hood, the engineer struggled to his feet and charged the inevitable. The floating man and his guards tried to stop him but were too late or feeble. With a final - and eloquent - Saxon curse Wulfstan dived into the eye and left the world behind, still substantially the man he'd been.

If he could Trevan would have clapped. He couldn't - but fully expected something similar from the congregation. He was wrong. On the contrary, they howled outrage and impotent hatred. Samuel then realised how outrageously pious these people were. A minor deprivation to their god outweighed even an inspirational act.

They were not willing to be robbed again. Untold hands rushed to pin Trevan and the Wizard hard to the ground. The 'spider' returned to Samuel's head, but waited, merely quivering occasionally in anticipation. He wasn't sure whether to be glad or sad at being left to last.

The Wizard forced his head round to face Trevan.

'Bye!' he said, brightly. 'Can't wait! I go from here to a better place.'

'Plus they're only saving *me* the trouble,' Samuel answered, holding back grudging regard. 'I was going to murder you myself.'

'Likewise,' replied the Wizard, smiling. 'Never mind. Some other time maybe....'

He went noisily and thus Trevan learnt that a magician's life left scars. Marked out by obesity, prone to loneliness, Rome had taught the Wizard things he'd rather not know. Then those skills had been put to full use - and not always in the cause of niceness. All in all, Samuel sensed far more kicks than caresses. Now it had to be relived, right from plump boyhood in Hull to terrible today. Also, he'd lied: the Wizard died a virgin.

When all the bad was taken there was little left save residual faith. They took the magical-dampener from around the Wizard's neck before slitting it, and then down he went, still gouting blood, slung into the eye.

'Final and most favoured, oh inspirer of our disturbance,' said the foremost speaker, floating close and caressing Trevan again. 'Who are you? Whence comes your lust to die?'

'I'm Pope Simon-Dismas, baldy,' said Samuel. 'Now get on with it.'

Humour was wasted here, let alone sarcasm. It was less than weightless. It instantly withered to nothing on meeting the air.

'Are there more of you to follow, or will this discourage? Who inspired such folly as to foul our peace? Will you speak or shall our god drag it forth?'

Trevan raised his head the maximum permitted.

'I can see right up your nose...,' he said.

That same nose flared, proving its owner wasn't quite as serene as he made out. However, there was no time for retribution, for the force from the eye grew impatient. Foremost speaker deferred to it instantly. The 'spider' within Samuel sank intangible teeth.

First titbit selected was the farewell to mother. Samuel lived again the news about his birth, then standing before her grave. It had been agony at the time and ever since, but now, gingerly probing the spot, he felt nothing. Memory was still there, he could behold the scenes, but they were sucked dry of content. He was no longer involved.

That could almost be construed as a blessing, but when the searing touch alighted further back he rebelled. The thing had found his first meeting with Melissa. She and Samuel - and it - stood in Church Twitten, in a variant replay of that pivotal time. Samuel felt it exult at finding such juicy strength of feeling.

'NO!'

It proved (just) possible to contest the theft. Samuel defended exclusive possession of that past moment. Repelled, the 'spider' drew back for a second - but then returned. It bit deeper and penetrated. Samuel's most precious possession started to drain away.

'*Please...!*'

Pointless. Another instance where saved Samuel-breath would have been better.

A new figure approached stage left. Trevan's watering eyes saw only the start of long legs. Trousers of some gold-coloured hide grew ragged over cavalry boots. But any, *any* distraction was welcome.

'Help!' said Samuel, hardly recognising his voice: let alone the sentiments. 'Someone help me!'

The reply was that of an intelligent machine; cleverly constructed but not sentient.

'Possibly....'

'Do not meddle!' That was the prime speaker, anxious to rein in his fury, though not entirely successful. 'The salvation journey is begun!'

He was ignored. The legs stooped and brought a parchment-pale face almost to Samuel's level. He now looked into almond eyes of gold. Trevan loved those eyes because whilst he searched vainly therein for pupils the feeding suddenly abated. He wanted more than anything to hold that a-bored-farmer-studies-a-sheep gaze.

Finally, the slim face arose and scented the air. It sought and found something.

'Your mother...,' the Elf mused. 'Oh, I *see*. If only....'

Trevan was frantic; the conversation must be maintained.

'What?' he gasped, pushing his face off the floor. "*if only*' what?'

The foremost speaker wanted to act but daren't. He and the other floating ones spluttered impotent anger.

'If only we had not met.' There was real regret in the Elf's voice, a vehicle not accustomed to conveying feelings. 'You are inimical.'

That seemed the literal truth. Whenever the Elf leant close to Trevan, a trickle of golden blood descended from his long nose. Also, he began to cough: a harsh unhealthy bark.

'No!' It was the foremost speaker's turn to protest now. 'You cannot!'

'Alas, I must.'

The Elf laid one hand on Samuel's shoulder. The guards' pressure, the 'spider's touch, went away. So too did the Elf's fingertips, blackened to a crisp where they touched Trevan.

He surmounted that great pain to speak.

'You will come with me.'

It transpired that even there and then the bottom of the barrel wasn't reached. Samuel had *sang-froid* to spare and ever after he was proud of that.

'Any port in a storm,' he replied.

There was an onrush of boots, outcry and even shots, but they each soon faded, no longer of concern. Trevan and his new friend had put such worries to one side.

CHAPTER 37

They were still present, but... displaced - at one remove from the resulting chaos. Likewise, the exact same scene was before Samuel's eyes, but now drained of colour and substance. He was no longer obliged to be involved. When a sabre traversed his midriff he flinched and cried out but came to no harm. The swordsman sought him in vain.

A more effective Elven blade put Samuel's bonds on the floor. Detached from him, they could then be seen and people rushed to the spot, slashing the air round about. Trevan weathered the futile blows and stepped away.

'You will travel in our realm awhile,' said the Elf. 'Welcome to the real world.'

Reinforcements arrived and formed an Elven circle about them as they passed, ghost-like, through the even greyer than hitherto congregation. Once, one of the floating ones somehow detected an Elf and laid stumps on him. Therefore a dagger was driven up into her palate and she died, albeit with obvious signs of gladness. Likewise, just before they left the 'cathedral', another sorcerer was brought up. He was able - with clearly painful effort - to glimpse the escapees. One of the defensive perimeter expired in cold blue flame, to be left behind without a second glance. Retribution or even taking notice appeared beneath elder-race dignity. A distant bell began to toll the alarm

They left by a different route, through scenes of horror, holocaust and pentagrams, traversing both the anarchy of demi-demons' nests and strict order of human barracks. Trevan came to appreciate his folly in blithely challenging this veritable town underground. Passages and tunnels travelled vast distances and to surprising places. Whole communities lived out pallid lives there. What presumption to think he'd win through when the Pope's finest had not! Such a warren was a project for an *army* and Grand-Wizards, not a businessman.

On the other hand, visiting was much easier when blessed with a sure guide and invisibility. As they went the Elf supplied what he called *'pre-emptive explanation'*. Though Samuel's life might be worth saving it seemed that his conversation was distasteful.

'These 'Bogomils' have stumbled upon something,' Trevan was told, 'and think it their god. We conduct occasional joint projects. Do kindly keep your distance.'

Samuel regulated his pace to put more room between them, since close proximity clearly caused distress. He'd still not adjusted to wraith-like status and passing *through* people.

'Will that suffice?' asked the Elf, more in hope than expectation.

'What? To explain?' answered Trevan. 'No, not really.'

'Tsk.'

'I mean, what do they *want*?'

The Elf pondered the most concise way of answering that. Samuel's overwhelming relief started to give way to vague offence.

'To quit their enemy's creation by the straightest path,' came the reply, 'short of suicide. Which is forbidden. Apparently. Meanwhile, they may freely abuse the flesh, theirs and others, just as they wish, free from so-called 'sin'. Please excuse me....'

Staunching a golden flow of blood provided cover to curtail speech, and Samuel's conscience prevented him from pressing the point. He noticed that the trickle froze upon the Elf's sleeve. Plainly it was a frigid substance that circled their veins.

Accordingly, the rest of the ascent passed in silence, save for the muffled sounds of ineffectual pursuit and the fading toll of that sonorous bell. They emerged into the light via a tunnel unknown to Trevan's painstaking surveys. He saw that Welcombe was nearby and had to resist the temptation to crumple earthwards and kiss the turf. Even torrential rain was greeted with joy. Evidently, summer downpours did not exempt the Elven realms.

At the Forge Inn the Sicarii took both inhuman visitors and seeing

Samuel again in his stride. Trevan and escort returned to mundane reality on the main landing, yet somehow, though snug in his room, the Negro had prior notice. However, when they entered, his defensive stance and levelled pistol were graciously abandoned as though accidental. Indeed, he seemed already on good terms with the Elf spokesman.

The two approached – but only moderately close - and made pretence of shaking hands at a distance. The Sicarii leant round to clue Samuel in.

'We've met before,' he explained, matter of factly. 'England is a strange country to me, so naturally I contacted the main players.'

Samuel saw the sense of that but hadn't until then fully realised the high strangeness of his own land.

The Sicarii resumed his interrupted shave. His guests found perches on the furniture and bed. The room was now crowded - but not convivial.

'I didn't know *you* were down there,' he said to the leading Elf, who remained standing and centre-stage. 'You never mentioned....'

'You never asked.'

Oddly, that was accepted as entire explanation.

'Just you?'

'No.' The Elf shook his head. 'We were merely passing. It's mostly your kin – estranged kin. Bogomils.'

'Oh, *them*.' The Sicarii carried on scraping away, flicking soap-froth from the blade into a basin. 'Much simpler. Any objections?'

'None. We are no longer friends. Burn them out. I will show you how.'

'Thank you.'

'We saw fit to save this one.'

'So I see. Why?'

The question was ignored as irrelevant. Again, the Sicarii refused to take umbrage; neither his perma-calm nor razor wavered. Instead, answer came to an unposed but more acceptable query.

'The rest were lost,' said the Elf. 'He will tell you the details. I shall leave him with you but he must be removed soon. They will seek him. All those who know of him must also go. There can be no trail.'

'I'll see to it,' said the Sicarii. 'But I repeat, why such concern for a *'newcomer'*?'

'We have further business with him. I'll call to collect. Meanwhile, he wants all kind of words: *explanations* even.'

'Naturally.'

The Elf smiled: a horrible sight. His teeth were all canines.

'To you, maybe,' he said.

And with that they left, just as Samuel, in their company, had left the 'cathedral'. It felt uncanny: having to assume their presence, departing but unseen. Both humans agreed to leave an interval of silence. Then, the more assured or impatient of the two, the Sicarii spoke.

'Well, *did* they?'

Expecting more of a welcome, Samuel felt disinclined to stretch himself.

'Did who what?'

The Sicarii left off shaving and somehow, just by pausing, implied that cut-throat razors could have all sorts of uses.

'Meet me half way, Trevan. I meant the 1702 expedition.'

'Then yes.'

'And?'

'They did and then died.'

'You're willing for our magicians to probe your bonce and check that?'

'If need be.'

Some final test was passed. White and gold teeth flashed in a smile.

'God is great! Now Mott will be pleased with you. And *I'm* pleased with you. You shall be *indulged*.'

The Sicarii took up a linen towel and started wiping lather from a newly smooth face. Then he went to the door and bellowed down the stairwell for tea.

'Now, my hero,' he said, returning, 'apparently you want explanations. Very well: are you sitting comfortably? Then I'll begin. The Bogomils are....'

****

'... somewhen in the tenth century. A town in Macedonia called Bogomila is said to be his place of rest, where he went to his maker in the fullness of years, sadly later rather than sooner. A former shrine to him there has now been erased by his Imperial Majesty's triumphant forces.

This turncoat shepherd and his disciples polluted their way through the Eastern Imperial provinces of Bulgaria and Thrace, even penetrating (*le mot juste!*) the capital, Constantinople. They foully preached an equal and co-eternal opponent to Almighty G*d, and ascribed this world to his evil invention, rather than the gift of our loving Father. It was also held (one shrinks to repeat it) that Christ both survived and descended from the Cross, to strive against his evil older brother, *'Satanael'*. The invention of such baseless fantasies is still a cause for nauseous wonder.

They accordingly abominate the symbol of the Cross and take all opportunity to slight it. This is one means by which you shall know them.

... the latitude permitted by despising the material has appeal to depraved sorts, and in this manner they recruit. No action towards the flesh (deemed the enemy's realm) is considered sin, as they seek the swiftest route home to the purely spiritual hereafter. They likewise shrink from the proper functions of marriage, reluctant to create new life, and thus practise the sin of the Cities of the Plain. This is another infallible token. In the same manner, they are joyless beings, refusing G*d's myriad blessings such as wine and laughter and the pleasures of progeny. Their stolid misery may well mark them out for you.

... the most thoroughgoing are their *'Perfecti'* who radically renounce the material by vow. Ever after they abstain from intercourse and eating flesh or any wholesome food. Some fanatics have even been known to truncate their extremities or self-destroy their G*d-given sight, blasphemously citing Biblical justification (Matthew, ch. 18, v. 8-9: *'if thy hand or thy foot offend thee, cut them off, ... thy eye offend thee, pluck it out.'*)

[NB. Inquisitors should prepare refutations against such satanic subversion of Scripture. 1 Peter, ch. 3 v. 15: *'... be ready always to give an answer to every man that asketh you a reason of the hope that is in you with meekness and fear.'*]

Likewise, whenever possible this so-called elite sorcerously eschew the ground, to symbolise severance from this earth. These sort should not be hard to spot....'

From: 'THE MALEFACTOR'S FOOTPRINTS: BEING A GUIDE (for Inquisitors & Reformers) TO PERVERSE SPIRITUAL STATES.

Prescribed for use in the recovered territories of Magyar-land, the provinces ascribed to Buda & Pest, the former Turk-vilayets of Transylvania and Bosnia, the Free-cities of Szeged, Pecs, Debrecen and Kecskemét, and such steppe land beyond the Danube as may come back to the Christian fold and the custody of his Imperial Highness.'

Resurgam Press. Vienna. 1848. Issued under Imperial licence.

Withdrawn from circulation by Papal decree *(Judex Crederis Esse Venturus)* 1902.

****

CHAPTER 38

Foremost speaker's busy-ness was interrupted by his god's return. The eye burst into splendour again.

He and the other floating ones quit their torturing of the negligent and sped back. The voice did not wait for them.

'*Where is the one?*' Plaintive tones were a shocking novelty. It sounded childlike and lost. '*Why was he taken from me?*'

Then, in contrast, the god-venom spat forth in unprecedented quantity. Scores were immolated or dissolved.

The dispersing congregation wavered - and then rallied, raising hosannas of welcome. There'd never been two such proximate visitations. This might still be the promised day of wonders.

The ground-spurners crossed the zone of devastation, skimming over the joyful dying. They were rapt and oblivious.

'Lord, lord,' shouted Foremost Speaker, 'we are blessed! Are we also forgiven?'

There was no direct answer. Speaker's breath was always deliberately shallow (to show his disdain for the enemy's element), but never more suspended than now. Distant ructions from beyond the eye mirrored his own concern. It was bad enough that their pious solitude and pure worship be disturbed, or that they should quarrel with ancient allies. These things were surmountable; ultimately just seepage from the silly, pointless, world above. Time would erase them in due course. What Speaker really feared, a tiny worry possessed of giant strength, was that they had *erred*. It shackled him to the meat-medium and would not let him soar. Maybe they had missed the crossroads and now strode forever along a wrong way!

Foremost Speaker punished the thought, exiling it along with other distasteful memories, like those of breeding and family, and the days before perfection. Yet sentence was disputed. The notion of ice-and-despair hammered for release with increasing force; its brain-cell prison door began to splinter.

Then three words completed the work. Worst-suspicion acquired freedom and reality and mockingly capered about, turning everything to bitter regret.

'*He was here*!' confirmed the visitant voice from beyond the eye. '***He was here....***'

'And we let him go...,' said Foremost Speaker, before his god could.

****

'He is our nemesis.'

'Then remove him.'

But the old Elf woman only spoke in jest, just to provoke. She knew better.

'The Ubiquitous Spirit would not permit, Joan, as you well know. Our survival is merely tolerated: nor can we expect favours. You yourself were present when that bargain was struck.'

She persisted out of mischief.

'So? We are tied but vermin are not. The life-haters were about the deed. You prevented them.'

Samuel's recent saviour languidly swerved that dart also. His tribe-sister had a real talent to ferment trouble. He admired her for it.

'That same Spirit would have thwarted them in some other way,' he said. 'Better the creature be in our charge.'

'In our debt,' said another of the older-breed present.

'Under our guidance,' added a third.

The Council was in broad agreement, as always. Free from all passions, they could reserve conflict for entertainment only. Their rare civil wars were painstakingly choreographed.

'Very well,' Joan decreed, speaking for all. 'He shall be kept from them. And diverted. Find out what the brute-beast wants. Then force-feed it. Stupefy the thing with fulfilment. Thereby save us.'

The Elf emissary nodded.

'It should be possible...,' he agreed, as indifferent as ever.

'Though the life-loathers will fight,' said Joan, smiling. 'Their search will be ravenous.'

There was a second allotted to mild amusement. Then one Elf round the table succumbed to open laughter: a thin and unnatural noise. His lapse proved infectious, but they subsequently excused themselves. The balance of power had changed: that much was now accepted. Even so, there was still - grotesque - humour in lower life like humans presuming to oppose their betters.

****

Father Omar felt the seizure coming. It gave fair warning in a moment of pure clarity: some final sunshine before nightfall.

He made it to his bedroom chair and so secured dignity for when he was found. Then there was time for the 'Last Things', like thanking God for this concluding mercy and all His other blessings; of which there'd been many. He also prayed for forgiveness - and received grounds for optimism on that score.

His brain was next commanded to release a clear memory of Jerusalem the Golden. It was just like being there. Only better.

Omar was still beholding those beloved domes and spires when a giant pinched his heart.

CHAPTER 39

The Sicarii somehow knew they were revisited, although Samuel couldn't see how. The Negro was prepared when the Elf was suddenly amongst them again without even a heralding displacement of air.

'It's all *go*, innit?' he (or maybe it?) said, in unkind mimicry of how humans sounded to him.

The Sicarii also proved up to imitating London gutter-tones.

'And even when yer get there yer don't fancy it, do yer?'

Abandoning the *Forge*'s supper, he walked over and shut the door to his room.

Trevan forced himself to remain seated. His alarm had been momentary. There were callers he'd rather see, but days of confinement with the Sicarii meant any diversion was welcome. Trevan had had to recount his story till it wore thin; plus the Negro's company was like continually handling lit fireworks.

The Elf slid a folded document onto the bedside table. It looked ancient though uncared for; thin and stained skin from some large animal. Once expanded Samuel saw that it was a map or diagram.

'About your lost monastery,' said their visitor, *sans* greeting or preliminaries. 'The way-barriers are still maintained against you. But there are also ventilation ducts. Even they do not know them all. This plan does. Pour down sufficient combustibles and the Bogomils will burn.'

'Thus saving the Inquisition the trouble,' said the Sicarii, taking up the sheet and studying it with unfeigned admiration. His eyes tracked its extent. 'Phew! There's *miles!* Good job Mott stockpiled plenty of *greek-fire.*'

Their guest leant over his shoulder.

'And increase the proportion of oil to tar and sand, here, here and... here. It should find living things on which to adhere. Their roaming death agonies will spread the flames.'

'Thank you, I'll see to it.'

'Do so soon. They are preparing to move.'

'Action this day.'

'Splendid. And speaking of movement: what about this one's associates?'

He meant Samuel, although his subject didn't even merit a look.

'Done,' said the Sicarii. 'Rounded up. Compensated. Placated. Intimidated. On their way to the ship. This hostel alone waits cauterisation.'

'Eh?' Samuel hadn't heard such orders given - but neither had he ever seen the Sicarii sleep: something he *must* surely do sometime. So, anything was possible. 'What d'you mean?'

'I mean your family,' answered the Sicarii, 'your employees and all those you've impinged upon here. Trevan Farm's already to let. This place will have new owners. A bright new future awaits them one and all.'

'Where?'

Samuel could tell the desired response was '*what's it to you?*' For the moment though, he was important (for some reason) and had to be humoured.

'Malta, probably.' The Sicarii shrugged. 'Or Rhodes, maybe: wherever they're needed.'

'How about the Bosphorus?' Samuel suggested. He'd thought of old Walter the London Watchman, and then of rifles and Tartars - and the Trevan Farm crowd in life-and-death competition with both.

The Sicarii considered the idea - with growing favour.

'Yes..., there's pretty lethal. That'd do, I suppose. Why not?'

Samuel was obscurely pleased. The least member of the family had finally made his mark on the rest. It didn't occur to him that there were others - bystanders - who deserved better. His former Whitechapel colleagues, for instance. Samuel could at least have sorted Egypt out for Jimmy Smith. But he was only thinking of the bigger picture – and himself.

'Have you got all you wish for from it?'

It was still a shock for Trevan to realise that the Elf was referring to him, and that the Sicarii went along with such contempt for his own species. '*It*!

'I think so, thank you: enough for my report to Mott.'

'Then I'll take it, as agreed.'

'Fair enough.'

The Elf reached out to Trevan: who could not prevent a flinching away.

'One other thing - before you go,' said the Sicarii, halting the pantomime. 'Just what *is* it down there?'

The Elf, gratefully it seemed, left Samuel alone. He looked down from his great height advantage and bared sharp teeth at the papal agent. It may have signalled amusement.

'Just a modest afterthought,' he mocked. 'A casual request for knowledge that has eluded your... Church for a thousand years.'

'But worth a try?' said the Sicarii, smiling.

'We are never unawares or careless, human.'

'No, I know that. Still; *is* it their god down there?'

The Elf considered blessing the dark, drawn, face with an answer.

'No,' he said eventually. 'No, it isn't. They are deluded: not even deceived but deluded.'

'So, what is…?'

The Elf repented of his generosity and grimaced at the ceaseless opportunism of 'vermin'. Did they never stop writhing about for advantage? Where was their *dignity*?

Samuel's shoulder was again grasped in those crab-flesh fingers and they jointly left the scene. Once more the touch caused distress to its begetter, made skin slough off, and gold-bearing veins to sunder. The hold was maintained with difficulty - and not an instant longer than necessary.

Trevan sought to free himself, not so desirous of rescue as before, only to find implacable strength within that grip. He was borne along like a kitten.

Liberation only came when they were beyond the room, out of the Sicarii's searching gaze. His captor then actually staggered back from him, glad to put distance between them. Samuel noted it and was pleased.

'I just don't agree with you, do I?' he said.

The Elf steadied himself against the landing balustrade and staunched his nosebleed with a ragged sleeve.

'No, you do not. You are *inimical*, as I've said.'

'So, why the concern? Am I for the chop now? Is that why he let you take me?'

This caused a wry smile set amidst golden smears.

'The predator-vermin could hardly prevent it. And I am conducting you *from* harm, not to it.'

Samuel hid the cavalry charge of relief under a brusque question.

'Why bother? Why help mere little me?'

It all seemed terribly clear and simple to his companion.

'Because others would make you more inimical. Then I would not be safe at any range.'

The Elf set off down the wide staircase. 'Follow me.'

'At what distance?' Samuel queried, determined to push his luck.

'Five paces is optimum. My influence will persist, whereas you will barely nauseate.'

'What about conversation?'

Trevan saw the elegant shoulders shudder.

'Only if you insist.'

Insults aside, it was memorable stuff, passing *through* the *Forge*; its space and staff and clientele alike, unseen and unperceived.

'Can I touch?' Samuel had in mind a parlour maid he'd treated as invisible till now (which was somewhat ironic given his present state). Her soft-palmed charms had been just one of many stern self-prohibitions: secret tests of dedication now utterly redundant.

'Not really,' the Elf answered. 'They – or perhaps we - are insubstantial. But the female may feel some mild sensation.'

That gave Samuel pause.

'How… how did you know I-....'

The Elf strode on and right through the soon to be former-landlord.

'Oh, farmyard thoughts are easy,' he said, a Parthian shot delivered in passing; no credit claimed for his good guess. 'They assault the air like shrieks.'

In the front courtyard resided an old all-purpose handcart. Samuel's luggage had travelled in it when he first arrived. Directly the Elf touched the handles it regained colour and solidity, incorporated into their present realm.

'Take this. You will need it.'

It sounded ridiculous. Come to that, Trevan was sure it *looked* ridiculous (could anyone see), but he obeyed, trundling the little cart along behind his leader.

It transpired that everything Samuel required had been right in front of his nose from the start. The Elves' treasury lay unguarded in open view, dumped by the roadside on the way into Welcombe. Perhaps the name should have supplied a clue.

Most was either bullion or gems. The Elf gestured him forward and Trevan needed no second prompting. Using his strong arms like scoops, the cart was soon awash with wealth - much of it antique and/or beautiful, although Samuel didn't pause to admire. When the first frenzy was past, he took to selecting the more negotiable stuff, like coin.

He was confident of being surveyed with disgust - but reckoned that a price worth paying. It didn't take a Hebrew goldsmith to tell him he was loading a fortune per minute.

'Enough.'

He'd been right: the Elf voice was twisted by distaste. Samuel ignored it in favour of packing down and filling odd corners.

'No more!' Disdain had soured into anger. Trevan turned and caught the departing signs of associated expression. Then, entire master of his face, the Elf resumed his usual bland mask.

'Can I keep it?' Samuel asked, pretending to be innocently touched.

'Yes. We intend a secure future for you. Now follow.'

There seemed no question of the Elf waiting for him. Samuel exerted all his strength and got the burdened wheels going.

'It's a risk, isn't it,' he puffed, 'leaving that lovely mountain out in the open?'

'It is removed from your domains.'

'Even so....'

'And is of no great concern to us. The material is easily acquired.'

'Legitimately?'

The Elf was amused.

'What does that mean? But no, of course not: not in your terms. Do *try* to understand. We only demean ourselves with it for vermin transactions, or for our rare children to play with. Only infants and animals like yourself attribute value to such dross.'

Samuel increased the pace to keep up. 'I really should resent these constant slights,' he said.

'But you will not. Amidst the wider opportunities presented you will find it strangely easy to be mild. Also, you are no match for me.'

'I could always come closer....'

'Ah yes, I forgot that.'

'And you forgot to *explain* as well.'

'No, not at all. The omission is quite deliberate.'

It was a dead end. So Samuel turned the conversation round.

'I still can't see why you don't knock me off.'

'No.' Mere agreement.

'And that's something else you'll hide, is it?'

'Yes.'

'Likewise, where we're going.'

'Wait and see.'

The sterile exchange was elbowed aside by Samuel noting something odd even by present standards. Their steps were traversing more ground than they ought - and increasingly so. Though bowing low before a lumbering cargo, Trevan was travelling at better than sprint speed and the colour-drained landscape was fairly streaking past. Which should have been cause for stumbling and sweating, yet he felt no call for either.

'We are not like you after-lifers,' his guide obligingly confirmed. 'Exemption from Judgement removes the obligation to tread each sequential point. Or experience every plodding second. Stay - moderately - close and you will be similarly blessed.'

'It's handy,' Samuel admitted as Bideford and then another, larger and unknown, town flashed by. 'But where are we-....'

'Here,' said the Elf, and they stopped dead, completely untroubled by mundane matters like momentum.

Samuel looked about. It was an English village; simultaneously a typical but also curious one. All the normal sights - thatch and fields, church and cattle-trough - were present and correct, but in addition the place was ringed with raised stones.

Trevan knew something about these: about how the pre-Flood people had erected circles and avenues of rock in which to worship demons, or maybe mark their Limbo-bound dead. Under Mr Farncombe's tutelage he'd read all about them, in books which buried bafflement under flimsy house-of-cards speculation.

Samuel set the cart down. 'Where's '*here*'?' he asked.

'I will not use the newcomer name. And our own is too sacred to relate.'

'Alright then: *why* here?'

Samuel saw that the Elf really had had enough of his company. The white brow furrowed as the brain beneath pondered all that remained to be said - and the swiftest way of saying it. The conclusions came out like bullets.

'Here we tried to teach you true religion, back when you first arrived. After our wars of extermination failed. But that went wrong too; the call of the sordid was too strong for your elevation. Too few would sacrifice eternity or 'soul', despite their drawbacks. However, some of our influence still lingers here. Call it residue missionary spirit. You will be more shielded here than elsewhere. Remain one week and do not stray abroad. There still remain dangers to you that must be liquidated. Meanwhile, we shall send you a gold merchant, one of our hybrids. He will convert your plunder into - I hate this word - *money*. Trust him but no one else. Then go wherever you chose.'

Following so long in Elf company and one epiphany after another, Samuel was almost reluctant to part. Might not normal life now seem insipid by contrast? What relish could there be in watered-down stuff: *'Adam's ale'* after champagne? Even more than death Samuel feared eternal beige.

'Will we meet again?'

Trevan had gained the impression that Elves had little strength of feeling, but a fair stock of it rode on the reply.

'I sincerely *hope* not.'

For some reason that did it where all the other insults hadn't. Good honest anger made Samuel leap forward and grab the Elf by his elegant neck. He was about to punch him in the face (though surprised he'd got that far alive) when it became clear there was no need. In every place Trevan touched, the Elf was burned to the bone. Smoke came from under Samuel's fingers as they visibly melted their way down. Shocked, he withdrew. The Elf fell without grace.

'Sorry!' Trevan always felt that way when he flared and won. Crocodile tears were fine, a permissible indulgence, so long as they came *after* victory.

The Elf would or could not speak. He made one, then another, attempt to rise; finally prevailing via a period on all fours. After a space for recovery he made a weak bow.

'The future arrives in anger,' he said, in a gasping vestige of his former voice, 'and I submit.'

'Do you?' Samuel was half aghast and half wary of being duped. He was still poised to strike.

'Yes. That is what this is all about. We must acclimatise....'

Trevan decided to go with it, never one to withhold his teeth from gnawing on advantage.

'Right then. Well, the stories say a beaten faery grants three wishes....'

The Elf attempted a smile but failed.

'Mere myth, alas.'

'Oh, well... how about three questions then?'

'Or what, vermin?'

Samuel lifted a fist as illustration.

'Another such encounter and I will die,' husked the Elf. 'Our flesh is more fastidious than yours.'

'So?' Trevan didn't really mean that - but it sounded good.

'*So* you would be stranded in our world, forever segregated from humanity.'

'Ah....'

'But I will comply, just the same. Strategy dictates that you be humoured. Clothe your dreary puzzlements in words.'

'What? Oh, right....'

He had to think quickly, but burning questions naturally bubbled to the surface in swift order.

'Well, for one thing: what *is* it down in the mine?'

Samuel succeeded where the Sicarii had not.

'A pimple from another state of being. A random, accidental, intrusion from a sentient elsewhere. An air-bubble in your world's brick, as it were. It is limited and bound and can only look, but it is also occasionally curious.'

Trevan reflected that the older breeds were not so delicate as they made out. The Elf was visibly recovering his former assurance and health.

'So, not a god then?' he said.

'Hardly; no more than its spy hole is a 'mine'. The creature first appeared under your *Bristol Channel* and slowly eroded its way to a better viewing point. It will come no further in. It cannot. Your rulers worry without call. Their monastery project was unnecessary.'

'So it's a demon?' ventured Samuel.

That produced a tired sigh and despairing accord.

'If you like.'

'And malign?'

'Not really. It will do favours and play games with whichever faction triumphs. But it knows the rules - just as we do. Next question.'

'Why am I such poison to you?'

The deep wounds Trevan had made were now 'only' black scars, but their unsightliness seemed to trouble the Elf far more than what went before. He'd drawn up his collar to hide them.

'You are not up to this,' he said. 'With a more educated vermin perhaps....'

'Try me.'

Another resigned sigh.

'Umm... well, I could say that we are borderline diffuse beings, blurred somewhat over the linear time you are trapped in. *So*, we sense the future coming, just as we feel the past die. You are a possible future - and a bad one. The closer you approach the deeper we experience it. And whilst we may not remove you there is hope that you may be moderated. Hence our help and gifts.'

'And don't think I'm not grateful.' Samuel thought it a fair stab at sincerity.

'No you're not,' the Elf batted back in complete confidence. 'Ingratitude is an intrinsic newcomer trait.'

Trevan didn't care for being so well read. 'This future...,' he growled. 'Tell me.'

'A *'revolution'*, in *'industry'*: I will show you.'

One long Elf finger outlined a frame in the air – and thus created a window into... elsewhere. It showed a world of black factories and smoke, of roads and haste. And little else besides.

'The image will be brief,' said the Elf, who seemed to have problems holding it stable, 'since it is far off. Mark it well.'

Trevan did. No one could call it a pretty scene by any means, but it looked like people were *improving themselves*. Samuel saw a go-ahead, prospering, sort of place and he wanted to see more, but the picture soon faltered and died.

'When?' he asked.

'Well, that rather depends on you - and your dangerous energy.'

The reply was prompt enough but unsatisfactory - and wilfully so. Only elder-breed cunning forestalled an angry follow-up.

'This,' said the Elf, hurriedly, 'will be clearer, because closer. Look.'

A replacement view, indeed crystal clear, showed a room Samuel knew well. Mr Farncombe was at ease in his parlour, in his shirtsleeves, washing Roman pottery sherds and far from prepared for visitors. When an ashen-faced Mrs Farncombe showed the Sicarii in, her husband's jaw descended like a trapdoor. Introductions brought only basic recovery and the terrifyingly friendly soldier had to step forward to shake Farncombe's dripping, drooping, hand.

'A brighter prospect, I think,' said the Elf, sweeping the vision out of existence.

'For me, anyway,' Samuel specified, almost daring to hope.

'That was my meaning. For the present it is you that counts.'

'So you say. Is that it or do I get a third question?'

The Elf shrugged. 'Why not?'

'I want to know who still thinks of me.'

'Surprising people,' came the laconic reply. 'But that is not what you mean. You want those who think *warmly* of you.'

'I suppose....'

'Two.' A blunt answer, drawn from lengthy Elven scenting of the air. He looked to be seeking out spoor from the ether. 'I find just two sticky lines of sentiment searching you out.'

'Who?' Again there was the pain of hope.

'One is your vermin-mate. *'Mel'... Melissa?* She is ardent. Must I probe for detail? It is disgusting for me.'

'Don't. Who else?'

'A parent or mentor. *'Mar'? O' Mar?* His spark is fading but currently fixed on you. He is due to depart. Was there some promise made to him? By you? About after his death?'

Samuel's stomach lurched. Acid abounded.

'There was.'

The Elf sniffed for particulars.

'He thinks of it in hope. He meanwhile worries about you. Also, he is recalling some foreign city.'

'Will he last a week?'

'No. And I warn you: though he yearns for it you must not go to him.'

Samuel thought about that - but not for long.

'I'll just have to miss him then.'

So be it. That was the way the world was. Trevan told himself pragmatism outweighed sentiment and was - almost - consoled.

'Presumably,' the Elf said, amused, 'you believe you'll meet again in your... 'afterlife'.'

'No. But I'll raise a statue to him in Lewes.'

Again, the Elf tuned in to a private transmission.

'That is not what he wants.'

'It'll have to do. I'm not arranging things I don't believe in. Masses won't serve his soul or memory. Better he should be remembered in the real world....'

Deliberately trailed bait. But because he didn't care what men thought the Elf didn't take it.

'Then our bargain is fulfilled,' he said.

Samuel was thinking of all the things he could have asked. But the chance was gone. No point begging. Let it go.

'Yeah, reckon so. Sorry about the... you know....'

He indicated the wounds he'd inflicted and, with a nod, the Elf implied they were nothing. By now it was nearly true.

'My actions postpone the future and I thereby heal myself,' he said. Samuel could not be bothered to comprehend.

'Well, thanks for everything....'

'Oh no, thank *you*, vermin,' said the Elf - and seemed to mean it. He forced himself to touch the human and they thereby parted.

Samuel found he welcomed the return of normal colour and shade, even if knowledge of the Elf's unseen presence detracted somewhat. He decided to assume that that problem - like so many others apparently - was speedily removing itself. Happily, the treasure hadn't followed suit. He sped to lay tight grip on it.

For a moment he basked in the renewed warmth of the sun, and likewise his revived good fortunes. Then Samuel Trevan squared his shoulders against the world and wheeled his cart down the main avenue of megaliths, into Avebury and the years to come.

****

****

Some days later he met a girl there, whilst out studying the stones. She proved as interested and informed as he, and likewise in a holiday mood. It seemed auspicious.

Up to then he'd been on tenterhooks, standing sleepless guard over his hoard till the promised Elf contact arrived. When he did, Samuel's red eyes learnt that Elf and human blood could prove an unhappy mix, blending faults from both. The stunted, corpse-cold, banker had no greetings, no conversation, and he bargained hard. When he and his armed servitors left, consistent to the end without a smile or farewell, Trevan held a thrice-checked draft in his favour. It was for more than he could spend in one lifetime, even trying hard. Samuel then slept the clock round, dreaming of celebration.

In consequence, this chance-met girl was just the ticket: curious, easy-going and good company. Just like him it was her first day off for ages; a break from drudgery at a nearby big house. Her being Welsh explained away the strange accent and reverence for the past. Few local girls would choose to spend their precious free time studying old stones. Ever cautious, Samuel looked long into her sloe-eyes but glimpsed no gold. Then that prolonged gaze decided it for them both.

Back at his lodgings he had her three ways, and then they had claret and guinea-fowl. Then they did it again as dessert. To himself, Samuel briefly queried her inventiveness and noisy delight, but put that down to her origins too. The 'Cymric arts of love' were acclaimed by men of the world throughout Christendom. Even procurers for the harems of the dual Caliphs had heard of them. So it seemed only natural when for whole moments at a time she was rampant and bestrode the wild frontier of strumpet-dom - but without ever crossing over. A certain fragile innocence to her was the tart sauce on top.

The only shadow over their encounter came with dusk and the girl's natural melancholy at thoughts of an early start to skivvying tomorrow. She'd got just a day off whereas Samuel was starting a whole life off.

What remained of Trevan's good heart was touched just as his grosser parts had been. He brushed back the black curls drooping over her moon-face, and for once the rush of impulse was not opposed. It was only the first of many such he could now indulge: a whole neglected army of them, long deprived of rations.

'Must you go?' he asked. 'In fact, *don't* go. No need. Stay. Tell you what, Jane - that's your name, isn't it? Marry me if you like....'

He shocked himself as much as her. He *heard* his voice saying so, but none of the expected 'common sense' cavils stampeded in its train. That wasn't like him either.

The offer hung in the air. It had put her mouth into an *O* of surprise. Then, presumably by way of consent, she slowly lowered it onto Samuel's cock. Which rose to the occasion.

Trevan recognised a contract when he saw - or enjoyed - one. He felt god-like and deserving of everything. Having risked so much and endured so much and worked so hard, it was now life's long overdue turn to fit in with *him*. He'd have whatever good things it could give - and not stint on them either. And if there remained any opposition, or should new problems arise, then his wealth or the Sicarii would sweep them all away. Or *crush* them.

So, what if this week he married this delicious wench and set her up somewhere convenient? There was no one to see or object, not to hand nor in Heaven. Who was around to say nay?

That being so, he'd damned well *do* it.

And next week he'd go to Lewes and marry again.

****

Attendance at Father Omar's funeral Mass was phenomenal. Half Lewes town turned up, and former St Philipians, many of them now nicely established, came from all over United England. The Bishop preached about good shepherds, the orphanage choir sang Purcell's sublime requiem for 'King James-the-True', and even prim people so far forgot themselves as to fight to touch the bier as it left St Pancras' priory church. A sharp summer shower, like the sudden fall of tears, did not disperse them or dampen their fervour. On the contrary, it seemed fitting.

Samuel would have enjoyed that honourable scrimmage and been first and fiercest among them. Not a few looked for him there but looked in vain. He had a pressing alternative engagement at that precise moment: mounting his Welsh fiancée.

Someone who knew Omar well had acquired some soil from the Holy City. A handful of it followed the deceased into the grave, landing on the shrouded face. Then the grown-up orphan boys, weeping or grim according to type, piled on the more homely but almost as loved earth of Omar's adopted Sussex.

That night the Town taverns did poor business. Some even shut as a mark of respect. The dead priest's name was commended to God from numerous devotions, and would be (though, naturally, at rapidly declining rate) for some time to come.

The Cathedral recalled deceased priests of the diocese every year at a special Mass. Their collective labours and dedication were thus brought to the Deity's attention, but there were just too many for individual mention. Likewise with St Philip's Orphanage 'founders-day' observances, when prayers were said for teachers past.

Omar left behind a pitiful sum, not even enough to purchase one year's *obits*; but his executors concluded that must be by choice. It was all too like him to prior disperse what little he had in charity.

Truth was, people assumed Omar Abdalhaqq ibn J'nna would not be long in purgatory in any case, and therefore unneedful of prayers. Perversely, the lack of arrangements was a tribute to his memory. They meant well. It simply did not occur to anyone that his wishes might be strongly otherwise.

Father Omar had entrusted that knowledge to only one other person - and died with misplaced faith in him intact.

****

****

THE SECOND
CONFESSION

'Nothing is true, and everything is permissible.'

Traditionally attributed to Hassan i Sabbah, *'The Old Man of the Mountains'*. (1034?-1124 AD)

****

'We should be careful

of each other, we should be kind.
While there is still time.'

Philip Larkin. *'The Mower'*. 12th June 1979 AD

****

****

JOHN WHITBOURN

****

****

THE YEAR OF OUR LORD 2020

'I am fain to find God's city,
That lies hid in Sussex hills....'

'The Hidden City'. Arthur F. Bell.

****

'For Lewes Town like Heaven is,
And Heaven is like Lewes Town.'

'St Peter & St Paul'. Sheila Kaye-Smith.

****

****

CHAPTER 1

'Dragons.'

Samuel looked again. It was always the same answer and he wouldn't have it.

'What d'you mean?'

'They be dragon's teeth, boss - what the Flood done for. I often comes across 'em.'

Trevan trusted the foreman in all his other professional judgements. There was no good reason to come over doubtful now. And yet....

He examined the array of regularities bound up in a matrix of chalk, tilting the thing this way and that, trying to make sense of it.

'So how come we don't see them nowadays then?'

For once the foreman's curiosity was dimmed. Show him an old-time knapped flint or pottery rim and he'd be over it like a sailor on shore leave, but this just failed to fire him.

'I already says: they drownded.'

Samuel persevered.

'What: *all* of them?'

'Pre-sumably. Noah wouldn't have 'em aboard. I don't blame him. Same with the giants and unicorns and such.'

'Evidently.' Trevan's tone was desert-dry.

Foreman plainly thought the place for such relicts was the spoil heap from whence Samuel had recovered it. *He* wanted to talk about the marvellous discoveries they'd made atop Mount Caburn; not freaks God had turned a cold eye on.

Trevan perceived that and was gentle. He said no more and replaced the small block - though noting its position for later. Unbeknownst to Foreman, his master had a fair collection of these mysteries now, gathered from all over.

'Show me this burnt stuff then,' he told his employee, and followed in his enthusiastic wake.

The labourers had cleaned and cleared the trench for inspection. They were a picked team, winnowed free over the years of secret scoffers and those bemused by careful delving in the earth. Some of them had actually 'caught the bug' and took a keen interest in their work. Trevan had been known to arrange reading classes for the best and then lend them books. He could - when he wanted - be a good boss. There was fierce competition for his post-shearing, post-harvest, seasonal employ.

The wind blew strong - as it usually did - across the top of Mount Caburn, and Samuel had wisely left his stovepipe hat down in the carriage in Glynde. Thinning hair a-dance he approached the hillfort's first rampart and was guided to the ladder down. He was no longer the explosion-waiting-to-happen of youth and young manhood, and there were crystal-conglomerates starting to restrict the freedom of his joints. All the same, he was still up to descending a deep trench unaided and assisting hands were batted away.

'Bugger off! Who d'you think I am: Old Father Time?'

That got some grins. Master was in a good mood and on fine form today.

Samuel reviewed the section, strata by strata, and finally approved. It had taken him untold curses and some sackings to get the diggings done as he wished, but now they knew how. Sides had to be plumb-bob straight and the base-layer brushed speck-less. He'd hammered home the point that Mother Earth would only answer precisely framed questions. She had to be seduced with trowel and hand-shovel, not ravished with a pick. Foreman had long ago got the point and then run with it. Now Trevan himself could not have done the work so well.

'Oh, I *see*....'

He'd spotted the thin layer of black carbon concluding the inner edge.

'That's 'er, boss. I reckon the fort was fired. There were a palisade on top and it tumbled down ablaze to 'ere.'

Trevan looked closer. The man was probably right. They'd lifted history's veil.

'And this just above is natural accumulation, I think,' said Samuel.

'Wind-blow and soil-creep,' agreed Foreman. '*So*, she weren't repaired or cleared. The visitors done the fort in and then left her be.'

'What about dating material?'

'Sea-pebble sling stones; nothing else yet.'

'*Belgae* Celts?' Samuel hazarded.

'Reckon so, boss. Caesar says they were slingers.'

Trevan was impressed. Foreman read with pointing finger and moving lips but he'd evidently battled through the ancient sources.

'So, maybe the attackers were Romans?'

'Could be, boss. I propose to take the ditch down to natural and then lift a strip of interior. That's where I hopes for pots and coins - for dating like.'

Samuel nodded. It was what he would have done.

'Good plan. Do it - but send word when you hit bottom. I want to sketch the rampart section myself.'

'Righty-ho.'

Foreman was already scratching at the burnt layer before Trevan was even halfway back up the ladder. He started the ascent cheerful enough but arrived disgruntled at being puffed out. There was always something there in life to spit on contentment.

'What - are - you - lot - staring - at?'

He knew the waiting workmen didn't deserve that and so felt even worse.

'Fine work though,' he added, after pause for breath and when the labourers were having trouble trying to ignore his gasps. 'Visit the *Lewes Arms* tonight: there'll be a pound behind the bar.'

That received a ragged cheer. It was enough for merriment but not oblivion. Everything Mr Trevan did seemed just as carefully judged. They were wary of him.

Work resumed and Samuel was left alone to wander off.

At Caburn's very top there was a view down into Lewes. He stood there and drank it in. For the thousandth time he told himself he'd won - and it still had the power to please.

From there Samuel could see St Philip's-in-Cliffe and the life-size Omar of bronze outside. Within, they'd be working on the St Guy's Day effigy he'd funded; their best and biggest yet. If it didn't win the Orphanage first prize for the third year running Trevan would want to know the reason why.

Up the rise of School Hill and High Street were Southover and Galen House, which he'd got from old man Farncombe and then glorified with marble. The Sicarii had squared *him* - and the Town panel - and everyone. Melissa said her father hadn't regained colour for two days after the Negro's call. Consequently, he'd gone to their grand wedding; apparently reconciled. Trevan and he even had some - halting - conversations in the years that followed, before father-in-law obligingly upped and died. Samuel had arranged a very decent headstone, considering. With the eye of faith, its white angel in St Michael's churchyard was just about visible from here. Samuel gloated over it. It was probably very cold in the ground this morning. He certainly hoped so.

Further afield was his Welsh wife, installed in comfort and Guildford, up in the distant Surrey hills. He'd also got another woman stowed in Pevensey-by-the-sea, whose conversation could keep him with her for a whole evening, even after they'd been to bed. Trevan thought of each - and all the others - fairly often, but they were really, at base (so to speak), just entertainments. The only one he *had* to have was nearby and kept close, currently doing whatever it was she did when he wasn't looking, in Southover.

Melissa had grown in girth just like Samuel (a man of the world complete with expanding equator). Likewise, she'd gone grey and lost her teeth. But there weren't two minutes together, not any day, when she wasn't in his thoughts one way or another. It was like longing for a thing and having it at the same time, *all* the time: cake and eating it: a perpetual festival. And if they hadn't been blessed with children to make things perfect, well: it wasn't for want of trying. Snow on the roof didn't mean the fire had gone out. They'd had - and still had - their fun, and meanwhile Melissa mothered the Orphanage instead. It seemed to suffice. Samuel had never so much as raised his voice to her, let alone a hand. There'd been no need.

It was November the second and an air of anticipation rose from the town like a buzz. From Trevan's vantage point he could count no less than seven huge bonfires in waiting. Everywhere people would be stockpiling fireworks and planning mild mischief. Samuel personally sponsored two of the societies in addition to the Orphanage effort. Lewes would have voted him Mayor if the Church had permitted. It should have been a faultless vista for him to behold.

But Samuel being Samuel, he sought faults to frown at and fight against. There was invariably something if you looked long enough. Today, he found it in the dun clouds over Horsham way. They were going nowhere at present but perhaps...? Trevan wondered if the rain would hold off, both from his excavation and the bonfire jollities.

And speaking of 'buzzes', the annoying inner resonance had returned to plague him. At first he'd thought it mere imagination, but recently that nice notion had been laid to rest. His doctor said Samuel just had to live with it; a real but mysterious malfunction of the ageing ear. And true, the thing was bearable, only an intermittent pain; but all the same....

Even so, considering his years he'd been pretty much blessed with good health. A lot of his contemporaries were already dead and buried. Whereas all he had to contend with were visits from the 'rheumatiz' and times when his parts refused to perform; plus maybe some recent fuzziness of vision and the 'buzzing' business. So, on the whole, Samuel Trevan still functioned just fine, and, to quote an old acquaintance, he was nowhere near *'dead yet'*.

Certainly, he was a figure in Lewes life, perhaps even a 'big cheese'; and no one there slighted him: not to his face anyway. Once, long ago, the Town had spat him out and he'd wandered abroad in exile. But then he'd returned: not as a beggar, not even as a Church charity-boy, but *vindicated*, and with *contacts*, and in triumph. And if they chanced to be contacts he mustn't mention, and a triumph he shouldn't discuss, well, you couldn't have everything. On that first return he'd crossed Cliffe Bridge feeling like a conqueror. There didn't have to be banners and maidens scattering rose petals. What he had sufficed, and the town seemed like his by right ever since that day. Looking back down the years Samuel reckoned he'd *done well*.

Health-related thoughts brought reminder he shouldn't brave the wind too much. Samuel Trevan might no longer believe in God but he had due regard for fate, and a new-ish aversion to tempting it. He'd spit with fury if a streaming cold confined him to bed through 'Bonfire'. He and Melissa *never* failed to see the procession pass, standing arm in arm at the head of Church Twitten.

So Samuel about-turned and quit the fort and view, wordlessly bypassing the dig (save to pocket the 'dragon's teeth' from the spoil heap), taking the steep path down to Glynde village. Haddad the coachman would be waiting there to ferry him back to the warmth of home.

And not a moment too soon either, Trevan admitted, just to himself. Lately, cold open spaces seemed to incite his ear affliction, and even stir up trouble in the eyes too. Sometimes, a newly arrived blurring on the very edge of vision developed instants of expansion, acquiring the power to play tricks; even threaten to take shape. The wind blowing straight down his ears was to blame, doubtless. He ignored it all, confident a mulled brandy-and-cloves made by Melissa's own fair hands would sort things out.

Samuel Trevan took extra care with his footing and overcame these fresh opponents - as he always had every other. So far.

****

'There you go, sir: hot and strong as pitch, just as you like it.'

The hotelier was quite right, both about the tea and Samuel's tastes, but he got no thanks for it.

'And the newspaper, sharpish!' Trevan instructed, and duly received it - slung in his lap. Native Lewesians were a sturdy - to the point of stroppy - lot. They expected courtesy no matter how much money you had. Samuel admired that quality and it pleased him to provoke them - or at least it used to.

What he *didn't* like was blind routine and being predictable. He now realised he'd come to Higham's Hotel most days this week, at about this hour, and always ordered tea. Trevan blamed the January chill and Higham's generosity with logs for the fire. Also, it was a well-ordered, respectable, place, ideal for reading the *'Times'* and local *'Intelligencer'* and wondering what to do next. The mercantile classes of Lewes used it as a meeting spot too. Trevan loved the low whisper of business-talk lapping round, even if he didn't join in.

He saw from today's paper that Mott was on a roll. A trade concordat with the Swedish Empire, ascribed to his presiding genius, would nicely freeze the Scots out of the Northern seas, thus adding impoverished isolation to all their other problems. Samuel wondered whether the

General's ambition even seeped over the border into that unhappy nation, or was it mere mischief for mischief's sake? Most likely the former, because if civil society there finally did go under then the Church might allow intervention. United England, out of the goodness of its heart, could send aid and troops - purely to restore order, naturally. If all fell right, *that'd* be an end to an old story....

Two pages on, Trevan smiled to read *'Edinburgh University in Flames - Mystery Arsonists Again'*. He heard the sound of intricate clockwork clicking into place in perfect working order - and it sounded sweet. Never averse to foxes amok in other people's - particularly foreigners' - henhouses, there might also be something in this for him. Just perhaps. *If* Mott remembered him and *if* an archbishop or cardinal owed Mott a favour, then maybe....

Samuel had these thoughts at least once a week. He wanted his life sentence commuted, he wanted to rejoin the community of commerce whose gossip teased his ears at that very moment. He wished to create again, not just spend. He yearned to go over to the two corn-factors by the fireplace and jostle with them for margins of advantage. General Mott could reinstate him there with just a few chosen words or a dash of his busy pen. That's all it would take. Sorted! Samuel Trevan Esq. would be useful once more: a player in Lewes - and shortly after further afield too.

He brooded over that, eyes glazing over the newsprint. How it galled him to know full well that local hauliers were ripe for reform – or replacement by underpricing. Some of them still used oxen! Given a free hand, those Sussex sleepyheads would all be out of business or working for him within a twelve-month! And as for the English gin trade; well, there was another low fruit positively gagging for someone to pluck it. Too timid to lobby the Crown about crippling Church tariffs; accordingly forced into bed with thuggish smugglers – pathetic! And... and... and *most* of all it galled Trevan that his letters to Mott went unanswered.

The Sicarii was the one he should consult. *He'd* straightened out Mr Farncombe and the whole of Lewes all in the space of one short afternoon in town. The people he'd interviewed that day never spoke of it: an infallible sign of unconditional surrender. Yes, *he* was the one to have on your side. The Sicarii would smile enigmatically and go off and... somehow wipe away the humiliating requirement to report regularly to a brother in Lewes Priory. Just not having to give monthly account of himself would be something. Samuel would settle for that. For a while....

But the Negro was probably long dead by now, or else adventures-in-many-continents past remembrance of Samuel Trevan. And even if memory persisted at all, his name would be only a footnote in a report about something infinitely bigger. No: no one significant recalled or thought about him any more.

'Hello.'

Samuel had already noted the young couple at a nearby table. They stuck out from Higham's usual clientele and were so wrapped up in each other as to flirt with expulsion. A single public kiss between - betrothed - lovers was just about permissible, but these two, good clothes and breeding notwithstanding, were sailing close to the wind. Their mutual passion had been observed and tutted over by the regulars.

For all Trevan cared they could mount one another over the tea-things, but he preferred not to have to watch affection. 'Romantic love' was just an invention of old-maid authoresses. Moreover, it was a lie that didn't last (barring he and Mrs T, of course). Besides which, these two needed feeding up far more than smooching. They'd do better to eat what they'd ordered instead of linking lips or addressing strangers.

'Are you talking to me?' Samuel asked, a welcome-free zone.

'Hello.' It was the girl this time, smiling wider and wider. Meanwhile, her thin arm didn't cease to twine round the beloved. '*Hello!*'

Trevan took pleasure in alarm: suddenly this was no longer normal or everyday. Perhaps they were well-spoken loonies, escaped from the priory bedlam. Or maybe they'd got out of a private asylum, the sort of place where wealthy families dumped those who failed the exam of life. But thereagain, would any warder let them dress so... fashionable?

Mr Higham himself detected matters were amiss and interrupted his cutlery audit. Then the girl's swift-drawn pistol sent him back to it in comic reverse stride.

The couple stood up and embraced across the crockery, exchanging a titanic, the-tongue-as-intrepid-explorer, type kiss. Somehow Trevan sensed it was long awaited. The casually brandished gun meanwhile kept him in his seat, more fascinated than threatened.

'I should have *so* liked to *fuck* you,' the young man told the girl, once disengaged. Samuel had rarely heard such adoring tones. The profanity reached and hushed even the distant beer-tap bar. The yeomanry there gathered round to look on through the hatch.

'In heaven,' the girl consoled her sweetheart. 'Soon.'

Both drew silver bodkins from their sleeves. Loving fingers gently parted shirt and bodice to lodge a needle-point above each heart.

Then they turned their perfect faces to Trevan.

'We are here,' they told him, speaking as one - and then fell forward, screaming in pain and joy.

CHAPTER 2

Since he didn't wish Melissa troubled, Samuel took his resultant thoughts to Pevensey - once the authorities had finished with him. A Justice of the Peace, an outlander from Surrey, had taken his deposition and, finding it supported in every way, was obliged to let him go. Trevan truthfully maintained that though the young people might have addressed him he did not know them. Higham the hotelier further testified as to their general peculiarity, and so that settled things for the moment. A King's Coroner's inquest was called for a week hence and Trevan told to be before it.

Samuel had already come to his own verdict - the most probable and horrible solution - before his feet boarded the carriage taking him away. Even so, he postponed acceptance. The chain of logic to the correct conclusion was long and vulnerable to attack in many places. Happily, there was (dishonest) comfort in that task and Samuel set about it as Haddad whipped the horses to the coast. Since the coachman loved his team dearly that hurt him as much as they, but his master had said to *'shake some action!'*, his face a mask drained of mercy. Poor Haddad had no alternative to cruelty and prayed for equine forgiveness even as he laid on.

Accordingly, they made good time, round Caburn and the gypsy camp at Southerham, pelting past Wilmington and its *'Long Man'*, barely slowing to fling out the toll at Polegate. The broad new road, commissioned to speed His Majesty to sea-bathing and mistresses at Brighthelmstone, made even January journeys feasible. Thus they travelled smoothly until obliged to branch off near Stone Cross. Thereafter, it was back to normal; progress being tempered by caution and great ruts and dips, the ravages of wear and tear. They were fortunate in that the month had so far been dry. Winter often made Sussex roads only fit for ox-carts.

Samuel didn't complain, for at least the lesser pace removed the cursed 'blurring' attendant on him since they left Lewes. Every time he looked from the window an emergent... shape seemed keeping pace with them. It proved so disconcerting that he almost drew the blinds, but once they'd slowed down the affliction fled. The gut-churning state of the Pevensey road was a price worth paying for that relief.

Then Trevan noticed a neat spray of bloodstains down his waistcoat; spurted droplets from the boy or girl's puncture wound. All his troubles immediately returned in formation.

In consequence, Pevensey Castle was an even more welcome sight than normal. Samuel had long ago warmed to the round of its Roman walls amidst the flatness of the 'Levels'. Plus there was a glimpse of the sea beyond. And looming up above the beach rose the *'Wizard's Palace'*: Papal Roman architecture improbably transported to darkest Sussex. This was the official abode of the Thaumaturgic Grandmaster for the south-east and... interesting tales were spun about it. Safely far off, Trevan could just appreciate the *frisson* it added to the scene, a dark mystery he need not probe.

Most of all though, Trevan liked the Castle because Susan lived beside it.

Haddad was directed to the 'Royal Oak and Castle' and given a guilt-inspired half-crown to play with. Samuel left him soothing the team, whispering to them of treats in store. Most of the money would probably go on sugar lumps.

Meanwhile, across the empty cattle-market square was Susan's cottage. Trevan sped off to burst into it - and, very shortly after, into her.

****

She was a hard-working but less-than-lucky young mother of three, left a widow by a lost fisherman. Or so it was assumed. His precise fate and whereabouts were known only to God and the fishes, although scattered wreckage washed up long after supplied a clue. It had been that kind of storm. Standing on tiptoe in Susan's upstairs room, you could see (should you care to) his token cross in St Nicolas' churchyard across the square.

Sometimes, afterwards, Trevan did care to. He viewed the already faded memorial and wondered if the man had gone down beholding the lights of home. And, if so, had that been a consolation or torment? No one would ever know. Then, faced with that dead-end, Samuel's thoughts would backtrack along less philosophical paths. It was ignoble and petty, but not to be denied, that tokens of his predecessor seen from that bedroom were a turn-on. Sight of that fading cross somehow made him feel Sultan-like.

It wasn't actually quite so bald or bad as that. Samuel and Susan had come to a comfortable arrangement some while ago, and were more solicitous of each other than many a long-wedded pair. He secured commissions for her sewing and embroidery, and also ensured that she got premium prices. Numerous Lewes properties of the more aspirant sort had Susie's cushions in them (though Galen House was not amongst them). Likewise, she catered for his needs. Their different hungers were thus satisfied.

That day Susan saw the infants to her mother-in-law's and then lifted her linen as Trevan required, without demur. Later on they'd have cocoa (if he'd brought some, broth if not), and conversation. Then, when he'd left, she'd find a guinea somewhere. This last part was never ever discussed, for fear of undermining what they'd built.

That time - those times - though, for all that he was in her there was no pleasure in her - or for her, because she could *tell*. Samuel looked down upon her honest Sussex face and saw other, less obliging, views.

He also suffered from grave distractions, such as the '*blurring*'s return and its crazed cavorting on the rim of sight. Plus the persistent sense that something was standing behind him, studying the up and down of the Trevan backside.

CHAPTER 3

'THE LEWES TIMES & PIOUS INTELLIGENCER'.

The 22nd of January 2021 AD.
P. Brazier. Secular and Ecclesiastic Court Reporter.

CHASTE SELF-DESTRUCTION

'Such was the melancholy conclusion of Coroner Champion, sitting at the Crown Inn yesterday, concerning the strange demise of two young persons on the 14th inst. The sad particulars according to Mr P. LAWS (witness) were that at midday in Mr HIGHAM's establishment, High Street, Lewes….

… enquiries conducted by the coroner's staff revealed that both were of good, Bristolian, family (whose name is here withheld in deference to their inconsolable state) of the rank of Gentry (Saxon), from whom they might expect every blessing and preferment in life, either together in matrimony or no. Testimony was also received from their parish priest and neighbours of quality attesting to each one's sovereign virtues and piety. Furthermore, a surgeon gave evidence of the young female's intacta state, thus disarming the malignant of any sordid speculation.

… Mr S. TREVAN (witness) of Galen House, Lewes, was formally reprimanded by the coroner for his taciturnity and 'sullen disposition'. Threatened with proceedings for contempt of court, TREVAN saw fit to quip that such a verdict would be 'uncanny reading of his inmost thoughts'. The witness was then discharged amidst most inappropriate merriment from the public gallery.

A suicide verdict was unavoidably reached, mitigated by references to a destablement of mind caused by falsely perceived barriers to their earthly love.

The cadavers are to be conducted west to their grieving families for burial, alas at a crossroads. The Bishop of Lewes, inspired by Christian charity, nevertheless granted an indulgence that they might receive a blessing and rest beside one another, awaiting the judgement of their infinitely merciful Creator.'

Samuel set the paper down. Of late he'd taken to keeping a pistol close by. *'Chaste Self-Destruction'* inspired him to check it still sat in his office desk. It did: ready and waiting. He had nothing to worry about. Samuel read on

He found only reassuring stuff: cattle-feed prices and banns of marriage: Lewes life going on, running smoothly along its Sussex rut. Which lasted until the *'Personal'* column on the back page. Normally it only amused him: endless pleas to St Jude for lost objects or self-defined 'gentlemen' seeking love. Therefore nothing whatsoever to do with Samuel Trevan.

Today though, he *was* involved. He was even impudently addressed. To his face! In front of everyone!

Trevan tried to but could not resist it. Another pointless but soothing revisit to his desk draw. Had his gun dematerialised in the last few minutes? No.

He read again, though he knew that nothing would have changed there either.

'To Mr S. T, citizen of Lewes.
Greetings from old friends who desire to renew a WELCOMBE acquaintance.
We are here.
Reply c/o Box 23. 'The Intelligencer' Offices.'

The paper went into the privy and Samuel (pistol in frockcoat pocket) went to *'Sharp's Ironmongers (Estab. 1685)'* in the High Street. There he spent like a lottery winner on new house and window locks of their sturdiest kind.

He also no longer deluded himself on another score. It ceased to be safe to deny it. Something on the periphery of vision was taking form and following him.

****

****

'You took your bloody time, Fynn. What's your game? The knocker went ages back!'

'Samuel!' Melissa chided him - though cautiously. He'd been like a bear with toothache lately; even marginally so with her. *'Pas profanum devant les domesticus!'*

With only a weak grasp of any of them, Melissa Trevan tended to mix and mangle her 'polite languages'. She took refuge in confidence that the lower orders wouldn't realise.

'It is the sheer *multiplicity* of locks, sir,' said the butler, in his own defence. He felt no call to shoulder blame that didn't belong. His brother ran a doing-nicely-thank-you print shop in the town: he'd see him alright if need be. 'Opening the front door after nightfall is now a complex task.'

Trevan glowered.

'You watch your lip, *Mr* Fynn, or you'll be going through that door yourself, open or otherwise. And who is it anyway?'

'They had no card, sir, but claim acquaintance. It may be merely business of course, but one cannot quite place their status. Accordingly, I thought it best to confer with you.'

'They're waiting?'

'On the doorstep, sir. And none too patiently, if I may say so.'

Melissa put down her book. Miss Austen's *'Pride & Piety'* had been causing her eyes to droop in any case, and now duty called. Galen House was *her* business and under Samuel's new interventionist regime it was all going to pot.

'Fynn! You may *not* leave visitors in such rude limbo. Either show them into the hallway or to the side door, but *don't-....*'

'Master's orders, madam,' the servant dared to interrupt. 'And there's been so many callers sent away of late I'm no longer clear who's to be admitted and who's not.'

'*What?*' That was news to Mrs Trevan and she wanted to hear more.

'I'll deal with them,' said Samuel, detecting a good time to be away. Meanwhile, Melissa detained Fynn to tell all.

'*Traitor!*' Trevan whispered to the butler as their paths crossed.

'*Truth,*' came the hissed riposte. Yet again, his employer wished the

Sussex servitor classes weren't so Leveller-minded.

Standing before the front door Samuel took a deep breath and then lifted the new and heavy latch. The callers were revealed. This time there was a pair of them.

'Come with us,' they said.

'No,' replied Samuel.

'Please.'

'Never.'

The youngest of them, a stunning girl dressed in London high fashion, pleaded with him. Her exhalations frosted in the air.

'You may have anything you wish of me! The flesh is of no account: we may give all quite freely. *All!* Imagination is the only fetter. And *I* can-...'

Trevan impatiently waved her to silence. She obeyed with lowered head. Jet-black curls tumbled down from her bonnet.

'What-do-you-*want*?' Samuel asked, an element of desperation in his voice. Their predecessors would only say in the most general terms, but these two looked more senior. Time was short though: soon Melissa would be down to pry.

'The future!' answered the male, bluntly. He looked like an elderly undertaker. Trevan's first action had been to check that the man's boots connected with the ground.

Getting no response the man had to expound. 'One future, much to our taste, flows only through you,' he said. 'We wish to describe its beauty and persuade you to let it be.'

'There's no common ground here!' Samuel exploded, though trying to keep his voice down. 'I don't share your cack beliefs!'

That caused them to wince, but they rode it in the interests of a higher cause.

'But you shall,' said the beautiful fanatic. She leant forward, her eyes fiery with the desire to save him. 'They are such sweet reason when embraced!'

There was food for thought in that, especially coming from her. But then Samuel noticed that underneath all her finery she was just skin and bone. The carefully contrived glimpse down her bodice showed a wasted landscape.

'Convinced or not,' said 'Undertaker', hurriedly, observing the failure to beguile, 'the promised days *will* come through you. All we ask is that you be informed of your destiny.'

'And do as I'm told.'

'And be *yourself*, Mr Trevan,' said the girl. It was hard to argue with her: she was so brimful with respect. 'What could be more natural than that?'

'Go forth: build businesses,' suggested the man, full of fervour, 'make things - anything. Employ slaving hordes-....'

That got Trevan's attention. 'But I'm not allow-....'

Undertaker swept all that aside. 'We have people in the highest places who will shield you. Be busy and bring on the new age!'

Samuel was troubled and confused. The now familiar fuzzy shape was coming up his drive to stand behind the two. They seemed to know it; the man-like form being back-up to their appeal.

'First off you try to kill me,' Trevan protested, 'and now you expect-....'

'Mistake! Mistake!' cried Undertaker, in honest regret. 'Our god put us to the test but we failed to perceive his sublime design. We have long mortified ourselves for that lapse....'

To prove it - and badly misjudging his audience - the old man whipped off one glove. The hand inside came with it. The remaining stump was moulded to mount a false extremity.

'I gave this for our wicked failure,' he said, '*and* for your forgiveness. Come with us!'

'Come with us,' echoed the girl, and licked her blue lips.

'Samuel?' said a far more feared voice from behind. 'Who is it?'

Trevan kicked the door shut in their faces and turned on Melissa to stand in her way.

'Peddlers,' he answered her.

She looked round him, as though the truth could be discerned through solid oak. Predictably the attempt failed.

'Peddling what?' she asked, far from convinced.

Samuel shooed her back. Reluctantly at first but then more freely, Melissa permitted it.

'Peddling meddling,' he told her.

****

****

When his wife was settled back in the parlour and wrestling with Jane Austen again, Samuel ventured upstairs to look out. The duo was still there in the dark, standing in silent vigil before his door. Indistinct movements suggested they might now be fully three in number – but only two of them human.

At long last reassuring fury arrived at being besieged *'in my own bloody house'*. It sealed off all bar one of the annoying branchways of choice. Trevan went to the kitchen and took a kettle from the range.

Back upstairs in the bedroom he flung open the sash window. Below, two pale discs turned skywards in earnest hope.

'It's a cold old night,' Samuel shouted down. 'Have a hot drink with my compliments!'

They took the scalding water full in the face and were seared. For a few seconds they shrieked - but then overcame and stifled further cries.

Trevan hesitated and stopped the flow. His victims looked up again. They radiated… love.

He didn't want it and so poured again. The recipients, complete master and mistress of their despised flesh, took it and even danced, cavorting under the steaming stream, accepting whatever *he* might offer without complaint.

CHAPTER 4

'His former - and soon to be again, and most solicitous thereto - acquaintances from WELCOMBE, *Devonshire, request the pleasure of the company of:*

MR SAMUEL MELCHIZEDEK TREVAN
at:
The Sheriff's Room, The White Hart Hotel, High Street, Lewes.
For warm refreshments (tho' of a differing sort than he lately provided <u>us</u>) and dinner.
5.30 for 6.00. Saturday, January 30th 2021.
Black Tie.
R.S.V.P. c/o Alfred Waterhouse, Proprietor.'

****

'To whom it might concern, c/o Mr A Waterhouse, The White Hart Hotel, Lewes (with apologies for his trouble).

From: S. Trevan Esq. Galen House, Keere Street, Lewes, Sussex. (No callers on business).

The 28th day of January, 2021 A.D.

Sirs: re your recent invitation:

Matthew: ch. 27, v 5.
Luke: ch. 10, v 37.
(And by the by, the lack of 'anno domini' in your missive was injudicious.)

I have no intentions to become, be or remain, sirs,
your obedient servant.

Samuel Trevan'

****

The Gospel according to St Matthew: Chapter 27, verse 5:
'Judas departed and went and hanged him himself.'

The Gospel according to St Luke: Chapter 10, verse 37:
'Go, and do thou likewise.'

****

'A Dinner in Honour of:

SAMUEL MELCHIZEDEK TREVAN.

The 30th day of January, 2021.
The White Hart Hotel, Lewes Town, Sussex.

❖   ***APPETISER****: Snails with black butter and garlic cloves,*
or:
Caviar
or:
Black Pudding.

❖   ***MAIN COURSE****: Rump Steak in black-pepper crust.*

❖   ***PUDDING****: Prunes in the Greek fashion (with soured curds).*

❖   *Followed by: **TOASTS**.'*

CHAPTER 5

'You must eat something. The manager will think it amiss.'

That actually made Samuel laugh, though said in all seriousness. It was an incongruous sound at such a party. The 'Sheriff's Room's Tudor fireplace was ablaze but it failed in combat with the company's intrinsic chill. The best function hall in Lewes' grandest hotel it might be, but this lot made it feel like a crypt.

'I should imagine he's already suspicious,' Trevan told the Bogomils, feigning concern for them. 'You're taking an almighty risk.'

Their leader inverted his usual expression to affect a smile.

'You are worth it, master,' he said, from the head of the banqueting table.

'Don't call me that.'

'Whatever you instruct.'

'Is that so?' said Samuel. 'Right then: *go away.*'

'Apart from that.'

Trevan marvelled. They really had achieved the detachment from the world that they sought. Not one of the dozen gathered in his honour perceived how repulsed he was by their black food and company. There wasn't even any respite to rest your eyes on: they had turned all the oil portraits of eminent Lewesians to the wall.

Samuel prodded at his nigh carbonised steak but made no headway. No one had asked him how he wanted it done: it just arrived that way. His companions seemed to relish theirs just as little, toying with the food's outer edges - although that was most likely some statement about appetite rather than good taste.

'I wish to God I knew why I came.' Samuel pushed his plate away and blood gravy slopped over its edge onto the fine linen.

'Then *wish* and he may tell you,' instructed one of the company in prissy tones, like a sanctimonious Sunday-school teacher. 'We call it *prayer*. You should try it.'

'There is no God!' Trevan flared - and was again glad this was a private dining room. Infidels were semi-tolerated now but that didn't mean they could be blatant. And no amount of official forbearance was any help against an angry mob of believers.

Their spokesman looked even more funereal and set down his fork.

'You heard him and yet you still *doubt?*'

Samuel fixed the man with his best pre-assault gaze. It was easily met and matched.

'I heard a voice - from a cave wall you've carved like an eye. That doesn't make it God.'

'Doesn't *not* make it God,' countered a hard-faced woman in a mourning crinoline. Her harsh bark detracted from a reasonable point.

'Your friends, the Elves, said otherwise,' Samuel taunted them.

'Ex-friends!'

'Betrayers!'

'False prophets!'

The denials sprang vehemently from all round the table. Samuel was curious that such passion persisted. It was clearly still a live issue.

'They also said to burn you out,' he told the angry silence which ensued. 'But I never heard whether-....'

'Many brethren died,' confirmed the spokesman, meanwhile playfully smearing shiny black sturgeons' roe up and down his forefinger. 'Just as we gathered in strength to seek you, fiery hell descended.' He thought on that briefly, not actually sad but saddened. 'The word of God was lost to us for a space.'

'How *did* you manage?'

There was growing confidence in Samuel's mockery. These skull-faces needed him: revered him almost.

Spokesman's finger was taken up by his female neighbour and slowly fellated clean; but his deep-set eyes never left Trevan all the while.

'As well as we could,' he answered eventually, 'adrift in an enemy world, with only memories for solace. But never fear for us, Mr Trevan: like Jews returned to Zion, we are *back*.'

Despite himself, Samuel was surprised.

'What? *There*?'

'Indeed. We again speak to our god and are guided. Once more there is a Master of the Dark for below, and a Master of the Revels – namely myself - for relations with the upper world.'

The tone alone said it was true: there was no need for evidence. And thus no choice. Trevan took delivery of the bad news.

'But how comes the Church allows-...?'

'Truth seeps in, Sam-u-el. Like water it is an implacable force, not to be denied forever, not even by greek-fire and sicarii.'

For the first time in years Samuel was tempted by wine. Some of the heady purple Lebanese stuff provided might admirably soften a few edges. He overcame that urge but the arid triumph made him tetchy.

'In my experience, error's likewise persistent,' he told them. It wasn't rewarded with offence.

'That is the difference between you and us,' replied Spokesman, now sounding like an annoyingly tolerant missionary priest. 'Between what *we* profess and both your past and present creeds. You once believed in a libel and now believe nothing, whereas we are in essence optimistic. That hope is our choicest possession.'

Death and everlasting oblivion were concepts that had jeered at Samuel from life's sidelines for some time now. They required regular stamping upon using reason or distractions. He therefore didn't care for other people's quiet confidence in such matters to be waved in his face. It made him want to snatch it from them.

'*Hope*', eh? Is that a fact? I suppose that's what keeps you all so cheerful....'

Samuel scanned his fellow diners. Not one wan face flickered or took the bait.

'The kindest favour we can pay the world,' said a handsome young man, 'is to look calmly on its degraded games.'

'Though there is the temptation to snigger,' added a woman, perhaps his wife, close beside him. Her faultless, pallid, visage did not look at risk from laughter-lines.

'But we resist,' her partner concluded.

Then Trevan noticed their restraint wasn't absolute. The man's hand was at and up her, working away under the table.

'For pity's sake!' Samuel protested. 'If anyone walks in....'

'And to think,' said Spokesman, somehow shouting him down with a voice not much above a whisper, 'that this man – this mere prude - is the vehicle for a new age!' He wasn't expressing scepticism, but wonderment at the ways of fate.

'A conduit for our deliverance,' purred the stick-thin schoolmarm type alongside Samuel. She began to caress his arm, affection swiftly transforming into exploration.

'I am *not!*' bellowed Trevan, shrugging her off. She pouted a little, shook her bonneted head at his wilful obstinacy, but never once wavered in her look of love.

It ought to have been enough that they didn't want revenge, but this long-term interest now seemed just as worrying. He'd come, he admitted it, against all better judgement, to face them eye to eye like he'd always faced up to every enemy. He'd wanted a resolution *that* evening, kill or cure. What wasn't envisaged was that they might twine themselves round him, like poison ivy, in life-long embrace. Even he couldn't keep up a fight that long.

'I'm *really* not,' he concluded, rather weakly even to his own forgiving ears. 'I just live quietly, off my own means, debarred from anything else. Can't you accept that? Like I do?'

Spokesman looked at him a moment before silently mouthing: *'No.'*

Samuel stood to leave. No one tried to stop him. It transpired they could deputise that to an unseen ally by the door.

Trevan felt its grip, could even glimpse it for random split seconds: a mannequin made up of frantic agitated particles. He most certainly perceived its hunger and antipathy.

The briefest of encounters revealed there was no point in struggling. It was his previous 'blurred vision' made manifest and it was stronger than he. Samuel fell back and was - reluctantly - released.

'The god gave it to us,' Spokesman explained, deriving no unkind pleasure from Trevan's fright, 'in order to hunt you down. We think it is an earth elemental.'

A number of lips curled at mention of such sordid origins.

Samuel's voice stumbled. 'I've seen - half seen - it before.'

Spokesman nodded. 'It located you some weeks ago and sent word.

He or she has been your faithful companion ever since.'

That was a concept Trevan refused to toy with. He resumed his seat before speaking.

'I thought it was the virgin suicides who found....'

'Emissaries, not scouts,' said the manipulated woman, in-between ecstatic gasps. 'A beautiful gesture to flush out our quarry.'

Samuel wondered at the choice of words: she was fairly flushed herself.

'They now tup in Heaven,' her partner reassured Trevan - as if he could care. 'Do not worry for them.'

'You... should not have known me,' said Samuel, trying desperately to think things through. 'Steps were taken....'

'And most thorough ones,' agreed Spokesman. 'We were put to great pains. All mention of you seemed gone from this world.'

'And a sicarii nipped off our enquiring fingers,' said the digital lovemaker (appropriately enough).

'So - we grew - our own – Samuel - Trevan.'

The young woman was approaching climax now and spoke in short, breathless, bursts. She just assumed he would understand - or perhaps she had better things to think about.

'Show him,' said Spokesman, indulgently.

There was one figure at the feast, heavily shrouded and stock-still, who'd not spoken yet. Samuel hadn't queried that, only wishing they were all so amenable.

'Stand!' ordered Spokesman - and for a moment Trevan thought he meant him.

In a way he did. The quiet figure rose and allowed itself to be unwrapped. Samuel saw that even the Bogomils were sickened.

It was him - more or less: mostly less. Removal of the coat and hat hinted at it; loss of the muffler made things crystal clear.

Samuel Trevan was in there somewhere, alongside bits of many others: all *sorts* of others; carelessly mixed. Numerous false-starts were either sterile-shiny or sealed off by cysts. Granted, all the correct features were present - but as if thrown on from a distance. The creature seemed crushingly sorrowed to be alive.

'Speak!' Spokesman commanded harshly.

The pseudo-Trevan flinched. Then its crooked mouth split. There were teeth and gums but all misaligned. A thick tongue played over them.

'SAM-U-WEL,' it mumbled, with botch-constructed chords, the very sound of cat-gut under torture. 'SAM-U-WEL TREE-VAN.'

'Enough!' ordered Spokesman.

Again it cowered. Samuel realised they must have had to educate their creation from scratch - and not been patient teachers.

Spokesman left his seat and crossed to behind the facsimile. He then looked across at the real thing as he massaged the travesty's shoulders. It clearly wished to shrink away from him but dared not.

'Even the most transitory of visits leaves calling cards,' Spokesman explained. 'A brush against stone equals a flaking of skin; sweat or tears contain a certain essence of the self. Not even your Church's dousing of fire could expunge them all, not when a puissant god directed our swabs and tweezers. Flesh from others could then make up the great defect. Eventually, encouraged and fed with blood, these scraps of... you predominated. In time, you could even be coaxed to speak - and you said....'

He applied all his height and power to a cruel squeeze of the muscles beneath his fingertips. The mock-Samuel bucked and lisped:

'SAM-U-WEL! SAM-U-WEL TREE-VAN!'

Each word equalled agony. The real Trevan didn't doubt old wounds were thus reopened. He even felt empathy - but directly stamped on it. Far better to be callous then admit kinship betwixt himself and... that.

'Which was sufficient for our supernatural hound,' said Spokesman, moderating his grip. 'A name, a - rough and ready - likeness: it was enough. Thereby you were at last found. We thought you might care to admire our handiwork.'

Samuel had that glass of wine now. Lost Holy Land summers came back to life in his mouth and revived him.

'You thought wrong.'

'Oh well, no one is perfect,' said Spokesman. 'At least, not till they take the vow. In any case, we no longer need this poor copy.'

And then he said something indistinct. The guardian of the door sped forward in a shimmering of sparks struck from the air. It started to devour the second Samuel.

At first, the creation shrieked out its torment, but then a curt order compelled silence. Trevan sought to avoid both watching *and* cowardice but failed on either count. Each time a large chunk was torn away by unseen teeth he had to turn aside, but then the sounds of consumption drew him back. At the end his doppelganger turned pleadingly to him/itself, so Samuel was there to see the light die in it/his eyes. Then they too were plucked out and went down into the electric maw. Finally, the demonic thing moved on to a noisy lapping up of the puddles and smears it had made.

Strangely, all Samuel found to think about was the mess and how it might be explained. It was *his* name on the invitations and menu.

'Mr Waterhouse, the manager, is a convert,' Spokesman informed him: though Trevan had not said a word. 'He will not complain.'

And that was the most frightening thing of all. They had apparent access to his thoughts.

'You asked, albeit rhetorically,' Spokesman ploughed on, smirking at Trevan's dismay, 'why you were here. I shall enlighten you. Destiny moves beneath your feet and propels you along like a tide. One may, of course, align oneself and swim with it, and so arrive faster. Or, as with you, one may even deny there are such *things* as tides....'

That got a group response from the devotees, too perverse and gloating to properly be called laughter.

'But you are swept along all the same.' Spokesman enounced each word very clearly, most anxious that Trevan should understand.

'To where?' It happily occurred to Samuel that he'd spent his life swimming against the tide. A few more years wouldn't hurt. But then he suppressed the rebellious thought lest it too should be read.

'You are the enemy of our enemy,' answered Spokesman, albeit indirectly, 'and therefore our friend. You will bring Hell to Earth - oh yes you will - and thus encourage souls to *our* god.'

'And if I don't - *won't?* What then? That?' Trevan indicated the remnant traces of the constructed him.

The very notion seemed to horrify them.

'No indeed,' said the post-orgasmic woman, now coiled languid and content in her chair. 'You are our promised one; our future. We would hardly abort *you!*'

Spokesman somehow curtailed their demon's dinner and had it re-attend the exit. The double doors were sullenly flung open and crashed against panelled walls. Samuel's would-be masters (whatever they might say otherwise) were dismissing him.

'Go forth, blessed one,' said Spokesman. 'Be yourself - and so be ours!'

Trevan wasn't going to turn down the chance. He'd obey the first part of the instruction - but as to the second....

What all-pervading revolution would it require, he puzzled as he descended the White Hart's stairs towards the street and freedom, to no longer be yourself?

****

'Oh *no*, not now, Carol. For God's sake, woman!'

Samuel just wanted to get home, to lock the doors, load his gun and drink tea. The last thing he needed after a whole evening spent with outlander maniacs was to be accosted by the local madwoman.

'It is!'

Short speech followed by silence was the last thing he expected of her. Trevan was taken aback.

'What is?' he asked.

'For *his* sake,' she answered.

'Oh Christ!' Samuel shouldered her aside and walked on up the High Street.

Mad-Carol was well known in Lewes. She sang nonsense all day long in never-ending private conversation, but was harmless enough save when she stole. The Justices had given up whipping her out of pity and exasperation. She slept with anyone for a brandy - and sometimes not even that. The nuns at St Anne's tried to take care of the young woman but they couldn't cure her wanderlust.

'Oh yes: for him too if you like,' she called after him. Trevan half turned.

'Look, it's late and it's cold, Carol. Just *go away* before I-....'

'Listen to me, vermin.'

That would have stopped him in his tracks at any time, but her voice had also changed. Turning completely, Trevan saw she'd let her eyes go golden.

'Ah...,' said Samuel, understanding all.

'Ah...,' Carol mimicked, and smiled. 'Yes indeed. *They* wish to speak.'

'*They*?' he queried.

'I'm only half-breed.'

'I see.'

'Their Ambassadress to Sussex.'

'Who would have thought it?' Samuel wondered whether he should bow.

'Not you for a start.'

'Nor anyone. Where?'

'The *Long Man*.'

Samuel looked up and down the High Street and despaired at the stupid powers of habit. In the present context did it really matter if someone saw him consorting with Mad-Carol?

'When?'

'Whenever. They will see you arrive.'

What other options had he? Samuel nodded. 'I'll be there.'

Mad-Carol sniffed the night air, a street-beggar looking into realms Mr Trevan, gent., was excluded from. And yes, sure enough, here was yet another one who knew Samuel's future better than he did.

'That's right,' she agreed, finding but not sharing the desired picture, 'you will.'

CHAPTER 6

'Ugh!'

It was as though the Elf had encountered a bad smell. He'd emerged from Windover Hill and the *'Long Man'* at speed, only to fall back before the full Samuel Trevan experience. There was no opportunity to enquire how he passed through solid ground or whatever lay beneath the giant hillside chalk-figure. His present difficulties seemed too great to even permit conversation.

'Sorry if I offend,' said Samuel, insincerely. 'I'll wear more cologne next time.'

The arrival certainly looked like Samuel's previous saviour and enricher, but gave no sign of recognition. Trevan had to concede that in their aquiline perfection the race tended to alikeness. Accordingly, it might well be someone else. Which would also explain his immunity to the hand of time. Whilst the Elf tried to compose himself, Samuel idly wondered what their womenfolk looked like and why one never saw them.

'It is *because*,' gasped his companion, recovering by sheer force of will, 'they can grow partial to lesser breeds' carnal vigour.' Greater control returned with every word and the usual disdain was clawed back. 'Such as your own, for instance. Alas, that perversion is easily acquired but hard to remedy. We therefore seclude the she-elves, restricting their options to each other and our own cool flesh.'

'I see....' Despite his heavy burden Trevan could not help but be intrigued. He even overlooked the blatant trespass in his mind. Accordingly it occurred again

'Murder that infant notion in its cradle, human. Even your proximity would cause them gross haemorrhage in those parts which most attract. Any Elf-mate would go gangrenous in minutes. I am hardened against you by spell and experience, and yet still I suffer. You have got worse.'

To be fair, it did look as though the Elf was afflicted. Sweat poured off him (though clearly not designed to) and he had to filter his words through a kerchief pressed to his nose. That gradually grew sodden as golden blood seeped through.

'Presumably,' Samuel tried to assist him, 'that's due to this future everyone's on about getting closer.'

'Presumably,' snapped the Elf - and then started to gag. Trevan allowed a pause for him to throw up, though nothing came of the retching. There was time to look around and be reassured by Wilmington village and priory, their closeness and normality. The winter sunshine did them both favours, enhancing their rustic charms.

'Well, anyway,' said Trevan, 'you wanted to see me....'

'No.'

'Oh.' That knocked Samuel back. He'd just assumed that they were there to spoon-feed him the solution to his problems like last time. He frowned. 'But your Ambassadress said-....'

'You wished to see *us*. We pre-empted you. Excuse me asking, but would you mind retiring a pace or two?'

Samuel obliged and the Elf's hacking cough immediately abated. Each step away allowed a better view of the *Long Man*'s chalk outline extending far above them. For a moment Trevan imagined this encounter as a bird soaring over the Downs might see it: two tiny figures at the feet of a giant. He found that perspective helpful.

'You know that they've found me,' he said.

'Yes.'

'Which has brought back all this *future* business....'

The Elf took the air and heaved again.

'Yes.'

'Well, what are you going to do about it?'

'Nothing.'

'Ah...,' said Samuel. Collapse of stout party.

'True, we did not foresee their dedication. It was envisaged that you would live out your life in untroubled ease. Pardon me again.' The Elf turned aside to spit out an unpleasant taste. It evidently proved impossible. 'However, we were wrong. Yet confidence remains that they have left it too late. You are old now. There is not enough time to pivot history round you.'

'*Thank* you.'

'What for?'

'It was sarcasm, skinny-ribs.' Samuel deliberately stepped forward, causing the wet kerchief to be gripped tighter still.

'Oh yes,' came the muffled response. 'I know: *'sarcasm'*. Strangely enough, we can't master it. Yet it's the one vermin trait I rather like. Please go back.'

Trevan obliged once again, but only because he needed to hear more.

'At the very least you could tell me things!' He hated himself for the desperation in his voice.

'Such as?' asked the Elf.

'You're the bloody mind readers: sodding well read!'

Likewise, he couldn't help but shout. The sound crossed Windover hill and the sheep looked up at them.

He meant the invitation literally and expected it taken up. Trevan lowered all guards and reserve, wondering if this was how his mistresses felt just beforehand. Which was not a nice notion to be framing as he detected silken Elven enquiry stroll through unmanned defences.

'Gracious, human; that was easy. You were what you'd call '*wet and willing*'.' The Elf was unmistakably crowing now, ransacking Samuel's private vocabulary and shining a light into the most secret corners. 'Goodness me!' he then exclaimed over some particularly sordid nugget. 'How revolting!'

'Answer me, you bastard, or I'll come and cuddle you.'

That received immediate reward; the invisible fingers directly restricted themselves to the matter in hand.

'So yes,' Trevan was told, 'your Welsh wife *was* our half-breed - but you've long suspected that. She kept us informed and ensured you were not the occasion of harm. Your exchanging of body fluids drained away time and energy that might have been put to more pernicious use: from our point of view, of course.

'Of course.'

'She trained in our Erotic College in Caerleon. A star pupil. Both a bishop and a Privy Councillor have succumbed to her delights. Fatally. You should be honoured to have her-....'

'Which I do,' Samuel snapped. 'Incessantly.' He'd sought to reverse the flow of crow - to nil effect.

'... and survive to tell the tale. What else? Oh yes, *that*. Well, it may help you to imagine your persecutors' 'god' as the tiniest fragment of a greater entirety, inexplicably protuberant into this world. We suspect it is one of the self-aware universes. The portion here stands in relation to the whole as a grain of sand does to Pevensey's shore. Its further penetration is forbidden by the Law. No, Samuel, I won't say whose Law....'

'You mean *can't*.'

'I admit we are just as subject to its arbitrary dictates as the 'demon' discussed. Do please excuse me....' The Elf had to pause and wheeze as things indigestible racked his frame, but failing to dislodge them then gamely pressed on. 'However, *it* revolts against the restriction for some reason: on rare occasion, in sleepy fashion. Why? That is *such* an idiosyncratic vermin question. You cannot just *do* or *be*, can you? Pitiful....' He regrouped again. 'Well, one presumes that the thing's motives are as random as its presence here, although I don't recall we've ever given it serious thought. Perhaps it derived a mission from the first surprised vermin met when it burned its way ashore. Your 'heretics' are prone to hiding in caves, are they not? And even universes can be terribly impressionable. Now please have compassion: kindly let me go....'

'Nope!'

Curiously, the Elf seemed at home with such mercilessness: even cheered by it.

'That's the spirit! Much more intercourse with us and you'll soon be just li-....'

'I was *always* like this,' interrupted Samuel. 'I'm not your handicraft: and I won't be distracted either.'

The Elf fashioned a smile..

'It was worth a try, Trevan-vermin. Very well then: yes, we really do think we've strangled that smoke-and-factories future. Readings indicate that we survive in more and more time-lines. We've had babies born to us recently; ones worth keeping. That's surely a sign.'

'I'm so happy for you. What about me?'

'I've neither wish nor skill to advise newcomer welfare.'

'Try. Downgrade your sensibilities to animal-doctor level. I *insist*.'

Persuaded? Intimidated? The Elf looked to the cloudless sky for inspiration, and then, finding something he disliked in it, lowered his sights to the green Weald.

'I still don't know what to suggest,' he said eventually, with transparent honesty by Elven standards. 'If you join them their ways would drive you mad. Bogomils would *not* be stable business partners. On the other hand, if you defy them they will... drive you mad. May I suggest a monastery?'

The sort of reply Samuel had in mind was said for him - or rather put into practice. Amidst more pressing distractions he'd barely registered the return of the 'buzzing' in his ears but it now forced itself on both their attentions. The noise grew loud - and then dominant - and then came screaming down the hill at them.

The creature was so near to taking form that they saw its shape and progress defined in mini suns sparked from the air. Small circles of turf browned and died at the touch of its feet.

On arrival, the Elf got similar treatment. He'd drawn a serrated knife from his boot but it couldn't harm the maelstrom besetting him. There was time to pass the blade once, twice, through the enemy, but soon after his sword-arm was no longer available for use. The thing briefly tasted the limb and then cast it aside.

It isn't true to say Samuel was rooted to the spot, although he chose to stay put. He'd simply seen the creature's turn of speed and decided there was more dignity in awaiting developments than flogging your guts out and *still* being caught.

Mention of guts made him look again at the Elf's dismemberment. He discovered that the species' body cavities were curiously empty. They made little mess when disassembled: fastidious to the end.

There was every opportunity to wreak similar havoc on Trevan but he was spared. Two tiny red coals that might be eyes looked out at him from the tornado. Samuel saw hatred there, but behind that (fortunately) a far greater restraining fear. So instead they regarded each other - and entirely failed to bond.

For some reason Samuel fancied fetching the Elven weapon: maybe as a souvenir of an... interesting day - but the creature blocked his way. He experimented with other directions and was similarly barred. The thing's swirl grew angrier, raising dust and Trevan's remaining locks - incidentally revealing the origin of the *'faery circles'* lately plaguing local farmers. Looking round for escape, Samuel noted one in an adjacent fallow field: a perfect circle of blasted grass. So that was where it had waited for them: perhaps listening, maybe reporting, before it swooped.

One route only was left open to him. Trevan was inexorably herded back to Lewes and his fate.

CHAPTER 7

'We-don't-want-none!' shouted Samuel. It was what lower-class Lewesians said to hucksters.

Back again, the callers' pale hides were proof against rebuff. They continued to occupy the threshold of Galen House.

'We are not selling anything,' replied the male, the one Trevan dubbed 'the Undertaker'.

'Makes a change.'

'We are tired of our visits,' said the old man. 'We also begin to tire of *you*.'

'Good. So push off.'

'More importantly, God wearies of you.'

'It's *not* God: I've told you. Or even *a* god. You've been had.'

'He spits on your stupid obstinacy.'

'It's rude to spit,' said Samuel. 'Look, will it speed things up if I stick this gun in your face?'

'No. Death is sweet liberation and thus holds no fear.'

Suddenly, all the ire went out of Trevan. He stared at the doorstep-missionaries with something approaching surrender.

'Look,' he said, nigh pleading, 'I was having tea. With my wife. Say what you must and then go.'

Undertaker's face was still reddened from Samuel's scalds. His young companion (who'd had her bonnet as protection) was contrastingly white with cold or bad diet - or maybe anger.

'We have something for you,' she hissed.

'I'd sooner have a farewell.'

'It may come to that.' The Undertaker stooped to open his valise. From that came a box: and from *that* - gingerly - a skull. He held it base up like a bowl.

'No thanks,' said Samuel, not looking. 'We've got plenty of ashtrays.'

The girl produced an instrument also made of bone: a perforated patella nailed atop a femur. Their parody of a holy-water shaker. Undertaker took it in his free hand.

'You frustrate,' he accused Trevan. 'You... disgust. I said that God spits on you. I meant it literally. You cause God to spew bile. See what you have done!'

The tool was dipped within the skull and then drawn out dripping with something Samuel had deliberately forgotten. It was the same stuff that had melted mine pumps and dissolved employees all those years ago. Trevan had zero wish to remember it, let alone renew the acquaintance.

'Go or I shoot,' he growled.

But he knew he wouldn't. Couldn't. *They* didn't care - but the Law did. The Law would hang him.

'The remains of a *perfecti* may contain it,' said Undertaker, indicating the skull, 'but nothing else. Only piety is proof against the wrath of God!'

He leant past Trevan and shook a few drops into the hallway. Landing, they melted the carpet and sank deep into the floor. Straightaway the area smelt like a brew-up of corpse and cheese. Ridiculously, Samuel's first thought was how to explain it to Melissa. She was fond of that Persian *'Armada weave'*.

When he turned back the pair were packed up and ready to leave.

'It is a terrible thing,' said the girl, sounding genuinely sorry for Samuel, 'to be spat at by the Almighty....'

****

Trevan couldn't argue with that. Galen House was going to collapse around their ears if the bombardment continued. Already the window frames were riddled with myriad pinpricks of corruption and threatened to fall out. An inspection of the outside brickwork revealed huge areas of honeycombing.

Samuel didn't believe it was all personally delivered: he patrolled the grounds day and night to fend off such attacks. Most of it must be a supernatural rain all the way from Welcombe.

Almost as bad was the stench. Neighbours first complained and then promised lawsuits. Samuel's best hope was that some immunity would develop - which was a sign of how low things and he had sunk. But day after day passed and the nausea remained ever fresh. Their very clothing became impregnated. People wrinkled their noses and avoided them on the street. Even Mad-Carol was more fragrant and socially acceptable than the Trevans.

Worst of all, the 'buzzing' - and thus presumably what it betokened - was now in the house.

Whilst servants queued to give notice, Melissa got out the scrubbing-brush and performed Trojan works of spring-cleaning. Her husband knew the effort was in vain but allowed the diverting activity. At least it tired her out, taking the edge off difficult questions and demands for explanation.

Then, one evening at dinnertime, the French-window just gave up the ghost and... melted into foul vapour. Fynn, dolling out onion soup for which they had no appetite, looked at the sagging gap for a spell and then simply walked out - out of the room and out of their employ. Samuel was almost glad of it, for the man's clanking armour-array of crucifixes, scapulars and amulets had started to annoy.

Melissa opened her mouth to ask... something. Simultaneously, the door chimes sounded for the umpteenth time that day.

Trevan knew who it was and, at long last, what to say.

'Would you excuse me a moment, my dear?' he asked his wife.

****

****

'THE LEWES TIMES & PIOUS INTELLIGENCER'.

The 19th of March 2021 AD.
P. Brazier. Secular and Ecclesiastic Court Reporter.

MAYHEM & FOUL MURDER?

'A most curious incident is reported in the Town last Tuesday night, when Mr SAMUEL TREVAN, gent., of Galen House, Keere Street, was witnessed amok in that vicinity and further abroad in Southover, all bloody with a sword and brace of pistols. Cries and shots are reported spread over a prodigious space during the time of darkness, and horrified onlookers testify to seeing bodies left just as they were slain in the street. These tales are supported by the quantity of ghastly gore which THIS REPORTER himself observed over the walls and cobbles of Keere Street, and, in particular, by the Holy Well in St Anne's Churchyard. However, strange to relate, the men of the Watch, coming upon the scene after seeking reinforcement, found none but the aforesaid TREVAN, armed and in a savage state. We dutifully relate that he offered no resistance to the forces of order and surrendered himself into custody.

Miss Juliet Eyeions, brewster and tapstress of the Lewes Arms, Mount Place, who freely spoke to THIS REPORTER, states on her faith as a Christian that, coming forth to query the commotion, she saw TREVAN, a man intimately known to her from commerce, discharge a pistol point blank into the pate of an old man (who disdained to beg for mercy), whereof he plainly died. I examined the designated spot and indeed found tokens suggestive of such a heinous act; yet of any cadaver not one sign.

TREVAN is committed in restraint to the Castle Keep on charges yet to be determined, arraigned for trial at the Spring Assize. Readers of this journal of record may be assured that they will continue to be apprised.'

CHAPTER 8

'You'll excuse me if I don't get up.'

It was meant as a joke but only made Melissa weep. Samuel could see that they were by no means her first tears of the day.

Actually, he was glad to see it, having assumed she would still be incandescent-angry. After correctly reading his face that fatal night, she'd barred the way, only to be lifted aside like a china doll and marooned up high on the mantelpiece. A servant had had to rescue her later. Even with all the other problems breeding like cancer around her, she'd not been a happy woman about that.

'Don't mourn yet,' Samuel ventured, mock-jocular. 'I'm still here. Just because I can rattle my chains doesn't mean I'm a ghost!'

Actually he couldn't, because they'd put him in a straitjacket as well. Otherwise though he'd hadn't fared too bad. His money secured him an above-ground private cell and ample food to live on.

Nevertheless, Trevan reckoned he deserved praise for jesting (however feebly) in present circumstances - but if so he waited in vain. Mrs Trevan seemed inconsolable.

'How's the house? Still surviving?' he enquired. That ought to get through: Melissa was very protective of her childhood and marital home. It was the factor that had fatally stayed Samuel's hand. Otherwise, he could have fled Bogomil persecution and taken her with him.

It did indeed do the trick, penetrating her enveloping sorrow.

'Restored,' she told him. 'The curse is gone.'

Samuel attempted a grin - and precariously achieved one.

'That's not a very nice thing to call me.'

He felt like he was succeeding - if a manacled man can be called any kind of success. Melissa mustered a weak smile back.

'Any messages?' he asked.

'Just the one.'

'Who from?'

'I don't know.'

It was difficult to arrive at any kind of inner peace, constrained in Lewes Castle gaol, under *'investigation'*, awaiting some or other trial; but at least he'd thought one particular fear dispersed. His stomach gave a preliminary churn at it being re-added to the pile of problems.

'Not the callers?' he enquired, anxiously. It was the description they'd settled on for want of him explaining about 'Bogomils'.

'No. They've gone too.'

'Right! Because I *dealt* with 'em! Who then?'

'They don't say. Read for yourself.'

Of course he couldn't. So Melissa had to hold the letter up to his face. Then she kept it there when he'd rather not read any more.

'*Ah*...,' he said.

It was spoken slowly, and solely to postpone what must come next.

'So *many* women, Samuel,' she said, amazingly calm, considering. 'And for so long and so often. Even another *wife!* And so many other secrets too. Is it true?'

'No.'

'Promise me.'

'As true as I love you.'

'Really?'

'On my oath, I swear!'

And then she left him without a word, and Samuel knew that the Elves or Bogomils or whoever it was, had supplied her with evidence. Good evidence. Better evidence than his oath. Which now was worthless currency.

He called after her but she didn't answer. The gaoler kept a straight face and slammed the door shut like death.

Their positions were now reversed. Melissa had left dry-eyed and it was Samuel's turn for tears.

****

Another day, another visit. The last.

'Please don't leave Galen House,' said Samuel. 'You grew up there. Look, *I* don't want it: I'll give it to you!'

'I don't want it either,' answered Melissa. 'It's tainted to me.'

Trevan sank back down to the cell floor.

'Where will you go?' A dead man's voice.

'Anna has offered me a room in her parents' house. For the time being.'

'What: your *maid*? The 'romantic' one? Anna from Malling? Flat chest but saucy bum? Well, well, well: I often wondered if there was something between you two. If I get out can I watch?'

Melissa looked down on him with pity.

'You've coarsened, Samuel.'

He didn't - couldn't - deny it.

'Maybe that's what happens when you get everything you want,' he said. 'The price for it....'

She shook her head, trying to hold on to the pristine memory of him.

'I thought.... I really thought you were the one, the man in a million.'

Trevan gave a bitter chortle, stretching the cord stitches of his straitjacket.

'Funnily enough, my love, it turns out I *was*, though not in the sense you mean. That's why I'm in so much demand.'

Melissa lowered her head and voice.

'Not by me,' she said. 'Not at the moment.'

He had nothing to say to that, not wishing to risk treading on any tiny embers that remained.

She lingered at the cell door, leaving it ajar and letting in an icy draught. A metaphor for what the rest of life promised for both of them.

'Goodbye, Samuel. Thank you for what you were.'

He said nothing, staring blankly ahead - but if looks could kill the world would have ended then. Had there been anyone around to mock him he might have burst his bounds, chains and all. All his days and years were passing by in review and he was spitting on each of them, as they'd spat on him.

The heavy door closed, separating them. Then Samuel was left alone in silence.

He didn't want to speak: not ever again, but words came unbidden. They were made, like him now, from equal parts of cruelty and concern. He called after her, hoping that she would hear.

'Don't worry,' he shouted. 'I'll send money!'

CHAPTER 9

Now that he was an old man, Field-Marshal Mott sometimes slept as long as four or five hours a night. It was an indulgence he permitted himself following a heavy day wrestling with the national interest. Tonight, after working into the early hours on the Scottish conundrum, and then treating himself to much postponed evening prayers, he was truly ready for bed.

What he wasn't prepared for was further pressing work pinned to that same bed: a grisly missive stabbed into his pillow by a stiletto of non-human provenance. The sight especially saddened him because his saintly sister had made that cherished hop-pillow. Now it would have to be disposed of, like she had.

That loss made him want to berate the sentries who stood perpetual guard before his quarters, but the sinful reflex passed. They could not be held accountable, poor boys. If it had been the work of Welsh assassins or a Leveller *Gideon*, then yes - but not these people (though that, of course, was the wrong word....)

Mott only thought of Elves when he had to, and believed in them on the same basis. Intellectually, he accepted that statecraft must involve him in spiritually perilous deeds. For that reason he had his own personal chaplain to confide to, when conscience revolted and *duty* demanded too much. These... *things*, though, they were beyond even that; they comprised his vilest, most degrading, association. As a young soldier he'd fantasised about a secret war of extermination against them, with troops who'd then be sent on hazardous crusade. But now he knew that wasn't possible - or even desirable. Shame.

The letter was extracted and held between thumb and forefinger up to candlelight. Mott hated anything written in other than plain black ink and plain English. Blood (not theirs, of course) was *such* a cliché – why bother when they'd made their point so many times? And so clearly.

And why, the Field Marshal next considered, did the name *Trevan* ring doleful bells?

****

Lewes had seen nothing like it, not since the 'Reformation-Devastation' Wars. The entire *'Wisbech and Spalding Regiment of Foot'*, the famed and infamous, English-but-foreigners, *'Fen Tigers'*, marched many miles just to escort Samuel Trevan from prison to his new home! A long way to come to facilitate a journey of mere yards. Yet someone thought it proportional.

A lone figure at the centre of a thousand-strong hollow square of soldiers, Samuel was now free. Free from Lewes Castle and manacles and straightjackets, free even from the threat of *'grave charges'*. Those who now watched over him could arrange all that with ease.

Just as they could compel him to go behind Lewes Priory's high walls. And stay there. Forever.

****

****

THE YEAR OF OUR LORD 2037

****

****

CHAPTER 10

Quite understandably, 'lay-brother Trevan' was refused permission to attend Melissa's funeral. He watched it from afar even so, spying across to Southover with a perspective-glass loaned by a kindly monk.

There was a fair crowd – though probably most were taunting Bogomils - but Samuel's attention focused solely on the tiny coffin. It held all he'd ever pinned his hopes on, and they, together with a large part of him, went into the ground with it. He said no prayers that day: said nothing. From then on he had few more words at all; for himself or anyone else.

The day-in, day-out, went on for further weary years, an exact parallel to the equally relentless siege of the priory. They still bombarded him with the 'god-bile' and entreaties after all this time. Once they grew impatient and even dared to assault the place in force, seeking to carry him off to be their messiah. Mercifully, the permanent garrison proved equal to repelling everything. Even the elemental was held at bay and had to buzz and spark its impotent rage beyond the walls. It therefore proved unnecessary to run the risk of shifting him to more secure accommodation like the Westminster Citadel or Rome itself. Or to consider even more drastic steps.

Things settled into a routine, the priory continuing its life of prayer and charity much as before. Soldiers and wizards came and went in rapid succession and Samuel lost track of the blur of faces. He learnt that this was a plum posting, the subject of intense competition, despite the dangers. Your pay was enhanced for the duration, and promotion often followed in its wake. Samuel hated it when bluecoats accordingly treated him like a combination of career opportunity and fragile antique. Everywhere he went there were unwanted helping hands. If he so much as paused, a chair would miraculously appear, if not two. Some days, Trevan positively waded through a treacly sea of cupboard-love. For a man of his nature it was customised torture. When it happened he hated his days.

Only occasionally did reality speak out. Once he'd overheard an Irish captain of archers enquire: *'why don't they just bump him off: quick and kind like; and do everyone a favour?'* But his men had howled him down, inspired by the goose/golden eggs imperative. Similarly, a priest, also earwigging, scolded the captain and put him on a charge (*'Machiavellianism'* might be practised but was proscribed). Samuel had surprised everyone by interceding for the man. He who might be expected to have least sympathy said it was a fair question. Apparently, he increasingly asked it himself.

Wasted breath. The Irish captain was demoted anyway – and, unfairly enough, never forgave Trevan for it. Thereafter, his minders minded their tongues.

Every night great warding spells were cast over him, and 'lockmaster' magicians wove their hands over the priory's main gate. It no longer mattered much to Samuel if they strove to keep him in or others out. Everything was indifference now and he was easy.

****

It was five years to the day after Melissa died; the year the *Kwa-Zulu* Empire converted.

'Arise.'

The voice was within his head. Trevan replied likewise.

'Don't want to. I want sleep.'

'By all means sleep on, Samuel-of-bitter-regret - but dream no more!'

'Who-....'

'Come with me.'

A strong hand wrenched the essential Samuel - a dry and shrivelled thing - from his slumbering form. He was drawn up far beyond the priory and into bluer skies.

'Behold, rascal-of-the-wrong-path: Jerusalem the Golden!'

Indeed it was, or at least as Trevan had always imagined it: a city of the best of everything, perfect and reflective under a blazing sun. They saw from on high; an eagle or an angel's view.

'Hold me or I'll fall!' shouted Samuel.

'Ha! I have never ceased to hold you, fool: not for one minute. No child-of-my-keeping shall *ever* fall.'

Samuel found he could speak - and yet strangely not break the silence.

'Is this heav-....'

'It is mine, son-of-sorrows, all mine! Here I worship the ineffable and infinitely expand with joy. Would you lose *this*?'

'No. What must I do?'

'Let go, Samuel-of-the-woeful-grip. Shed your armour: split the shell!'

'I... can't.'

'Observe!'

The view was wider now, Jerusalem just a diamond speck central in an illumined landscape. Its glow was met and matched by other islands of light. They ranged from powerful beams shed by cathedrals and communities, to the candle flickers of lone souls treading their own way. In-between, there was both grey as well as black, and each shade ebbed and flowed against the other. The pattern and balance shifted constantly. Samuel saw some lights wink out and the dark flood in to cover their space. Elsewhere, new sources flared into being and the gloom retreated.

'Observe closer,' said his companion, proudly. '*I* helped make this!'

They were back over St Philip's in Lewes. Samuel had not known it until then, but the orphanage was a fiery star in the Sussex hills. Its light was almost blinding. And he saw himself nearby, still sleeping, a sunspot upon it, a black detraction.

'The fevered dream is almost done, oh Samuel-so-silly: childhood ebbs away. You must now make a man's decision. Once and for all - for always.'

It proved easy. The biggest but easiest thing Samuel Trevan had ever done.

'I'm... sorry,' he said.

'What for?' asked the voice, slightly puzzled.

'For breaking my vow: your funeral Masses: Melissa - and everything!'

Samuel heard that old familiar bellow of a laugh and for a moment was happy again. He'd clean forgotten what it felt like.

'Do you *still* not see, Trevan-so-thick-of-head? We forgave long ago, didn't we, Melissa-of-the-beguiling-smile? No, it is not *us* you must say sorry to....'

****

****

The first monk awake found Trevan prone before the great oak cross in the middle of the cloisters. He was fervently calling on Christ and His Church for forgiveness.

The prior was summoned and, though his charge was plainly raving, agreed out of kindness and concern to hear his confession. Nothing else would serve to calm him.

Samuel freely admitted this was only his second adult visit to the sacrament. Therefore he had much to tell and was thorough. Absolution and a mild (considering) penance seemed to comfort the fevered brain. Then he spent the remainder of the day asleep - and the rest of his life almost as passively.

To anyone who'd listen, Trevan said that he repented with all his heart. He had been wrong and therefore, *'logically speaking'*, those who'd thwarted him must be right. The bronze statue of Father Omar outside nearby St Philip's had told him this, passing words of wisdom over the wall. From then on it often spoke to him (though no one else was so favoured), supplying faultless guidance.

The monks smiled gently on such delusions. It was only fitting, if alas mere fiction, that the well-remembered giant should provide instruction for his charges at their sunset, the same as at their dawn. False or no, the laudable effect was that henceforth Trevan spent his days in prayer and even the Bogomils gave up on him.

Shortly after, Samuel Trevan made what was termed *'a good death'*. Pious rumour recounted that at the end he greeted persons unseen, naming both beloved wife and tutor.

Trevan's final words on earth were *'We should be careful'*. Followed by: *Thank God!'* They travelled on his dying breath.

His edifying example, often retold, lived long after him; a lone and unexpected legacy - but small return, surely, for such a... *busy* life. When you think about it....

****

****

EPILOGUE

****

****

CHAPTER 1

The Pope and Elf studied each other in mutual incomprehension. These meetings were always uncomfortable and Simon-Dismas II thanked his Maker for the solace, indeed the diversion, of the setting. He still missed his native plains, although there were many compensations in this new life. Like now, for instance. The Vatican gardens were an official 'Wonder of the Modern World', consciously designed to inspire thoughts of ever-higher harmonies. Likewise, the numberless fruit trees and flowers stood as metaphors for the flowing generosity of the Divine. And their totality symbolised His great favour in simply permitting beings to *be*, even in this short life, let alone the one to come.

Knowing his soul-less guest to be excluded from that eternal bounty, the Pope wondered why she should be as entranced as he.

She might well be the one they usually sent, though it was impossible to tell and, if so, would make her implausibly old. Simon-Dismas had learnt from the helpful notes left by his predecessor on the throne of St Peter that it was best not to speculate on the subject, but to simply arrange what was needful and then be sparing with words. He'd also counselled charity towards such poor creatures.

Across the gardens the Pope could see the *Torre Dei Venti*, home of the Vatican Observatory. From that venerable tower had come the calculations that set the name of Gregory XIII on the universal calendar. Likewise, the 'Meridian Room' at its top established a base time as well as zero map axes for all Christendom. In fact, most things seemed to have their beginning and end here in the Eternal Rome conquered by Christ. Through it this world was delivered to Him - and who knows, one day, places further afield too. For Simon-Dismas sometimes mused upon the star-maps his astronomers published and, sitting wine glass in hand, allowed his speculative faculties to soar....

What Simon-Dismas knew for sure was that within the *Torre* at that very moment Jesuit acolytes from *'The Sacred Congregation for the Cosmos'* would be preparing their telescopes for the watches of the coming night. There were increasing problems with the smoke pollution of the Roman sky, and so recurrent talk of relocation to Abyssinia, but meanwhile they worked on with infectious zeal. Only last month there'd been a correctly predicted meteor return, and yesterday the Congregation's general had come to announce discovery of yet another *'galaxy'* (apparently a whole *imperium* of stars!) in the constellation of Orion.

Afterwards, in a parallel to Simon-Dismas' private wine-sipping and star-map sessions, the two princes of the Church had chatted over tea and biscuits, discussing whether one day news of the Redemption might be passed to any beings inhabiting those far parts. And, if so, how?

That it would be a project for long after both men were dust; maybe another millennium of progress away, did not deter them discussing it. There need be no sprinkling of melancholy on such conversations, as with the pagans: no need to lament the little life of individual men. If God willed it then it would come to pass; and which particular here-today, gone-tomorrow, humans were around to see hardly mattered. All would get to hear of it in due course, whether whilst on earth or during what followed.

That was another advantage of serving a two thousand year old institution given cast-iron guarantees: you could adopt the long view. Which was very relaxing.

It was the same with being Pope Simon-Dismas II (Xavier-Geronimo Ludwin as was, lately Archbishop of Maryland, son of a Kiowa-Apache accountant). As rulers of half the world went (with influence in the remainder and the Hereafter), he was a fairly jolly sort of fellow, and certainly more easy-going than most emperors in history. That attitude sprang naturally from knowing all would be well. Eventually. However messy it might look from time to time.

The Pope then recalled that meanwhile there were still some on earth unblessed by that knowledge: his present companion on the balcony for example. Their evangelisation had been essayed in the past, only to be received with indifference or laughter. It was not openly admitted but no further attempts were planned.

Simon-Dismas obliged himself to consider the final item on their agenda: last but by no means least; the foremost petition in his prayers some evenings. Accordingly, it was casually broached.

'Oh, by the way; about the... what was it: *Tre-van*, person...?'

'What of him?' queried Joan. 'He's dealt with.'

'Quite so. Nevertheless, suppose there's someone similar out there?' The Pope waved his naturally copper-toned but now also tanned hand in the warm air, encompassing Rome, but meaning Christendom, or even the world.

The Elf-woman remained unconcerned.

'We think not. A few of us can see *far* forward. There's nothing remotely like him visible. Trust me: that future's strangled.'

'*Trust*' was asking too much, but, with no means of checking, acceptance was always an option.

Now the play of sunlight over the potted orange trees looked even more charming than before; more... *enduring*.

His Holiness Pope Simon-Dismas II looked into the distance - and smiled.

'Turned out nice again,' he said. 'Hasn't it?'

CHAPTER 2

The world might well be finished with Samuel Trevan but his business there proved incomplete just yet.

Melissa had kept Samuel's large collection of *'dragon's bones'* to the end, just like she'd treasured everything of his, even though they no longer met. But when the pneumonia carried her off no one coveted the boxes of dusty old rocks. Her executor, a distant cousin of pious disposition, wanted nothing to do with such vaguely blasphemous relics. Years later he sold them, unpacked and unseen, for a shilling at public auction.

They were bought by one Dr Mantell of Lewes, a surgeon and 'natural philosopher' of enquiring mind. He examined them the very day of purchase, sitting in his study and pondering the giant teeth and jaws and vertebrae over a glass of port.

Out of nowhere came the shocking idea that these were much, much more ancient than 4004 BC, the date Genesis and the Church gave for the creation of the world. Yet how could that be? One or the other notion could be right - but not both.

Likewise, professionally familiar with the developing human frame, Mantell half-glimpsed a suggestion of mutating forms therein, one species morphing over eons into another. Yet surely that also contradicted tenets of Holy Writ?

Perturbed, somewhat guiltily, he thought on all that evening, sipping at his drink until Mrs Mantell called him to bed. Even then his scandalous ideas would not go away, though he rather wished they might.

Next morning the Doctor was still unsure and, being an honourable

Christian gentleman, felt obliged to act upon his doubt. He considered the advisability of a privately printed essay; or maybe a lecture to the Lewes *'Philosophic Society of St Luke'*. It was at least arguable he concluded, that there might be service to religion in these *fossils*, and in proving the scriptural account of the Flood. He saw no harm in jotting a few ideas about *that*.

Intending only the most respectful choice of words, that evening Dr Mantell took up his pen and - to the Bogomils' eventual delight - commenced subverting a civilisation.

THE END (1)

CHAPTER 3

The world might well be finished with Samuel Trevan but his business there proved incomplete just yet.

Melissa had kept Samuel's large collection of *'dragon's bones'* to the end, just like she'd treasured everything of his, even though they no longer met. But when the pneumonia carried her off no one coveted the boxes of dusty old rocks. Her executor, a distant cousin of pious disposition, wanted nothing to do with such vaguely blasphemous relics. Years later he sold them, unpacked and unseen, for a shilling at public auction.

They were bought by one Dr Mantell of Lewes, a surgeon and 'natural philosopher' of enquiring mind. He examined them the very day of purchase, sitting in his study and pondering the giant teeth and jaws and vertebrae over a glass of port.

Out of nowhere came the shocking idea that these were much, much more ancient than 4004 BC, the date Genesis and the Church gave for the creation of the world. Yet how could that be? One or the other notion could be right - but not both.

Likewise, professionally familiar with the developing human frame, Mantell half-glimpsed a suggestion of mutating forms therein, one species morphing over eons into another. Yet surely that also contradicted tenets of Holy Writ?

Perturbed, somewhat guiltily, he thought on all that evening, sipping at his drink until Mrs Mantell called him to bed. Even then his scandalous ideas would not go away, though he rather wished they might.

Next morning the Doctor was still unsure and, being an honourable

Christian gentleman, felt some obligation to act upon his doubt. He considered the advisability of a private-printed essay; or maybe a lecture to the Lewes *'Philosophic Society of St Luke'*. It was at least arguable he concluded, that there might be service to religion in these *fossils*, and in proving the scriptural account of the Flood. He saw no harm in jotting a few ideas about *that*.

Finally, after distracted hours of chasing consequences, and likewise pursuing them in prayer, Doctor Mantell carried his problem (as Mother Church advised) to his confessor.

Fr. Perry, priest of St Michael's, proved persuasive. He argued the wisdom of not lifting a shroud deliberately draped by God, and of ditching these disquieting remains in the Winterbourne.

With residual regret, Mantell complied. On a cold, wet morning early in the third millennium of Man's salvation, he stood and watched that fast flowing stream bear the rocks away; taking a certain future - much pleasing to the Bogomils - along with them.

THE END (2)

CHAPTER 4

The world might well be finished with Samuel Trevan but his business there proved incomplete just yet.

Melissa had kept Samuel's large collection of *'dragon's bones'* to the end, just like she'd treasured everything of his, even though they no longer met. But when the pneumonia carried her off no one coveted the boxes of dusty old rocks. Her executor, a distant cousin of pious disposition, wanted nothing to do with such vaguely blasphemous relicts. Years later he sold them, unpacked and unseen, for a shilling at public auction.

They were bought by one Dr Mantell of Lewes....

...

THE END (> ∞)

www.ingramcontent.com/pod-product-compliance
Lightning Source LLC
Chambersburg PA
CBHW051334250626
47155CB00007B/2592